A HACK'S PROGRESS

Phillip Knightley is the author of many books, including *The First Casualty*, *The Second Oldest Profession* and *Philby, KGB Masterspy*. He divides his time between London, Bombay and Sydney.

D0488740

ALSO BY PHILLIP KNIGHTLEY

Phillip Knightley

A HACK'S PROGRESS

VINTAGE

Published by Vintage 1998

2 4 6 8 10 9 7 5 3 1

Copyright © Phillip Knightley 1997

The right of Phillip Knightley to be identified as the author of this work has been asserted by him in accordance with the Copyright, Designs and Patents Act, 1988

This book is sold subject to the condition that it shall not by way of trade or otherwise, be lent, resold, hired out, or otherwise circulated without the publisher's prior consent in any form of binding or cover other than that in which it is published and without a similar condition including this condition being imposed on the subsequent purchaser

First published in Great Britain by
Jonathan Cape, 1997

Vintage
Random House, 20 Vauxhall Bridge Road,
London SW1V 2SA

Random House Australia (Pty) Limited
20 Alfred Street, Milsons Point, Sydney
New South Wales 2061, Australia

Random House New Zealand Limited
18 Poland Road, Glenfield, Auckland 10,
New Zealand

Random House South Africa (Pty) Limited
Endulini, 5a Jubilee Road, Parktown 2193,
South Africa

Random House UK Limited Reg. No. 954009

A CIP catalogue record for this book
is available from the British Library

ISBN 0 09 977281 7

Papers used by Random House UK Ltd are natural, recyclable products made from wood grown in sustainable forests. The manufacturing processes conform to the environmental regulations of the country of origin

Printed and bound in Great Britain by
Cox & Wyman Ltd, Reading, Berkshire

To the late A. F. Osborne, my master in English and History at Canterbury Boys' High School, Sydney, who taught me to distinguish what is important in life.

Hack: A common drudge; especially a literary drudge; hence a
       poor writer, a mere scribbler.

But also,

Hack: A half-bred horse with more bone and substance
       than a thoroughbred.

And as a verb,

Hack: To make rough cuts, to deal cutting blows.

CONTENTS

ACKNOWLEDGMENTS

I was encouraged to get on with this book by Ian Jack, editor of Granta, who ran an extract from the first few chapters, and by David Godwin who read it and rang to tell me what every author longs to hear – 'I laughed out loud'. My agent, Rachel Calder, and all her colleagues at the Tessa Sayle agency, worked hard to find me the right publisher. At Jonathan Cape, Dan Franklin and Tom Maschler had faith and advice and my editor, Pascal Cariss, had time for the vital finishing touches before departing for different fields. My son, Kim, improved the manuscript no end by ruthlessly cutting out all my little darlings and urging me to defy years of self-conditioning and write subjectively.

Michael Cudlipp deserves special mention because he gave me my break in Fleet Street (Gray's Inn Road, actually) without which there would have been nothing to write about. And a twenty-one gun salute to the old *Sunday Times* and all who sailed in her under Thomson (father and son), Denis Hamilton, and Harold Evans.

The quotation from David Mason's book, *Thalidomide: My Fight* is by courtesy of his publishers, George Allen & Unwin. The quotation from David Hickie's book, *Chow Hayes: Gunman*, is by courtesy of his publishers Angus & Robertson. The song "Till We Meet Again" by Richard Whiting (music) and Raymond Egan (words) are quoted by kind permission of Redwood Music Ltd. and EMI.

Finally, what follows is how I remember it but I accept that others who were there at the time might have a different view.

THE FRENCH DEFECTION

I rang the American embassy in London and asked to be connected to the CIA station. And such is the openness of American society that the woman on the switchboard showed no surprise and seconds later a mellow, film star voice said, 'Bronson Tweedy.' I said shakily, 'Mr Tweedy, my name is George Phillips. You don't know me, but I was in Paris a couple of weeks ago and I met this French spy who might interest you. He says he wants to meet you.'

Tweedy heard me out, interposing a question or two, and then said, 'George, with the best will in the world, without knowing a lot more about either you or Pierre there's no way I'm prepared to meet him. Now what's it going to be? Are you going to tell me about yourself, or am I going to give you a few questions to put to your French friend and you can get back to me when you've got the answers?'

I had no wish to tell Tweedy my life story, so I noted down half a dozen questions that he wanted me to put to Pierre. They were simple, but the answers would be revealing. Which French secret service did he work for? Which department was he in? How long had he been there? What was the name of his departmental head and the deputy head? Which CIA officer from the Paris station acted as liaison officer with his service?

I came back to Tweedy three days later with the replies. He offered to ring me with his decision in an hour or so and laughed when I said that, no, I would ring him. When I did, his manner had changed. He was suddenly enthusiastic. 'Yes, George, we'd like to meet your friend Pierre,' he said. 'Let's get him over from Paris for a day or so. Why don't you book him into the Hyde Park Hotel for next Thursday and Friday. Tell him we'll contact him after lunch on Thursday.' Wouldn't it be better, I suggested, if Tweedy's office did the hotel booking? 'No,' he said. 'We'd rather you did it.'

So I followed orders and made the booking, and rang the hotel to check that Pierre had arrived and then I reported back to the man who was now, in effect, my CIA controller. Then I was left alone until Friday afternoon when Pierre telephoned me from Heathrow airport on his way back to Paris. The meeting had gone very well. There would be other ones. He was deeply grateful for all I had done for him. Next time I was in Paris we must get together for a drink. But I should ring him before coming because he was not certain how much longer he would be in France. He might be going to live in America. Oh, and Tweedy said I should ring him in a week's time.

It had started in Paris two weeks earlier when, as Phillip George Knightley, I sat at the rear of Harry's Bar, 5 Rue Daunou, drinking a pastis and waiting for Pierre. I had arrived in France three days earlier to cover a political kidnapping for the *Sunday Times*. It was a sensitive affair and I had discovered exactly nothing. In an ideal world I should have been able to telephone the *Sunday Times* foreign editor, Frank Giles, and ask for another week. But modern journalism is not like that. The kidnapping was this week's story; next week the world would have moved on, so I was expected to write *something* now, even though later events might render it incomplete and perhaps inaccurate.

So I had telephoned a French friend, a leftwing lawyer who had been helpful in the past. He listened sympathetically. 'I'll get someone to ring you,' he said. 'He's in one of the secret services. The Service de Documentation et Contre Espionage, I think. If he can't help you, he'll know someone who can.' Pierre rang within the hour and we arranged to meet. I told him that I was bald, bearded and looked like Lenin. He said he was tall, mid-thirties and would be wearing an English blazer.

Suddenly I saw him pushing his way through the other drinkers. He held out a large hand, apologised in excellent English for being late, ordered a pint of Watneys, and got straight down to business. 'All off the record,' he said, 'and I'd rather you didn't take notes. They have a nasty way of reaching the wrong people.'

It turned out that Pierre not only knew the inside story of the kidnapping but offered me several names and telephone numbers of people who subsequently confirmed all he so generously told me. However, all the time, in the back of my mind, I kept asking, why is he telling me all this? What's in it for him? But the information was so tempting that I persuaded myself that there would be no reckoning. I merely invited him to dinner and, when he declined, extended the invitation to the next time he happened to be in London. I'd probably never hear from him again, but I still felt an instinctive foreboding.

Back in London, with a note of congratulations from the editor, I got on with other things. Yet when the call from France came through and the voice on the other end of the line said it was Pierre I knew immediately that repayment time had come. 'I am considering leaving my job so I'm looking around for a new employer,' Pierre said. 'Do you know anybody with that big American company? No? But I'm sure you have contacts who could help. What I want you to do is set up a meeting for me in London with someone from the American company. I'm sure you can do that. I'll ring you at the same time in two days and you can tell me what the arrangements are. Don't try to contact me, either directly or indirectly. It could be dangerous – for both of us.'

I did not like his tone and I did not want to be involved. But I was in his debt and if I let him down I would also be letting down the French friend who had introduced us, and I knew enough about how things worked in France to realise that this would be a mistake. But once I had done what he wanted then that was it. I certainly had no intention of calling Bronson Tweedy again.

But in the end, the temptation was too great. Maybe I could still salvage something from the affair, something I could write about, if not now, then perhaps later. 'George,' Tweedy said, his tone very friendly. 'Can you make lunch at the Connaught tomorrow? Just the two of us. There's a lot to talk about.' I was now so far into my new role that I found myself taking a roundabout route to the Connaught. I took an office car to Grosvenor Square, then a walk to Selfridges, a quick turn through the food department, back to Grosvenor Square via Park Lane, then fifteen minutes hanging about outside the Connaught until I thought it was safe to go inside. I wanted to arrive at the meeting before Tweedy so as to gain an initial psychological advantage, but he was already at the table. Tweedy was about forty, well-built, greying slightly, and very English in manner and dress: on this bright London autumn day he wore light grey trousers and a dark-green Harris tweed jacket. You would never pick him as the CIA station chief in London.

Then again, maybe he wasn't. He *said* he was Bronson Tweedy, but this being the spy world and since I had only spoken to Tweedy over the telephone and had no way of knowing what he looked like, I would not have been surprised if this cosmopolitan American at the restaurant table holding out his hand was actually one of Tweedy's minions using his name. All spies have lots of names – it confuses the opposition and provides an escape hatch if things go wrong. I remembered that at his Old Bailey trial during the Profumo scandal poor old Stephen Ward told the court he had been working for MI5 and his case officer was a man called Woods from the War Office. The prosecution's barrister told the court that Mr Woods was totally unknown at the Ministry of Defence. Of course he was unknown – Woods was actually one of the many names of the MI5 officer Terry Wagstaff but no one from MI5 was about to tell the Old Bailey this.

Anyway, it did not matter because I was not me, either. I was there as George Phillip. So if it was not really Bronson Tweedy then at least we were starting off even and I settled down to absorb everything Tweedy was about to tell me. But to my disappointment all he had to say over lunch was that any service that treated its officers like Pierre had been treated deserved to lose them. Then, to my alarm, he moved on to a book, *Philby, the Spy Who Betrayed a Generation*, about Kim Philby, the British Secret Intelligence Service officer of nearly twenty-five years' standing who turned out to have been working all the time for the KGB. I was a co-author of the book, but did Tweedy know that?

'Great book,' he said. 'Those *Sunday Times* guys reconstructed Philby's life from interviews with people who knew him. He gave them no help whatsover. But what puzzles us is that the British authorities did nothing to stop publication. They use the D-notice to stop all sorts of things. Why didn't they use it on the *Sunday Times* when it ran those articles on Philby? Why didn't they use it on the book?' I said I did not know. Tweedy looked me right in the eye. 'Maybe it was a controlled operation,' he said.

'Controlled?'

'Yeah. Maybe the British authorities didn't care if the whole damned mess came out as long as they controlled the way it emerged. The *Sunday Times* thought it was getting a scoop but it was really SIS running the show.' The thought worried me but Tweedy was watching me so I managed to reply as casually as I could that I had gathered from the book that anything was possible in the spy world.

'We don't care much one way or the other,' Tweedy said. 'We've moved on from the Philby business. Written it off. It still bugs the FBI, though, and Hoover would love five minutes alone with Philby in a dark street.' He pushed back his chair. 'Better get back to the office,' he said. 'Let me get you a taxi.'

We stood in the street for a moment. As the taxi pulled up Tweedy looked at a point somewhere over my shoulder. 'George . . .' he began, and then paused. I quickly turned my head to see who he was talking to. '. . . it's been nice meeting you.' He grinned broadly and turned to the taxi driver. 'Take Mr Phillip George Knightley back to the *Sunday Times*,' he said. Then he strode off towards the American embassy.

I felt a keen humiliation. Tweedy had blown away my professional and moral disguise. I should have known in journalism you never get anything for free and that you mix with spies at your peril. Yet in order to procure and pay for information I had entered into a pact with the French and American intelligence services that I thought I could control by clumsily disguising my name. Tweedy, of course, knew that dealing with spies at arm's length is impossible.

In the taxi on the way back to the office I decided that although journalism is riddled with people working for intelligence services, I would stay clear of the game and never become George Phillips again. I would remain Phillip George Knightley, special correspondent, the *Sunday Times*. No more, no less.

CHAPTER ONE

THE LAST ISLAND TRADER

My maternal grandfather, William Iggleden, died before I was born but my mother used to let me play with his pistol. It was of some obscure Italian make with four barrels, one above the other. When you fired the first, the next rose to meet the firing pin and so on. This made it difficult to aim which may explain why Grandfather, who, in the early years of this century used to travel around the New South Wales outback for the Sydney general store Marcus Clark, never shot anyone. I cannot say the same for Uncle Les, my father's brother. He was working in Queensland after the Second World War and made the mistake of seducing a travelling cane cutter's wife. When her husband heard what had happened he walked into the pub where Uncle Les was having a quiet beer and knocked him to the floor with a single punch. Les, who was only five foot six, got up, went home, returned with his .22 rifle, said, 'Cop this, you mongrel,' and shot the cane cutter through the shoulder. He got three years, came out, and disappeared. Auntie Noreen said he was either too ashamed to get in touch, or, more likely, he was dead. Otherwise, she said, he would certainly have helped her after she lost her job as a conductress. (The driver let her drive their tram over the Sydney Harbour Bridge and an inspector caught them.) I mention all this only to show that my family was a bit out of the ordinary – even for an Australian one.

We had big families in those days. My mother was one of four and my father one of fourteen. My mother's family came from Kent and my father's from Northamptonshire, but over the years in rural New South Wales the men married a series of Irish barmaids, so later Knightleys never seemed to know whether they were Catholic or Protestant, an important distinction in Australia. When my paternal grandmother, worn out from having all those children, died at thirty-four, the older children stayed with their father and were brought up as Protestants and Freemasons, while the younger ones went to a Catholic orphanage and came out defiant Catholics.

It did not seem to worry any of my aunts and uncles or my thirty-two cousins – big families get bigger – even though the question of whether you went to a Catholic school or a public (state) school had undue influence on how your life developed. Catholic-educated boys (girls did not look beyond the house as a career then) tended to go into the Public Service or the police; those from public schools into the professions or business.

My parents sent me to Sans Souci public school on the shores of Botany Bay. As you drove south out of Sydney you passed through an industrial area reeking of tanneries and tallow works, then you emerged into a series of sandy suburbs named after places back 'home' in Britain – like Brighton, Ramsgate and Sandringham – and then, suddenly, you came upon this strange, French-sounding place. It was pronounced the English way because no one knew it was French, let alone what it meant. Nor did they care. France was where Australians had fought in the First World War, and uncles with their trouser leg pinned neatly back to hide their stump would tell you it was a dirty, foreign place – it rained all the time, the inhabitants ate filthy food like frogs and snails, and never had a shower. My father, then a signwriter, said he chose Sans Souci simply because it was cheap. He bought a block of land there in 1924 for £45 and a local builder put up a two-bedroom brick bungalow for him for £800.

He nearly lost it during the depression when he could not meet the mortgage repayments. But the State premier, the Labor leader Jack Lang, forced the banks to offer a moratorium on mortgage repayments until the depression was over. This turned my father into a life-long Labor supporter. He blamed those British investors in London who held Australian bonds for demanding their interest payments when everyone in Australia was suffering, and from then on refused to stand up for 'God Save the King' in the local cinema despite glares and the occasional threat from other patrons.

Although I was a child of the depression – I was born in 1929 – I do not remember any great hardship. This is not to say that there was none, just that I don't remember it. School photographs show most of my class without shoes but I think that was from choice. The soles of our feet became tougher than leather – when the January sun melted the bitumen on the roadway in our street, I could stir the hot tar with my big toe.

In fact, seen through the hazy mist of memory, my childhood was idyllic. The walk to school took me past the local fruit and vegetable shop, the place my mother called 'the Dago's' because in those politically incorrect days what else would any native-born Australian call an Italian shopkeeper? Next came the hay and corn shop with its musty smell of long-stored grain. Then a Chinese market garden on poor, low-lying ground that no one else wanted. Occasionally I would meet one of the Chinese hurrying, eyes lowered, on some task that took him reluctantly out of his garden. The Chinese in Sydney kept a low profile in those days, wisely so. One of my uncles told me that on the day the First World War broke out, gangs of Australians went looking for Germans to beat up. But Germans were scarce in Sydney, so, my Uncle explained proudly, they beat up the Chinese instead.

Each day at school began the same way. We all assembled in the playground and led by the headmaster recited, 'I honour my God, I serve my King, and I salute my flag.' The God was the Protestant one, the King was George V, and the flag was the Union Jack. We celebrated Empire Day on 24 May each year and, just to remind us of our place in the order of things, there was a huge map of the world about the size of a football pitch in the playground with the British Empire coloured in red. One by one we had to stand on New South Wales and recite the names of the countries in the Empire and their capital cities.

Highlight of the school year was the summer holiday, half of December and all of January, six weeks of long, hot days at the Sans Souci swimming baths, going slowly brown – no concern then about skin cancer – with the start of school too far away to worry about and the only problem being the choice between a lime ice-block or a double chocolate malted milkshake, drunk with the thrill of the scoop of ice-cream hurtling down the inside of the aluminium container towards my sunburnt and peeling nose.

No, I lie. There was one cloud. Bubba Smith, from the top of the street, who must have been all of ten, persuaded Patty, who was nearly eight, to drop her knickers under Mrs Small's house every afternoon after school. Bubba had recruited some of his friends to this little orgy at a penny a time and I unwisely paid my dues. We might have got away with it had not Bubba and Patty, unable to defer their passion, crept away at morning recess to a spot behind the blackberry bush at the top of the school playground. Unknown to them, it was overlooked by the kitchen window of a nearby house. The woman at her sink nearly dropped the dishes and promptly got on the telephone to the headmaster. (I often wonder how, in those sexually repressed days, she described what she had seen.) Patty quickly told all and named everyone. I knew that our secret was out when I saw a delegation – Patty's mother, Bubba's mother, Lorraine's mother (Bubba had been expanding his stable) and the headmaster – opening our front gate. I sought refuge on the top of the garage roof and refused to come down until my father arrived home. I knew I was safe when I heard him laughing so loudly that my mother had to warn him that the neighbours might hear. A medical examination showed that Patty was still virgo intacta, so the parents settled the affair among themselves and we all got off with a 'good talking to'.

My 'talking to' came from my mother and consisted of a confused lesson in sexual ethics and a warning about homosexuality. I doubt whether she had discussed this with my father beforehand because although their relationship seemed perfectly amicable their conversation was almost entirely in clichés, something which I found strangely comforting. I knew that every night at the dinner table my mother would serve my father a piece of grilled steak with vegetables and as he cut it she would say, 'How's the steak, love?' and he would reply, 'Tough as old Harry.' Then my mother would say, 'Put your foot on it,' and they would both laugh. My whole life as a boy growing up in Sydney had this sort of predictability about it. Every Sunday an uncle and aunt would come to visit for afternoon tea or we would go to visit them. Tea at either house was always the same – home-made scones, nut-loaf and fruit-cake. Once a year the whole family from both sides would gather in the Botanical Gardens for an enormous picnic – seventy or eighty people – which went on all day. It always ended with a rousing rendition of 'Till We Meet Again' which left all the old aunts weeping:

> Smile the while,
> You kissed me sad adieu,
> When the clouds roll by I'll come to you,
> Then the skies will seem more blue,
> Down in lover's lane, my dearie.
> Wedding bells will ring so merrily,
> Every tear will be a memory,
> So wait and pray each night for me,
> Till we meet again.

Canterbury Boys' High was one of several selective schools which creamed off the smartest twelve-year-olds from all over metropolitan Sydney. This meant I had to travel two hours a day to get there. I caught a steam tram from a stop at the bottom of the street. I listened for the engine's whistle as it turned into the main road because this gave me thirty seconds to get out the front gate and run down the hill in time to jump on the footboard of the last carriage. At Kogarah main line station I caught an electric train to Sydenham where I changed and caught another train to

Hurlstone Park. Then I walked a mile uphill to the school. Comparing notes years later with a distinguished fellow Cantabrian, Dr William McBride, the man who alerted the world to the baby-deforming drug thalidomide, we found that our right arm was an inch longer than our left from carrying a Globite case full of text books that two miles each day for five years.

The school staff, descended from generations of Scottish schoolmasters, drilled their subjects into us with dedication. Fear and corporal punishment kept us in line. 'No move, no speak and be able to repeat the last sentence' was the school rule, and six strokes of a bamboo cane on the hand of your choice was the punishment for breaking it. It worked – up to a point. I can still quote parts of Caesar's *Gallic Wars* in Latin from memory and translate Victor Hugo at sight but when I eventually got to France I could not even ask where the toilet was. In Australia in the 1940s foreign languages were for learning, not speaking.

Our school ground was disfigured with slit trenches in anticipation of Japanese air raids which never came. In fact, Sydney had a soft war, even though its citizens used to complain that butter was rationed and beer hard to get. There was a midget submarine raid on Sydney Harbour and a larger submarine shelled the eastern suburbs from out at sea, all of which made many a local decide to pack up and move to safety inland. Property prices plummeted and European refugees, who were all accustomed to bombing and shelling, could not believe their luck. They bought luxury houses at the bottom of the market and thus laid the basis of postwar fortunes.

The end of the war in the Pacific came in the middle of the school's annual athletic carnival. The headmaster announced victory over the loudspeaker. Right had triumphed over the yellow menace, as it always would, but we should be prepared for other wars. Mankind could no more abolish war than dogs could stop fighting. He then gave us a holiday and we went into the centre of Sydney to watch American servicemen seducing Australian girls. Then, aroused by what we had seen, we tried to get a celebration of our own going with the girls from St George's High School. At our urging they asked the headmistress's permission to have a Victory dance. She said yes, providing it ended by 10.30 pm, they wore their school uniform, and they did not invite any boys.

My matriculation grades were not good enough for an arts course at Sydney University, so my mother said that while I thought about whether to re-sit some subjects I had to go to work. Consolidated Press, owned by Sir Frank Packer, father of Kerry and publisher of the *Sydney Daily Telegraph*, the *Sunday Telegraph* and the *Australian Woman's Weekly*, was looking for copy boys and I started there on the night shift – 6pm to midnight. The copy boys sat in a row on a wooden bench facing a series of buzzers, watched over by the head copy boy who was at least sixty-five. If a buzzer went, the boy at the top of the bench ran to answer the call and the whole line moved up one. But the reporters and sub-editors seldom used the buzzer. They simply roared 'BOY!' and you tracked down the source of the roar. We were called copy boys because we carried copy – the handwritten or typewritten material for publication – from one part of the newspaper office to another and finally down to the composing room where it was set for printing.

But this was only part of our duties. We ran messages for reporters, collected their laundry, bought them hamburgers and sandwiches, put them on the train or tram when they were drunk, lied to their wives and girlfriends about their whereabouts, and escorted in and out of the building the many women who called to see Sir Frank Packer. In return for all these extra duties we hoped that some of the skills of our heroes would rub off and that one day we would be rewarded with a cadetship. Four years as a cadet and you became a fully trained journalist and able to shout 'BOY!' yourself.

The king of the reporters' room was a lanky, sallow-faced former war correspondent called Sam White whose reputation preceded him. White not only had the glamour of having been a war correspondent in the Middle East but he wore the first pair of suede desert boots ever seen in Sydney. This was a brave thing to do because the toughest cop on the Vice Squad, Sergeant 'Bumper' Farrell, the man who chewed the ear off a fellow Rugby League footballer during a scrum, had decreed that only poofters wore suede shoes and therefore anyone caught wearing them could be arrested for homosexuality, then a terrible crime in Australia and punishable by life imprisonment. True, not many homosexuals actually got life, but ten years was a common sentence.

Unfortunately Sam White was not there long enough to teach us much. There is a mean streak in many Australians, a desire to punish anyone who seeks to soar above the crowd. Anyone who had been 'overseas' had to be brought back down on his return. No one actually said to Sam, 'Just because you've been a war correspondent, mate, don't think you can bludge back here. You're on court rounds.' But the chief of staff did send him to Darlinghurst Court, where the biggest case would have been about pimping, prostitution or consorting with known criminals, a catch-all charge that made it possible for the NSW police to arrest just about anyone any time. Sam stuck it for a week, then came into the office late in the afternoon, flung his copy on to the subs' table and announced, 'This isn't fucking journalism,' and resigned. He left a week later for Europe, settled in France and as correspondent for Lord Beaverbrook's newspapers found the fame he justly deserved.

The reporter with the most envied job was Dave Barnes, who ran the *Sunday Telegraph* Beach Girl competition. During the summer months, Barnes spent several hours every day wandering along Sydney beaches looking for candidates for that week's beach girl. When he found one, the *Sunday Telegraph* photographer would either take her picture on the sand or ask her to come into the newspaper studio later that day. At the end of summer, the paper's readers voted for the beach girl of the year. Barnes took his job seriously and as far as I knew never took advantage of the power it gave him. I cannot say the same for the photographers. Swimming costumes in those days were usually one-piece and very modest. The photographer, alone with the beach girl in the office studio, would take the discreet shot that would be used in that week's newspaper. Then he would say, 'Now let's have one for the boys in the darkroom,' and insist that the girl drop the top part of her costume and expose her breasts. It was a revelation how many would agree. 'They can't resist the camera,' the photographers would say cynically, as they produced their collection for the copy boys. In these days of topless and bottomless Sydney beaches, no one would find the photographs erotic, but for eighteen-year-old copy boys the thought that we had seen a photograph of the bare breasts of the incredibly beautiful girl that Dave Barnes had escorted through the newsroom that afternoon made us tremble with lust.

One day there was a printers' strike. The journalists' union called the reporters out in sympathy and the reporters told the copy boys to come out too. In the Irish pub on the corner of Park and Castlereagh streets they lectured us about worker solidarity. 'There's only two classes in this world,' said one of the sports writers. 'Bosses and workers, and you lot are workers. When youse are old enough you can join the union. Then you've got every bloody worker in Australia behind you, providing you stick together and don't scab.' Anyone who would stay at work when his mates were out on strike was a dirty, rotten bastard, lower than a fucking snake's belly, probably a Pom, and should never, ever be forgiven. There was once such a journalist, they said, who defied the union and stayed at work to help the management produce the paper. When he finished his shift in the early hours and tried to catch the night tram home, the conductor threw him off. The next day when he tried to get a beer, the barmaid would not serve him. His regular restaurant turned him away. And when the sanitary men, who in those pre-sewage days collected your full lavatory pan and replaced it with a fresh, empty one, heard about the scab they let him stew in his own shit. Here was an example, they said, of Australian worker solidarity, and, like a lot of other things in Australia, the best in the whole bloody world. All this, it turned out, had happened years before, but the reporters spoke of it as if it were yesterday, and their hatred for the scab, still being punished, was undiminished. It all had a powerful impression on the copy boys and made me, forty years later, as emotionally incapable of crossing any picket line as I was then.

After a year as a copy boy there was still no chance of a cadetship because returning servicemen had priority for any spare jobs. But they all preferred the city, so I began writing to editors of country newspapers asking if they had a vacancy for a first-year cadet. The *Northern Star*, a daily paper in Lismore, a flourishing dairy centre in northern New South Wales on the Queensland border, said yes. My mother, who had not forgotten the Patty and Bubba Smith incident, found me accommodation at Miss MacNa-mara's Boarding House for Professional Young Gentlemen and Ladies, a big, pre-First World War wooden house with a rusting, corrugated iron roof on which the drumming of rain during the wet season was sometimes so loud it kept those on the top floor awake half the night. Miss MacNamara, a white-haired spinster in her middle seventies, promised to keep an eye on me herself. We slept two to a room – men in one part of the house, women in another – and ate in a big community dining room served by two waitresses who were even older than Miss MacNamara. The other guests were police constables, nurses, office workers, school teachers, and one other journalist, a Scots immigrant called Frank Cleary, who had clearly run away from something nasty in the Old Country.

I think it was at Cleary's suggestion that the editor threw me in at the deep end: the annual meeting of the Country Women's Association, the weekly swimming carnival, the opening of a new baby health centre, the monthly meeting of the Returned Servicemen's League, weddings, funerals and twenty-first birthday parties. When the one woman reporter, Gwen Lyle, went on holiday, I even wrote her weekly column, 'Roundabout, by "Suzanne".' It was wonderful training. The idea of interviewing someone on the telephone never occurred to us – we went out and met people face to face. We were part of the community. We knew everybody and everybody knew us. If I got someone's second initial wrong, they would stop me on the street to complain. If I got the whole story wrong I would never hear the end of it. The *Northern Star* taught me to be accurate, that people had feelings, and that you could not use your privileged access as a journalist to come into their lives, suck them dry, and then leave again. You had personal and civic responsibilities. Take Alderman W. G. Walker, the mayor. Walker was a popular figure and good at his job. But he was poorly educated, and his grammar made his speeches something of a joke to anyone who, like a reporter, had to listen to what he actually said. One day, when he was particularly incoherent, I handed in as a joke a verbatim report of his speech. The editor was furious. What if the story had made its way into the paper by accident? The mayor's reputation would have suffered and so would that of the newspaper. Was this what I wanted? In future I would do as everyone else did – without changing the mayor's meaning, I would polish up his speeches in all my reports. Why? Because it was not a journalist's job to make fools out of honest public figures. If they were dishonest, that was another matter, but if I wanted to get on in journalism then the gratuitous humiliation of other people was not the way to do it.

But even at that stage of my career in journalism there were indications that not everything the reader learnt from his paper was necessarily true. On one long, hot, humid summer afternoon, Cleary got up from his typewriter in the reporters' room and announced he was going for a cold milkshake. 'Here,' he said, handing me a file, 'it's time you had a turn doing the stars.' I looked at the folder. It was labelled 'The Week Ahead – Your Future in the Stars, by Taurus'. Until then I had believed that the *Northern Star* had a regular astrologer who wrote the weekly column. Now it appeared the reporters did it. Cleary noticed my bewilderment. 'Don't worry, it's easy,' he said. 'Go down to the file room and dig out a copy of the paper from ten years ago. Copy out its stars column then mix it around a bit.' He headed for the door, then stopped. 'One other thing. Don't give the same people bad stars two days running.'

At the end of a year in Lismore I was restless. I felt that I had learnt all that the *Northern Star* had to teach me. Cleary, in a rare communicative mood, said that it did not matter what you did to earn a living because the best training for journalism was life. 'Piss off from here,' he said. 'Get any old job. You'll always be able to come back to reporting.' The very next day there was an advertisement in the *Sydney Morning Herald*: 'British company requires trainee South Sea Island traders. Young men with initiative and a sense of adventure are invited to apply for long- and short-term contracts.' To a nineteen-year-old steeped in Conrad and Somerset Maugham, the challenge was irresistible and after a long interview in the Sydney offices of Morris Hedstrom – at which they seemed more interested in what sport I had played at school than in my academic achievements – I got the job and left for Fiji the following month.

In those early post-war years, before tourism, the few people who wanted to go to Fiji did so by boat, in six or seven leisurely days on old steamships which had been rescued from troop-carrying to re-open the San Francisco-Sydney run. But my new employers splashed out on a seat for me on the Pan American clipper plane which boasted bunks that folded out of the cabin ceiling. After a few drinks and a freshly cooked meal, the stewardess made up your bed, you snuggled down between crisp sheets to the comforting roar of the engines and woke up in Nadi, Fiji's international airport. A day's taxi-ride over dirt roads past miles of sugar-cane fields took you to Suva, the capital.

It was exactly as I had expected – straight out of *Lord Jim*. The docks were crowded with inter-island vessels, most of them still sail-powered. Beyond the Customs sheds, wooden buildings with wide verandahs shaded footpaths along which Fijians, Indians, Chinese and Europeans moved leisurely about their business. A dirty canal ran from the harbour through the town to the warehouses. In the offices and shops ceiling fans struggled to stir the humid air. And over everything, pervasive and persistent, was the sweet, heavy smell of copra and the rhythmic thud-thud-thud of the town's mill crushing coconut meat to make oil for a fat-starved Britain.

It was fortunate that Suva was so romantic because being an island trader turned out to be unspeakably boring. Morris Hedstrom bought copra from the Fijians and, in return, sold them British-manufactured goods. My job was to keep track of all those goods. I met the 'home' ship when she came in, helped supervise the unloading, entered the stock, and at regular intervals did the stock-taking. Indian clerks, descendants of the Tamil labourers Britain had imported in the nineteenth century to work the sugar plantations, did the counting. I did the sums: six dozen and three four-inch brass countersunk screws at £1.7.6 a gross, equals what? After an hour or so of this in those pre-calculator days I would doze off at my desk, at first guiltily and then, when I noticed everyone else nodding, with equanimity. I made a vow then that I would never take an office job again.

In the evenings I escaped into the colony's social scene. This was on many, highly regulated levels. At the top there was the Governor, known to all as 'H. E.' (His Excellency), and his staff, representing His Majesty's Colonial Office. They mixed happily with each other and seldom appeared in public. When they did, the Governor wore a pith helmet with plumes of ostrich feathers, his spotless white uniform heavy with gold braid. Then came the old Fiji families – English and Scots traders who had been in the colony for more than a generation – followed by Australian and New Zealand businessmen recently arrived to make a quick killing. The others told stories about this lot's greed for profit. One, a cattle rancher called Bailey, lived miles from anywhere in a house that did not even have electricity. A windfall made him decide to import a kerosene-powered refrigerator from New Zealand. When it arrived, he drove to Suva, proudly cleared it from Customs, took it back, installed it, and the next day invited some neighbours over for a drink. For the first time in years, he boasted, he had hard butter and cold beer. One of the neighbours said, 'I'll give yer ten quid more than you paid for it.' 'Done,' said Bayly, and sold it on the spot.

The various groups seldom mingled. The top rung had its clubs (the Fiji, the Defence, the Yacht Club) all of which operated a colour bar – whites only. The town's top hotel, the Grand Pacific, then one of the great hotels of the world, did not. But Fijians, Indians, Chinese and the white workers seldom went there anyway – it was too expensive.

The unmarried Morris Hedstrom staff ranked well down the social scale and stayed in the Bachelors' Mess, which was run like a military one. Head mess boy was a Fijian, Jimmy, who fed us, organised our laundry and went around in the middle of the night with a club killing cockroaches as big as sparrows. The bachelors played billiards, gave parties, and drank a lot. Perhaps we were depressed because at the end of a couple of months it became apparent that far from being trainee island traders we were actually white indentured labour. Most of us arrived with a few pounds to tide us over until pay day, only to learn that Morris Hedstrom paid monthly in arrears. Not to worry, the kindly Morris Hedstrom manager said. As employees of such a respected company we could open credit accounts wherever we wished. Soon we all had accounts with the tailor, the taxi company, the laundryman, the liquor merchant, and at most restaurants. Our pay cheque arrived on the last day of each month. The bills came in twenty-four hours later. By the second of the month we were broke again. Older hands told us that after two years they were no closer to becoming solvent than when they arrived. Their contracts had expired but they could afford to leave the islands only, as every now and then one did, by secretly booking an airline ticket and fleeing their employer and their creditors in the dark of night.

I fled after six months. Not from the islands, but back to journalism. A group of local businessmen decided to try to break the newspaper monopoly enjoyed by the *Fiji Times and Herald*, whose editor, a former New Zealand schoolteacher called Len Usher, was trying to mould it into a South Pacific version of *The Times* of London. The idea was that the new paper should be more like the *Daily Mirror*. The backers bought a flatbed press that the London Missionary Society had imported a hundred years earlier to print bibles, recruited an editor from New Zealand and found a sub-editor in the unlikely person of Bryan Hanrahan, a former British army officer in the Royal Artillery who had washed up in Fiji after a good war in India. With a flash of inspiration, based on the fact that Fiji is just to the west of the International Date Line, where the world's time starts, they called their paper the *Oceania Daily News* and gave it the slogan 'The First Paper Published in the World Today'. Theoretically, every day it would scoop not only the *New York Times*, the *Washington Post, Le Monde,* and *The Times* of London, but every other newspaper. The challenge was irresistible. I gave up business for ever and became its only reporter.

The job brought me into contact with a Fiji that I had not known existed. Underneath an apparently calm and orderly exterior, all sorts of strange things were going on. The Indian community, which even then made up nearly half the population, seethed with internal violence, usually over land disputes, arranged marriages that had gone wrong, or quarrels over dowries. Judging from the court cases I covered, the favourite method of settling these arguments was not litigation but to break someone's legs with an iron bar. The other popular criminal pastime was rape, usually of Fijian women by Fijian men. The court interpreter was a stony-faced Chinese who always seemed to have trouble in getting the women to describe the state of the rapist's sexual organ, since a statement that it was erect was deemed a necessary part of proof of the crime. From the convoluted answers he dragged from the reluctant accusers, translated for the benefit of the British magistrate, I concluded that most Fijian women seemed to think that a man's penis had only one form – stiff.

Occasionally there were events of international interest. I watched one morning as the home boat towed into Suva Harbour a former United States navy torpedo boat. It was minus most of its superstructure and I could just make out a bearded, half-naked figure on deck. When it dropped anchor, I rowed out in a borrowed dinghy and met the owner. He was a New Zealand adventurer called Ronald Johnson. Johnson had been sailing around the South Pacific in his 62-foot yacht *Thelma* and had put into Pearl Harbor, Hawaii, just as the US government was holding one of its periodic war disposals sales. Surprised at the low prices, Johnson sold *Thelma* for $10,000 and promptly bought US torpedo boat 761, which he renamed *Purple Sea*, two floating docks, four landing barges, twelve marine engines, seven launches, and 5,000 gallons of petrol. After he had paid, the port authorities revealed the catch – Johnson had twenty-four hours to clear his purchases from Pearl Harbor or forfeit his money. The same day he did a deal with a freighter captain. In return for all but the *Purple Sea* and two marine engines, the freighter would tow him and his engineless ship to Tahiti. There, Johnson believed, he could install the engines in the *Purple Sea*, and get rich trading out of Papeete.

Two days out from Pearl Harbor, on 9 October, 1947, the tow line broke in a storm. The freighter skipper said he had no time to try to get another line on board so Johnson would have to abandon the *Purple Sea*. Johnson signalled, 'No way,' so the freighter steamed off and left him drifting in the middle of the Pacific. On 23 October the freighter captain, covering his tracks, reported to the Papeete authorities that Johnson and the *Purple Sea* had gone down in the storm. But Johnson was far from dead – in fact he was enjoying himself. There was sufficient water and food on board for two and a half years, and a well-stocked library of books ranging from Dickens to *Practical Navigation*. Johnson told me, 'The weather was good, so I set up a deck chair and for the first month I just read and loafed in the sun. Then I got bored so I found a roll of canvas in the hold and rigged up a sail. She sailed best going astern, which slowed her down to about a knot or so, but sailing kept me occupied. I set a rough course for Fiji and settled down to wait for land.'

Johnson drifted for four months. He grew sick of tinned food so fished and cooked his catch on deck on an open fire fuelled by hacking down pieces of the superstructure. Then on 12 February 1948, the British freighter *Fort Cadotte* on its way from London to Suva via the Panama Canal radioed that it had picked up a small craft, with one man on board, drifting 200 miles east of the Wailagilala Lighthouse in the East Fiji group of islands. It towed Johnson and his *Purple Sea* into Suva three days later. Today Johnson could have sold his story for a fortune and then have gone on to work the after-dinner speakers' circuit. In 1948, all he got from me was a few beers which, since the *Oceania Daily News* did not run to expense accounts, I was unable to reclaim.

Life as a reporter in Fiji was wonderful. I covered everything, and even started a gossip column which I called, naturally 'Round the Town with Suzanne'. The column turned out to be a terrible error of judgement. At first informants fell over themselves to tell me what was really going on in the colony – politically, socially, sexually. In innocence, I wrote it all: 'Who was the lady in the red polka-dot dress seen emerging from bushes near the Cable and Wireless station in the early hours last Thursday accompanied by Mr R. And did her husband know?' The circulation of the *Oceania Daily News* soared.

My first inkling that not everyone enjoyed reading 'Suzanne' came when I went as a paying passenger on Johnson's boat to Levuka, the old capital, on the island of Ovalau. There we were to meet up with the Yacht Club for a weekend cruise. Levuka was at its peak in the nineteenth century when Bully Hayes, the notorious South Pacific 'blackbirder' or slave trader, used to navigate his way into harbour by following the trail of floating empty rum bottles left by other schooners, and the town could boast of fifty-two bars on the short main street. While we waited for the Yacht Club to arrive, I wandered up to the Royal Hotel where Somerset Maugham once stayed, and then on to the cemetery off Beach Street. There I found the grave of John Brown Williams, the United States Consul for Fiji, who died in 1860, and is buried under a breadfruit tree. The story goes that it was Williams's inflated claims for compensation from Fiji for looting after the consulate was burnt down during a Fourth of July party that decided King Cakobau to cede Fiji to Britain's Queen Victoria before the American sent him bankrupt.

Just before the cruise had left Suva, I wrote a small item for the *News*. I still have the yellowing clipping dated Wednesday, 20 October 1948. 'Big event of the year for yacht club-ites is the cruise this weekend. Known as the closing weekend it provides an excuse for a party on Saturday night. There's some very tall (or are they?) stories around town of the amount of liquid ballast some of the boats are to carry.' This was a perfectly justifiable reference to the heavy drinking for which Yacht Club members were renowned but in the middle of the night I was seized from my berth by a bunch of drunken Yacht Club heavies chanting, 'Suzanne is a dirty old man. Oink, oink. Suzanne is a dirty old man.' I put up a token resistance for honour's sake and then surrendered. They carried me to the end of the pier and threw me into the sea. When I clambered out, they gave me a rum and told me to be careful what I wrote lest I confirm the Fijians' worst views of the whites.

Word of this, and of the lady in the polka-dot dress, must have reached Government House because I received a telephone call – could I have afternoon tea with the Governor's secretary? He turned out to be a tall, languid young man, not much older than me, a little like the British attaché in Evelyn Waugh's *Scoop*, and we had a chat over Darjeeling and Osborn biscuits in a drawing room that looked as if it had been transposed intact from Mayfair.

He handled it brilliantly. He began by asking me how journalism worked. Who thought of a story? How did you go about getting it? Who decided how long it would be? Gradually he steered the talk around to an item I had written about a hurricane which in December 1948 had devastated some of the outer islands in the Fiji group. I had used the Weather Bureau's code name for the hurricane, 'Margaret'. It was a brilliant story, he said, but he felt that the use of a woman's name for the hurricane tended to detract from the seriousness of the disaster. 'In fact, dear boy,' he said, 'one has to be careful about publishing women's names in general. Things like that could damage our reputation in the eyes of the

Fijians and cause problems. I know H. E. is very keen that we must be seen to be beyond reproach. I'm sure you understand.' And he actually winked.

Soon afterwards the editor of the *News* left for a better job in Australia and the paper fell apart. The new editor, another New Zealander, drove Hanrahan, the sub-editor, mad with lectures on pedantic points of grammar. Late one night, overcome by the heat and tension, Hanrahan listened to half an hour on the use of the pluperfect, then snatched a painting off the editor's wall and smashed it over his head. Understandably, the editor fired him. The printers, who had more to do with Hanrahan than the editor, went on strike in his support. The clerical staff, who had more to do with the editor, went on strike in *his* support. Since I comprised the whole of the editorial staff, I had to choose which picket line to join, and since I was a paying guest in Hanrahan's house, I joined him. The proprietors, under pressure from the Governor not to allow either strike to succeed because of the example it might set the native workers, sacked everyone and shut down the paper for good.

This put me in an awkward position. There was a law intended to prevent beachcombers from settling in Fiji. It said that anyone without a job, or a bank balance sufficient to provide a living, could be deported. I made one or two desultory attempts to find a job, knowing all the while that no one in the colony was likely to employ a man who had been on strike, and when I had no success, retired to a remote Fijian village, hoping that my absence from the streets of Suva would encourage the immigration officers to forget about me.

Village life was very revealing. Nature provides just about everything a Fijian needs. Food grows wild, fish rush to take the hook, and a system of co-operative living means that the village undertakes the responsibility of providing housing for anyone who needs it. In those days Fijians had little sense of personal property – everything belonged to everybody, so if a neighbour had something you needed, you simply took it, the only inhibition against doing so being that he could always do the same to you. This practice was not conducive to success in the retail trade, and generations of British administrators had given up trying to establish Fijians as shopkeepers and let the Indians take over this section of the economy.

What little work needed doing was done mostly by the women. The men lounged around, played rugby, drank kava, a mouth-numbing drink made from the crushed roots of a Polynesian plant, used for its effect rather than its taste, which was unbelievably foul. (One of my fondest memories is of watching the Duke of Edinburgh, forced by protocol to swallow a coconut shell full of ceremonial kava during the 1953 Royal visit to Fiji, desperately trying not to grimace or throw up.)

The carefree life that Fijians led made it hard for them to understand European concern about responsible behaviour. An old-timer who had been in the Colonial police told me that he had been on duty the day after Charles Kingsford Smith and Charles Ulm landed in Fiji in 1928 on their historic flight across the Pacific from the United States to Australia. Suva had no airport, so Smith had managed to land their three-engined Fokker, the *Southern Cross*, in Albert Park, opposite the Grand Pacific Hotel. But once the plane was loaded with fuel, the park would be too short for the take-off. So the *Southern Cross* was towed to a nearby beach long enough for take-off, and it was re-fuelled there. Both pilots were fanatical about clean petrol — a blocked carburettor jet over the ocean could cost them their lives — so they personally strained every gallon through a piece of chamois leather before it went into the plane's tanks. This operation left the area near the plane reeking of petrol fumes, so my police officer friend said he had posted a guard of five Fijian constables around the plane with orders to keep everyone away until take-off at dawn. 'In the middle of the night,' he said, 'I woke up worrying about something. I couldn't put my finger on it, but it was disturbing enough to make me dress and drive down to the plane. A light drizzle of rain had started and, rare for Suva, it was actually a little chilly. When I got to the plane the Fijians were shivering and to keep warm and shelter from the rain they had gathered under the plane's wing and there — and there — they had lit a little fire. They couldn't understand why I bawled them out. I didn't have the courage to tell Kingsford Smith. In fact, I didn't tell anyone.'

I wore out my hospitality in the village and returned to Suva where I moved in with a local family called the Wilders, part European, part Fijian. They owned a derelict launch and I filled in my hours repairing the engine and getting the hull seaworthy. I had visions of following Johnson's lead and becoming an island trader. In the meantime I thought I could at least provide the Wilders with fish caught from the coral reef about two miles offshore. The launch made it to the reef where I dropped anchor and, when the tide had gone out, stepped on to the coral to look for fish trapped in the reef pools. At sunset I reboarded the launch to return to Suva, but the engine refused to start. Darkness fell, the wind got up, and I had no way of knowing whether the anchor was holding. If it did not, the launch would be pounded to pieces on the reef and I might well be, too. The lights of Suva seemed frustratingly close but midnight came and went and I was just considering soaking a rag in petrol and lighting it when there was the sound of a powerful engine and a launch from one of the freighters in harbour loomed out of the darkness. A Fijian deckhand threw me a line and the launch towed me back to town. Hanrahan, who knew of my plans, had noticed that I had not returned and persuaded the freighter captain to lower the ship's launch and look for me.

Word of this adventure went around town and within days I received two worrying letters. The first was from the secretary of the Masonic Lodge of Suva. The letter said that the Master and other officers had noticed the company I had been keeping and had decided that the lodge was not prepared any longer to welcome me as a visitor from Australia. The second letter asked me to call on the immigration officer as soon as possible.

I replied to the letter from the lodge saying that the phrase 'the company you have been keeping' must refer to Polly Wilder, one of the prettier and younger Wilders, and that the lodge's objections could only be racial. I found one of the Jehovah's Witnesses who periodically visited Fiji and persuaded him to give me a half a dozen quotations from the Bible about brotherly love and racial tolerance and peppered my letter with them. I concluded by saying that if this was an example of the brotherhood of freemasonry, then I no longer wanted any part of it. I wish I had kept a copy because it must have sounded as smug as only a self-righteous nineteen-year-old could.

There was nothing to say to the immigration officer. He made it plain that he would be calling on Morris Hedstrom, who had deposited a bond with him when I first arrived, to pay my fare back to Australia. I could either book the ticket myself and go the route I chose, or he would do it. Either way, I had two weeks. Ten days later I sailed for New Zealand in a little passenger ship, the *Matunga*, standing sadly at the stern until Suva disappeared below the horizon and the haunting smell of copra was finally swallowed in the ship's wake.

It was an unfinished chapter in my life so, forty-two years later, I went back. By then the old Fiji had vanished, to be replaced by a multi-million dollar tourist resort for Americans and affluent Australians – tennis ranches, golf courses, luxury hotels and lavishly equipped cruise ships. On the surface all had changed, and yet . . . Morris Hedstrom was still there, though not under the same ownership. It did not recruit abroad any more but employed Fijian nationals, so there was no longer any need for a Bachelors' Mess. Fiji became independent in 1970; the Governor and all the elegant young men who worked for him had gone.

But not before he abolished the colour bar at a stroke. It was the custom for the Governor to do a round of the clubs at midnight on New Year's Eve and announce the names on the Queen's New Year's Honours List. Suddenly, the incumbent Governor, Sir Brian Freestone, bending to the winds of change, let it be known that when he next looked in at the clubs he had better see some brown faces among the white, or else he might not be calling again. Change came overnight. Even the Masonic Lodge, which had given me my comeuppance, opened its doors to all races and creeds and at the time of my return visit, the masters of the two lodges which met in Suva were both Roman Catholics – one an Indian and the other a part European. Polly Wilder would be amazed.

Some of the old hands had stayed on, regretting the fact that no one dressed for dinner any more and that the Grand Pacific Hotel had become a shadow of its former self, a back-packers' refuge, unable to compete with the luxury hotels on the other side of the island. Just before my return visit, my old boss at Morris Hedstrom had died at the snooker table in his club, which his friends said was appropriate because that was where he had spent most of his life. Len Usher, the young editor of the *Fiji Times and Herald* had become Sir Leonard Usher, KBE, CF, and there was a street named after him. The *Fiji Times*, now owned, of course, by Rupert Murdoch, had taken over the slogan of the *Oceania Daily News*, so the first paper published in the world today lived on in spirit, if not name.

In Suva, except when there was a cruise liner in town, life ticked over as it always did. The dark old warehouses were still there and the docks still smelled of copra. Giant Fijian men in skirts still strolled hand in hand past women fishing off the sea wall. On my last night I walked from Morris Hedstrom down the main street to Albert Park, watched some Fijians playing rugby, and tried to imagine what it was like for Kingsford Smith and Ulm coming in to land after crossing half the Pacific Ocean and seeing below them the little green handkerchief of the park. Then I crossed the road, ordered a cold beer on the lawn at the Grand Pacific, listened to the rustle of the coconut palms as the sun went down and the tropical night took over, and decided that Fiji was much the same. All that had gone was my youth.

CHAPTER TWO

MURDOCH SENIOR AND JUNIOR

The *Matunga* took five days to reach New Zealand and as soon as it docked and I had found accommodation, I began the round of the Auckland newspapers looking for work. There wasn't any but someone in a pub said that there was good money to be made on the wharves. The wharf labourers' union did not have sufficient members to handle the increasing flow of imports as the New Zealand economy began to pick up after the war, but it was reluctant to recruit new members in case the situation changed. It had compromised by agreeing with the employers that they could use casual labour when needed. The employers recruited these workers from a compound on the wharves at 7am every morning. We were known as 'seagulls' because we hung around hoping to pick up the scraps that regular wharf labourers rejected.

It was demeaning to be herded into the compound with its high wire fences and then looked over by the men from the stevedoring companies assessing your physical strength, but the money made up for it. Those selected were taken by truck to the ship being unloaded and then added to the union gangs already at work. The union organiser explained the unwritten rules. Each day he would inspect the hold to see that it was properly lit and that all the safety regulations had been obeyed. He would then examine the cargo to see that the correct rate had been agreed – dirty or dangerous cargoes justified higher rates. A gang comprised eight men but the job rarely needed more than four at one time so it was understood by everyone, including the employers, that four men would work two hours while the other four 'rested', and then vice-versa. On your two hours off you could even go into town as long as you were back on time. None of this applied if the job was so unattractive that no union men wanted it and the gangs were all seagulls. Then you worked until your back cracked, loading, say, 112lb bags of flour into slings, emerging from the hold at knock-off time looking like a ghost and as thirsty as only a wharf labourer can be.

After two months there was a lull on the waterfront, seagulling declined, and I had to seek another job. By this time my hands were hard and I actually looked like a labourer, so the New Zealand Posts and Telegraph department took me on as a linesman. I thought this meant hanging from telephone poles, but the P and T was in the process of going underground and it actually meant digging ditches in which to lay cables. This was all done by hand and was boring pick and shovel work unless we hit rock; then it became fun. The foreman was a licensed explosives expert and he would bring out a stick of dynamite and a detonator. One gang would drill a hole into the rock in which to place the explosive while another drove to the nearest area of bush and cut six or so leafy saplings. These were used to deaden the blast and stop small pieces of rock from flying about. When the foreman had wired the detonator to a small generator we drew lots for the privilege of cranking the handle that set off the explosion.

We inched our way south for six months and then I decided I had had enough. I booked a sea passage to Sydney on the weekly trans-Tasman service and spent the entire voyage in my berth – the Tasman Sea must be one of the roughest in the world. There were still no jobs on any of the Sydney newspapers, so in desperation I appealed to Sir Keith Murdoch – father of Rupert Murdoch, the multi-media magnate – who ran the *Herald*, the only afternoon newspaper in Melbourne. I wrote to him personally and told him that I had met two of his reporters in Fiji, where they had been offloaded from a Swedish oil tanker diverted from its original destination, San Francisco, to Indonesia. The reporters had been working as ships' stewards hoping to make it to London, Fleet Street, fame and fortune, in much the same adventurous way as young Keith himself had done thirty years earlier. Mentioning them gave me a valid excuse to recount my own role in Fiji and to suggest subtly that I too was an adventurer. Murdoch replied by telegram asking me to meet him on his next trip to Sydney. I did and was hired as a fourth-year cadet. I hitched a ride to Melbourne on an inter-state freight truck and started work the following week.

It was my first experience on an afternoon newspaper and the system was as rigid as in any military establishment. The chief of staff and his deputy started work at 5am and ploughed through the morning newspapers – the *Age*, the *Argus*, and the *Sun-Pictorial* – looking for stories that could be expanded or developed. A newsroom diary listed all forthcoming events and those occurring that day were added to the list of possible stories. By the time the first reporters arrived at 7.30am, the assignments had been compiled and the straightforward ones set out in typewritten notes which were placed in each reporter's mail box. Reporters allocated complicated assignments were given a personal briefing from the chief of staff or his deputy.

As well as general reporters, of which I was one, there were 'roundsmen', senior journalists who looked after specific 'beats'. The western roundsman looked after the western end of the city which included the railways and the transport unions. The police roundsman covered crime, the court roundsman the courts, the state roundsman the goings-on at the state parliament. The shipping roundsman met incoming ships, and the industrial roundsman covered all industrial disputes. Sometimes a story straddled two areas and then there were fierce battles between roundsmen defending their territory.

One day I had been assigned to shipping because it was the regular roundsman's day off. It was late afternoon, nothing was happening, and the final edition – the *Herald* produced about five a day – was due to press in about an hour. The *Florentia*, a passenger ship from Malta, had docked that morning carrying wives and relatives of Maltese men who had emigrated to Australia ahead of their families to set up home. These men, many of whom had not seen their families for a year or more, had arrived at the wharves before dawn to meet the ship.

Despite the post-war immigration scheme that had brought hundreds of thousands of southern Europeans to Australia, local officialdom remained very suspicious of them. Immigration officials acted as if every document the immigrants carried had been forged, Customs automatically assumed that they were all smuggling drugs, arms and alcohol, and the quarantine officers knew for certain that they would be carrying sausages full of foot and mouth disease or other typically foreign organisms.

So while wives, children and parents lined the ship's decks and waved to their menfolk waiting patiently on the wharf in the sun, these officials slowly and painstakingly worked their way through the immigrants' documents and baggage. I had left the wharf at noon to do other shipping stories so I decided now to go back and see if it had all concluded smoothly.

I walked through the dock gates into a riot – the Maltese were storming the ship. A Customs officer who had tried to stop them entering the Customs examination hall had had his ear bitten off and was staggering around with a bloodstained handkerchief clasped to his head. The Maltese were winning, but over the noise of battle was the distant whine of police sirens.

Was this a police rounds story or a shipping one? Once the police arrived, the police roundsman would not be far behind and his office car was equipped with two-way radio so he could dictate stories direct to the *Herald*. But until he arrived, it was a shipping story, my story – if I could find a telephone and send it. At the far end of the Customs examination hall, well away from the fighting, was an empty office. The door was locked but a hard push sprang the catch. I got on the telephone and told the chief of staff what was happening. Then I dictated five paragraphs to the copy-takers – fast touch typists, all women, who worked with earphones, typing one paragraph to each short sheet paper, then ripping it from the machine to pass to the sub-editors' desk for processing.

I had just started the sixth paragraph when two Customs officers burst in. 'Get the fuck off the phone,' the first one said, reaching for it. 'I'm from the Herald,' I said. 'I'm sending my story.' He wrenched the telephone from me. 'Dave,' he said. 'Chuck this bastard out.' Dave escorted me to a loading ramp and made me jump down to the street. As I walked through the wharf gates, I saw the *Herald* police rounds car arrive, and the roundsman leap out and run towards the riot which appeared to be petering out. He was too late. I had my first front-page scoop.

Whether word of this reached Murdoch or not, I never knew. But a week or so later his secretary called me to her office and said, 'Sir Keith likes to meet new members of the editorial staff. He's going to Canberra for a couple of days tomorrow. He wants you to go along as his secretary. It's a good chance to see how he runs his papers. Here's your ticket. You'll be staying at the Rex. He'll be at the farm but he'll be in touch with you when he needs you.' In Canberra, I checked in at the hotel and waited. Sir Keith rang early next morning and said he would pick me up outside the hotel in an hour. I watched a procession of government limousines and the occasional Bentley come up the driveway. Would Murdoch have a Bentley or a Rolls? Finally a battered, dirty, utility truck pulled up with Murdoch in the passenger's seat and a young man about my age driving. Murdoch got out to let me in, and I squeezed my knees around the gear shift. 'This is my son, Rupert,' Murdoch said. We shook hands and the truck lurched off for the Indian High Commission.

I had, of course, heard of Rupert because there had been rumours in the reporters' room that he was going to fill in some of his time between finishing at Geelong Grammar School and going up to Oxford by working as a cadet on the *Herald*. My first impression was that he was an image of his father. He had the same sturdy build, the same features, the same wavy hair. He had also inherited his father's relaxed easy manner – what someone was later to describe as 'deadly charm'. 'Have you been to Canberra before?' he asked. I confessed that I had not. 'If Dad doesn't need you this afternoon, I'll show you around. The War Memorial's well worth a visit.'

At the Indian High Commission, Murdoch and the High Commissioner and his wife chatted over tea while Rupert and I waited patiently. The High Commissioner was pressing the Murdochs to come to a reception he was giving that evening to mark India's national day. Murdoch was protesting that the reception was black tie and he did not want to drive back to the farm to change. Finally he yielded. 'Okay,' he said. 'We'll come. We'll buy something in town.' Ah, I thought, how wonderful to be rich. Your dinner jacket is back at the farm when you need it for a black tie reception, so you simply buy another dinner jacket. When we got back into the truck and drove to the Rex, Murdoch got out, fished in his pocket for his wallet, drew out a single pound note and handed it to Rupert. 'Buy a couple of black ties for tonight,' he said.

Murdoch had lunch with the Prime Minister, Robert Menzies, and I went along to hand out the cigars and field telephone calls. Then he dictated a letter to his fellow newspaper proprietor Sir Lloyd Dumas, of Adelaide. It gave a summary of what had been discussed over luncheon, including four or five paragraphs on what the Prime Minister had said about the likelihood of an alteration in the currency exchange rate between Britain and Australia and advice on what Dumas should do to take advantage of this inside information. I could have sworn that Murdoch said that, according to Menzies, a 'revaluation' was likely in the next three months and that was what I typed and then signed on behalf of Murdoch and posted. But when I mentioned it to a business reporter on my return to Melbourne, he alarmed me by saying, 'That can't be right. A *devaluation* is on the cards but certainly not a revaluation.' I spent an anxious three months worrying that when the devaluation occurred Sir Lloyd Dumas would lose a fortune and the blame would be traced back to me. In the event nothing at all happened; Sir Lloyd Dumas never complained; and I felt the first splinter of doubt about the effect of political and economic information.

The shipping round continued to produce good human interest stories. The ships' pursers were happy to tell me if there were any unusual passengers on board and there often were. On the *Orion* I found the self-proclaimed ju-jitsu champion of the world, 67-year-old, 6-foot 6-inch, 16-stone Leo McLaglen, brother of the film star Victor McLaglen. McLaglen said that he had learnt his skills from a Japanese nobleman, Prince Shimara, and had then taught ju jitsu to Allied troops during the Second World War and to police departments in Britain, the United States, France, Germany and Australia. I suspected a little show-business exaggeration here, so I asked him to show me a trick. He put his hands around my neck, pressed, and I fell unconscious on to the floor of his cabin. I was out for only a few seconds and it seemed fun – and a good story – at the time, but today I wonder whether encouraging him to cut off the blood supply to my brain, however briefly, for the sake of a few paragraphs in a newspaper showed a very responsible attitude on my part – or his.

On some occasions a story emerged from the most unlikely source – proof of old Cleary's dictum that everyone had a story if you could only winkle it out of them. On one passenger liner I was reduced to interviewing a father and son business partnership who had come to Australia to start a toy factory, hardly stop press news. But I persisted with questions and it turned out that in Britain they had manufactured furniture and had never made toys before. 'Why the switch?' I asked. Father and son looked at each other and the father launched into an explanation. The furniture business in Britain was going through a bad spell. It was subject to economic cycles and when things were down, people made do with their old furniture. One day the son had said, 'Let's find a business that is recession-proof.' So he went through statistics looking for the last products people stop buying when money is tight. 'What do you think they are?' he said. I confessed I had little idea. 'The main two are fairly obvious,' he said. 'The last thing people stop buying is food. The second last thing they stop buying is clothing. But what do reckon the third last is? – toys. No matter how bad things are, when it comes to Christmas and birthdays, mum and dad can always scrape up enough cash to buy the kids some toys. So we're going into the toy business.'

Immigration stories were always news because this was a period when the Australian government was vigorously recruiting migrants in Britain and Europe. I interviewed the largest family ever to migrate to Australia, that of Bernard Davis (58), his wife, their children, and their sons-in-law, nineteen people in all, from Leigh-on-Sea, Essex. I interviewed a 24-year-old typist, Margaret Jarrett, from London, who had written to the Lord Mayor of Sydney saying that she wanted to marry an Australian and had then received 800 proposals of marriage.

I also reported what happened to Mohammed Razak and Mohammed Sadiq, two Muslim Indians from Fiji who jumped ship in the hope of being able to join all these lucky immigrants in Australia. The immigration department told them that they would not be discriminated against on the grounds of race or religion, but that they would have to satisfy the department of their educational level by taking a short dictation test. An officer then provided pens and paper and dictated fifty words to the men – in Italian. Straight-faced, he told the Magistrate, 'Neither man managed to write one word.' The Indians were then sentenced to three months' imprisonment pending their deportation. The 'White Australia' policy was such an integral part of Australian life that I saw then neither the injustice nor the hypocrisy.

But I did become uneasy over the way the *Herald* seemed to slant its coverage of anything to do with the Communist Party. It was 1951 and the Prime Minister, Robert Menzies, was gearing up for a referendum in an attempt to get the Communist Party declared illegal. I wrote a small story about the Party moving out from its Melbourne offices and the fact that I had been unable to find out where it had gone. The *Herald* put a headline on this story which read 'Local Reds Bolting', and wrote into my text a line saying that 'all incriminating documents have been removed'.

But just how far the *Herald*'s anti-Communist policy went I did not discover until after a visit to the Bonegilla migrant camp, outside Albury-Wodonga on the border between Victoria and New South Wales. The camp was used to process non-British migrants, many drawn from Displaced Person (DP) camps all over Europe. In return for eventual Australian citizenship, these DPs had signed a contract agreeing to work for two years anywhere they were sent by the Australian authorities. They were taken directly from the ships to the camp, their luggage under bond, and all Customs and Immigration formalities were performed during the first week at Bonegilla. I persuaded the chief of staff that it would be an interesting story if I were to follow the fortunes of one DP from the time of arrival at Port Melbourne, through processing at Bonegilla and on to the first job. I did not tell him that I already had one DP in mind, a beautiful 22-year-old Czech girl called Eva Hajek who had been elected 'Miss *Hellenic Prince*' during the *Hellenic Prince*'s seven-week voyage to Australia. She was the first girl who had interested me since I arrived in Melbourne. There were some attractive women reporters on the *Herald* but in those pre-liberation days they were seen as rivals and dangerous as girlfriends. I had gone out with one or two secretaries but ran into trouble as soon as their families realised that I was a reporter. I gave one Hemingway's *A Farewell to Arms* only to have it handed back to me the next day with a note from her mother saying she considered it a dirty book that should be banned. I took another out to dinner and the next time I called to collect her I was met by her father who told me 'No gentleman would take a decent girl to a Chinese restaurant.' Miss *Hellenic Prince* was the sophisticated European woman I had dreamed about.

Bonegilla was a hot dusty place. The camp consisted of twenty-four blocks each with its own kitchen and dining room, all surrounded with barbed wire. There was nowhere to go and little to do. Nevertheless the story and my relationship with Miss *Hellenic Prince* were both going swimmingly when a Customs officer caught me after lunch one day and said, 'I might have a story for you. Come and have a look at this.' He took me to a storeroom behind the Customs examination hall, unlocked the door and ushered me inside. It was like entering a Nazi shrine. Two tables were covered with Nazi memorabilia – busts and photographs of Hitler, Goering, Hess and others I did not recognise, SS daggers, Nazi flags, copies of *Mein Kampf*, photographs of officers in SS uniform, Nazi party cards and pamphlets. 'Found it in the bastards' baggage,' he said, 'I reckon some of them must've been in the SS.' 'How did they get past the Immigration officers in Europe?' I said. He shrugged his shoulders.

I made a list of what the Customs officer had found and got the *Herald* photographer to photograph it all. Then we raced back to Melbourne to file the story. I could already see the headlines: NAZIS IN AUSTRALIA. SS MEN BEAT IMMIGRATION CHECK. HOW MANY ARE WAR CRIMINALS? We handed in the story and the photographs and waited for the reaction. Nothing for two days, then a summons to see the editor. He had the article and the photographs on his desk. 'This is a good story,' he said. 'Well done. But I'm afraid we can't use it. I don't doubt its accuracy and you're to be commended for digging it up. But I'm sure you see the problem. We'd be handing the Communists a gift. This is just the sort of thing they'd use for propaganda. But don't worry. I'll pass your story on to Canberra and I'm sure that the government will take the necessary steps.'*

I naturally mentioned the fate of my Bonegilla story to my colleagues on the *Herald*. They were all sympathetic but two, Bill Irwin and Charlie Henderson, were especially so. Irwin was the Melbourne correspondent for the *West Australian* which had an office in the *Herald*. Henderson was an ex-serviceman, a late-comer to journalism. They started inviting me home for dinner and afterwards we would discuss the state of the world and what could be done about it. Then one night Henderson asked me if I would help him distribute some pamphlets in his neighbourhood. When I wanted to know what sort of pamphlets he produced one. I don't remember the contents in detail but it was a Communist Party text, an appeal for support over some strike that was currently making news in Melbourne. When I hesitated, Henderson said, 'Look at it this way. When you come to the end, don't you want to be able to say, "All my life I have striven for the liberation of my fellow man"?' I don't know where he got this quote from,

---

* It did. But it took nearly forty years. It was not until 1987 that the Australian government, after fourteen months of parliamentary debate, decided to set up a Special Investigations Unit to root out any war criminals who may have crept into the country in the mass migration of DPs after the war.

but it was effective. I crept around the darkened suburbs of Melbourne stuffing pamphlets in letter boxes, expecting at any time the heavy hand of the Special Branch to fall on my shoulder and my career in journalism to come to an end in the local Magistrate's Court: HERALD REPORTER REVEALED AS UNDERCOVER RED. But the strike ended and Henderson called off our pamphlet raids. Instead Irwin invited me to a 'Solidarity Evening'. There were about ten other guests, some of them also from the *Herald*'s editorial staff. We drank beer while Irwin played us tapes of various comrades from around the world exhorting us to stay shoulder-to-shoulder against the capitalist menace.

My flirtation with Communism came to an end when Irwin rounded off one of his discussion evenings with an appeal for funds for the Party. Beyond the embarrassment of being asked for money at what I and the others had considered to be a social occasion at a colleague's house, I sensed that behind Irwin's appeal was a demand for commitment – with the handing over of cash a barrier would have been crossed. Later experience of the KGB and other intelligence services confirmed that I was right and that the giving or acceptance of cash is a psychologically important moment in clandestine relationships. I never went to Irwin's again and although we remained friends, the relationship was not the same. Years later when the nature of the Soviet regime had become more apparent, I called on Irwin during a visit to Melbourne. I tried to steer the conversation to politics but he was not interested. He was engrossed, he said, in the theory that wheat was the origin of many modern ailments and he had been doing research on the relationship between early man's development of agriculture and the occurrence of disease. I wonder if Irwin was a born outsider and, like his wheat theory, Communism had been only another expression of his 'outsiderness'.

The most glamorous round at the *Herald* was the police one. Chief police roundsman was Alan Dower, a tall, distinguished man with a military moustache and bearing, whose act at parties was to borrow a broomstick, pretend he was on the parade ground, and carry out drill as ordered by an imaginary sergeant major. His deputy was Lionel Hogg, who could well have been a detective himself had he not opted for journalism. It was Hogg's job to give an occasional lecture to the cadets on the mysteries of reporting. One sticks in my mind. 'A little twist to the most mundane of stories can turn it into a front-page lead,' Hogg began. 'Now take what happened to me last week. The police got a call to a restaurant where the chef had just beaten off an armed robber. I interviewed him and asked him how he had done it. He said he chucked a plate of food in the man's face and the guy ran away. That's a pretty boring story. But I noticed that the restaurant was a Hungarian one. So I asked the chef what the plate of food had been. He said that in the excitement he hadn't noticed. So I wrote a lead that said the chef of a Hungarian restaurant had foiled an armed robber by chucking a plate of Hungarian goulash in his face. It made page one.' We thought about it for a second or two and then one of the cadets said, 'But, Lionel, that wasn't true.' Hogg laughed. 'No,' he said. 'But it should have been.' Hogg had a point and over the years I have come across countless newspaper stories in which the facts fit together so neatly that I suspect the reporters had all been taught by Hogg.

Hogg arranged for each cadet to accompany a night police patrol car crewed by three detectives so we would get the feel for police work. On my night we crawled around the darkened inner suburbs of Melbourne hoping that the radio would crackle to life with some exciting crime in our area but the only message we got was an order to check out a man sleeping on a bench in a park near the state parliament building. He did not speak English and the detectives were losing their patience with him so I felt justified in intervening and, with some schoolboy French, discovered he was a crew member of a ship in harbour and had missed the last bus back to the docks. Instead of being grateful the police became wary of me. Squashed between two of them in the back seat of the squad car we maintained an uneasy silence until they spotted an old drunk urinating against a tree in St Kilda Road.

'Dirty bastard,' the driver said. 'Teach him a lesson.' The two detectives in the back of the car jumped out. One grabbed the old man's hat and flung it far into park. The other began methodically kicking him in the backside as the old man staggered away mumbling muted protests and then fell over. The detective gave him one final kick and then came back to the car. The exercise must have made them hungry because we headed off to the city centre and stopped at a late-night restaurant. The proprietor, a Greek, came hurrying up. 'Oyster soup and steaks, Tony,' one of the detectives said, 'and put some bloody oysters in the soup.' When we were leaving I made an effort to pay for my share. 'Put it away,' one of the detectives ordered. 'It's on the house. We look after Tony, he looks after us.'

Did I write any of this? Did I tell the *Herald* readers that their police were less than perfect? I did not. Hogg had made it clear that we were guests in the squad car and that anything that happened had to remain confidential, otherwise the cosy relationship between the police and the *Herald* police roundsmen would be endangered.

The most eccentric reporter on the *Herald* was undoubtedly John Pitcairn.

He appeared in the reporters' room one day, a slight, red-haired figure with a drawling British accent. He had been on a tour of the Pacific, he said, and had just arrived in town from Tahiti. He peppered his chat with French words, spoke confidently about the international situation, and told tall stories about all the Tahitian chiefs he knew and how obliging their daughters had been. Yes, he was related to the Pitcairn of Pitcairn Island and his family knew the Murdochs because his nanny, while his father had been posted to the British army in India, had later gone to work for Dame Elisabeth Murdoch. In fact, he said, he was staying in Rupert Murdoch's room while Rupert was up at Oxford.

Pitcairn was often late for work because Sir Keith Murdoch gave him a lift in his car and Murdoch started work later than the newsroom. The *Herald* executives did not quite know what to do with Pitcairn and his time-keeping. They did not want to be seen to be easy on the boss's guest but neither did they want him to complain to Murdoch, and the feeling was that, being English, Pitcairn could not be trusted. Pitcairn went about his duties oblivious to it all. Some days we both drew suburban court reporting and the courts were often close enough for us to meet for lunch. He began to tell me stories of life in the Murdoch household. Most of them were mundane family gossip but one I remember well.

According to Pitcairn, the British Council had got in touch with Murdoch to ask him if he would help entertain a distinguished British author, Eric Linklater, who was visiting Australia as a guest of the Council. Murdoch readily agreed and had asked Pitcairn to prepare him a little brief on Linklater's achievements. Pitcairn boiled it down to: private in the Black Watch, a wartime career in the Directorate of Public Relations in the War Office, rector of Aberdeen University, Lieutenant-Colonel in Korea, and a list of all Linklater's books, plays and films. He then added what would turn out to be an unfortunate line – that Linklater was a connoisseur of fine French wines.

Pitcairn said that, for reasons he never understood, Murdoch had taken an instant dislike to Linklater and the dinner had proceeded in an atmosphere of deep chill. After one particularly long silence, Murdoch suddenly said, 'I understand, Mr Linklater, that you are something of a wine buff.' Linklater replied that he liked good wines and, yes, he did know a little about them. 'Hah,' said Murdoch, pouncing. 'Then perhaps you could tell us what we have been drinking this evening?' And he gestured to the middle of the table where the Murdoch family butler/chauffeur, Ted Penticost, had placed a wine bottle which he had wrapped in a snowy-white napkin. Linklater picked up his glass, drank in the aroma, took a deep sip, and then rolled it around his mouth before swallowing it.

'Well,' he said, tentatively. 'A claret, of course. Not a distinguished vineyard. Certainly not from a château. Recent vintage. A perfectly drinkable table wine. In fact, delicious.'

A delighted smile spread over Murdoch's face. 'Really,' he said. 'Then no doubt you'll be surprised to know, Mr Linklater, that you've been tasting one of the best wines in my cellar, one I myself drink regularly. We're talking about a Château Pape Clement, a grand cru classé. Bottled by the Château itself, of course. Penticost, show Mr Linklater the label.' Pitcairn said that everyone turned to look at Penticost who was standing frozen, white-faced, eyes glazing over. Everyone, that is, except Sir Keith Murdoch who was watching Linklater. 'Come on, Penticost,' Murdoch said impatiently. 'Show him.' Penticost moved slowly to the table, lifted the bottle, peeled off the napkin, and robot-like turned the label towards Linklater. Linklater peered at it. 'Yes, well,' he murmured. 'as I said.' Murdoch suddenly caught on. Penticost had deceived him, probably not every night, but certainly this time. He clenched his jaw, changed the subject, pretended nothing untoward had happened, and quickly brought the evening to a close. Pitcairn claimed not to have known what Murdoch later said to Penticost, but insisted that the man did not lose his job.

The other unusual reporter was Graeme Edwards who was blind. Edwards had started as a night copy-taker with the *Herald*'s sister paper, the *Sun-Pictorial*, a morning tabloid, and had eventually convinced the *Herald* editor that since a lot of afternoon newspaper work is done over the telephone because of pressure of time, there was no reason why he could not conduct interviews and write stories. He turned out to be brilliant at it.

He had a special telephone similar to those used by professional telephonists on big switchboards. He would dial the number by touch, pose his questions, and then take down the answers on a small machine that produced braille shorthand. He would read back his notes and touch-type his story, checking it with a colleague just to make sure that he had not over-typed any lines or had run off the bottom of the page.

Like many an Australian from that period, he later went to London hoping to break into Fleet Street but found London editors less willing to give a blind reporter a trial than those in his native Melbourne. He did some broadcasting for the BBC and then embarked on a book about life as a blind journalist called *Keep in Touch*, which did very well. He met and married a Spanish woman, Christina, then returned to Australia where he worked in the publicity section of the Immigration Department, an example of what you can achieve with sufficient courage and determination. I was proud to be his friend.

It was Edwards who said to me one afternoon after I had been at the *Herald* for nearly two years, 'How much longer are you going to hang around here?' I said I didn't know. 'You've learnt all you're going to,' he said. 'If you stay on you'll slip into a niche and it'll be so comfortable you'll never move on.' He was right. Yes, I could stay in Melbourne and climb the ladder into the *Herald* hierarchy – reporter, senior reporter, A-grade, Super A-grade, sub editor, chief of staff, deputy editor, even editor. But far more appealing challenges lay over the horizon in Fleet Street. An earlier generation had proved it could be done – George Johnston, Osmar White, Chester Wilmot, Alan Moorehead, Ronald Monson, Noel Monks . . . Monks had even lost his wife to Ernest Hemingway, for Christ's sake, and Johnston was giving up journalism to be a real writer and live on a Greek island. So on humid Melbourne nights I would join my fellow reporters in someone's back garden in St Kilda, lie back woozy with beer and wine, watch the Southern Cross and dream of foggy evenings in London, feeling my way from Australia House to the Strand Palace, which everyone said was *the* place to stay. 'But slip the porter at the Savoy a quid and get your mail sent there,' said one of us who had heard it from someone recently back who had done it. 'It impresses the Poms.'

Edwards's advice was sound – 'do it now' – but I did not have the money to go to London, so I thought I would give Sydney another whirl. In the 1950s it was the journalistic capital of Australia, and, so everyone said, a great place to be a reporter.

CHAPTER THREE

VACUUM CLEANER SALESMAN

There were no jobs in journalism in Sydney and my savings quickly ran out. An advertisement for salesmen caught my eye. It promised extensive training, good money, and opportunities for advancement for anyone with a car and ambition. The speed with which the world-weary head salesman hired me after the most cursory interview should have made me suspicious . . . but it didn't. Training began the following day and lasted six hours. Ten of us sat in a tiny office in downtown Sydney in front of a table and a blackboard. On the table, its chrome trimmings glinting in a spotlight, was a vacuum cleaner. On the blackboard were the messages 'Once you are inside the front door, a sale is virtually assured' and 'The secret of selling is to close the sale'.

I was wondering what this actually meant when the chief salesman began his lecture. He pointed to the vacuum cleaner. 'This is what you are going to sell,' he said. 'You charge sixty pounds for it. You get fifteen of that. Any mug can sell one a day, so you're going to be making at least seventy-five a week. But if that's all you make, I'm going to be very disappointed in you. Bill was top salesman last week. He sold eighteen. He took home two hundred and seventy pounds. How do you feel about that?' I could have told him – we felt very good indeed.

'You may be asking yourselves – who needs a vacuum cleaner?' he went on. 'Don't. We don't give a shit who needs what. We're going to make those women buy a new vacuum cleaner whether they need it or not. That's what being a salesman is. That's why we don't waste money trying to get you leads like some other companies do. You don't need leads. You could drive me out into the suburbs right now, pick a street, pick a house – all at random – and I'd bet you a fiver I could knock at that door and sell the woman who answered it a cleaner in under half an hour. That's what being a salesman means. Now I'm going to tell you how to do it.'

37

For the next two hours he did just that. The company would give us two vacuum cleaners – a demonstration model and a new one, pristine in its cardboard box. Then we would drive off to anywhere we liked, but the closer to home, he said, the less driving each day to get to work. Then we would knock on doors. When the housewife answered, we would launch into our pitch which, he advised us, we should learn word perfect.

'Good morning. My name's Phillip Knightley and I'm from Vega Vacuum Cleaners. Now I'm sure you've heard our offer on the radio? You haven't? Never mind, I'll tell you. This week we're offering a free check on any of your electrical appliances. Are they all working all right? They are. That's good. Now how about your vacuum cleaner? People often forget about their vacuum cleaner. How long is it since you've had it checked? You've *never* had it checked? Oh. Well, I'll be happy to do it for you right now and for absolutely no charge.' At this point, the head salesman said, you move resolutely forward and nine times out of ten the woman will step aside and let you into her house. The sale is now virtually assured, he said, as long as you remain determined that you will not leave that house, no matter what she says, until she signs and pays up. 'It's just a matter of outlasting her.

'So the woman produces her vacuum cleaner and you produce yours and you put it right alongside hers on the carpet. Hers is old and grubby. Yours is new and shiny. She cannot help but notice the contrast. If at that moment she says, "How much is that one?" then you forget everything else and produce your sales contract. Anyone who asks the price is three-quarters sold. If she doesn't, you say, "Okay, let's test this old machine." You clean a small area of carpet with her machine then set it aside. You say, "Now we'll clean the same area with the Vega machine and see if yours has left any dirt behind." You detach the nozzle of the Vega machine, pull out a spotless white handkerchief from your pocket, wrap it over the nozzle and replace it. You clean the same section of carpet, detach the nozzle and lo and behold, your handkerchief will be stained black with dirt.' One of the trainees risked a question. 'What if it's not?' he said. The head salesman grinned. 'Don't worry. It will be. No vacuum cleaner in the world gets up all the dirt in one pass.

'You look at the dirt, you show it to the woman, and you say, "Oh dear. I'm afraid your cleaner has had it. It's not cleaning at all. It's leaving all this dirt and germs behind. It's leaving your carpet filthy. I suppose it could be repaired but it would cost almost as much as a new one." And then you sign her up for a new one. Now she may try a few excuses to wriggle out of it. Can anyone suggest what those excuses might be?'

'I can't afford a new one,' said one trainee. 'Unlikely,' said the salesman.

'People don't like to tell strangers that they can't afford something. But if she does say that then you make her feel guilty. You reply, "Madam, you can't afford not to. Do you really want to leave that dirt and those germs around to make your family ill?'

'I'll have to ask my husband,' said another trainee. 'Yes,' said the salesman. 'They often say that. And you reply, "Does he ask you before he takes decisions in his office? It's your job to run the house and he wants you to do it as best you can. If you need a new cleaner then I'm sure he'd want you to have one." But if they insist then you leave the new cleaner behind and you come back that night when the husband's at home. You can bet a tenner that the woman will have used that machine in the meantime and she'll want that machine and that the husband will want to appear the big, generous spender in front of you. You'll close the sale.'

That afternoon we rehearsed the sale, the trainees taking it in turn to play the housewife. Try as I would, I could not make my sales pitch sound convincing. I did not believe that any woman, no matter how ingenuous, would fall for such an obviously contrived approach. The head salesman noticed my diffidence. 'Look, mate,' he said. 'Believe me, it works. Don't try to analyse it. Just bloody well say it.'

I tried. The next day I began knocking on doors. I hated it. It seemed such an invasion of people's privacy – even worse than tabloid journalism. But I had to admit that when I stuck to the pitch that we had been taught, the doors opened, old vacuum cleaners were dragged out, sections of carpets were cleaned, housewives were horrified, and cleaners were sold. But not many. I sold three in the first week, two in the second and none in the third. I was not ruthless enough. When it came to closing the sale, I could not ride roughshod over the woman's last shreds of reluctance to buy. They sensed it and backed out. I began cutting my commission so as to be able to drop the price to the housewife, a serious error. 'Never cut the price,' the head salesman had told us. 'The value of the cleaner is immaterial. And if you quote one price and then cut it to clinch the sale, the woman will become suspicious.'

The more I failed, the less hard I tried. I took to going out late in the morning, calling at one house, and when I failed to make a sale, knocking off immediately for lunch. One day I called at a house and the woman turned out to be the mother of a school-friend. 'Oh,' she said. 'Is this what you're doing now?' The head salesman had warned us that friends might look down on us and that we should mentally compare the huge sums we were making with what they might be earning and laugh silently to ourselves. But the tone in this mother's voice kept me from knocking on doors for two days. The final blow was when the salesmen organised a

party to celebrate the amazing achievements of the man who had won the
the salesman of the year award for the third year running. He was retiring
and had bought a cottage at the seaside where he planned to spend a lot of
time fishing. I gave him a lift home and on the way confessed I was not
doing every well.

He said, 'I never followed all the bullshit Vega try to pump into you. I
went up to the door and knocked and when the woman answered I said,
"Do you want to buy a new vacuum cleaner? They wear out, you know,
and you need to buy a new one from time to time." If she said she was
interested, then I'd sell her one. If she said no, then I'd say, "Thanks very
much," and I'd try next door. You guys were lucky to do ten houses a day.
I'd do a hundred. I got a lot of knock-backs but I made a lot of sales, too.'
The thought of cold-calling on a hundred doors a day so depressed me that
I resigned from Vega the next day. I was cured for the rest of my life of
ever wanting to sell anything to anybody.

Well, almost. I got a part-time job with an advertising agency so small
that it could not afford a full-time copywriter. Its main account was for a
new brand of refrigerator called, with singular lack of imagination, Colda.
Colda sponsored a radio play once a week and I wrote the advertisements
that were read between acts. 'Colda refrigerators keep your food colder
longer. Its powerful compressor unit and high technology insulation fight
off summer heat. Don't run the risk of sickness from spoilt food. Make sure
your children grow older with Colda.' I lasted long enough to decide that
advertising was not for me – there was something of the door-to-door
vacuum cleaner business about it, something slightly but definitely shifty.

The *Sydney Daily Mirror* came to my rescue. I had bombarded its news
editor, Charlie Buttrose, with job applications and his secretary rang one
day and asked if I could come in for a week's trial as a D-grade general
reporter. The *Mirror* and its Sunday stable-mate, *Truth*, were owned by
Ezra Norton, a newspaper czar in the Citizen Kane mould. Norton had
made his money from *Truth*, which specialised in juicy divorce cases and
attacks on the Roman Catholic Church. Norton's father, a fiercely anti-
British immigrant from Ireland, realised that, unlike Britain, New South
Wales law allowed anyone to publish all the evidence in divorce hearings.
There were very limited grounds for divorce in New South Wales at that
time. You could either wait three years after the spouse had left home and
then sue for desertion, or go for a quick divorce on the grounds of adultery.
Adultery won easily. But the courts, again unlike Britain, would not accept
as evidence an overnight stay at some Brighton love hotel. In Australia, the
couple, either by arrangement or ambush, had to be caught in the actual act
of illicit sex.

This provided regular employment for an army of private detectives who specialised in springing from concealment in hotel wardrobes, or from under beds, or crashing through windows, camera with flash gun in hand and a ready quip such as 'Hello, hello, what's going on here?' The private detective would then describe the event in great detail to the divorce court judge, and it all would be reported in the next issue of *Truth*, usually under a joky headline. Thus, when the international golf star Norman von Nida was caught with his lover on the back seat of a car near a golf club's seventeenth fairway, the *Truth* headline read: CHAMP GOLFER CAUGHT IN WRONG HOLE.

Truth reporters prowled the courts looking for other juicy sex stories, especially ones involving Roman Catholic priests. But, in an effort to show some good taste, these were not given joky headlines, but alliterative ones So a case of homosexual relations between a member of the Marist Brothers order and a teenage pupil carried the headline: BEASTLY BROTHER IN BED WITH BOY.

Anyone in conflict with the Catholic Church could be assured of support from *Truth*. Some orders of nuns ran laundry businesses in Sydney suburbs and novices were expected to work long hours at tubs and ironing machines. Every now and then, a novice would realise that she did not have a vocation and would leave surreptitiously at night, scaling the high fences surrounding the order's headquarters. In *Truth* jargon, it was a case of: ANOTHER NUN OVER THE WALL AT ARNCLIFFE.

Norton hated Freemasons almost as much as he hated Roman Catholics. I can state this from personal experience. Not long after joining the *Mirror*, the editor, Len Richards, sent for me and said, 'Mr Norton has a job for you. Come on. We'll go and see him at the city office.' Norton's office was spacious and elegantly furnished, but I did think it odd that he had two busts of Napoleon on his desk. Norton was short, dark-complexioned, immaculately groomed and with an expensive taste in suits. He got up as we came in, walked around to the front of his desk and shook hands. Then he gestured to two chairs and returned to his own. We waited. Suddenly Norton turned to me and said, 'That was a fucking Masonic handshake you gave me, wasn't it?'

I was stunned. Honesty seemed the only defence. 'Yes,' I said.

'Well, listen to me, sonny,' Norton said. 'If you want to get on in my fucking papers, then you don't go around giving fucking Masonic handshakes. I don't want any fucking Masons on my papers and I don't want any fucking Catholics. All I want is fucking reporters. Is that fucking well clear?' I was still stunned but managed to say it was.

'All right,' Norton said. 'Now what do you know about Professor MacMahon Fucking Ball?'

I said I knew that MacMahon Ball was professor of international relations at Melbourne University, one of the few such departments in Australia.

'Well, I reckon he's a fucking Commo,' said Norton. 'And we're going to get him. I want you to do me a dossier on him. Everything you can find out. And then we'll fucking well crucify him in *Truth*.'

On the way back to the *Mirror* in the office car I asked Len Richards what I should do. 'Exactly as Mr Norton says,' he replied. 'It'll never be published. Too libellous. But if you don't do it, Mr Norton'll sack you.' I asked around. Richards was right. Norton had a reputation of terrorising and sacking people. His chief accountant, a mild, confident and beautifully mannered Englishman called Harold Parrot, had been reduced to jelly by Norton who would ring him at least once a day and shout down the telephone, 'Is that you Parrot? Then get down off your fucking perch and come and see me.' The news editor of *Truth* was an amiable Irish old-timer called Jack Finch whose face had been reduced by years of drinking to a hue of deep rosy red. He, too, went in fear of Norton, who would ring him late on Saturday when Finch was busy getting the paper to bed and roar, 'What's the lead, beetroot puss?'

Norton also had a reputation for feuds that sometimes ended in fisticuffs if he had had enough to drink. He hated Frank Packer with great passion, probably because the two were so alike – both newspaper owners, both horse-racing enthusiasts, both big drinkers. During the war, Norton resented the fact that Packer had been given a commission in the Australian army, and worked out a bizarre revenge. He ordered a *Truth* photographer to go to the races every Saturday and photograph Packer enjoying the racing. Sunday after Sunday for several months, *Truth* published this photograph with a caption that never changed: 'Captain Frank Packer at Randwick races yesterday. Captain Packer will be leaving for the front shortly.' Norton ceased tormenting Packer only after the two met in the members' bar at the races and began wrestling, one trying to strangle the other by tightening his neck tie, although who was being strangled and who was tightening the tie depended on who told the story, a *Truth* man or a *Sunday Telegraph* man.

Not wishing to cross Norton so early in my career, I set about compiling a file on Professor MacMahon Ball, pretending to myself that if I stuck to the truth it could be called journalism. I gathered all the academic reference books and then began telephoning his friends and enemies and finally contacted MacMahon Ball himself. The tactics were not very different from those used today by journalists on quality newspapers who want to write an anonymous 'profile' of someone in the news. But in my case I had to disguise the real purpose by pretending to be working on a survey of academics and their lifestyle. It took me a week or so to finish and then I sent it off to Norton and never heard another word about it. I learnt later that he had dozens of files on all sorts of prominent Australians whom he disliked and had never published any of them.

I was probably saved from further work like this by the editor of the *Mirror*'s historical page, Bill Joy. Norton's formula for a successful afternoon tabloid, he told his editors, was 'the right mix of cunt and culture' and every day he would send them a memorandum setting out his verdict on that afternoon's paper – 'Too much cunt' or 'Too much culture' or, rarely, 'You got it right today.' The first ingredient was provided by photographs of pretty girls with deep cleavage – a technique noted by Norton's successor as owner of the *Mirror*, Rupert Murdoch, who transferred it intact to Britain when he started the *Sun* – the *Sun* was modelled on Norton's *Mirror*. The second ingredient, culture, proved more difficult in culture-starved Sydney until Joy, a British immigrant, began editing the historical page. The idea was to tell the story of an important moment in history in a lively, vulgar manner, concentrating on the people involved rather than on the events. Joy, a cosmopolitan, well-educated Englishman, nevertheless liked lots of blood, gore, rape and plunder and his choice of subjects reflected this. The page was immensely popular with *Mirror* readers, many of whom wrote to say that they had cut out the stories and had saved them to read at leisure when they retired.

Joy had a staff of three writers, which was never quite enough, so some reporter was always being seconded to the historical page for a week's work and now it was my turn. It was pleasant journalism in pleasant company. Joy's journalists considered themselves a cut above the ordinary reporters and the leisurely pace left time for discussion and debate. Joy would tell us stories about life on Fleet Street, about newspapers where a reporter always carried his passport to work in case that day, at a moment's notice, he would be sent to Africa or China. Fleet Street, Joy said, was never-ending excitement and adventure and its newspapers reflected this.

Sydney offered nothing like it, although the lottery beat could sometimes be mildly exciting. New South Wales had a state lottery which was used to finance hospitals and, later, the building of the Sydney Opera House. It was drawn every day and the first prize was then £6,000 – about £80,000 in today's values. It was drawn in the morning and the name of the winner was known within minutes. This made it a natural afternoon tabloid story because a *Mirror* reporter could wait in a radio car outside the lottery headquarters for the winner's name and address and, if he was quick enough, be the first to break the news to that day's lucky person. The *Mirror*'s rival afternoon newspaper, the *Sun*, also had a radio car on the job and the lottery story became a race each day to see who would scoop whom.

Off we would go from the lottery office, tyres squealing, out into the endless suburbs of Sydney. Then a run up the driveway, the bang on the door, and the cautious questions in case we wrongly raised someone's hopes – 'Are you Mrs Simpson? Did you have a ticket in today's lottery? What did you call it?' (It was the custom to give the ticket a name.) 'Then I'm happy to tell you Mrs Simpson that you've won first prize.' Stand out of the way to let the photographer blaze away with his 5×4 Speed Graphic; exploding flashbulbs; Mrs Simpson's joy captured on film for ever; a few quick questions to get the guts of the story; run back down the driveway into the car and on to the radio; and then dictate the story off the top of your head because if you took time to write anything, the bastard from the *Sun* might scoop you. Scooped once and you're in the dunce's corner; scooped twice and you're out. It did not take me long to work out that this was more a means of keeping the reporters on their toes than any serious risk of loss of circulation. Most readers bought one afternoon newspaper or the other, not both, so did not know who had scooped whom and any idea that a *Mirror* reader would say, 'The *Sun* scooped you on the lottery story today, so I'm changing papers,' was ludicrous then and remains so today, in Britain as well as in Australia. Scoops are a journalist's way of assessing his or her colleagues and of interest only to journalists.

After the initial thrill of being able to break good news to someone every day, the lottery beat became boring and depressing. Sudden riches seem to bring out the worst in people. One woman I interviewed had run a syndicate with two friends. They each contributed a third of the cost, took it in turns to do the actual buying of the ticket, and since they trusted each other completely, the one who did the buying put it in her name. One week the ticket took first prize. But the woman who had bought the syndicate's ticket for that week, the woman to whom I broke the good news, digested the information and then said, 'Actually I bought two tickets this week – one for the syndicate and one for me. And it's the one I bought for myself that has won.' There was a long drawn-out court case and since there was no way of proving which ticket belonged to whom, she was eventually forced to share the prize with her friends. But, of course, they were friends no longer.

The other thing I noticed was how reluctant winners were to celebrate with outsiders. No one ever said to me and the photographer, 'Here's a fiver. Have a drink on me on your way back to the office.' Or, 'Come on inside and we'll open a bottle.' Or even, 'Let's have a nice cup of tea.' Once they knew that they had the money they seemed determined to keep every penny of it. I remarked on this one afternoon to the crowd of *Mirror* journalists who used to meet in the pub near the office, the Evening Star. 'Christ,' I said. 'If I ever win the lottery, then it'll be on for young and old. Drinks for anyone and everyone.'

Ten years later I am back in Sydney from London looking for work as usual and getting by on a day's casual here, a night there. Although I am thirty-three, I am living at home with my parents because I cannot afford anything else. One morning my mother says, 'I read my stars in last night's paper. It says I've got to buy a lottery ticket with an Aquarian. You're the only Aquarian I know, son, so buy a ticket between us on your way to work, will you?'

'Mum,' I say, 'I used to write those star columns on the paper up at Lismore. It's all bullshit. Let's not waste our money.' 'Just do it,' she said. 'Humour me.' So I stop at a lottery seller on my way to the Australian Broadcasting Commission's offices where I have a day's casual work and I buy a ticket. I think I'll be witty to annoy my mother so I call the ticket 'A Queer Corn' – to reflect that it belongs half to me, an Aquarian, and half to my mother, who was born under Capricorn, and who has painful corns. I give her the ticket and I forget about it.

Three days later I am at home because there is no work that day and the telephone rings. It is a reporter from the *Mirror*, one I had once worked with. 'Phil,' he says. 'Have you got a ticket in today's lottery?' 'Yes, why?' He ignores my question. 'Did you call it A Queer Corn?' 'Yes.' 'Well, mate, it's won first prize.' I refuse to believe him and accuse him of an elaborate practical joke. He gets indignant and says he will ring off while I telephone the lottery office and check myself. I do and he is right. I relay the news to my mother and she doesn't even look up from her knitting but infuriatingly says, 'I told you so.' Then the telephone rings again and it is the *Mirror* reporter. 'Mate,' he says, 'I'm told you once said that if you won the lottery it'd be on for young and old.' 'That's right,' I reply. 'And it will be.'

I go into the Evening Star and consult the licensee, telling him frankly of my dilemma – I want a big party but I don't want to blow the whole prize. He confides in me the wisdom gained from twenty-five years in the public house business. 'Now what we're gonna do is this. Anyone you invite, tell 'em when it's on, but don't tell 'em when it's gonna be over. Just say, "She's on at the Star after work."' I ask why. 'Because if they know it's on for two hours then they'll pace their drinking. If they don't know when it's gonna finish they'll knock it down as if there's no tomorrow because they'll think each one could be the last. And they'll all be pissed within the hour. It'll cost yer next to nothing. You'll see.' I look doubtful because he adds, 'If you want to make sure, then we'll hit them with champagne about half way through. That'll really finish 'em off.'

He was one hundred per cent correct. Journalists came from all over Sydney. They packed all the bars at the Evening Star and for the first hour the bar staff could hardly keep up with the demand. Then the drinking suddenly slackened. Bill Jenkins, the *Mirror* police roundsman, an athlete and a drinker of renown who regularly downed six schooners (pints) an evening, spread over two hours, was weeping quietly into his third because he felt unable to finish it. Then came the champagne and the speeches and less than two hours after the party began, it was over because no one could stand up.

I had one part of the celebration left to complete. My mother had shown so little excitement at our win – almost as if it was merely confirmation that the stars are right and sons are wrong – that I was determined to shake a reaction from her. So, the next day I went to the bank and I withdrew her £3,000 in one pound notes and I broke the seals and crammed them into a big brown paper bag. And as she sat shelling peas I crept up on her and emptied the money into her lap, where the notes spilled over her pinafore and cascaded into the pea saucepan. 'Here's your share,' I said. And my mother looked at the notes and then at me and said, 'You silly bugger,' and went on shelling the peas. Later she realised that she would have to keep the money in the house overnight until the bank opened in the morning so, according to my father, she stuck it under the mattress and woke up every hour to check that it was still there.

To be a crime reporter in Sydney in the 1950s was to be a prince of the city. There are theories that crime in Sydney is different because of the unique origins of the place – no other city began its life with only two types of citizens: criminals and police (the convicts and their jailers). The natural enmity between the two was exacerbated by some of the most stringent laws governing social behaviour in the world. It was illegal to drink in a pub after 6pm. Since most people did not finish work until 5pm this left just an hour to down as much beer as possible before everyone was thrown out onto the streets – the notorious six o'clock swill. Although there was a pub on nearly every street corner, the bar staff had trouble in handling the rush between 5pm and 6pm so experienced drinkers would order four or five glasses of beer when they first reached the bar, line them up and drink them in rapid succession, only to repeat the exercise until 6pm arrived or they fell senseless to the floor. An American visitor told me that Sydney was the only city in the world where he had actually seen the legendary 'face on the bar-room floor' – as he drank with an Australian friend he looked down to see a man lying against the brass footrail, hat still on his head, staring up at him with glazed eyes. 'The amazing thing about it,' he said, 'was that the other drinkers took not the slightest notice of him.'

You could not get a drink in a restaurant or café unless you had a full meal with it. You could not get a drink in a nightclub unless you ordered your alcohol when you made a table reservation, which had to be done before 6pm. You could buy alcohol to take away and drink at home only from pubs, which, of course, closed at 6pm. Naturally, illegal liquor shops, 'sly grog joints', existed all over the city. You got an address, usually a private house, from a friend, knocked at the door, identified yourself, and if the owner was satisfied you were not a policeman, you were allowed to buy a bottle or two at an inflated price.

You could bet on a racehorse only by going to the racecourse. This was the only form of gambling allowed – no casinos, no poker schools, no card games for money even in private homes among friends. Again, there were illegal betting shops and gambling clubs, especially for the Australian national game: two-up, where two coins are thrown into the air and the gamblers bet on whether they will fall with the heads up or the tails, or one of each.

This was all victimless crime and not even the police believed that such repressive laws could be enforced. So over the years an understanding had grown up between the police and liquor and gambling czars. In return for a share of the profits, the police would turn one blind eye to sly grogging and gambling – only one blind eye because there had to be an appearance of enforcing the law lest the public lost faith in the police force.

So the sly grog joints were raided regularly but not too often and the owners were warned in advance when their turn had come. There was an even more accommodating arrangement for the biggest two-up school of all, Thommo's, in Surry Hills. Thommo's had been founded in 1910 by a boxer who fought under the name of Joe Thomas. It boomed during the war when American servicemen were its biggest patrons and then became fashionable in the 1950s, a place where politicians, lawyers, doctors, radio stars and businessmen mixed with boxers, jockeys, labourers and criminals. By then Thommo's, also known as 'The Game', was being run by Joe Taylor, a high-class criminal, who also ran the Celebrity nightclub in York Street. Taylor used to claim that American entertainers he engaged for his club, stars like Diana Barrymore and Peter Lawford, also patronised Thommo's.

Taylor had a special arrangement with the Sydney police to make sure that his patrons were never caught in a raid. One of Taylor's associates, the notorious Sydney gunman Chow Hayes, described to his biographer, David Hickie, how it worked.

Each Monday morning between ten and eleven, a young plain clothes copper from the CIB [Criminal Investigation Bureau] would arrive at The Game in his own private car with a briefcase. He'd hand the briefcase to Taylor personally and Taylor would take it into his office. I don't know exactly what amount of cash went into it – but it would have to be massive because both games [the Big Game and the nearby Little Game, known as the 'Snake Pit'] were operating twenty-four hours a day.

Taylor told me that there were only two keys to that briefcase. Taylor had one himself and the top copper at the receiving end back at police headquarters had the other one. Taylor would put the cash in the briefcase, lock it again and then hand it to the young copper. He'd take the briefcase back to the top police in town where it'd be split up between the top cops. Meanwhile, local uniformed coppers would also arrive at The Game in pairs from surrounding police stations in Darlinghurst, Regent Street, and Central. Those police would receive ten shillings or a pound.

Whenever Thommo's was due to go off [be raided by the police], the organisers would round up a bunch of derelicts from Belmore Park and take them over to The Game. They were paid two pounds each to stand inside and be rounded up in the fake raid. There'd be thirty or forty of them, and as soon as they were taken off to the police station, the real game would start up again.

Everyone in Sydney knew of Thommo's and Taylor's deal with the police and I can't recall anyone I ever met who condemned it. The author C. K. Stead has described this sort of acceptance as 'the simple system of good lawlessness and evil lawnessness . . . something I recognise instantly as "Sydney" – as particular as the Harbour Bridge and the Opera House; or as the Catholic cathedral with its statue of an archbishop inscribed "God's Gift to Australia and a Worthy Son of Ireland".'

The criminals who ran the sly grog, gambling, protection and prostitution rackets quarrelled frequently among themselves over territory, money and women. They had their own code of ethics. It was acceptable to 'bash' someone with whom you had quarrelled – either with fists, bottles or staves of timber. If the quarrel had escalated beyond a bashing, then you could shoot him, but preferably only through the shoulder or in the stomach, since this offered him a chance of survival. In turn, he was obliged to tell the police nothing. When they arrived at his bedside in hospital, usually St Vincent's in Darlinghurst, he would explain his mangled head by saying he had fallen over when drunk, or his bullet wound by saying that some bastard had shot him but it was dark and he had not been able to see who it was. If the dispute had gone beyond a beating or a wounding, then the murderer was expected to do the shooting openly, face-to-face, preferably in a public place like a nightclub, and then take his chances with the police.

All this was wonderful grist for all the Sydney journalists covering police rounds. Rivalry between them was intense and each had his own detectives whom he cultivated and promoted in his stories. The split seemed to be on sectarian lines. The *Mirror* police roundsman Bill Jenkins was a Catholic and associated with Catholic detectives. His rival, Noel Bailey, of the *Sun* newspaper, was a member of the Masonic Lodge and thus friendly with many Masonic policemen. Jenkins says that the competition was so fierce that he used to lie awake in bed at night wondering what Bailey was doing. Sometimes the apprehension was too much to bear and he would get up and telephone Bailey's house. If a dazed Bailey answered he would hang up and go back to sleep but if Bailey's wife replied, Jenkins would immediately telephone around his contacts and could only relax when he knew from them that nothing untoward was happening. Both Jenkins and Bailey paid some of these contacts – an acceptable facet of journalism in those days – but most of them were drinking companions which meant that a Sydney police reporter had to have a clear head and an iron liver: Jenkins once told me that he spent four to five hours a day drinking with detectives which made me wonder when the detectives ever found time to catch criminals.

Even crime in Sydney that was not committed by professional criminals was out of the ordinary. Shirley Beiger was a young Sydney fashion model who lived in King's Cross with her lover, Arthur Griffith, a bookmaker's clerk. Early on the evening of 9 August 1954, Griffith told Beiger that he had an appointment with his dentist. Beiger followed him to Chequers, a Sydney nightclub and saw Griffith with a nightclub dancer. Beiger went back to her flat and took from Griffith's room his .22 calibre rifle. She loaded the rifle with one bullet and put six in her pocket. Beiger waited in the car outside Chequers with the rifle across her lap. When Griffith emerged and walked towards the car, Beiger shot him dead on the pavement.

In those pre-*Female Eunuch* days, the killing split Sydney on gender lines.

Women said that Griffith was a two-timing bastard who deserved everything he got. Men said that if women were allowed to shoot every two-timing bastard in Sydney, there would be not enough cemeteries to hold them. What intrigued me as I covered the coroner's inquest, and then followed the murder trial, was that it was apparent from early on that Shirley Beiger was going to walk free. It was my introduction to the way skilled lawyers can manipulate juries and the beginning of my long fascination with lawyers and their profession.

There was no doubt that Beiger had shot Griffith. There were witnesses and she readily admitted it, so there were three possible verdicts – murder, manslaughter, or accident. Beiger's lawyer, J. W. Shand, QC, scorned the manslaughter defence. He was determined to get an acquittal and opened his defence by bluntly telling the jury, 'The circumstances of this death amount either to murder or pure accident.' And then he took Beiger through an account of the shooting and her motives. Beiger said that she loved Griffith deeply and had been hurt and upset to see him with another woman. When she took and loaded the rifle she was thinking that if only she could give him a fright he would come back to her – 'If only I can fire this gun and if he will think I am hurt he will come back to his senses.'

'When Griffith came to the car,' Shand told the jury, 'Miss Beiger was extremely tense. She had forgotten about the gun lying across her knees. Griffith pushed her and the gun went off.' The court heard Beiger herself tell the same story. Dressed entirely in black, with a demure hat and wearing little jewellery, Beiger said that she knew Griffith had other girls because he had told her so. 'He was still in love with me, but he seemed to need to have someone else, too.' You could almost read the thoughts of the women in the courtroom and on the jury – 'Typical.'

Beiger said that she could not even remember Griffith approaching the car when he left the nightclub because she was so tense and upset. 'The first I remember he was at the window. It was down. I can't remember what was said except that he said he would be home later.'

Mr Shand: Do you remember what happened then?

Beiger: He just gave me a push, as he usually does.

When Beiger uttered the words 'as he usually does', thus planting in the minds of the jury the suggestion that Griffith was habitually physically aggressive with her, she collapsed and the judge had to adjourn the court to allow her to recover.

On her return, she moved immediately to the crucial part of her evidence. 'All I remember is him falling away from the car. I remember him trying to reach through the window. I realised something dreadful had happened.'

Shand then summed it all up: here was a happy young couple in love. Then Griffith had cruelly hurt Beiger. So she had taken the gun to give him a fright and win him back. She did not know it was cocked and when he pushed her it went off. The only possible conclusion was pure accident and the only verdict was not guilty of murder. The jury agreed and the whole court broke into cheers when it announced its finding. Beiger seemed confused (she said later she had not heard the 'Not' part of the 'Not guilty' verdict) but when two smiling policewomen ushered her from the dock towards her father, she collapsed into his arms crying, 'Oh, Daddy.'

Although my main work was for the *Daily Mirror*, I used to do an occasional Saturday shift for *Truth* and stood in as its news editor from time to time. It was easy to fill the main part of the paper with the usual divorce cases and Saturday's sport but the front page was always a problem. Unlike British Sunday newspapers, no one on *Truth* began working on a major news story until Friday or Saturday and if nothing sensational had emerged by Saturday afternoon, panic followed.

One week I had two reporters working on an exposé of Sydney's milk suppliers, an idea I had sold to a reluctant Jack Finch who was worried Norton might have some friends in the milk business. Government regulations specified that the butterfat content of the milk had to be a certain minimum level. Dairy farmers had told *Truth* that they produced rich milk well above that level, therefore the milk suppliers must be watering the milk down to the minimum legal requirement. *Truth* reporters had bought sample bottles of milk from all over Sydney and *Truth* had paid to have the butterfat content analysed. If one or two bottles had been watered down to a level below the legal minimum we had a story. The trouble was that we had not started on the story until Thursday and the laboratory did not come up with the results until late Friday afternoon. Every single bottle was above the minimum butterfat level.

The race now began to find a replacement front-page lead. At 4pm we had nothing. Jack Finch's face had become so red that I feared he would explode. 'For Christ's sake find *something*,' he said. 'You're an imaginative fellow. Use your fucking imagination.' Then he went and hid in his office. I went through the week's newspapers for a fourth time. There was a small item from Wednesday's *Sydney Morning Herald* about a youth convicted in a suburban court for indecent assault. He had used the evening rush hour crush on a suburban train as an excuse to press his groin against the girl squeezed against him in the train corridor. To my everlasting professional shame – I can only plead that I was just twenty-four and very ambitious – I obeyed Finch and used my imagination. I invented a story about a pervert known only to his victims and the police as 'The Hook'. The Hook, who was unemployed, spent his days travelling the Sydney train network armed with a length of wire cunningly contrived from an old coat hanger. The wire ran over his right shoulder and down his coat sleeve where it stopped in a hook just short of the cuff. The Hook, while pretending to read a newspaper, would sidle alongside an attractive and unsuspecting girl as they stood in a crowded train, drop his shoulder to extend the hook which he would then slip under the girl's skirt and surreptitiously raise it to look at her stocking tops. The Hook would then quickly slip his device back up his sleeve and continue reading his newspaper, a picture of innocence. I quoted an anonymous police officer as saying that suburban police had been inundated with complaints but that they did not know where to begin their inquiries. An equally anonymous girl spoke of her horror at discovering her skirt rising mysteriously above her stocking tops and her vow never to travel by train again until this pervert was caught. Finally I got a staff artist to draw his impression of The Hook at work. The more I worked on my fairy story, the more I enjoyed it. There were no inconvenient facts to get in the way of a perfect narrative. Like Lionel Hogg said – it was how it should have happened. Finch was delighted and made only one change to my copy – he had The Hook active that very Saturday evening among crowds heading into Sydney for a night out. Then he wrote a headline: HOOK SEX PERVERT STRIKES AGAIN.

It made a good front page and had the opposition struggling desperately to catch up. Some rival journalists may well have guessed that it was an invented story but knew better than to try to tell that to their news editors. I learnt later that they spent hours telephoning duty officers at Sydney suburban police stations trying to find one who either knew of The Hook or would brand the story a fake, but, of course, all any of them could say was that, no, no one at his station had heard of The Hook but he could not answer for the others.

I came into the *Mirror* on Monday moring confident that I had got away with it. *Truth* did not believe in by-lines ('No fucking journalist is going to get fucking famous at my fucking expense,' said Ezra Norton) so there was unlikely to be any come-back from the police unless someone at *Truth* told them who had written the story. My telephone rang and a voice laden with authority said, 'Sergeant Williamson here. Did you write that stuff about The Hook?' He obviously knew, so there was no sense in lying. 'Yes,' I said. 'Right. Well, I just want to thank you and let you know that we got the bastard this morning.' Had I heard right? 'Got him?' 'Yeah. Arrested him at Punchbowl station. Caught him in the act. You might want to write about it.' I checked with the police roundsman. They really had got him.

Over the next few weeks I waited for The Hook to appear before a magistrate but he never did and I did not want to press my luck by asking the police about him. Thinking about it, as I still do from time to time, I came up with several explanations. It could have been a copycat crime: some idiot read the *Truth* story, decided that he would emulate The Hook and got caught on his first time out. Or, there really had been a Hook out there and my imagination had paralleled the truth. Or, the Sydney police, who had a reputation for massaging crime statistics to polish their public relations, got rid of a case which promised to be a PR disaster by arresting some pathetic minor sex offender and nominating him as The Hook. I decided that the last explanation was the most likely and, filled with guilt, I swore that would be the first and last time I would ever make up a story. This turned out to be a vow that was not easy to keep, because I soon fell in with the Fleet Street Royal press corps, which made up stories all the time.

The Royal press corps had come for the Queen's tour of Fiji, New Zealand and Australia in December 1953 and January 1954. The *Mirror* was ambivalent about it all. It was the first time a reigning monarch had visited Australia and loyalist newspapers like the *Sydney Morning Herald*, which tended to import Englishmen as its editors, had become very excited and were planning extensive coverage. But Norton was a republican and anti-English, and was certainly not going to follow the *Herald*'s lead. So in the end the *Mirror* decided on a compromise. It would assign a junior reporter to the job and under no circumstances would any story refer to the Queen as 'Queen of Australia'. I was junior enough and I had also lived in Fiji, where the Mirror's coverage was going to start, so I got the job and left for Suva the following week.

The British press had been travelling with the Royal party from London. To an impressionable colonial who had grown up on British B-movies about country house weekends, where the hero arrived in his MG with the top down and wearing a snazzy striped blazer, all these Fleet Street reporters appeared to have come straight from West End casting.

A lot of the men were either half drunk all the time or fully drunk half the time. At one stage of the tour I shared a room with Patrick O'Donovan, of the *Observer*, who was usually sober in the early part of the week, when he did not have to write anything, and then drunk on Friday and Saturday, when he did. In Wellington, New Zealand, he typed his story lying full length on the hotel floor because he was incapable of sitting on a chair without falling off it. But when I had to take his copy to the cable office because he had passed out, and naturally had a peep at it, it turned out to be legible, coherent, irreverent and funny. In fact I decided that O'Donovan drunk was a better reporter than some of the other reporters sober.

The women amazed me. They buzzed with gossip about the Royal party – not so much the Queen and Prince Philip, but the ladies-in-waiting, the secretaries, the bodyguards. Anne Matheson of the *Australian Woman's Weekly* had covered more Royal Tours than she could remember and knew everyone. ('Hello, Annie,' the Queen would say at the start of yet another tour. 'Nice to see you again.') She acted as messenger in a mild flirtation between one of the ladies-in-waiting and one of the reporters, the dashing Bruce Grant, of the *Melbourne Age*. But this was unusual; most of the Royal party treated the press in the same way as Prince Philip did – a persistent irritation that you ignored as far as was possible.

Gwen Robynson was covering the tour for the London *Daily Mirror* and since our papers had the same name, hotel staff sometimes confused our incoming messages. This introduced me to the confusing world of 'cablese', a language invented by desk-bound foreign editors ostensibly to save money (cables were charged by the word) but actually to lend them and their empire of foreign correspondents an aura of secret romance. They went something like this:

PROROBYNSON EXFORNEWSED CANST FILE EARLIEST FRIDMORN GMT UPWARDS EIGHTHUNDRED HOW HM COPING HEATWISE STOP BBC SAYS DUKE EXPRESSED CONCERN PROHER HEALTH ETDEMANDING SCHEDULE CUTS STOP WHAT SAYST OTHERS QUERY ADVISE WHEN AUCKLANDWARDING ENDS

PROROBYNSON EXFORNEWSED YOUR HM HEALTH PAGEONE LEAD STOP OTHERS HAD UPCHASE LATER EDITIONS STOP CONGRATS PROGOOD WORK STOP ONFORWARDING EXES SYDNEY ENDS

It was catching. Within days I had a cable from the *Mirror* in Sydney.

SUN SAYS QUEEN WILL SIT CROSSLEGGED ON GROUND AT TONGAN FEAST AND EAT ROAST PIG WITH FINGERS STOP WHY YOU NO FILE THIS STORY QUERY SMITH

In a flash I understood the art of being a foreign correspondent: it was not reporting what had happened today – the agencies did that – it was telling the reader what was going to happen tomorrow, or the day after. It did not matter that if what you confidently said was going to occur then did not, because by that time both you and the reader had moved on to the next prediction. For example, the Queen did not sit cross-legged on the ground at the Tongan feast – she sat in a chair – and she ate her roast pig with a knife and fork, as did her host, Queen Salote of Tonga, but I did not get a cable from Smith saying:

YOU RIGHT ABOUT QUEEN AND FEAST STOP SUN WRONG AND HAS APOLOGISED TO READERS STOP WELL DONE ENDS SMITH.

So after that I left the reporting of the record to Reuters, the Associated Press, the Press Association, the Australian Associated Press and all the other agencies, and concentrated on the strange little happenings, the accidents, the faux pas, the social oddities and the mechanics of a Royal Tour. How, for example, did the Royal bodyguards go about their business? 'Well,' said one of them, only too happy to talk about this work. 'All our planning is based on the fact that the British are not by nature assassins. So we concentrate on the foreigners. We get a pen sketch of everyone who is likely to come into contact with HM and we discuss anyone we are doubtful about with local police. There are all sorts of precautions we take, searches we make, positions we take up. But I've got to tell you that if any one maniac was determined enough, then there is little we could do to stop him.'

How could the tour organisers be certain that the Queen would draw a crowd? Wouldn't it be terribly embarrassing if, when she drove through the streets of Sydney, there was no one to line the route, wave flags and cheer? The answer, from one of the Buckingham Palace staff, turned out to be so simple I was ashamed I had not already thought of it. 'The host government must agree when the tour is arranged that it will declare a school holiday for the specific purpose of allowing the children to see the Queen. The schools themselves then arrange transport to take the children to the tour route and lay on flags for them to wave: This alone ensures the basis of a crowd. But when the mothers learn that little Jimmy and Amy are going to see the Queen, they go along too, to watch their kids watching the Queen. Presto, you've got your crowd.'

As the tour progressed I developed a theory, later confirmed on other Royal tours, that there was an unwritten agreement between Buckingham Palace and the press. It was as if the Palace had said to Fleet Street, 'You need us to bring in your readers, most of whom love Royal stories. We need you to tell the Queen's subjects what she is up to and what a wonderful person she is. So you can write anything you like about the Royals – as long as you don't question the actual institution of the monarchy.' So Fleet Street cheerfully made up all sorts of stories about the Royal family – arguments, rifts, romances, pregnancies – and Buckingham Palace seldom denied them, never banned or even remonstrated with the reporters concerned, and even laid on a cocktail party or two during tours so that the press could actually meet the people they had been writing about.

During processions, the tour organisers provided limousines for Fleet Street to follow the Queen's car and when curious crowds waved at the reporters, as they had waved at the Queen when she had passed, the reporters felt they had the right to wave back. After all, they were part of the show. In Milaura, Victoria, I was standing in the crowd when this happened. 'Who're they?' said one rural Australian as the press limousines swept past, the reporters fluttering their hands. 'All the Royal bastards,' said his companion, and I thought, 'He's got it right.' I didn't write that, of course, and I didn't write about my own moment with the Queen. She was visiting a village in the interior of Fiji. The visit was nearly over when the Royal walkabout made an unscheduled stop and the Queen disappeared inside a large bure, a Fijian native hut. Minutes passed and she showed no sign of re-appearing but nothing important could have been happening because the Royal party and the press were making their way back to the cars. Bored, I wandered along a path that turned out to lead to the back of the hut where there was a large window, with a palm frond shutter instead of glass. The shutter was propped open, so I thought I'd just take a quick look inside. I had to stand on tip-toe to see over the ledge. For a moment I could see nothing in the darkened interior. Then, as my eyes became accustomed to the gloom, there was the familiar face of the Queen, reflected in the mirror of a dressing table, literally powdering her nose. Our eyes met for half a second, then I shrank back to the ground and slunk away, wondering if this was a hanging offence, or just a life-long ban on covering Royal Tours.

Being on tour was a corrupting experience. You were your own boss, and providing you did not miss a major story, your office left you alone. You stayed in the best hotels, ate the finest food – all on expenses – met people and saw interesting things. How could I go back to reporting suburban courts after all this? I did try, and the very first case I covered convinced me that I would have to leave Australia as soon as possible.

Dr Bernard Lake, a Sydney antique dealer, had been charged with exhibiting an obscene object calculated to cause offence to the general public, to wit a native wood carving. There was a long history of such charges. Gino Nibbi, an Italian writer who ran the Leonardo Art Shop in Melbourne in the 1920s was visited by the Victorian police because he placed a reproduction of a Renoir nude in his shop window. The police told him that the reproduction was obscene and that there had been thirty telephone calls of complaint to police headquarters.

Lake was not so lucky. A detective walking past his shop near Circular Quay noticed a wood carving from the Sepic River area of New Guinea. It depicted a Sepic River native in a crouching position. Since the carving was intended for use as a water vessel and needed a handle, the wood carver had extended the man's penis from between his legs to his mouth. The detective said that he had looked at the carving carefully and had decided its obscenity offended him. That was all that was required under the law in Australia at that time, so Lake was hauled into court and charged.

The case went on for days. Learned anthropologists trooped into the witness box to testify for the defence that this was a genuine New Guinea artefact of anthropological interest and had not been deliberately carved so as to cause offence to a Sydney policeman. The constable himself had an embarrassing moment during his own evidence when the lawyer defending Lake placed the carving on the edge of the witness box, and put it to the policeman that this was not a penis at all, but simply a handle. It was definitely a penis, said the constable. There was no way it could be a handle. 'Could you just pick up the carving and show it to his worship, constable,' said the lawyer. The poor policeman's hand reached out for the carving, stopped in mid-air as its owner sought desperately for a way to pick up the carving other than by the penis/handle, then gave up and did so. It did not help. Lake was convicted and fined.

So, that same year, was Harry Robinson, the owner of the Moulin Rouge Café, in Sydney's King's Cross, for exhibiting on the café's wall a copy of Toulouse-Lautrec's *Woman Adjusting Her Stocking*. Detective-Sergeant Roy McDonald of the NSW Vice Squad said he saw the mural by looking through the café's plate glass window and decided at once that he found it obscene. The director of the National Art Gallery, Hal Missingham, told the court that the mural was a well-done copy, a work of art, and that if he had the chance of hanging the original in the art gallery he would be prepared to do so. It made no difference; Robinson collected a criminal conviction and was fined £5.

Suddenly life in Sydney seemed terribly stifling. Dr Herbert Evatt, the Labor leader, had lost the Federal election and the country braced itself for at least another three years of Robert Menzies. Immigrant friends painted a beguiling picture of life in Paris, Prague and London, and wondered why they had ever left Europe for a country which persecuted artists and writers, where the quality of debate was deplorable, and you could not get a drink after 6pm. The *Mirror* had a London office, so I began lobbying for a posting there. The editor-in-chief quickly disillusioned me: Mr Norton did not approve of the sending of journalists abroad, especially to Britain. If, however, I was to get to London at my own expense and turn up at the

Mirror's bureau there, then no doubt a job could be found for me. I sailed with the Italian shipping line Lloyd Triestino, waving goodbye to Sydney without a trace of regret. In Europe I travelled overland from Naples and arrived in London just before Christmas 1954. The *Mirror*'s office turned out to be in Red Lion Court, rather than Fleet Street, but it was a start.

CHAPTER FOUR

AROUND THE WORLD IN THREE DAYS

The clerk in the ticket office at Dover railway station introduced me to the British class system. I asked for a ticket to London and he replied 'First or second class, sir?' What was I? On the grounds of cost, I opted for second class, deciding to defer the real decision until later when I had got over the shock of the cold and gloom. As the train rattled through dreary suburb after dreary suburb I sat shivering, peering through the smog, trying to see something I recognised from all those Ealing B pictures, realising only later that most of them had been shot in the summer.

I spent the first days wandering around the West End gaining confidence from landmarks that were familiar from books and the cinema. In Piccadilly Circus I was happy to learn that Britain in the Fifties was indeed a country where eccentricity was respected. As I waited for the lights to change, I heard the blast of a hunting horn and a rider in full hunting rig came galloping down Regent Street, weaving his way in and out of the traffic. He shot an amber light opposite Eros, skidded around the corner and, with a clatter of iron hooves and another blast of his hunting horn, headed for Trafalgar Square. (I discovered later he was part of some field sports organisation on its way to lobby the House of Commons.) Apart from me, no one took the slightest notice. In Australia, the crowd would probably have done its best to unseat him, and he would certainly have been arrested by the Vice Squad.

After a week in the Hotel Russell, Russell Square, most of it spent wandering its echoing corridors looking for a bathroom with a shower, I found lodgings in a house at Shepherd's Bush, choosing it from the *Evening Standard* not because of its location – I had no idea where Shepherd's Bush was – but because of the price. It was an ugly terraced house with a kitchen that smelled of cabbage and damp clothes which the landlady dried on some sort of wooden hanger suspended from the ceiling over the cooker.

We fell out immediately. I had a bath every night before going to bed because the rooms were unheated and a hot bath was the only way I could face the icy sheets. She complained, not because of the cost – I had to feed shillings into a meter – but because the noise of the running water disturbed her.

Christmas was five days away, so I arranged a dinner party with three other Australians who had travelled on the same ship. I was on my way home from the *Mirror* office, where I had gone to look around before starting work on New Year's day, when I saw a wine bar in Fleet Street called El Vino. I went in and was greeted with a fog of cigarette smoke, a wall of animated conversation, and the earthy smell of wine. I recognised the drinkers as journalists; I even knew the faces of some, and immediately felt at home. I had a solitary glass of hock and when I saw someone buying a bottle of claret, I decided I'd stock up for our nostalgic Christmas dinner. We wouldn't be able to drink frosty beer and go surfing afterwards, but we could remember Sydney. I addressed a large, red-faced man behind the counter: 'Could I have a bottle of good Australian claret, please?' He looked at me for a moment and then he grinned and turned to the drinkers lining the bar and the staff serving them. 'Did you hear that?' he said. 'This gentleman wants a bottle of good Australian claret.' Then he chuckled. 'Bit of an oxymoron, I'd say, wouldn't you?' There were smiles and some low laughter. He turned back to me, suddenly serious and pompous. 'I'm afraid, sir, that we don't stock any Australian wines. Or South African. Or Cypriot. No colonial wines at all. They may be drinkable in their own country but they don't travel.' And then he left me. I crept out into the gloom and have never been back to that El Vino again.

My trouble, I soon realised, was that I had arrived too late. The first wave of Australians-on-the-make had hit the beaches years earlier – Peter Finch, Shirley Abicair, Dick Bentley, Bill Kerr, Keith Michell, Leo McKern, Joan Sutherland, June Bronhill, Sidney Nolan, Arthur Boyd, Jack Brabham, Frank Ifield, Rolf Harris. We had even got a man into Buckingham Palace – Michael Parker – and had had a Lord Mayor of London – Sir Leslie Boyce. Add to them the Australians who had stayed on after a good war and the precedent was daunting. And they had all so smoothly integrated into London life that hardly anyone remembered that they were Australians. (Who would ever have said 'the Australian, Robert Helpmann'?)

But by the time I arrived, the novelty the Australians held for the English had worn off and we were back to the one historical factor that colours all Anglo-Australian relationships – the fact that Britain started Australia with a boatload of thieves, prostitutes, trade unionists and Irish rebels, all transported to Botany Bay for the term of their natural life, later reinforced by the 'get-rich-quick migrants' and then the post-war £10 passage scheme. All migration to Australia was thus largely involuntary and came principally from the lower-income bracket in Britain. No wonder that Winston Churchill, lamenting the fall of Singapore, and in deep conflict with the then Australian Prime Minister John Curtin, called us 'bad stock'.

Equally, Australians did not have a very high opinion of the British. Not for us the image that, say, Indians held of them – tall, impressive men in plumed helmets. For Australians the typical Englishman was short, cloth-capped, pasty-faced and whingeing. This gave my generation of Australians a conditioned reflex to Britain. Those descended from the Irish were told that the English drove their forefathers out of Ireland. Those descended from the radicals were brought up on tales of dark, satanic mills, and the sons and daughters of the 'get-rich-quick' believed that economic necessity forced their forebears to leave the Motherland. So although I had no experience of the Raj, I could understand the feelings of an Indian cricket writer talking about Bradman's career, 'We Indians looked on Bradman as a kind of Avenging Angel as he reeled off century after century against the common foe – England.'

None of the Australians in my wave knew any English people socially. Early on, I had looked up some of the Royal Tour correspondents who had been so free with their invitations when they were in Australia. One of them invited me to lunch. When I arrived, she was with an Australian girl, another reporter she had also met while on the tour. She introduced us to each other and then disappeared, pleading an unexpected engagement. One of the other reporters in the *Mirror* office, Rex Lopez, a Gibraltarian, assured me it would all change once I had been here five years or so. I pointed out to him that he had arrived in 1940 and now, fourteen years later, he still knew hardly any English people. And yet . . . Driving to work one day in a BMW bubble car I had bought for £250, darkly unshaven after a late night, I forced a pedestrian to break into a run as I swung out of Admiralty Arch into Trafalgar Square. He whirled around and as I went past he whacked the vinyl roof of the car with his tightly rolled umbrella and yelled, 'You bloody Greek bastard.' (Cyprus was in the news.) And I found myself indignantly shouting back, 'I'm British. I'm British.'

I had a miserable Christmas and reported for work wondering whether I could last out the six months I had set myself as the minimum time that I could stay and still return to Sydney with some dignity. The *Mirror* office in London was unique in the history of journalism. It reflected Ezra Norton's Irish ambivalence about Britain. On the one hand he recognised that

London was still the major centre of overseas interest for most Australians and that his newspapers would have to cover what happened there. On the other, he refused to buy a service from any of the big news agencies because he felt that they would reflect too British an attitude. So he created his own service, staffed it with Australians, and expected them to cover Britain from an Australian point of view. But having done this, he began to wonder if he could trust them. On the eve of war he had sent a flamboyant New Zealand-born reporter, Eric Baume, to report from Britain. Baume had run 'The *Daily Mirror* World Cables and *Truth* Special Service' out of a suite at the Savoy and had written the front-page lead of the first issue of the *Mirror* on 12 May 1941. Baume had employed Lady Margaret Stewart, daughter of Lord Londonderry, as a war correspondent and feature writer and Norton suspected, quite correctly, that Baume was having an affair with her. When Baume wrote that he had met George VI through the Secretary of State for War, Oliver Stanley, Norton decided that Baume had been well and truly 'duchessed' – his description of how the British establishment seduced Australians away from their anti-English stance by sucking them into aristocratic circles. This view was confirmed when after the war Norton told the London office to stress in their stories the theme 'Britain is done for' and Baume proved less than enthusiastic.

So Baume was recalled and the enlarged London office was staffed with Australian reporters assigned to cover the British scene – but ordered to have as little contact with the British as possible. It worked like this: the London editor was George Hawkes, a former Australian army officer. Under him was Keith Hooper, a former Australian war correspondent, who had the title of chief sub-editor. There was one feature writer, Eric Jessup, a former clerk in the British navy who had taken his discharge in Australia and had worked there as a jackeroo. Then there were seven journalists, of whom I was one. Because of the time difference between London and Sydney, five of us worked from 6pm to midnight and two from midnight to 6am. We sat around a big U-shaped table, with Hooper inside the U, and we 'stole' stories from all the British newspapers. Of course, we did not steal them intact – that would have been illegal – we took the facts, and – this is the creative part – we rewrote everything. We shuffled paragraphs around, putting the first paragraph second, paraphrasing the third, turning a direct quotation into an indirect one or vice versa, adding a sentence or two from the same item in another newspaper. Then Hooper went through the rewritten story, added a touch or two of his own, and handed it to the teleprinter operator, a Cypriot-born Armenian called Victor Krikorian who had served in the British army in Cyprus, and he sent it off to Sydney. Even Jessup's feature stories were scarcely original, since he gathered all the facts from the *News of the World* clippings library to which Norton had reluctantly bought access. This recycling of news occasionally produced strange results. Sometimes we so thoroughly rewrote a story that by the time it appeared in the *Sydney Daily Mirror*, where it had been given the tabloid treatment by a Sydney sub-editor, it looked fresh and original. Then the Australian correspondents of the British newspapers would pick it up and send it to London, just in case Fleet Street had missed it. And every now and then, in its new form, it got back into the very same paper whence it had originated.

The work was mind-numbingly boring, relieved only when Sydney — which thought everything in Britain ran like it did in Australia, only on a bigger scale — made some impossible request, usually at 11am Sydney time, which was 2am in London. EXSMITH RING BUCKPALACE ASK REAL REPEAT REAL REASON WHY MARGARET NO MARRY TOWNSEND.

Or, EXBLUNDEN UPWAKE HOMESECRETARY ASK WHETHER INTENDS HANG RUTH ELLIS. We spent a lot of time devising replies that disguised the fact that Buckingham Palace did not have a 24-hour answering service and that no one in the London office knew the Home Secretary's private number and would not dare ring it at 2am if he did.

Occasionally, very occasionally, something out of the ordinary raised new questions for me on the nature of journalism, particularly the one that journalists argue over all the time: what is news? I was wandering through Harrods one afternoon, filling in an hour or two before work, and in the basement, I found the pets' corner. It seemed to have everything — puppies, kittens, hamsters, birds, rats, even snakes. And there in a remote corner, huddling in his cage, was a small kangaroo, looking as homesick as I was. I felt compelled to write about him. I painted a real tabloid picture: Australia's national emblem, brutally removed from the sunny plains of New South Wales, shivering in the English winter, waiting for some rich Englishman's spoilt child to demand brief possession of him as a Christmas plaything before committing him to his fate with the RSPCA. 'Nice piece,' said Hawkes and then we all forgot about it. Four days later Hawkes handed me a teleprinter message from Sydney: PROHAWKES TRUTH READERS GREATLY DISTRESSED KANGAROO PLIGHT HAVE CONTRIBUTED FORTY STERLING PROHIS RESCUE STOP BUY HIM FIND GOOD HOME FILE EIGHT HUNDRED WORDS AND PIX HAPPY ROO WITH NEW OWNER STOP FINCH. 'Here,' said Hawkes. 'It's your story. Draw forty quid from Miss Dwyer and go and buy the bloody kangaroo.' 'But what'll I do with him when I've bought him?' I asked. 'That's your bloody problem,' said Hawkes.

Rex Lopez came to the rescue. The Duke of Bedford had recently opened his stately home to visitors and one of the attractions was a small zoo. 'The Duke'll take him,' Lopez said. 'Ring his gamekeeper.' I did and it was all arranged very quickly. I would buy the kangaroo and have him crated and sent by rail. The gamekeeper would meet the train, the kangaroo, me and a photographer from the Keystone Press Agency. We would get a cup of morning coffee with the Duke, Duchess and one of the sons and then they would pose with the kangaroo in the stables. It was amazing what a Duke would do in those days for a bit of publicity.

I went down to Harrods, planning on the way a little fun with the poncy sales assistant in the pets' department. I broadened my Australian accent. 'Listen, mate,' I said. 'I've got some friends from Sydney coming over for dinner on Saturday and I want to give them a bit of a treat – kangaroo tail soup, freshly made. Have you got any kangaroos?' His expression did not flicker. 'We do have one, sir,' he said. 'I'll take him,' I said. 'Will that be cash or account?' 'Cash,' I said. 'And will sir be taking him with him, or does sir want him delivered?' I surrendered.

The gamekeeper met me at the station and took me back to the stately home where the Duke and Duchess were charming over coffee. Then we adjourned to the stables. A wooden box with a large Harrods label stood near the door. The Duke and Duchess arranged themselves alongside it, the gamekeeper began levering it open with a crowbar and the photographer levelled his Speed Graphic. 'Maybe Your Grace could give him a bit of a pat,' I suggested. At that moment the lid of the box came off. There was a thump, a brown blur, another thump and a glimpse of a kangaroo's tail disappearing over a six-foot wall in the stable yard. 'Shit,' said the photographer. 'He's bolted.' He had indeed. I wrote a lame story for Finch about the kangaroo taking happily to the wild acres of Duke's estate and the Duke's insistence that the animal could not be photographed being patted in case it disturbed the settling-in period. I learnt after that the kangaroo had come from a breeding farm on the Isle of Man, was accustomed to Britain's climate, and must have found some other kangaroos on the Duke's estate because there were soon so many that they had become a nuisance. Should I have told those *Truth* readers the real story?

It did not take me long to find out that everyone else in the *Daily Mirror* and *Truth*'s London office was as bored with the job as I was but since they had been at it longer, they had all found other interests to keep them occupied. Eric Jessup had bought an old Norwegian fishing ketch, the *Northern Light*, and was converting it to a luxury yacht which he planned to sail to the West Indies and there make a fortune in the yacht charter business. His weekdays were spent chasing elusive parts from ships' chandlers and his weekends in carpentry and mechanics. Hooper had bought a large run-down house in Wimbledon and was decorating and refurbishing it. The office picture researcher, Philip Harris, had been a lieutenant in the Australian army in France in the First World War where he founded and edited *Aussie*, a front-line newspaper for the Australian troops, and a censor in London in the Second World War. Although he was now over seventy he spent his time applying for other jobs in Fleet Street that might have 'better prospects for promotion'. He was not having much luck. 'There's plenty of papers who want me,' he'd say, 'but they can't find a way of fitting me into their pension scheme.'*

The only reporter trying to get on in journalism was Rex Lopez, who wanted to make the leap from Red Lion Court into Fleet Street. He kept quoting the example of Murray Sayle, an Australian who worked on the *People*, as proof that it could be done. One Saturday night he took me around to Sayle's flat in Notting Hill Gate, where I was delighted to learn that he had also been to Canterbury Boys' High School in Sydney. Sayle, a tall, raw-boned man with a large broken nose (a dance hall scrap between arts and medical students while he was at Sydney University) ran a salon where expatriates gathered to rail against the English and discuss ways of beating the system. Sayle was our beacon, and free with encouragement and advice. Three years earlier he had knocked on just about every door in Fleet Street before getting a week's trial on the *People* as assistant to the legendary crime reporter Duncan Webb. Webb was then in the middle of exposing the Messina brothers, five Maltese who ran most of London's brothels. Webb would establish that some West End address was being used by prostitutes. Then he would trace the ownership of the premises back to the Messinas. The first step was often the most difficult and Webb himself could no longer do it – the Messinas had rumbled him and his picture was on display in every brothel in London. This is where Sayle came in. As Webb explained it to him: 'I need someone who couldn't be me, and couldn't be a copper. As a big wool man straight off the boat, looking for a bit of the old you-know-what, you'd be perfectly convincing,

---

* Harris came into his own when Rupert Murdoch took over the *Sydney Daily Mirror* because his father had known Harris in 1914–18. Rupert increased Harris's salary, invited him to his hotel every time he came to London, and paid for his funeral and wake when Harris died in 1971, aged eighty-six.

digger.' And how did one actually establish that premises were being used for prostitution?

'You have to get a definite offer of sex,' Webb had told Sayle. 'Get them to disrobe and name a price. Like, how much for a short time and how much for an all-nighter. Don't actually hand over any cash, though. Sam [the *People*'s managing editor] would never stand for throwing the firm's money around like that. Then you make some sort of excuse and leave.'

Sayle had gone on to prosper on the *People* – leaving only to write what is arguably the best novel on journalism, *A Crooked Sixpence* – and remembered Webb with admiration: 'Webb set a standard of honest reporting later to flower in various Insights, Daylights and other forms of group-grope investigative journalism which have since chewed up so many Finnish forests. But no one ever did it better, or produced a worse set of bad guys than the Messinas.'

But in 1955, we Australians in the *Sydney Daily Mirror* office could only encourage ourselves with the thought that since Sayle had broken into Fleet Street, then maybe, one day, we would too.

I don't know whether it was all the talk about prostitutes with Sayle or the fact that, in those days, it was impossible to walk down Park Lane without being accosted every ten yards or so by a girl, some very attractive, but one lonely Saturday night soon afterwards I was tempted. I was on my way to a coffee bar near Grosvenor House when a girl of about eighteen standing in a doorway said in a shy Irish voice, 'Are you looking for company?' I said I was and we took a taxi to a warm, neatly furnished basement flat in South Kensington. I was all for a cup of coffee and a preliminary chat but from the moment we stepped inside the front door she was very businesslike. 'Can I have the five pounds, please?' She took it and tucked it under a vase on the mantelpiece over the spluttering gas fire. Then she went to a single bed near the window and without drawing back the bedcover, lay down, pulled up her skirt, drew up her legs and said, 'Come on.' I knelt by the bed and tried to kiss her. 'No kissing,' she said, impatiently. 'Come on, come on.' It was a waste of time. The whole thing was so choreographed, so detached, so mechanical, that my desire faded as quickly as it had come. Her attitude suddenly changed. 'Never mind,' she said, getting up, 'I'll give you credit. You can come back another time. In the afternoon, perhaps.' Now I couldn't stop her talking. She made me coffee and told me about her life on the streets. I told her about life in Sydney. After about ten minutes there was a knock on the door and a young man with a South London accent came in carrying a glass of orange juice and two tablets on a saucer. He smiled at both of us. 'Time for your vitamins,' he said. As he left he winked at me. 'Got to keep her healthy,' he said. The Irish girl saw me to the door. 'Come back one afternoon,' she said. 'Any time you like. I'm always home in the afternoon.' But I never did.

When I told Lopez about this the next day he looked at me with pity and amazement. 'Lots of lonely girls in London,' he said. 'But the trouble is that most of them live in the suburbs. If you take them out on a Saturday night then you've got to be prepared to hack it down to Streatham and back. But if you're willing to work a bit harder, then you can try your luck with me in the West End convents.'

'Convents?'

'All these Spanish and Italian girls come over here to learn English. Their dads put them into convents to be certain they're safe. But they have to go out each day to the language schools. You can pick them up there. Or in the coffee bars near the schools, or you can hang around outside the convents, but that's a bit risky – sometimes the nuns call the coppers. Wherever, it's best when the girls have just arrived and before they cotton on to London. But you have to be able to speak a bit of Spanish or Italian or French. Later on, they'll want to practise their English on you.'

'Count me in,' I said. 'Where do we start?'

'There's a nice little convent in the Old Brompton Road,' Lopez said. 'The Virgo Fidelis.'

A week or so later I had a chance to repay Sayle for all his advice. A researcher from the BBC telephoned the *Mirror* office and said that a programme called 'What's My Line?' was looking for someone who had been a beachcomber, and since Sydney was in the South Pacific she had reasoned that a reporter on the *Mirror* might suggest where she could find one. I said I could – me. Wonderful, she said, and explained the programme. Four celebrities – Gilbert Harding, the crusty, short-tempered media star, was one – asked questions of the participants and hoped to find out what they did. 'You're one beachcomber,' she said, 'but the producer thinks it would be a good joke to have two, one after the other and fool the panel that way.' I said that I happened to know another one: Sayle had been a beachcomber in Cairns in northern Queensland. She snapped him up.

On the night it all fell apart when the compère accidentally revealed everything after only one or two questions had been asked. But that made for a lot of joshing from the panel and the audience seemed to like it. The lights went down and everyone began to wander off through the props and electrical cables – the compère and the panel in one direction and the participants, ushered by the producer's assistant, in another. We ended up in a small hospitality room where there were plates of tired cheese and tomato sandwiches and a pot of coffee. Sayle and I were in something of a daze. Two lads from Canterbury Boys' High school in Sydney, Australia, had just appeared on the BBC in London. Had we made it? Was this the beginning of The Big Time? The assistant invited us to help ourselves and then disappeared.

'Something odd's going on here,' Sayle said after a while. 'What's happened to Gilbert Harding and the others? Aren't they coming here? Have they gone home? Let's go and see.'

So we wandered casually out of the coffee room, down a corridor, turned a corner and bumped into Harding coming out of a thick oak door, a large whisky in one hand and a smoked salmon sandwich in the other. 'Dear boy,' he said, spotting Murray. 'Coming to join us?' – they knew each other from the *People*. And he showed us into a brightly lit room with potted palms, uniformed waitresses, tables laden with drinks, and the stars of tonight's show. The producer's assistant glared but said nothing. Sayle poured us both a big drink and emphasised the lesson. 'This is the way it goes over here,' he said. 'No matter how well you reckon you're doing, you can't be too complacent. There's always Another Room.'

My BBC appearance did not bring in offers of work, but at last there was an unexpected break from the routine of Red Lion Court. The Australian Rugby League football team, the Kangaroos, had been touring Britain and everyone in the London office had by now been too long out of Sydney to appreciate what big news this was back home. In the early hours of the morning the teleprinter chattered out a message for Hawkes: EX-RICHARDS SUN BEATING US HOLLOW ON KANGAROOS STOP UPSTEP COVERAGE IMMEDIATELY ENDS. Within hours I was on my way to Ilkley in Yorkshire where the Australian team was staying. I was to cover their last match in Britain and then tour France with them. Within days I faced the dilemma of all sports reporters – do you write what really goes on and then get so frozen out by the players and officials that you never get another story, or do you keep your mouth shut, write anodyne nonsense, and enjoy being accepted as a non-playing member of the team?

The very first night at the small hotel in Ilkley, when I had not yet presented myself to the Kangaroos' manager, I was dining anonymously in the small restaurant. Four Australian players were seated at the bar when a local businessman and his attractive wife walked in and were shown to their table. 'Hey, darling,' said one of the Australians to the woman. 'Would a quick fuck be out of the question?' The woman blushed and her husband immediately pushed his chair back and stood up. So did the four Australians at the bar. The man registered their size, realised who they were, and thought better of whatever he had been planning. He took his wife by the arm and left. I mentioned the incident to the hotel manager who said that his takings had dropped dramatically because none of his regular customers would come to the restaurant or the bar out of fear of Australians. I did not write the story.

It got worse in France. After a match at the Parc des Princes, the team decided to visit a brothel in Montmartre. The man from the *Sydney Sun* and I decided to go along. A few modest Kangaroos went off to private bedrooms but most of the action took place in one large room with two seasoned women and one famous forward on the bed, and ten players and two journalists as the audience. The forward was drunk and could not perform. The two French women did their professional best, without success. 'Il ne vient pas avant demain matin,' one of them complained when what seemed like half an hour's oral sex failed to produce any result. The forward now became aggressive and demanded his money back, threatening to drop-kick both women between the brass bedposts. The manager, a small man wearing a green leather apron, appeared in the doorway, assessed the scene, went away and returned remarkably quickly with an equally small French policeman. He was not in the least troubled by the size of the opposing team. He began to speak quietly in French, saying that it would be best for everyone if the Australians now left. If, however, they did not wish to do so, he explained, his voice rising, they could stay. He would then beat their heads to a bloody pulp, an action he graphically described and even illustrated, pounding to pieces with his baton a small bedside table. This was language the Australians understood and the *Sun* man and I watched in amazement as they filed quietly out of the room and on to the street. We did not write the story.

The French players were equally unpolished. One of them, a Catalan called Poux, had a French wife who was the image of Brigitte Bardot, then every male's erotic fantasy. In a bar in Perpignan, with the pastis flowing freely, Poux watched quietly as one Australian after another made a crude pass at her. Then he punched out the bottoms of two wooden chairs and, as an encore, challenged the Australians to a test of manhood. He took a heavy ceramic ashtray from the bar, held it flat against the wall, and then headbutted it until it broke in two. The Australians abandoned the Bardot lookalike to prove that they too had foreheads of steel. The game stopped only when the bar ran out of ashtrays. Everyone appeared at breakfast the next morning with a large red weal in the middle of his forehead. I did not write the story. That is the way it goes, then and now. While sports writers give the impression of being only too willing to criticise sportsmen, it's all froth and bubble – they never write the most interesting stories because they have to live and travel with the people they write about.

After the Kangaroos' tour I began to wonder if I was cut out to be a journalist. Compared with any nine-to-five job, journalism was all a big adventure – excitement, freedom of movement, a chance to use your wits and initiative, a sense of being – if not a part of mainstream events – a close-up observer. But it could also be a bit seedy. To be successful you had to betray the trust of too many people. You winkled your way into their presence, won their confidence, got them to tell you things they should not, and then exposed them to the world at large. I was amazed that people could be so innocent as not to realise the journalist's intention. A colleague went to interview an elderly, retired couple and the next day exposed them as one-time Soviet spies. When the story appeared he sent them a big bunch of flowers and a note in appreciation of their help. He showed me their reply. Part of it read: 'Your flowers cheered us up enormously on what was otherwise a most miserable day.' It did not occur to them that the flowers had come from the very man who had made their day so miserable. Or how about a reporter known to her colleagues as 'The Seamstress of Fleet Street' because of her skill at stitching people up? She wanted to write about the murderer Peter Sutcliffe, the 'Yorkshire Ripper'. She got to him through his wife, Sonia, even going on a two-week holiday with her. This was called 'befriending Sonia professionally'. Sonia would no doubt have another name for it.

Pondering over what I would do if I gave up journalism, an advertisement in the local newspaper caught my eye. 'Be your own boss. American vending machines can pave your way to a fortune.' In an attic in Soho a slick salesman convinced me that five machines dispensing peanuts, strategically placed in pubs around London, could bring me £50 a week, nearly three times what I was earning at the *Mirror* office. All I had to do was to buy the machines at £200 each and contract to buy the peanuts only from him. I took Lopez on as a partner and we persuaded five publicans in the East End – 'Big drinkers down there,' Lopez said – to allow us to install the machines. A week later we returned to top up the peanuts, empty the cash, pay the publican his 10 per cent, and bank our money. We ran into a barrage of abuse: the peanuts were stale, the machines gave out only twenty-five nuts for a shilling, and the customers were incapable of putting one hand under the dispensing spout while turning the operating handle with the other so peanuts showered all over the pub carpet and were trodden deep into the pile. 'Get it outta here,' said the licensee of the Iron

Bridge in the Old Kent Road, 'before I chuck it out and you after it.' Lopez and I tried to get our money back from the Soho entrepreneur. 'No money back, lads,' he said. 'Not company policy.' But his nuts were stale compared with those in the High Street. 'Stale mine may be,' he said. 'But they're a bigger nut.' In the end he agreed to swap our peanut machines for ones dispensing bubble gum. But we had already lost heart and instead of doing deals with newsagents to place the bubble gum machines outside their shops, we installed them in our flat and adjusted the money slot so that drunken guests could help themselves.

Sayle advised us to stick with what we knew, journalism, so three of us, Lopez, Philip Harris and I, started Global News and Features – a worldwide agency that offered to provide discriminating subscribers with a range of news stories, feature articles, columns and photographs. The problem of where to obtain all this editorial material was easily solved – we had it all at hand in the *Mirror* office. We would take all the material that came in from newspapers, wire services and picture agencies, then tailor it for our subscribers. We rented an office in Chancery Lane with one desk and a telephone manned during office hours by Harris. We designed a lavish brochure listing Global News and Features offices in all the major capitals of the world, actually addresses of friends and relatives. We sent the brochure out to every newspaper in Britain along with a sample sports column written by Jimmy Jones, the former champion tennis player who had turned journalist. Nobody answered, nobody rang. In the second week the features editor of the *Birmingham Post* telephoned. Would we get our office in Paris to cover the French motor show for him? Certainly – 2,000 words and a selection of photographs for £100. The trouble was that our man in Paris was a friend's mother who made dolls for a living, and we had neither the time nor the money to go to Paris to cover the motor show ourselves. So our editorial staff swung into action. Lopez got all the press releases from the organisers of the motor show and began to rewrite them as if he were there. I persuaded a darkroom assistant at Keystone to superimpose a photograph of me alongside the new car Renault had unveiled in Paris. Then we sent the whole package express to Birmingham: a personal report on the Paris motor show by Phillip Knightley. The telephone rang the next evening, rerouted by Harris from the Chancery Lane office. It was the Birmingham features editor and he was very angry. 'What do you take me for, lad, a bloody idiot? I've read all the Paris handouts and I can spot a rewrite a mile off. Is this all you've got to offer?' I said I would get on to our man in Paris and see what he could do. That was Global News and Features's only assignment but it was not the end of our venture.

Six weeks later George Hawkes announced that the entire editorial staff
was suspended while a special investigator – sent from Sydney by Norton –
examined the office's work practices and established the truth or otherwise
of some serious criminal allegations. Norton had somehow learnt about
Global News and Features but thought that the whole office was involved.
The investigator invited me to submit a statement confessing everything.
There was no sense in denying it, so I did, but added a sentence that saved
me from the sack and perhaps prosecution. It said, 'All I was trying to do
was to take the first step to becoming a newspaper baron. Since Mr Norton
is one himself I am sure he will understand the attractions.' We all escaped
unscathed – except poor Victor Krikorian, the Armenian teleprinter
operator. Unknown to most of us he had been moonlighting at the Soviet
newsagency, Tass, and in the atmosphere of confession engendered by
Norton's investigator, someone betrayed him. Hawkes got a secretary to
ring Tass and ask for Victor and since the Tass staff were used to women
ringing him at all hours, they put the call through. When Victor came on
the line, he heard not the voice of one of his girlfriends, but that of
Hawkes. 'Victor,' he said. 'You're sacked.'*

Now and then there would be news from Sydney that proved that the
repressive atmosphere had not changed. In 1956, the famous conductor
Eugene Goossens, who had been running the Sydney Symphony Orchestra
and enriching Australian musical life since 1947, returned after a five-
month trip to Europe. The Sydney Vice Squad was waiting for him at the
airport. In his baggage detectives found seven brown paper parcels
containing more than a thousand pornographic items – photographs,
books, films, statues, carvings. In court Goossens pleaded guilty to a charge
under the Customs Act and was fined £100. But the story had made front-
page news and Goossens's career was finished. He left Australia as soon as he
could, never to return, making mysterious comments about threats and
blackmail and a vindication that never came.

Goossens's third wife, an American pianist, had remained in Europe and
when the scandal broke took refuge in a convent outside Paris with two of
Goossens's daughters. From Sydney came the message: EXBLUNDEN
INTERVIEW LADY GOOSSENS STOP DOES SHE STAND BY
HUSBAND STOP WHAT THINK CHILDREN QUERY. I flew to
Paris, hired a car and drove down to the convent in a little village in
Normandy. I was standing in the sleepy main street wondering whether to

* Hawkes did not know it at the time but he did Krikorian a favour. He rose through the
ranks at Tass to be an economic journalist and, eventually, adviser to the Soviet government
on international commodity prices and then, when the USSR collapsed, a successful antique
dealer in Surrey.

try telephoning the convent first or whether to walk up to the gates and ring the bell, when a woman and two children came around the corner and went into the boulangerie.

I waited near the door and as the group came out I could hear their conversation. It was in English. This could only be Lady Goossens. All I had to do was introduce myself and rattle off my questions before she could get away. Even if she refused to reply and hurried off, as she probably would, there would be enough for a front-page story. SHAMED LADY GOOSSENS FLEES. But as she passed she gave a polite smile and I imagined this turning to cold contempt when she learned who I was and what I was after. I couldn't do it. I let her go and I went back to London and told Sydney that the convent would not open the door.

Lopez had been right. The Virgo Fidelis girls were wonderful, and by 1959 one of them, an Italian from Rome, had become a regular girlfriend. She'd taken a job as au pair to a Scottish businessman, Archie McNair, who was the financial brains behind several Chelsea coffee bars and restaurants, like Alexander's, named after Alexander Plunket Greene, Mary Quant's husband. He chatted with me one night while I waited for the Roman to get ready. I told him that I was looking around for something outside journalism. 'Hmmm,' he said. 'I've got this nice little restaurant up the wrong end of Kings Road. It's closed at the moment . . . a bit of trouble with the council, but it has tremendous possibilities. It's got a garden with a big tree at the back. There are not many restaurants in London with a garden. We could be partners. I'd put up the premises. You do it up and run it. Fifty-fifty. Are you interested?'

Of course I was. It was not far from that other fashionable coffee bar in the Fifties, Le Rêve, and I already dreamed of luring away its famous regulars. If I couldn't make The Big Time as a journalist, I'd do it as a restaurateur. The place had a flat above it and a week later I had moved in and was spending all my spare time re-painting it. I planned to be a journalist by day and greet my famous customers by night. We opened a month later, July 1959. McNair had been right, the premises had natural charm, and all I needed to have done was to have opened a simple, medium-priced restaurant serving Continental-style food, a place where local residents could afford to eat regularly. But I had just come back from a holiday in Austria and I decided instead to open London's first Viennese restaurant, complete with Austrian cuisine, waitresses in Tyrolean dress, and, at the weekends, a yodeller or two.

There were no Austrian chefs in London, as a quick ring-around of the catering employment agencies revealed. I had to settle for Tadeusz, a Pole who swore he understood Viennese cooking. At the launch party, with German champagne, apfelstrudel and a Sachertorte flown in from Vienna, he was a terrific hit with the customers, wandering around the tables, chatting about the food, accepting the occasional small drink. 'Where did you find him?' McNair said. 'He's going to make us a fortune.'

The following morning, Tadeusz failed to show up. I drove to his room in Battersea and dragged him, red-eyed and complaining, to work. He was sober for a week and then hit the bottle again. When he was drinking, his slender grasp of English quickly deserted him. He would stare, puzzled, at the waiter's order slip until a word registered. If the word was Wiener, then it did not matter because it only occurred in Wiener schnitzel. But if the word was chicken, then we were in trouble because there were ten chicken dishes on the menu and thus a one chance in ten of getting it right. Customers who ordered roast chicken and got chicken salad began to stay away. The kitchen porter left because he said Tadeusz had made a drunken pass at him.

If only I had read *Down and Out in Paris and London* before I opened a restaurant. George Orwell's indictment of the hotel and restaurant business would have saved me from the worst of what was about to happen. In short, there is something about the catering trade that brings out dishonesty in all who are associated with it. Everyone tries to rob everyone else. If I did not weigh the ingredients as the tradesmen delivered them then I found that a hundredweight of potatoes was only 100lbs. Unless I put a lock on the refrigerator, the cleaner helped herself to steak and eggs for breakfast. I decided that people did not regard the taking of food, especially in a restaurant when you are surrounded by so much, as stealing. I confess that I was no better. The first thing Tadeus taught me was how to get four legs from a chicken – 'Buy boiling chickens, then the legs are so big you can cut them above the knee joint and it looks like a whole leg.' But aren't boiling chickens tough? 'Not when you boil them enough.' But then there's no flavour. 'Not when you fry them in butter.'

The other things he taught me have been very useful in subsequent years of dining out. Do not believe the waiter when he offers you the choice of your dish grilled or fried. In a busy restaurant everything is fried – if the customer has specifically asked for grilled fish, it is fried and then the fat dried off with a few seconds under the grill. Never order cooked oysters in any form – today's oysters naturel are tomorrow's oysters Kilpatrick. Avoid pasta in restaurants other than Italian because it is half-cooked in the morning and then simply plunged into boiling water for a few seconds when someone orders it in the evening. Soup is often kept going for three or four days, simmering away in a bain-marie. Steak so old that it is beginning to smell can be revitalised by rubbing it with lemon juice.

Other aspects of the restaurant business I learnt by trial and error. For instance, if you are going to sack a kitchen porter, give him thirty seconds' notice. I felt bad about giving one porter only three days. In that time, he quietly but systematically smashed all the crockery and secretly disposed of the pieces until, the night after he had gone, we discovered we were down to place settings for only one table. Keep an eye on women dining alone, especially on how much they are drinking. One drank two bottles of wine and three brandies, then locked herself in the toilet and flatly refused to come out. The waiter and I broke open the door and found her sitting on the floor with her arms and legs wrapped around the bowl. With great difficulty we managed to prise her away and get her to her feet and then, watched curiously by the rest of the diners, we led her towards the door. 'You may now cease holding my arms,' she said. 'I'm perfectly capable of making my own way out of this terrible place.' We released her, whereupon she swung her handbag in a vicious arc and caught the waiter behind his left ear. A resting actor, he crumpled gracefully to the floor, where he lay stunned, bleeding gently into the carpet.

By this time McNair had given up any hope that the Old Vienna was going to be another of his successes. I had been negotiating to sell the place anyway. The trouble was I was selling the Old Vienna as a going concern so I had to keep it open until the new owner, a Bangladeshi who wanted to redecorate and rename it the Patna Rice, had signed the contract. The chef had gone, complaining he had nothing to do, so there was nothing for it except to run the place single-handed and hope no customers came in. Those who did were greeted at the door by me in my waiter's guise. I would take their order and send it down to the kitchen in the dumb waiter. Then I would run down the stairs, slip on an apron and cook the meal, then rush back up the stairs again to receive the dishes in the dumb waiter and serve them. No wonder, then, few customers came back.

During the day the Old Vienna was a coffee bar, but here too, I had trouble. An inspector from Kensington and Chelsea council came by one day and inspected the Gaggia espresso machine. 'It's been plumbed all wrong,' he said. 'The water intake is direct from the mains. If the pressure in the mains drops below that in the machine, the water will flow back from the machine into the mains, polluting the water supply.' I did not believe him but, sure enough, a few weeks later a neighbour came in to complain that when she had turned on the tap in her kitchen that morning, coffee-coloured water had come out. 'I thought it was just dirty,' she said, 'but I tasted it. It was a double espresso.'

The end, when it came, was spectacular. I was woken in the middle of the night by a light shining in my eyes. Above my bed stood a large, dark figure with a torch in one hand and a truncheon in the other. He was saying something but I could not hear him because I wore earplugs to keep out the noise from the Kings Road traffic. When he finally allowed me to remove them, I learnt that he was a policeman and that someone had been seen breaking into the restaurant. Who was I? The owner. Would I accompany the police party while it searched the premises?

We crept downstairs. There was a dim light in the kitchen. The police pushed me behind them and burst in. There was Frank, the kitchen porter from British Guyana who had left weeks before to study art, deep into a bowl of rice and chicken stew. The police hauled him to his feet and pinned him roughly to the wall. Frank's story was that he was on his way home from an art students' party in Fulham, felt hungry, and remembering the many meals he had had in the kitchen of the Old Vienna, had shinned up a lamp-post, crossed the awning and come in through the first-floor window. The police were all for arresting him for breaking and entering and were disappointed and angry when I said it was not like that. As they left the sergeant said, 'I wouldn't ring us if you have trouble in your restaurant, sir. We could well be a long time in coming.'

I reduced the price and signed with the Bangladeshi the following week. When I drove past a month later the Patna Rice was packed. Before it was pulled down to straighten the road, the locals said it had made a fortune. Frank, as a reward for not sending him to jail, gave me one of his paintings – a black woman in childbirth on a dark night – but I lost it in a move somewhere. I heard later that he went to the United States, was acclaimed as a genius, and his work was now selling for thousands.

I took a holiday. All the Australian backpackers returning from hitch-hiking trips around Europe inspired me to try it myself. But instead of going to the south of France, the Costa Brava or Portugal, I chose Algeria. On a lonely road outside Algiers, trying to get to Oran, a French settler stopped and picked me up. I could not help but notice, snug in a leather holster under the steering wheel, a large automatic pistol. The Frenchman saw me looking at it. 'It's dangerous to hitch-hike,' he said. 'Don't you know there's a war on?' I said I did, but that it was between the Algerians and the French. I was not involved. I was an Australian. He looked at me with pity for my ignorance. 'Is it written on your forehead?' he said. He left me at his turn-off and I was still worrying about his warning when an Algerian in a battered old taxi stopped for me. We chatted amiably for an hour or so as the taxi wheezed its way up a hillside to a small town where I planned to spend the night. The taxi-driver bombarded me with questions. How old was I? Was I married? Engaged then? Girlfriends? He stopped just outside the town and pulled the car off the road. 'You can stay at my place tonight, if you wish,' he said, switching suddenly from 'vous' to 'tu'. I declined, he insisted, I declined more firmly. 'Okay,' he said, 'goodbye, my friend,' and he leant forward for the two-cheeks kiss. I tolerated it but then, his eyes bright with passion, he said, 'Et maintenant, sur la bouche,' and pulled my head towards him. In the next thirty seconds I suddenly appreciated what women suffer, and silently apologised for my occasional transgressions in this area. I simply did not have sufficient hands to push his head away, stop him from trying to unzip my trousers, reach for the handle of the car door, and try to rescue my rucksack from the back seat. Abruptly, he gave up, pushed me out of the car, threw my rucksack after me and drove off in a cloud of oil fumes. I have never hitch-hiked since.

Back at the *Mirror* office, Jessup made me an offer I could not refuse. 'The *Northern Light*'s almost ready,' he said. 'Six months or so and it's bye-bye Fleet Street and off to the West Indies. Why don't you come along?' He had made the same offer to Lopez and we discussed the details that night. We wouldn't have to put up any money, just our time and labour in getting her ready for sea. Jessup had been in the Royal Navy and had been taking navigation courses, so he would not expect any great displays of seamanship from us. We consulted Sayle. 'You'd better get the ranks right,' he said. 'Who's going to be captain? Jessup's the owner but is he captain?' We had another meeting with Jessup. Sayle was now expressing interest in joining us for the first leg of the voyage, to the Canary Islands, so he insisted we sort out the ranks. 'What I propose,' he said, 'is that we make the *Northern Light* the first democratic sailing ship in maritime history – a crew without any rank whatsoever.'

'Nothing doing,' Jessup said. 'I'm the owner and I want to be the bloody captain.'

'How about this, then?' Sayle said. 'You stay the owner, but we'll *all* be captains.'

Jessup thought for a moment. 'Okay,' he said. 'But which captain will take decisions?'

'Democratic vote,' Sayle said. 'One captain, one vote.' To celebrate, Lopez dug out a popular Spanish record, 'Yo no soy marinero, soy capitan, soy capitan'. We got Joshua Slocum's *Sailing Alone Around the World* out of the library and subscribed to *Yachting Monthly*. Soon we had learnt all the jargon and could hold our own in conversation with the workmen at the Teddington boat yard where the *Northern Light*'s mainmast was being repaired and some of her copper sheathing replaced. She was a magnificent vessel. She was 44 feet long with a 15-foot beam and drew nine feet. She had oak frames, teak planking and a flush deck that still left full headroom below. Jessup had divided the interior into a large stateroom with attached galley, navigation area and two folding bunks. Forward of that there was a double cabin and a single bunk forecastle. Aft was the engine room, shower and toilet, and a bank of batteries and their generator.

He had installed a 44hp, two-cylinder Kelvin diesel engine that had a reputation of continuing to run even when upside down. You started it on petrol by swinging by hand an enormous flywheel and then, after it had chugged a few revolutions, you shoved a lever and switched to diesel. To hell with sailing, I thought after getting it going the first time, this can take us around the world on its own.

In June 1960 we took her down the Thames to Gravesend to have the mast fitted and then back to St Katharine's Dock to do the rigging, ballasting and take on supplies. By now we had all left the *Mirror* and journalism, hopefully for ever. Life as wandering yachtsmen was going to be much more rewarding. But as the final fitting-out expenses mounted we began to wonder whether our money was going to last until our first charter in the winter season in Barbados or St Lucia – we had not yet decided where we would make our West Indies headquarters. An old friend, William Harcourt, an Australian who at that time was public relations officer for the Federation of British Industries, came to our rescue. He put a paragraph in the Federation's newsletter telling members of our plans and inviting them to offer samples of their products so that the *Northern Light* could become 'a floating showroom for the best that is British, a sure-fire way to win lucrative export orders'. We were inundated with calls and, reluctant to turn anyone away, we became agents-at-large for about twenty products ranging from umbrellas, leather luggage and handbags, to bilge pumps, galley stoves and several varieties of tinned food – we calculated the samples were enough for three meals a day for the next two years.

We sailed from St Katharine's Dock on a bright August afternoon, waved farewell by dozens of friends, some in tears, and a few of our keener sponsors. We promised to write and send orders the moment we received them. The only ominous note was provided by Robert Close, author of the banned novel *Love Me Sailor*, and who had been an apprentice before the mast, waving from Tower Bridge and then cupping his hands to shout, 'YOU'LL BE SORRY.' Down the Thames under motor was easy, although owing to a misunderstanding between Captain Jessup and Captain Lopez, we did hit a large buoy, but not hard enough to damage anything other than our paintwork. We managed to put into Dover Harbour that night after Captain Sayle flashed a morse message with our masthead light requesting permission to enter from the Harbour Master (an act that convinced me that we were all real seamen now).

We sailed at dawn the next morning for Falmouth, where we were to pick up many cases of duty-free liquor. It was a glorious late summer day with a light breeze and a flat-calm sea, so we crossed the Channel under sail, the *Northern Light* behaving beautifully, turned right when the French coast came in sight and meandered past all those Normandy seaside resorts straight out of history – Honfleur, Arromanches, Barfleur – and then put into Cherbourg for one last farewell meal in France. The seafood was so good and so cheap that one meal became two, and a few hours' stay became an overnight binge. The next day we struggled to get up in time for an early lunch – soupe de poisson, plat de fruits de mer, fromage, a litre of house wine each and several calvados to make a trou Normand or two.

We cleared the harbour late afternoon in bright, clear weather but an hour later heavy clouds gathered, the wind changed, the sea got up, the *Northern Light* began to pitch and roll and waves started breaking over the bow. We voted on whether to reduce sail and decided four to nothing to do so. Captain Lopez and I wanted to vote on whether to return at top speed to Cherbourg but Captain Jessup said that although all the captains could vote, as owner he decided the agenda and returning was not on it. At this Lopez and I retired to the stern and got rid of our lunch. Then, too late, we took some highly recommended anti-seasickness pills which within fifteen minutes turned us into zombies, incapable of doing anything. While Sayle and Jessup wrestled with the sails, Lopez and I grasped the wheel, stared uncomprehendingly at the compass, and fought off sleep. All that kept us awake was a frequent drenching in sea and rain water. At least the self-draining cockpit, one of my better pieces of boatbuilding, was working, but from down below the crash of crockery, glasses, pans, and tins of food was evidence that the catches on the galley cupboard doors had been installed by men who had never been to sea in a small boat.

Halfway through the night we gave up trying to sail and started the engine. This eased the *Northern Light*'s motion enough for Sayle and Jessup to take a break. Sayle fried a tin of honey ham, covered it with sliced Malaysian pineapple and Dijon mustard and ate it in the cockpit with such relish that Lopez and I lost the last of our lunch and, with it, our pills. Sayle then confessed that as a small boy he used to ride up and down in department store express lifts because he enjoyed the stomach-churning sensation.

Sometime during the night, as I clung with one hand to the wheel and with the other to my safety-line, drugged with seasickness pills but nauseous just the same, my boots half-filled with water, rain trickling down my neck between my oilskin top and my seaman's sweater, looking into the wall of blackness surrounding us and wondering when we were going to be run down by some huge tanker, a question popped into my mind and refused to go away: what am I doing here?

Dawn found us wet and miserable off Falmouth, where a local fishing vessel guided us into harbour. We dropped anchor, fell into our bunks and slept until late afternoon when a Customs launch woke us. We told the officer where we had come from and explained the condition of the *Northern Star* by saying we had had a rough time, we'd run into a gale in the Channel. 'Gale?' he said. 'That was a Force Three. Little more than a breeze.'

The captains met in the stateroom an hour later. Captain Jessup said he had an announcement to make. After careful consideration he had come to the conclusion that he did not like yachting and he did not like foreign places. This had come as a surprise to him because he had devoted the past ten years of his life to this venture, but there it was. He had decided therefore to abandon the voyage. We could go ahead if we wished but we would have to insure the *Northern Light* and find a competent professional seaman to take his place. Captain Lopez and I hastened to say that, everything considered, we too had decided not to carry on. Captain Sayle said that he had planned to get off in the Canaries anyway, so he would vote with the majority.

A week later Jessup, Sayle and I crewed the *Northern Light* from Falmouth to Southampton where Jessup had found a yard to keep her until she could be sold. Apart from the fact that I was seasick all the way, the passage was uneventful until we reached the Solent. A squall hit us off the Isle of Wight and Jessup decided to shelter up the Medina. As we motored sedately past the Royal Yacht Squadron, Britain's most exclusive club, through the rain we could see telescopes trained on us from the verandah. It took a while to realise why. The *Northern Light* was flying the Australian flag and the Squadron must have thought that we had just arrived from Australia, were heading for a mooring no doubt arranged by the club, and would be at the bar that evening.

They were disappointed. Half a mile up the river, Jessup decided that there was nowhere safe to moor overnight, so we turned the *Northern Light* round, clipping someone's immaculate motor cruiser with our bowsprit in so doing. With the fast-flowing current behind us, even the engine in reverse failed to slow our race downstream. We narrowly missed a ferry hauling itself across the river on its cables, and barely twenty minutes after being welcomed to Cowes, we shot past the clubhouse under the startled gaze of its members and out into the Solent again.

It was dark by now and as we searched for a mooring we saw the lights of a freighter underway out of Southampton. It was hard to be sure, but it appeared to be on a collision course with us. While we were voting on whether to change course, and if so, which way, the freighter took evasive action. As it drew abreast, an officer came out on the flying bridge and shouted, 'It's bastards like you who give yachting a bad name.' But we had made two passages by now and Captain Jessup was not about to be told off by the mate of some dirty British steamer with a salt-caked smokestack. Without a moment's hesitation he lifted his loudhailer and roared, 'Fuck off.'

Full of maritime satisfaction, we found a sheltered spot and dropped anchor, but when we tried to raise it next morning it seemed to have fouled a submarine cable of some sort. We tried everything but it was stuck fast. I was all for paying out a few more fathoms of chain and then motoring full ahead so as to break the anchor loose. Jessup voted against this on the grounds that such a manoeuvre could well drag the *Northern Light* under. If it did not, it might still sever the submarine cable and black out the Isle of Wight. With great reluctance we unshackled the chain and abandoned an expensive anchor. At the yard we unloaded all our personal gear from the *Northern Light* and said goodbye to her and our dreams.

But, it turned out, she had inspired Sayle and Jessup to feats neither knew they had in them. In 1972 Sayle, who had continued his sailing career under the tutelage of Bill Howell, an Australian dentist and a remarkable yachtsman, convinced the *Sunday Times* that it would be a good jape if he were to enter a *Sunday Times* yacht in the *Observer* Single-handed Transatlantic Yacht Race, especially as it would cost the newspaper not a penny: the BBC paid Sayle £5,000 for making a film on the crossing, 'Alone on a Wide, Wide Sea', and he used this to fit out the boat, insure and equip it. If he won, or did reasonably well, it would be a great coup. Even if he did not, the *Observer* would be obliged each week to report the progress of its greatest rival. In those days of buoyant advertising revenue and huge editorial budgets, Sayle's idea seemed a wonderful summer story. After a couple of months' preparation, he set sail.

First news of his disaster came, oddly, by telephone. He rang from the middle of the Atlantic to tell Jenny Phillips, his editorial assistant (who is now his wife), that he had been dismasted in a gale and was about to go over the side to cut the mast away before it holed his hull. Jenny swung into action and next morning Sayle was taken in tow by an American coastguard cutter which waived salvage rights in return for Sayle's agreement to lecture the crew on single-handed navigation – they could not believe he had given his position so accurately using only the traditional sextant and chronometer. It all made for rattling boys' own adventure journalism. Sayle has since sailed the Atlantic each way several times.

Jessup brooded over our failure with the *Northern Light* for the next twenty-eight years. Then in 1988, retired and with few responsibilites, he announced to his wife and friends that he was going to try again. He bought a 38-foot glass-fibre ketch, the *Lucy B*, moored her at Brighton Marina, and at weekends took her out into the Channel and taught himself to handle her. When he felt confident, he sailed her to the Canary Islands, picked up an amateur crew, and arrived in St Lucia in January 1992 after a seven-week crossing, low on water, a stone lighter, but spot-on with his navigation. He had made it. Back in Britain, his lifelong ambition achieved, Jessup fell ill and died in 1994. His last words were an enigmatic, 'Sink her . . . sink her.' His ashes were scattered in the Channel, a reminder to his crew of the long and courageous course he had sailed from those early days on the *Northern Light*.

Lopez and I crept back to London after our round-the-world sailing venture that had got as far as Falmouth, and went into hiding from the friends who had bade us farewell us only ten days earlier and from the sponsors who were anxiously awaiting export orders. The only alternative to falling on our swords was to leave town in a hurry. I went to Victoria Station and asked the ticket clerk what was the longest railway journey he could sell me. 'Vladivostock – but it'll take you six months to get a Soviet visa,' he said. Otherwise? 'Basra on the Persian Gulf. Orient Express to Istanbul, the Taurus Express to Baghdad, and then the metre gauge to Basra. End of the line.' I bought a second-class single for £40 and the next day put journalism behind me for the moment and set off for the end of the line.

CHAPTER FIVE

RECRUITED BY THE CIA AND THE KGB

In Basra I discovered that the British India Steamship Company, the parent of P & O, ran a regular service to Bombay and from there I could take a liner to Sydney. So it was nine days down the Gulf in the SS *Dumra*, travelling second-class (there were five classes), getting used to sleeping in the long, hot afternoons ('Silence Time: 2pm to 4pm', said the notices in the gangways), and in the crystal-clear evenings reclining in a deck chair sipping gin and tonics, watching falling stars and wondering where life was taking me. India, I decided, would just be another brief port of call on the way back to Australia.

Then, on 13 December 1960, Bombay, standing outside the Customs shed with my one suitcase, wondering: what now? I was thirty-one, I had £65 in travellers' cheques, 200 Gulf rupees, ten American dollars, and a ticket on the next ship to Sydney – which I had discovered did not leave for another five months. Could I last out? I stayed on for two years, found a new life, began a new career and later married an Indian woman, thus acquiring at one stroke some two hundred and ten Indian relatives. Even today, more than thirty years after leaving Bombay, I cannot meet an Indian outside India without wanting to talk to him, because I feel sure he will know some of the nine hundred million I know too. If this sounds emotional it is because I found India an emotional country. The struggle to survive that is the lot of so many Indians gave me a greater awareness of my own good fortune and deepened my appreciation of the simpler delights of life, while the proximity with death – the grey face covered with flowers that is carried past you when you are on your way home from the cinema – seemed to heighten all feeling from sex to sentimentality. Trying to grasp the essential difference between my time in India and my time in Britain, I can only come up with this: In India I missed none of the props that now seem such desirable goals in London – a house, a plump bank account, an insurance policy, a television set and a car. It was enough then to be alive and well and living in Bombay.

On that very first day I moved in with an Australian artist, Roy Dalgarno, and his wife, Betty, whom I had met in Paris a few years earlier – she lived in a Left Bank studio so small that her baby daughter slept in a cupboard drawer. Roy was art director of Lintas, the international advertising group, and Betty represented a German film company. They swept me immediately into the fantasy world of the Bombay advertising, film and racing crowd – morning coffee at Gaylords in Churchgate, talking in lakhs (hundreds of thousands) of rupees when I did not have hundreds, then a swim at Breach Candy with the English jockeys down for the winter season. I had absolutely nothing in common with the jockeys but I cherished a hope that one would slip me a tip that would win me a fortune at Mahalaxmi racecourse on Saturday afternoon. It was exciting but unreal, a prolonged holiday that I felt must have a delayed reckoning. Then, surprisingly, I got a job. A new English-language literary magazine called *Imprint* was about to start and I was offered the post of managing editor – Rupees 1,200 a month (£95), four weeks' annual holiday, and a return airline ticket to Australia.

Three months after I had arrived I was living in a two-bedroom flat in fashionable Colaba. I had a German girlfriend, an Indian manservant and an account at the tailor's. Since India was then in the grip of prohibition, I also had liquor permit No. ZO 4035 entitling me to four bottles of whisky or thirty-six bottles of beer a month as a 'foreign alcoholic by birth'. This was not enough, so I had also acquired a bootlegger who delivered regular supplies of 'country liquor', a concoction made out of banana skins, which was drinkable if mixed with lime juice and soda but which, nevertheless, produced excruciating hangovers. I also had Iraqi amoebic dysentry, picked up in Baghdad.

In an emotional depression following an attack of dysentry exacerbated by a country liquor hangover, came a revelation. I was living like an expatriate, a sahib, and apart from the different physical surroundings, I might as well have been back in London. The real India was slipping away from me. Fortunately I met Dr Aurelio Massa, who changed my life. Dr Massa was an Italian, a spiritual Easterner who by mistake had been born in the West. He was vague about his background and never fully explained how he came to be in Bombay. One of his patients said that Massa had been touring India when the Second World War started and had spent 1939–45 in an internment camp. Trained in orthodox Western medicine, he had used these years to study homeopathy. When I went to see him he was practising a blend of all known medical systems.

He was the first and only doctor I have known who treated a patient as a whole human being instead of a collection of symptoms. His consulting room was the living room of his flat. He sat on the sofa with you and you chatted and had tea together. His prescription for the dysentery was brief. Drugs will cure it but you will probably get it again. In the long term it is better to help your body cope with it. You need less food in India than in Europe, so eat sparingly. Don't drink alcohol before meals and keep up the afternoon nap habit. Then he moved on to the whole human being. 'Man was not made for work alone,' he said. 'Everyone needs a consuming interest outside his work. Find yourself a hobby or a sport, something you can do every day, something you can look forward to during office hours. See life as a whole in which work is only a small part.'

Mulling over this advice, it seemed to be a recipe for living like an Indian. Broadly, Westerners eat and drink too much, take their work too seriously and think that sleeping in the afternoon is decadent. Indians don't eat enough, take work so casually that they can always have 'unaccountable leave' to play in a mid-week tennis tournament or see a Test match, and can sleep anywhere at any time. Since I was in India, why not try the Indian way. So I moved out of my Colaba apartment and took a Rs 150 (£12) a month room with a Parsi family and a crow that came through the window each morning to wake me up. I ate nothing for breakfast, dal (lentils) and a chapati for lunch and had a light dinner. I bought a motor scooter (I considered a bicycle but everyone said that would be going too far), wore Gandhian handloom clothes, took up tennis, cut my living allowance to £1 a day and never felt better in my life. I got my lunch from a colleague at work, Dolly Irani, whose grandmother sent her tiffin all the way from Bombay Central. Dolly's grandmother made the best dal in India: thick, deep yellow, scattered with burnt onion and topped with little patches of glistening ghee.

Deciding which tennis club to join posed a problem because the wrong choice could have taken me straight back into the world I was trying to escape. But the United Services proved ideal. It was more Indian than other Bombay clubs, its Service people friendlier and its location magnificent – at the end of Colaba Point, out past the Afghan Church with its marble plaque inscribed: 'In memory of the officers, the non-commissioned officers and private soldiers who fell mindful of their duty by sickness or by the sword in the campaigns of Sind and Afghanistan 1838–1843.' Since it was in the middle of the army and navy cantonment, you reached it along neat and clean streets, through parched parade grounds bordered by officers' bungalows with wide verandahs, high ceilings and large electric fans turning lazily in the afternoon heat. The clubhouse was almost lost behind ancient banyan trees and rampant creepers, but its lawns were always freshly mown and watered, its bamboo chairs comfortable and, if you were prepared to wait long enough, a wrinkled bearer would bring you Assam or Darjeeling tea, toasted mutton sandwiches, pakoras, bhajias, and finger chips with tomato sauce. Until I was expelled on suspicion of being a British spy – of which more later – the United Services Club became my home.

In the office, I took more interest in my colleagues. Why had Mr Khatri become an accountant? Where had Devidas Gawaskar learnt to draw? What was life like for Sheila Trace in the Bombay YWCA? Soon I knew more Indians than Europeans: the mechanic who fixed my motor scooter, the leather worker who made my belts, the juice squeezer outside the cinema, the jamadar who cleaned the office, the tennis professional at the US Club. I made a point of trying to negotiate Indian life without an intermediary to shield me from its stresses. I queued for hours to take my scooter riding test. I spent a whole day at the docks to clear a parcel from Australia. I visited the magistrates' courts, wrote letters to newspapers, and was caught in a Prohibition raid on a private party. (The Indian in a white dhoti on whom I had been pressing drinks turned out to be an undercover inspector in the Anti-Corruption Squad.)

I began writing film scripts, first for a small production company and then for the Government of India Films Division: how to understand metric weights; why farmers should use fertiliser; and then in that traumatic month of November 1962, 'give your blood for Indian soldiers on the Indo-Chinese frontier'. I began to feel Indian, aggressively defensive over the 'liberation' of Goa, fiercely patriotic over the border trouble with China, and patronisingly tolerant of the first tourists, 21-day birds of package who would never know the real India.

Occasionally someone famous in the West would visit Bombay and all the English-speaking, Westernised community would come forth in force to worship its heroes. So when the Terrace Theatre Unit at Warden Road announced that it had booked the beat poet Allen Ginsberg and his companion Gregory Corso for an evening of poetry reading under the winter stars, every seat was taken. The Terrace Theatre had a design flaw – the entrance and exit doors were behind the stage. This meant that once you had taken your seat, you could not leave until the interval because you would have to cross the stage to do so. The audience on this night was predominantly female – bright, young college girls, dressed in fashionable salwar kameez, anxious to catch up with all that was new and radical from the United States. Ginsberg lolled in a chair, Corso at his side. 'This is a new poem,' he said. 'I wrote it yesterday.' There was a hush as we all waited eagerly for the master's words. 'My father's cunt is winking at me in the darkness,' Ginsberg began. Silence, followed by a rustle as several people half rose to leave and then realised that they were trapped. For another forty minutes Ginsberg bombarded us with every four-letter word in the English language. Then he announced a break for coffee and there was a stampede for the exits. When the bell rang after the interval only ten people, all men, took their seats. Ginsberg left it to Corso to round off the evening.

In September 1962 I went to Delhi to make a documentary for the Second Punjab Regiment, the oldest in the Indian army, which was celebrating its 200th anniversary. It was a fortnight of rehearsals and drill, interspersed with an endless round of parties, music recitals, films, cocktail parties and formal dinners. Every British officer who had served with the regiment and was still alive was brought at the regiment's expense from retirement in Britain to take part. The presentation of colours was followed by a ball and then the junior commissioned officers' dinner at a table creaking under silver collected over two centuries, and – could I have imagined it – at my table a young Sikh captain steadily munching his way around the rim of a champagne glass until only the stem was left. 'Take no notice of him,' his wife said. 'He does it at every party.'

From Delhi I took the third-class sleeper to Pathankot and then a bus to Srinagar in Kashmir. The road had been washed away and the the journey took two days. At lunch on the second day at some roadside hotel, the South Indian couple at my table found that the waiter, not surprisingly, spoke no Tamil and no English. They, on the other hand, spoke English but no Hindi. I surprised myself by interpreting for them. I spent a week sightseeing in Gulmarg, longing for the plains, and then took the train back to Bombay. I remember well that the ticket cost Rs 56 (£4.30) and thinking that if I saved furiously for a while I could spend the rest of my life on the road like Kim, travelling the railways of India, eating toast dribbling with butter and drinking endless cups of incomparable Indian railway tea.

Meanwhile my work at *Imprint* had been taking some strange turns. The original idea seemed an admirable one: Western books in India were prohibitively expensive, so *Imprint* would condense four or five bestsellers and publish them in a magazine which because of its advertising would cost only one rupee a copy. It would overcome nationwide distribution problems by soliciting subscriptions by direct mail. The direct mailing shot, one of the first ever done in India, produced an enormous response, something like a 25 per cent success rate. We even had letters from people complaining that we had not been in touch with them, 'My neighbour, a

Jain, has had an offer from you to subscribe to your new magazine, *Imprint*, the best of books each month. I have had no such offer. Is this because you are discriminating against Muslims? Please advise.'

My job was to condense the books, read the proofs and answer readers' letters. I loved the letters. 'Dear Managing Editor: Contrary to your usual policy, you have not condensed *To Kill a Mocking Bird* into one part but into three. This did not greatly concern me because I could look forward to three nectaries instead of one. Part one arrived on schedule, as did part three. But part two did not arrive at all, thus totally fucking the continuity. Yours sincerely.'

It was pleasant, relaxing work and the editor, Glorya Hale, and her husband, Arthur, who ran the business side of the venture, were amusing, cosmopolitan Americans and fun to work for. They lived on the fifth floor of 'Bakhtavar', a modern, high-rise apartment block, more luxurious than most London or New York flats, that looked out over the approaches to Bombay Harbour. They installed *Imprint* on the sixth floor and since there was plenty of space, suggested that I should live in one suite and turn it into an editorial office by day. Sitting on the balcony one evening after everyone had gone home, enjoying a quiet beer and watching the lights of the small fishing boats come on as the day faded, I became aware that someone in the next block was doing the same thing. We nodded to each other and raised glasses. Then he called across the gap, 'What are you drinking?' When I told him it was beer, he said, 'Come over and try vodka.' I went down in the lift, across the courtyard and up the lift in the next block to the sixth floor where I noticed that a sign on the bell that I was about to ring said SOVEXPORT FILM.

Inside I met Igor – I never got to know his other name and even if I had it was probably not his real one. Ostensibly Igor represented the Soviet film industry in India. He tried to persuade Indian distributors to show Soviet films and kept an eye open for Indian films that might do well in the Soviet Union. He was not very busy which was fortunate because he also had another agenda which slowly revealed itself over the next six months. He would invite me to Soviet consulate parties to celebrate various national days, or just to get drunk. One of his colleagues, who lived in some style on Malabar Hill, one of Bombay's better suburbs, had been a tank commander in the battle for Moscow and could tell gripping stories about the Great Patriotic War. The drinking at his parties was, even for India, formidable, and would go on long after all the women guests had left and the sun was beginning to creep through the slats of the venetian blinds. The Indians would pass out first, quietly crumpling to sleep in armchairs or on rugs on the marble floors. The British would creep off to find unoccupied bedrooms until, with unconscious bodies everywhere, the whole flat looked like a first-aid station on the Western Front circa 1915. Finally, there were only Russians and Australians upright, and then the Australians crashed where they stood, Roy Dalgarno on one occasion bringing down with him a heavy brocade curtain complete with all its rods and drawstrings, and crushing under him an elaborate, pierce-carved Burmese side table. It was the only time I saw the tank commander angry. As we carried a semi-conscious Dalgarno through the front door, apologising for the accident, the commander kept saying, 'Not accident. Deliberate anti-Soviet act.'

Eventually Igor came to the point. He invited me to his flat, sent his wife out of the room, put a bottle of vodka, two bottles of mineral water and two glasses on the table and said, 'I have something to confess to you. I want to be journalist. I want you to teach me.' I said I saw no problem, but I knew nothing about Soviet newspapers or magazines or what sort of articles might interest them. 'Leave that side to me,' Igor said. 'You and I will write articles on India. Political articles. True stories with inside information. I will sell them to the Soviet press and we will divide the income equally.' We shook hands on the deal. Our first article was about the India that Bulganin and Khrushchev would not see on their impending visit – the poverty-stricken shacks, the notorious caged prostitutes of Bombay, the illicit liquor stills, the villages given over entirely to gold smuggling.

Igor placed it in a Soviet magazine with surprising speed. Again he invited me to his flat where he showed me the tear sheets. Then he produced a small wad of rupee notes and a sheet of paper with several sentences typewritten in Russian. 'I must send the editor a receipt showing that the fee has been received and properly divided. You know bureaucrats. Please sign here.' The faint tinkling of alarm began deep in my head and I hesitated. As I did so, Igor looked simultaneously eager and shifty. 'Look, Igor,' I said. 'I don't really need the extra money.' As I said this I took a quick look at the figures, the only part of the receipt I could read. The amount was large enough to be tempting but not so large as to create suspicion. This confirmed my decision and I pressed on. 'Please give my share to the children's hospital.' Igor looked very disappointed but was professional enough not to press me. We finished the vodka and I left promising to meet again soon. He never invited me anywhere again and dodged all my invitations to him.

I learnt later that Igor's pitch was typical not only of the KGB but of most intelligence services. If I had accepted the money then I would have crossed a barrier. The next payment would have been bigger and the third bigger still, until I came to rely on the extra money. If I wanted to pull out there would have been my signature on receipts, something I would have found hard to explain. Our joint articles would have delved deeper into areas in Indian affairs that should not have concerned us and if I had complained that the sort of information Igor's Soviet 'editors' wanted was not readily available, he would then have suggested that we try to find an Indian who did have access to such information and pay him for it. I could have found myself a principal agent running a ring of sub-agents for Igor. I had quit just in time.

If I had been naïve about Igor's intentions, I was simply stupid about *Imprint*. Arthur Hale went to Delhi regularly, in order, he said, to argue our case for an increased newsprint allocation. I thought nothing about these trips. I knew that Hale had been in the American army in Burma during the Second World War in psychological warfare operations. It did not click. Odd Americans dropped by en route from Saigon to Delhi or Hong Kong and stayed with the Hales. I never gave them a second glance. When I look back now over those early copies of *Imprint* I see that many of the books we chose to condense lauded the American way of life and painted a grim picture of the lack of freedom in the Soviet Union. I did not notice that at the time.

Then there was this subsidiary publishing operation. At the Hales' request I was writing short histories of American folk heroes – Johnny Appleseed, Casey Jones, Davy Crockett – which *Imprint* was publishing as lavishly illustrated children's books and putting on the Indian market at a ridiculously low price. It seemed a nice, innocent idea. There was one incident that puzzled me briefly, something that stirred a tiny tremor of doubt. I was out sailing one Saturday afternoon with Arthur Hale and we were talking about the rights and wrongs of the Indian border dispute with China. I said that, hard though it was for me to admit it, perhaps there was more to China's case than we knew. I said I had heard about an Indian academic, a Professor J. G. Ghose, who had been working in the national archives in Delhi when he had accidentally come across a survey map which the British had drawn up in the nineteenth century. The map clearly showed the disputed territory as being within China's borders. Hale appeared to absorb this without much interest. But back at the landing at the Gateway of India, Hale said, a little too off-handedly I thought, 'That Professor Ghose . . . what were his initials again?'

Twenty years later I was in Washington working on a documentary film about the exploits of the notorious British traitor Kim Philby, the British Secret Intelligence Service officer who was, all along, an agent of the KGB.

The film crew and I had travelled to Virginia to have lunch with Harry Rositzke, former chief of the Soviet Bloc division of the CIA. Rositzke was sitting at the head of the table and I was on his right. I became aware that down at the other end of the table Mrs Rositzke was talking about India with the production assistant, an Australian girl who was into yoga. I said to Rositkze, 'Were you and Mrs Rositzke in India at some stage?' He said, '1960 to 1964. I was at the embassy under Ken Galbraith.' I said, 'Oh. What were you doing?' He looked puzzled – presumably because he thought I would have researched his career before coming to see him. 'CIA station chief,' he said. 'We were very interested in India in those days. Delhi was friendly with us but also in bed with Moscow and that made India one of the few places in the world where we had any interface with the Soviets.'

I told him that I too had been in India in the early 1960s. 'Yes?' Rositzke said. 'And what were you doing?' I said, 'I was with a little magazine in Bombay, a literary magazine called Imprint.' Rositzke grinned. 'I knew it well,' he said. 'It was one of my little operations. Shake hands with your ex-boss.'

I must have gone grey because he added with some concern, 'Didn't you know?' And then he explained it all to me. The CIA had become concerned about Soviet influence in India in the early 1960s. Not only was the Indian government friendly with Moscow, but the bazaars of India were being flooded with cheap but beautifully produced and lavishly illustrated children's books about Soviet folk heroes, published not only in English but in many of the regional languages. 'A whole generation of Indian kids were growing up to believe that the only heroes in the world were Russian ones,' Rositzke said. 'We had to get in there with some American folk heroes before it was too late.' The obvious answer would have been to publish the books in America and then ship them to India. But the CIA did not work like that. Since – as is usually the case with intelligence operations – money did not matter, the CIA decided to set up a publishing operation in India to produce the books. Once that was agreed, the idea just grew. Why not also publish a magazine with a subtle pro-American slant? The spin-offs from having a genuine publishing house in Bombay clinched it: a legitimate bank account which could provide funds for covert activities; a safe house for visiting officers and agents; a listening post for all the snippets of political and social gossip that go to make up raw intelligence. I suppose that, as intelligence operations go, it was one of the more benign ones, but it was still something of a shock to learn that, however unwittingly, I had been an employee of the CIA.

Now Igor's attempt to recruit me made sense: he was not after an

Australian itinerant journalist who was passing through Bombay; he was after an employee of a CIA front. He must have known. It could not have been just coincidence that the KGB's own front operation in Bombay, Sovexport Film, was right next door to the CIA's front operation in Bombay, *Imprint*. What a joke it all was. What a waste of time, money and talent. Or was it? Indian film-goers got to see some Russian masterpieces, thanks to Sovexport Film. Thirty thousand Indian subscribers got to read a few good books that they would not have been otherwise able to afford, thanks to *Imprint*. And I got to live for two years in Bombay, one of the great cities of the world.

My little brush with the international espionage community was not over. My contract with *Imprint* came to an end and I left India, deciding however to keep up my membership of the United Services Club so that whenever I returned to Bombay I would be able to enjoy its pleasures. So it was something of a shock that many years later I received in London a letter that said, in blunt military style:

Sir,
1. In pursuance of instructions received from Service Headquarters, I am instructed to inform you that the managing committee at its meeting held on Monday, 29 Aug 88, has ruled that your membership of this club is terminated with immediate effect.
2. You will be sent intimation about any outstanding bills or credit in due course.
3. Kindly acknowledge.
   Thanking you,
   Yours faithfully,
   Lt Col I. P. Lobo (Retd)
   Secretary

What was going on? There was no sense in writing to Colonel Lobo. His instructions had come from Delhi, so it was to Delhi that I protested.

General V. N. Sharma, PBSN, ABSN, ADC
Chief of Army Staff,
Army House,
4 Rajaji Marg,
New Delhi 10011

Dear General Sharma,
   I have been a civilian member of the United Services Club,

Bombay, for 28 years. I recently received the attached letter terminating my membership. As you will see, no explanation is given. I suspect that it may have something to do with security because a year or so ago, the club banned foreign guests.

If the reason does pertain to security, then I appreciate how difficult it would be to make an exception. But may I make the following points: I have had a long and close association with India for almost 30 years; I am married to an Indian, several of whose family served in the Indian army; I made blood-donor films for the Indian army at the time of the Indo-China war; I have many friends in the Indian diplomatic corps.

All of this may seem to be making a mountain out of a molehill, but I have a sentimental attachment to the club and the loss of it means a lot to me. As you will appreciate, a man's club is a part of his life. If security is the reason for terminating my membership, perhaps I could be confined to the main clubhouse and excluded from the golf course and swimming pool, both located in the coastal defence area.

Yours sincerely,
Phillip Knightley

Army headquarters must have mulled over the case for a while because the answer came two months later from a Colonel B. M. Kapur, 'MA to COAS, DHQ, PO New Delhi.' It was brilliant, in that it switched responsibility back to me, and appealed to me to sacrifice myself for the good of a club I clearly loved. It read:

Dear Mr Knightley,
1. Please refer to your letter of 17 October 88 on the matter of the termination of your membership of the US Club, Bombay.
2. The Chief of the Army Staff has given due consideration to your admittedly genuine concern for the continuance of your membership and he understands and appreciates your sentiments. You would, as an old member with the good of the club at heart, see that such a broad policy decision, taken in overall service interest, would also naturally affect desirable members such as yourself; but diluting the policy to accommodate exceptions may negate the very reasons for which such a policy is being introduced in the first place, and hence the inability to accommodate your request.

Yours sincerely,
B. M. Kapur

What could I do but surrender gracefully? But every time I visited India I made discreet inquiries to try to discover what was behind it all. Was the army aware of the origins of *Imprint*? Was everyone who had worked for *Imprint* suspected of being a CIA agent? Had the army learnt of my association with Sovexport Film? The truth turned out to be very different. A longtime Bombay resident, an Englishman with a naval background, was a member of the club. He took every opportunity to socialise with officers of the Indian navy. Over the years the nature of his questions to these officers during club social occasions raised a suspicion that the Englishman might be working, at least as a part-time agent, for the British Secret Intelligence Service. The club faced a dilemma. To expel him – and only him – would not only draw attention to a situation which may have already led to security breaches, but leave the club open to a lawsuit from the Englishman, one which in litigious India would drag on for years. Service headquarters in New Delhi was consulted and its solution was practical but drastic – to expel immediately without giving any reason all foreigners who were members of the club.

It worked, but since all the foreigners were white, it left the club and its members open to accusations of colour discrimination, a charge they are very sensitive about. My own feelings? When I am in Bombay and have a few drinks with Indian friends, they sometimes go on to the United Services Club to continue the evening. I go with them to the clubhouse gate, which is as far as I am allowed, and then when they have gone in, I watch for a while through the trees. And I know how Indians felt during the Raj.

Thursday in India is guru's day so one Thursday I went down to the Sri Satya Sai College of Arts and Science at Whitefield, twelve miles from Bangalore, to see Satya Sai Baba, a remarkable new Yogin hailed in India as the most impressive holy man in centuries. My taxi trip there was nearly disastrous: the car's steering track rod fell off and we ploughed across the road to miss an oncoming truck by inches. Unfazed, the driver produced a large stone from the boot and pounded everything back into place. 'Sai Baba saved us,' he said as he worked. 'If we hadn't been going to see him we would have had a terrible accident.' But it was clear that he did not entirely believe this because we covered the rest of the distance at a speed of no more than 10mph and I arrived late to find the best places already gone and Sai Baba not due to appear for another two hours.

We all sat on a circular concrete platform under a corrugated iron roof through the centre of which grew a large tree. Women sat on one half of the platform, men on the other. A path strewn with freshly picked flower petals ran up the dividing line to a throne with a red rose on each arm and a crisp white towel on the seat. The crowd was predominantly Indian but here and there a pink face stood out, especially that belonging to an American girl in a yellow sari who sat motionless in a yoga position, staring into space. Two German men in white, homespun dhotis with white tika marks on their foreheads led the male voices when a harmonium announced the start of hymns, which then went on for the next two hours.

At 11am Sai Baba appeared. There was an immediate rush towards him and the ushers were kept busy manhandling people back to their places. The master was smaller than his photographs suggested, about five foot seven, but his frizzy, Afro-style hair added about another six inches. His heavy growth of beard was powdered, a mole on his cheek stood blackly out, and his lips and mouth were bright red from chewing betel-nut. He was wearing a long, immaculately tailored saffron robe, fastened at the neck with two plain gold studs. The robe had full sleeves and was long enough to sweep the ground and hide his bare feet as he walked. The reason for this became apparent as Sai Baba approached where I was sitting: the devotees flung themselves at his feet and attempted to kiss them, but the ushers leapt forward and pulled them back. Other devotees pressed letters on Sai Baba requesting private audiences. He passed them to his assistant. He walked up to a woman in a wheelchair, blessed her, and then moved to two tall American men sitting near the platform. Obviously knowing what was expected of them, they held out their hands. Sai Baba made a pass in the air and a pinch of ash suddenly appeared between his fingers. He placed it in the men's upturned palms and they immediately ate it.

The singing grew louder as Sai Baba stepped on to the platform and walked along the flower petals to his throne. He stood alongside it, tapping his fingers on the arm in time to the rhythm of the hymns, slowly turning his gaze to take in everyone. Then he wiped his lips delicately with the towel and walked back to the gate. The American girl in the yellow sari had not moved for two hours, but now she turned her head to follow him. Her look could only be described as one of ecstasy. I managed to catch the two American men as the crowd broke up and asked them where the ash in Sai Baba's fingers had come from. 'He materialised it right out of the air,' one said. 'It came from nowhere. Look at my hand. You can still see the residue.' What did they think of Sai Baba? 'Sir, he's a holy man. The holiest.'

Sai Baba's powers took on two main forms: materialisation and wonder cures. Of the materialisation examples, the most common was the production of holy wood ash, such as I saw Sai Baba produce for the Americans. But, according to his followers, the ash could also grow on Sai

Baba's photographs when he was hundreds of miles away. It could begin as a spot and spread slowly, or it could appear all at once, practically burying the photograph in a moment. The wonder cures performed by Sai Baba could happen at a distance, or they could occur by Sai Baba taking on the person's illness and then rapidly recovering from it. All accounts from followers should, of course, be treated with scepticism, but there is a well-documented cure concerning an illness apparently suffered by Sai Baba himself and which nearly killed him.

In June 1963, Dr Prasannasimha Rao, the assistant director of medical services in Mysore, was called to attend Sai Baba. Dr Rao said later that over a period of three days Sai Baba suffered four severe heart attacks and a stroke. His left side became paralysed, and the sight in his left eye and his speech were both impaired. Dr Rao warned Sai Baba's followers to prepare themselves for the worst. Then the Yogin improved slightly and said that he had taken on the illness of a follower in order to save him. Eight days later Sai Baba was carried from his sick bed to attend an Indian religious festival. He managed to struggle on to the platform by himself, but walked with what a doctor present described as 'the characteristic hemiplegic gait'. Then he called for some water, sprinkled a little on his paralysed left leg and left hand and stroked them vigorously. He stood up, addressed his followers in a normal voice, sang a number of religious songs, walked normally from the platform and, finally, climbed the stairs to his room unaided. The next day Dr Rao could find no sign of Sai Baba's heart attack or stroke – he had apparently made a full recovery.

I found it hard to make up my own mind. If Sai Baba was indeed able to transform matter by using his own energy, presumably we would have to write off the whole basis of Western physical science as nonsense. On the other hand so many things in India are inexplicable to the Western mind. If pressed for a conclusion I would have to say that I think Sai Baba is a clever conjurer and justifies his trickery on the ground that if he is to perform good works, he must first grab people's attention – something every journalist understands. His philosophy cannot be faulted. 'The Lord can be addressed by any name that tastes sweet to your tongue, or pictured in any form that appeals to your sense of wonder and awe' is as a good a plea for religious tolerance as you are likely to hear. But the one that impressed me – because it applies as much to India as to Sai Baba – was this: 'No-one can understand my mystery. The best thing you can do is to get immersed in it. There is nothing to be gained by arguing the pros and cons. Dive and know the depth. Eat and know the taste.'

I dived and I ate and I knew the taste. Even when I left India I could not stay away. Over the years I noted and regretted the changes as Western marketing techniques took over and Indians began discovering wants they never knew existed. Still, no matter what happens, no one can change the India of 1960–62. It is part of me. I remember the time slipping easily by, the years turning over with that soothing certainty peculiar to a calendar marked by religious festivals. Every day seemed a joy, every night held the promise of sexual adventure. I would play tennis until nearly dark, watch the sun set over the Arabian Sea and ride back from Colaba Point along a roadway lined with freshly bathed people out for their evening walk, sniffing smoke from the wood fires and watching the lights blink on along the verandah of the Navy Hospital. The rest of the world was going mad, the Cuba missile crisis threatening everyone with oblivion, but the India I knew was there for ever.

CHAPTER SIX

FLEET STREET

After India, Australia seemed dull and provincial. Life was too easy, too predictable. I reported horse bloodstock sales for the Australian United Press, courts and human interest stories for the Australian Broadcasting Commission, and wrote the occasional historical feature for my old newspaper, the *Sydney Daily Mirror*. I was marking time, gathering the courage for another go at Fleet Street. When I had first left Sydney ten years earlier I had been one of the few. Now everyone was going, and London was getting crowded. I was now thirty-four, and at what age does one cease to be a promising young man? I had already booked a passage to Genoa with Lloyd Triestino when, as described earlier, I won the New South Wales state lottery.

I would now have enough money to live in London for a year or two while I concentrated on getting into Fleet Street without being forced to take a stop-gap job with an Australian bureau. Elated, I postponed my arrival in London to spend August in the Riviera. Stanley Meadows, an actor and member of the Meadows nightclub family (Churchills, and the 21), had a suite in the Martinez at Cannes and let me stay in the chauffeur's room up under the eaves. I spent the mornings playing tennis, the evenings playing boules, the nights wandering the Croisette observing the French observing August. Meadows drove me to London via Geneva where I called on Murray Sayle, now working for an American financier called Bernie Cornfeld who was coining millions with the Fund of Funds, a mutual fund of mutual funds.

Cornfeld's company, I.O.S., was holding a conference of its salesmen who had flown in with their wives from around the world. While Cornfeld re-motivated the salesmen, Meadows and I sailed the wives around Lake Geneva in the company yacht. I might have been tempted to stay on but the conference ended, the salesmen and summer departed, and Geneva settled into its winter mode. As we drove across France, the roof of Meadow's pale blue Ford convertible now firmly up, I planned my last-chance assault on British journalism.

It turned out to be surprisingly easy. I arrived in London in the middle of the great Argentinian beef scare. Typhoid had broken out in Aberdeen and tinned corned beef was thought to be the source. One night at a dinner party I met George Clarfeld, who described with some indignation how useless the Ministry of Agriculture's restrictions on meat imports were. 'You can't import corned beef to Britain unless it's been processed in a packing plant recognised by the Min of Ag from beasts inspected by veterinarians and slaughtered in abattoirs inspected and approved by Ministry officials. Okay?' I said it seemed a sensible precaution to me.

'Right. Tomorrow I'll show you a tin of corned beef with a label that says it was packed in Gibraltar, a British colony. So everyone assumes that it must be safe. Right? Well, how many head of cattle do you reckon there are in Gibraltar? Twenty. They use them for fresh milk. So where did all the beasts come from to make this shipment of Gibraltarian corned beef? I'll tell you. From Ethiopia. And if you think all those Ethiopian cattle would have passed the Ministry's tests in Britain, then you can think again.'

'Christ,' I said. 'That's a good story.'

'Why don't you write it? I'll help you.'

If I realised at the time that Clarfeld had an interest to promote – he imported quality tinned meat and was anxious to put his cheaper rivals out of business – I did not let it worry me. This was the story I needed to get a start in British journalism.

The next morning I walked into the offices of the *Sunday Times* in Gray's Inn Road. I could have gone to the *Observer* – both papers had been reporting the typhoid scare with equal vigour – but the *Sunday Times* happened to be closer to Paddington, where I lived. By such mundane choices are our lives decided. The commissionaire rang the news editor and passed me the telephone. I briefly outlined the story and the news editor said, 'Hang on a minute. I'll be right down.'

Soon afterwards I was shaking hands with Michael Cudlipp, the man who gave me my break in Fleet Street. 'The story's a good one,' he said. 'The problem is that I don't know you, so I can't let you write it. On the other hand it wouldn't be fair to take it away and give it to one of my staff reporters. So how about a compromise? Are you willing to work with a staff man and I'll pay you as if the story was entirely yours?'

I spent the following week sitting alongside a staff reporter as, point by point, we confirmed Clarfeld's information. The story got a good run but by the following week, with public interest waning, I was wondering what

I could do for an encore. On Tuesday the telephone rang. It was Cudlipp. 'I wonder if you'd be interested in doing a little item for the Atticus column?' he said. 'There's a story in today's *Mail* about pupils at Eton writing off to Communist Party headquarters for posters of Marx and Lenin. Is Eton going Communist? You could interview the headmaster and a couple of the pupils.' I said I was very interested. 'Keep in touch with the Atticus editor. He's Nicholas Tomalin.'

I rang Eton from the public telephone in the hall of the rooming house in which I was living. The headmaster's secretary said she was sure he would not mind seeing me, but Eton had just appointed a public relations officer and she had been told that all press enquiries had to be referred to him. She gave me his number but when I found some more change and rang he was out and not expected back until that evening. Anxious to show Tomalin that I was making progress I telephoned him and told him what had happened. He sounded incredulous. 'Eton's appointed a PR?' he said. 'Christ. That's a good story. Much better than the Communist posters. Forget about them. Interview the PR. How does he see his role? What image of Eton does he want to project? Why was he appointed in the first place.'

Enthused, I changed a pound into small change and kept ringing the PR until finally, at about ten o'clock that night, I got him. He was not helpful. 'I'm the man behind the scenes,' he said. 'I'm meant to arrange interviews for other people, not give them. I can fix it for you to see the headmaster. No trouble at all. But I don't really think it'd be appropriate for me to give an interview myself, I really don't.'

Crushed, I rang Tomalin early the next morning. 'What do you mean, he doesn't want to be interviewed,' he said. 'That's a load of nonsense. I've found out he's a journalist himself. In fact he's our stringer in Windsor. Leave it to me. I'll lean on him.' And he did, because to my mortification, there in the following Sunday's Atticus column was a long interview with Eton's new public relations officer in which he answered all the questions I had hoped to put to him.

On Tuesday afternoon I had a telephone call from Cudlipp. 'Tomalin would like to see you,' he said. 'Can you come in? And after you've seen him, pop into my office for a minute.' Tomalin came straight to the point. 'You lost that Eton story because you gave up too soon,' he said. 'An important lesson for journalists – most people are modest or like to give that impression. So when you want to put them in the limelight, they'll say no. But they don't mean it. They're waiting for you to ask again, to push them, so that finally they can surrender gracefully and modestly. That PR was delighted to be asked to be interviewed for Atticus but he felt he had to say no as a matter of form and he was deeply disappointed when you took his no as final. Lesson: in journalism – no no is ever final.' Then he softened. 'Never mind. Perhaps it was different in Australia. I've got nothing for you this week, but I think Michael has. And there might be some holiday relief coming up.'

I walked around to Cudlipp's office repeating, 'In journalism, no no is ever final,' a piece of advice from a master journalist that was later to have a resounding effect on my career.

Cudlipp said, 'If you don't mind odd hours and boring work, then you can join the team doorstepping Churchill. He may die in our time and even if he doesn't we'll carry a colour piece on his last hours. You can do the six to midnight shift Thursday, Friday and Saturday if you like.' So I stood outside Churchill's London house along with twenty or thirty other reporters and photographers, slipping guiltily off every few hours for a cup of tea in Palace Gate. ('The greatest Englishman this century has just died,' says Cudlipp in my imagination. 'Describe the scene outside his house.' 'I can't,' I reply. 'I'd gone off for a cup of tea.') The boredom would be relieved from time to time when Churchill's son, Randolph, would come staggering drunkenly down the road, or Churchill's doctor, Lord Moran, would emerge and read yet another bulletin on Churchill's chances of survival which, considering the time he had hung on, seemed limitless. A joke went around the press corps. The door to Churchill's house opens and the press, expecting Lord Moran yet again, rush forward. Instead it is Churchill himself in his dressing gown. In full Churchillian tones, he reads from a sheet of paper. 'It grieves me deeply, more than I can adequately express, to have the mournful duty of reporting to you that my loyal and faithful physician, Lord Moran of Manton, expired peacefully at 11.44 this night.'

Churchill eventually died and as a reward for my doorstepping duties Cudlipp assigned me to the team reporting his funeral. Then Tomalin went on holiday and made me Hunter Davies's assistant on the Atticus column. I was slowly becoming a fixture around the *Sunday Times*. I had found a vacant desk and a telephone, the switchboard knew my extension, and Cudlipp expected me to come into the reporters' room every Tuesday without being told. I had even impressed the managing editor, a tough Scotsman called James Dow. I had written what I considered to be a run-of-the-mill story about a horse at Buckingham Palace that was in remission after treatment for cancer. I had reckoned without Dow's news sense and skill at headline writing. The story appeared on the front page under the headline QUEEN'S HORSE RECOVERS FROM CANCER. The following Tuesday Dow called me to his office. 'Great story,' he said.

'Almost the perfect English story. Touches all the chords – the Queen, a bloody horse, cancer, and a happy ending. If you could've worked in the fucking corgis it would have made journalistic history.'

In retrospect, I was lucky in that I had arrived at what turned out to be the beginning of the golden age of the *Sunday Times*. Denis Hamilton was editor-in-chief and under his strategic command it was expanding. It was Hamilton who felt that there was a market for a more analytical, in-depth approach to the week's news, something that the daily papers did not have the time to do properly. It had been Hamilton who had decided that there was a hunger out there for journalism that explained what had taken place during the war, not only among ex-servicemen who had been minor cogs in major events, but among civilians who knew we had won but did not quite understand how it had been achieved. He was not a writing journalist but an editorial executive who had a gut feeling for what people wanted to read, and who would spare no expense to bring it to them. Although he had had a distinguished wartime career, he was not the type to give pep talks to the troops. They did not need it. In the late 1960s you could not enter 200 Gray's Inn Road without feeling the undercurrent of excitement throughout the building.

And what a strange building it was. The front on Gray's Inn Road was modern – aluminium and copper glass. But this concealed the old Kemsley headquarters where such ancient papers as the *Sunday Graphic* and the *Empire News* had been produced. The back of the building faced the Post Office headquarters at Mount Pleasant and was a warren of corridors and abandoned offices, secret stairways, ancient lifts, concealed doors, docking bays, wrapping and bundling areas, all capped by a sprawling composing room with row after row of linotype machines. It was all so vast and unplanned that there were rumours that from time to time someone was found in an unlisted back office still working for some branch of the Kemsley empire, and unaware that a Canadian called Lord Thomson had taken over.

On the old *Sunday Times* there was none of the formality of a modern newspaper office, with its individual contracts and its human resources department. The *Sunday Times* staff reporters were interviewed, engaged and paid monthly. Since no one was ever sacked, no one knew what redundancy terms applied. James Dow was the link between management and editorial, but this required so little of his time that he was also a senior editorial figure who helped produce the paper.

Those reporters not on the staff, like me, were paid weekly. It was all very relaxed. On Fridays, Michael Cudlipp's secretary would ask me how many days I had worked the previous week. It was usually three. She would type out a memo to the contributions department, which was run by an old India army hand, Ron Meakins. Cudlipp would sign it, Meakins would countersign it, and I would take it to to the cashiers, one of the largest departments in the old part of the building, who would count out £18 for me. Cashiers also paid out on pink slips. A pink slip was an advance on expenses. If you received an assignment needing an immediate outlay of cash – a lunch with someone, for example – you could get any senior editorial figure to sign a pink slip directing the cashier to pay you, say £10 'for lunching senior civil servant'. At the end of the month you submitted a list of the expenses you had incurred in the course of your editorial duties, got it approved – usually a formality – and the cashiers then deducted what they had already paid you under the pink slip system, and gave you the balance.

It was a logical accounting system but, of course, open to abuse. Domestic and personal financial crises were regularly solved with pink slips, and with enough ingenuity you could work the system to pay out on almost anything. Murray Sayle joked that the pink slip system was money for old rope and for a bet offered to prove it. He was about to compete in the 1972 *Observer* Transatlantic Yacht Race and had been buying equipment, so he submitted a genuine pink slip reading, 'To purchasing 50 yards of second-hand line for *Sunday Times* yacht – £20.' The cashier raised his eyebrows but paid out. 'There you are,' said Sayle, flashing the cash. 'Money for old rope.'

The *Sunday Times* was everything I felt a newspaper should be. This was real journalism, not the parochial trivia of Sydney but important national and international stuff. I believed that the *Sunday Times* and me, in my small way, were playing a role in shaping the nation's future. My desk was in a corner of the newsroom adjoining the colour magazine. To my right was a reporter using a strange typewriter with a typeface so large I could read what he was writing from five yards away – speeches for Lord Thomson who had notoriously bad eyesight. In front of me, on the rare occasions when she was there, sat Kathleen Halton, a strikingly beautiful woman who was working on some project for the magazine. I did not realise who she was until one day her telephone rang when she was out. I answered it and offered to take a message from the man at the other end. 'Just tell her Ken T-T-T-Tynan called,' he said.

In the foreign department, Donald McMormick, a former officer in naval intelligence, would tell stories of life under Ian Fleming when he was foreign editor, and of running Fleming's network of foreign correspondents, the Mercury foreign news service, which, it later emerged, also acted from time to time as an intelligence-gathering ring for the British Secret Intelligence Service. In the features department, Reuben Ainsztein, a Polish Jew, a former RAF air gunner, and by then an historian and a journalist, would tell thrilling stories of being on the run as the German army swept across France in 1940. 'I was in Le Havre trying to get a fishing boat to England. The Germans were trying to show how nice they were and had set up a soup kitchen. I was starving so I risked going there. I was having a quiet bowl of soup and a bit of bread with a couple of Frenchmen when, to my horror, two German soldiers joined us, produced a bottle of wine, and insisted we share it. Then they wanted to drink a Bruderschaft. So I had to link arms with the German soldier on my right and toast each other as brothers. After a while I saw the second German soldier looking very hard at me, and finally he said, 'What's your name?' There was no sense in lying because it was on my papers, so I said, "Reuben Ainsztein." Then I got up and walked towards the roadway. As I left I heard the German say in shocked tones, "Hans, du hast Bruderschaft mit einem Juden getrunken." Then there was silence. I kept walking, waiting for them to order me to halt, already feeling the bullet in my back. But they let me go.'

I now knew most of the reporters, I had been invited to a couple of office parties, and had played for some of the editorial sports teams. These events were great for name-dropping in letters back to Sydney. The cricket team played the *Sunday Express* and the *Express* captain was Denis Compton. The soccer team played the *Sun* and the *Sun* fielded Jimmy Greaves. The Rugby Union team played the *Observer* and Clem Thomas was in the *Observer* team. Once a year there was a football match against the House of Commons and you got a chance to chop the legs out from under your local MP.

Had I finally made it? Was this The Big Time? Cudlipp's secretary no longer asked me how many days I had worked – she just put through my weekly payment automatically. But I still felt insecure. What I needed, I decided, was one story that I found myself, one that only I could have done, something that Cudlipp and the other editorial executives would remember when they next came to appoint a staff reporter.

During my first spell in London I had met an African revolutionary, Abdulrahaman Mohammed Babu, who came from Zanzibar. He was employed as a Post Office clerk in Ealing but his real work was plotting the overthrow of British rule in Zanzibar. 'The British government doesn't take us seriously,' he would say at late-night drinking sessions. 'One day I'll blow up the Post Office in Dar-es-Salaam. That'll change their minds.'

He never got around to planting the bomb but he certainly plotted it and in 1962 the British authorities imprisoned him briefly for sedition. In 1963 the British got out of Zanzibar and the following year who should come to London as Foreign Minister of the new state but Babu. He stayed, naturally, at the Park Lane Hilton, and one of the first things he did was to give a party for all those people who had known him when he was a Post Office clerk.

It was a wonderful party. Babu had a string of stories about what it was like being a foreign minister of an emerging African country. In Geneva he had been having a quiet drink at the bar in the Hotel Richmond when an American slipped on to the stool alongside him and struck up a conversation. He said that among other things, he represented an American shipping consortium which felt that it might be of some help to the new government of Tanzania in finding space to ship cloves abroad. When they had arranged how to explore this possibility, the American then moved on to Babu's personal plans. 'Would you like your kids to receive an international education?' he said. 'Well, that's expensive. But we might be able to arrange it. American schools, American universities. All possible. You help us, we'll help you.' How could he help the American, Babu asked. 'Well, we're rather ignorant of politics in your part of the world,' the American said. 'We need someone like you to act as our adviser, someone to keep an eye on what is going on, someone on the inside, as it were.'

By now, Babu told us, he was intrigued and willing to play along to learn more. He had asked how would he report what he learnt. 'Someone will get in touch with you back home,' the American said. 'Here's a little gift for you.' He handed over a Rolex wristwatch. Here's the guarantee. Look what I'm doing. I'm tearing the guarantee in two. Here's one half for you. If someone gets in touch with you and shows you this other half, then you'll know he's come from me. Is that clear?' Babu said it was.

'That's fixed then,' said the American. 'And this is to cover any expenses you might have.' And he reached into his jacket pocket, took out a thick white envelope and handed it to Babu. Then he raised his glass, said, 'Here's to a long and profitable relationship,' and left. The white envelope, when Babu opened it, contained $10,000 in $100 notes. What did he plan to do with it, we asked? 'I'll hand the money over to the government,' Babu said. 'But I'm going to keep the watch.' We agreed that this sounded like the actions of an honest man. (Babu told me much later that no one ever turned up with the other half of the Rolex guarantee which, he said, either meant that the CIA decided not to go ahead with the operation, or they had found somone better placed than he was to be their agent.)

A drink or so later Babu told us how he had paid off a long-standing grievance with British Customs who had always hassled him in his earlier guise. (With his mop of frizzy hair, straggly moustache and unconventional clothing, he no doubt fitted a drug smuggler's profile.) Two days earlier he had driven from Paris and had been examined by Customs in Dover. The first thing they found when they opened his suitcase was a Luger pistol wrapped in an old shirt. The Customs officer lifted it gingerly out of the suitcase. He said, 'What's this?' Babu replied, 'A handgun.' The officer read an inscription engraved on the butt: 'To Babu from Fidel.' He said, 'Is this Fidel, *the* Fidel Castro?' Babu admitted it was. The officer called his boss and he called his boss who called Special Branch. Only then did Babu produce his diplomatic passport. He said it was one of the most satisfying moments of his revolutionary career.

The party spread out to two floors. In one suite Princess Elizabeth of Uganda was hostess. One floor lower Babu entertained, disappearing upstairs from time to time. Next morning I remembered only two things clearly: one was restraining a young African who was determined to jump out of the window and who was very ungrateful for my intervention. The other was meeting a West Indian called Julian Carniffsen who spoke enthusiastically about a business venture he was about to embark upon – the clove trade in Zanzibar, the island's main export. Was there a story here?

I found Carniffsen's number and called him. Carniffsen said he had stumbled on the business opportunity of a lifetime. Zanzibar shipped most of its cloves to Indonesia because Indonesians like a clove in their cigarettes and there were an awful lot of Indonesian smokers. Big shipping companies would get the contract to ship the cloves from Dar-es-Salaam but the cloves still had to be moved from Zanzibar to the mainland.

'My group has the use of a former British navy motor torpedo boat,' Carniffsen said. 'We're busy converting her now. Come down and see her. She's at St Katharine's Dock. We're going to sail her to Zanzibar in a couple of weeks and, bingo, we're in business.' The following weekend I went to see the boat. She seemed a sturdy craft and in good repair. One of the partners in the project, a German engineer, was working on the engines and gave out an air of competence and common sense. 'Let me know when you're about to leave,' I told Carniffsen. 'I'd like to write something for the *Sunday Times*.'

Two weeks later he rang. There had been a disaster. Their boat had hit something in the Thames, had nearly sunk, and was now beached at a boatyard in Kent. He was sorry to disappoint me, but there was no story any more. I went down to the boatyard and spoke with the owner. 'We heard this boat coming downstream. The tide was running out and she was going too fast. She hit a buoy, lost power and started to settle. We went out and boarded her. She was full of black guys. One of them was still asleep in his bunk with the water lapping around his blankets. It was a devil of a job to wake him.

'We got them all off and towed the boat in here and beached her. She had no charts, no navigation instruments, nothing . . . Well, there was a school atlas and a ruler. One of the black guys said they originally had a compass and a sextant but they had to sell them to raise money for food for the trip. They said they were headed for Zanzibar. I asked them how the hell they expected to get there and this black guy says they were going to get out into the Channel shipping lane and find a ship heading for Gibraltar. Then they'd follow her. Once they got to Gibraltar they'd turn left into the Med. There was only one way out of the Med, the Suez Canal. He said they'd go through the Canal, down the Red Sea, turn right, follow the coast of Africa and sooner or later they'd hit Zanzibar. Can you believe it?'

I checked with Carniffsen. It was all true. The German engineer, the only technically competent member of the partnership, had fallen out with the others and had withdrawn. His departure had encouraged further defections and the group was suddenly down to three. Carniffsen had been forced to recruit in his nightclub haunts – 'All nice fellows,' he said, 'but not much maritime experience.'

On Tuesday I told it all to Cudlipp. 'Great story,' he said. 'The Ship That Died of Shame. Write it just like you've told me. I'll get a photographer down there this afternoon.' I rang Carniffsen for some extra detail.

'Phil, I'd rather you didn't write anything just yet,' he said. 'I'm trying to re-finance the project. I'm talking to Shirley Abicair who's interested, and a couple of other people. It's not the right moment for publicity, okay?'

What could I say? Could I tell him that my career at the *Sunday Times* might depend on this very story, that I would have to weigh my personal interests against his, that the story was true and that there was no legal way he could stop me from writing it, or the *Sunday Times* from publishing it? And what would he reply? That I only knew about the story because he had told it to me as a friend, and that as a friend he was now asking me to delay publishing it. What would I say to that? I could hardly claim that it was in the public interest that the story be printed. It was a comic human interest story with a tinge of racism (would it have been as funny if the crew had been white London teenagers?)

What I said was: 'Don't worry, Julian. The publicity will probably bring you more offers of backing than you can handle.' And as I said it, I knew it was untrue. Cudlipp must have sensed my unease. He came over to my desk when the first edition arrived with the headline he had predicted: 'The Ship That Died of Shame'. 'Nice story,' he said. 'Carniffsen and his friends should thank you. If they'd have gone ahead they would probably all have drowned. You could say that you've saved their lives.' The reality was that no backers came forward to save Carniffsen's project and he went on to other things. He eventually forgave me but even today every time I see him I spend time afterwards trying to justify to myself what I did to him.

I felt I was doing well enough at the *Sunday Times* to justify buying a second-hand Ford Popular and getting married. My wife, Yvonne Fernandes, was an editorial secretary at the ancient British publishing house of Eyre and Spottiswoode, who, when they heard of the marriage, promptly sacked her – 'We don't employ married secretaries. They tend to talk about company business with their husbands.'

The photographs of the wedding reception show lots of Indians, many Africans, several French people – including a young, mysterious lawyer called Jacques Vergès, later notorious in France for defending the Nazi war criminal Klaus Barbie and the international terrorist Carlos the Jackal – and my expanding circle of British friends. My new feeling that maybe the Poms were not so bad after all was boosted when we went looking for our car which I had parked outside the Pimlico flat where we had held the reception. It was gone.

At the Victoria car pound, the night duty sergeant explained that the police had towed it away because it was parked too close to the corner. Then he said, 'Do I detect a slight Antipodean accent there, sir?' I confessed to being an Australian. 'And since the car had a string of empty tins tied to the rear bumper, and a sign saying just married, can I take it you are about to leave on your honeymoon?' I admitted that I was. 'Well, I think in those circumstances we can let you off with a warning, sir. Here's the keys of your car. Nothing to pay. A little wedding present from the Met.'

CHAPTER SEVEN

THE WORLD'S WORST
WAR CORRESPONDENT

The *Sunday Times* had only a small foreign staff but supplemented it with volunteers from the reporters' room when a major foreign story occurred. On 24 May 1967, the foreign editor, Frank Giles, asked me to join a team that the paper was sending to the Middle East to report on the crisis that had arisen over the Sinai: the United Nations peace-keeping force that had been keeping Egypt and Israel apart had been ordered out by President Nasser. War was in the air. The paper's best men had already left for Israel; would I be prepared to go to Cairo? (I had already reported to Australian friends that British newspaper executives were incredibly polite. They never ordered you to go anywhere – they asked if you would mind doing it. The contrast with Australian executives – who were not adverse to dragging a reporter out of the staff toilet to send him somewhere – was striking.)

One of the compensations of foreign reporting is being able to arrive at an overseas airport, clear Customs and Immigration, walk to the taxi rank and say, 'Take me to the best hotel in town.' The reason is a practical one. A foreign correspondent is only as good as his communications – as we will see later – and the best hotel in town is more likely to have the best telephone system and an efficient staff able to take and send reliable messages. The fact that fine food and wine seem to go hand in hand with reliable communications is an incidental bonus.

After settling in at Cairo's best hotel, the Semiramis, the next thing I did was to join the best sporting club in town as an overseas visitor. I thought the club would have many members from the diplomatic corps and a chat with them after a game of tennis would be worth far more than a formal briefing at an embassy. Only then did I look for Don McCullin, the *Sunday Times* photographer on this assignment, and arrange a taxi to take us next morning down to Suez and across into the Sinai so that we could at least look at the territory causing all the trouble. Then we went to dinner.

The dining room of the Semiramis was already crowded with that international club of foreign correspondents who flock to war and crises like nineteenth-century camp followers. At other times their paths seldom cross, but when they meet on the job they greet each other like brothers and – in recent times – like sisters. They exchange gossip – who's died, who's moved papers, who's new – get drunk together and tell the same old stories about stupid foreign editors, intransigent censors, lost passports, mangled cables, minor triumphs and great scoops. It is a way of life they would not change for any desk job no matter how highly paid. They are addicted to the excitement, that pump of adrenaline that taking part in world-shaking events, no matter how peripherally, provides.

Thanks to O. D. Gallagher, formerly of the *Daily Express*, I felt I knew them all. I had recently interviewed Gallagher, the last of the old-time greats among correspondents, for a book I was writing about war and propaganda, *The First Casualty*. O. D. was a survivor. He had covered the war in Abyssinia, the Japanese invasion of China, and the Spanish Civil War. When that ended he had a few weeks in Britain before becoming a correspondent with the RAF in France where he remained until Dunkirk. He was on board the *Repulse* when it was sunk by the Japanese in the Gulf of Siam. Rescued from the sea and taken to Singapore to recuperate, he rushed off to cover the war in Burma, arriving in Rangoon just before it fell. Then he decided to join the army, reasoning that it could hardly be any more dangerous than being a correspondent for the *Daily Express*.*

Gallagher had taken me through Evelyn Waugh's *Scoop* and had pointed out that far from being a novel about the nature of journalism, it was actually all true, and only thinly disguised at that. In *Scoop*, Lord Copper and the *Daily Beast*'s foreign editor, Salter, are uncertain where 'Ishmaelia' is and Boot ends up being sent there by accident. Gallagher told me that the real life Lord Copper (Lord Beaverbrook) and the foreign editor sent him to Abyssinia because Gallagher was a South African and 'Abyssinia is in Africa, isn't it?' Boot goes off to war with so much equipment that it needs a whole aircraft to get him to Marseilles to catch the steamer. In real life Gallagher bought a mule train, while George Steer of *The Times* bought a large truck, fitted it with a sign saying '*The Times*', and used it to carry his equipment, his bearers and his brace of guns for duck-shooting expeditions.

In *Scoop*, the hundred and twenty correspondents in Addis Ababa form

---

* Gallagher died of a stroke in 1986 while out for an evening walk with his wife in the hills near Loch Ness.

themselves into an association to deal with a government which has refused to allow them to go to the front. In real life the correspondents formed the *Association de la Presse Etrangère* and in negotiations with officials learnt the real reason they were not allowed to go to the front – no one knew where it actually was. In *Scoop*, the *Daily Beast* complains bitterly about the cost of cables. In real life cable costs were so high that the correspondents were forced to invent the most complicated cablese in order to cram as much as possible into a message – for instance, SLONGS for 'as long as'. Gallagher told me that by the time this had been tapped out in morse to London by a telegraph operator who did not understand English it was almost unintelligible. Fleet Street foreign editors did their best to unravel it and then made up the rest, so that when the correspondents received clippings of their stories they were not only amazed at what emerged but often unable to identify what the original story had been about.

In *Scoop* incoming cables are delivered to Boot by the landlady at the German pension who usually reads them first and often waits until ten or twelve have arrived before handing them over. In real life cables from London were delivered fifty at a time by a delivery boy who could not read, so he simply handed the lot to the first correspondent he happened to meet. Gallagher and Noel Monks of the *Daily Mail* took advantage of this to try to bring down the imperious Steer a peg or two. They slipped a concocted cable into the delivery boy's bundle. It read: STEER TIMES ADDIS ABABA WE NATION PROUD YOUR WORK STOP CARRY ON IN NAME YOUR KING AND COUNTRY – ASTOR [proprietor of *The Times*]. It backfired. Word of the cable reached the palace where it was accepted as being true and the Emperor, impressed, sent for Steer and gave him a long exclusive interview.

In *Scoop* poor old Boot is constantly scooped by crack correspondent Sir Jocelyn Hitchcock who pretends to go to nonexistent places and makes up stories. In real life the *Daily Telegraph* correspondent was Sir Percival Phillips who copied out large chunks of his dispatches from an old book called *In the Country of the Blue Nile* by Colonel C. F. Rey. Phillips scooped the rest of the press corps so often that Gallagher received an imploring cable from the *Express*: BEG YOU EMULATE PHILLIPS STOP NOT ONLY YOUR JOB BUT MINE AT STAKE SAYS CHRISTIANSEN [the editor] – SUTTON [foreign editor]

Gallagher told me that, desperate, he too dipped into Colonel Rey's book and, with help from his friend Monks, updated the material and put it into the context of the war. He got congratulations every day for a week and on the Saturday the final cable read: PHILLIPS BRILLIANT IN TELEGRAPH BUT YOU EXCEL HIM STOP KEEP IT UP. Gallagher said he and Monks were astounded and Monks had made a remark as perceptive today as it was then. He had said, 'Well, now we know – it's entertainment they want.'

I had mulled over all this in the plane on the way to Cairo. Would I try to send sensational but exclusive stories – which Evelyn Waugh rightly said was a paradox? I could not imagine the *Sunday Times* being interested in entertainment, but on the eve of a possible war, there might not be much else to write about. The real question of interest – will there or won't there be a war – would probably be impossible to answer because of the military value of surprise. Nevertheless, I decided to concentrate on that. Tomorrow was Wednesday. I had four days to make sense out of what was happening, write it in 2,000 crisp words and make it not only accurate, fresh and penetrating but so interesting – as the editor of Insight, the *Sunday Times*'s investigative department, Bruce Page, had once said – that it could successfully compete with the cat on the old lady's lap in Eastbourne for her attention. It was too much to think about so after dinner McCullin and I joined the other correspondents in the penthouse bar, got drunk, listened to the air raid sirens practising (we hoped) and watched the lights go out over Cairo.

The drive across the desert to Suez was uneventful. We tend to imagine desert as being all rolling sandhills but often it looks more like a building site after the bulldozers have been through. With mile after mile of nothing but parched and barren landscape broken occasionally by the wreck of a car, we had nothing to do but talk. The taxi-driver chatted happily about President Nasser, the Israelis, and life in modern Cairo. He showed photographs of his children, mentioned which restaurants near our hotel were worth a visit and said that if we had the time he could offer a cheap rate for a trip to Alexandria. Then, when we reached Suez, he betrayed us.

Instead of crossing the bridge into the Sinai, he drove us straight to the local headquarters of the secret police, already alerted for our arrival, probably by him. We were ushered inside where we were greeted by a young inspector. 'Welcome, English,' he said. 'Welcome back to Suez.' While he ordered tea for us, we hastened to assure him that we personally had nothing to do with Britain's 1956 invasion and that we were just a couple of newsmen looking for a story. McCullin entertained him with an account of life in Egypt as a young British National Serviceman and of how he used to swim the Canal, his box Brownie tied to his head, to take photographs of local whores for the amusement of his fellow recruits. I suspected he was making it up, but with McCullin you could never tell. It made no difference. 'There's no story here,' the inspector said. 'Nothing.

The Sinai is a closed military area. You cannot visit there, English. Go back to Cairo and tell your colleagues they definitely cannot come.' A day wasted.

Next morning, leaving McCullin to his own devices, I called on the Indian embassy. India was non-aligned so more likely to be impartial. Indians are great gossips anyway and could give me a summary of what the diplomatic community believed was likely to happen next. There I learnt something I should have considered earlier: the commander of the United Nations peace-keeping force was an Indian, General Indar Jit Rikhye and he was in Cairo and staying at the Nile Hilton. Who better to give me an assessment of whether the expulsion of the UN force was likely to provoke an Arab-Israeli war?

I rang the general's room from the Hilton lobby and his ADC, a helpful Swedish captain, came down to see me. The general was having his breakfast and I was welcome to join him. It was a large, Punjabi-style breakfast with many eggs and piles of toast. (An Indian wife once told me that it was easy to keep a Punjabi man happy – 'All he needs is five or six good meals a day.') So for the next two hours General Rikhye gave me a military-style briefing on his assessment of the situation. It was lucid and utterly persuasive and its conclusion was that there would be no war now or in the immediate future.

At the Gezira sporting club, a Czech first-secretary and a Soviet cultural attaché (probably KGB) told me that they agreed with this assessment. Mohammed Hassanan Heikal, the editor of *Al Akram*, thought that war was unlikely. Anthony Nutting who had resigned as a Foreign Office Minister of State over Suez and who was in Cairo to see President Nasser, agreed. And this was the thrust of the story I sent on the Saturday 3 June 1967. After I had sent it, I spoke with Frank Giles and said that since there was not going to be a war, I could see no point in remaining in Cairo any longer. Giles reluctantly agreed so McCullin and I flew back to London the next day.

I got out of bed in London on Monday morning to hear on the BBC that the Six Day war had started. Rehearsing my excuse that Israel had fooled a lot of people more knowledgeable than me, I went straight into the *Sunday Times* where – did I imagine it? – my reception was a little chilly. The problem was that not only McCullin and I had returned – the paper had also pulled out the entire team of reporters and photographers from Israel. They had been flying over Italy on the way back when the El Al captain announced the start of the war on the aircraft's public address system.

The rush was now on to get everyone back again. Since the Israelis have always been better at public relations than the Arabs, the team for Israel was back in Tel Aviv by that evening; not so McCullin and me. The Egyptian government said that those correspondents already in Cairo could stay on at their own risk and if they submitted all their stories to the censors. No new correspondents would be allowed to enter the country. In vain we pleaded that we were not new correspondents: we were old ones who had left too soon. McCullin abandoned the effort and flew to Israel. Since I had been considered the paper's man on the Arab side, I wrote a memo to the editor, Harold Evans, headed 'Some Arguments for the Arabs'. I suggested that the Arab case tended to go by default because they did not understand the need to present their arguments via the modern media and they got swamped by the Israeli propaganda machine. 'From *Exodus* to the photographs of pony-tailed Israeli girls on the way to the front, Israel appears in the West as a much more attractive cause to champion than Egypt (especially since the average Englishman's attitude tends to be coloured by his wartime experiences in North Africa). The Arabs feel that no matter what the merits of any dispute in the Middle East, Britain will side with Israel. This feeling is understandable when even the BBC Middle Eastern Service during the early stages of the current crisis led its bulletin – beamed to a hundred million Arabs – with stories of Britons rushing to volunteer for service in Israel.'

Bruce Page, who was co-ordinating the paper's war coverage, read it and assured me that the *Sunday Times* would present a balanced view.* Since I could not get back to Cairo, he suggested that I try to cover the Arab side from Jordan. Direct flights there had been suspended so I left that night for Beirut, intending to make at least one Lebanese rich by taking a taxi through Syria and on to Amman.

Despite the promise of large sums of money, Beirut taxi drivers were reluctant. It was dangerous, they said. Israeli fighter planes had been seen over Lebanon. They might attack cars on the road. We might get into Syria only to find the border into Jordan closed. Eventually one relented and we set out. It was a lovely Middle Eastern day, hot and sunny with a cloudless sky. And in it, so high you could hardly see them, tiny jet fighters etched white lines across the blue. At the border I lined up behind a couple of Roman Catholic nuns and waited to see the Syrian immigration authorities. I had changed my Australian passport for a British one because

---

* It did. The paper produced a much-acclaimed supplement on the war that broke new ground in war reporting. Rather than relying on one or two star war correspondents writing personal accounts, it flooded the war with reporters and at the same time drew on every other source of information it could locate. Page's theory was that this multiplicity of sources, this saturation coverage, would cancel out individual bias. It was an expensive experiment which is probably why it has not been much used since.

it required fewer visas but now, as the Syrian officer examined it, I wished that I had not. He finished his inspection, looked up at me, then sent the passport spinning across the desk and on to the floor. 'English shit,' he said. 'Filthy English shit.' I picked up the passport. 'Does this mean you are refusing me entry to your country?' He beckoned a sentry. 'Get out,' he said. 'We don't want English shit in Syria.'

I returned to Beirut and hung around with correspondents exploring other routes. Every day there were new rumours – the Lebanese had arranged with the Syrians for a bus to take all the journalists to Jordan; a boat was leaving tomorrow morning to creep down the coast; the correspondents in Cairo were having a rough time and had been smuggled out of the Semiramis hotel and into the British embassy disguised as Arabs. ('How do you disguise two Englishmen as Arabs?' someone said. 'Make them hold hands.') These kept us all going until Friday when it was clear that the war was over and that Israel had won. In London, a team was putting together a whole section of the paper devoted to the war. So far I had been able to contribute nothing, but there was one last chance. The foreign ministers of all the Arab countries were gathering in Kuwait for a meeting to decide the Arab world's response to Israel's victory and to the triumphalism that this had engendered in the West.

I managed to get a Middle East Airlines flight to Kuwait despite the obstructive tactics employed by the airline's employees: 'No traveller's cheques, no credit cards. If you want a ticket you must pay cash. No. No dollars, no pounds. Only Lebanese money.' In Kuwait every hotel room was reserved for the foreign ministers and their retinues but I finally found a room in a hotel that seemed to be occupied entirely by bodyguards – huge, dark, bearded, sullen men armed with swords, daggers and heaven knows what else. They regarded me with suspicion.

The meeting started at 10am on Saturday and went on all day. I hung around the conference centre learning absolutely nothing. There were no other reporters, Arab or Western, present, so no one to consult. There was no chance of grabbing a foreign minister on his way to coffee or lunch because they were all escorted from the hall to their cars by bodyguards who, I was certain, would behead me first and ask questions afterwards. Sitting morosely in my hotel restaurant at lunchtime I was joined by a young Arab wearing a London-tailored lightweight suit. He announced that he was in charge of security for the conference and quizzed me about my identity and plans. Satisfied, he began chatting about his days at the London School of Economics. He was, he said, a *Sunday Times* reader. Good arts pages, witty book reviews, pity about its politics. I tried to convince him that times were changing, that an influx of newer, younger blood would make the paper's politics less predictable.

We got on so well that I risked a direct question. 'What are they talking about at the conference?' He leaned forward in his seat. 'You don't really expect me to answer that, do you?' I admitted that I did not. Then he said, 'But why don't we discuss what *we* would talk about if *we* were foreign ministers.' So we did. We decided that Israel would probably always win any full-scale armed conflict with any or all of the Arab states. 'Our Israeli cousins seem better at waging war than we do,' the security chief said. 'And although the West is happy to sell us arms, they are never going to let us defeat Israel. So what can we do to redress the balance? The answer is right underneath us. God has seen fit to put most of the world's oil underneath Arab lands. All we have to do is present a united front in the way we exploit this oil, how much we produce and – above all – what we charge for it. If we can do this, then we'll have the West over a barrel, as it were.'

I felt obliged to contribute something: 'Of course, we can't do this immediately. Our economies have to recover from this war and there will be many disputes to resolve. But we should begin to work towards such a united front as soon as possible with the aim of achieving it within a year.'

'A little longer I would have thought.'

'Agreed,' I said, and in our role as foreign ministers we shook hands.

He took a sip of his orange juice. 'Well, if that's what we've decided, you can bet that they've decided much the same sort of thing. In fact, I'd say they've decided *exactly* that.'

'I've got to go,' I said. 'Work to do.'

In my room I began writing an account of the Arab foreign ministers' meeting. I described the high security, and the fact that there would be no communiqué, but implied that reliable sources had given me an outline of what had been decided. Since the meeting was not due to end for another three hours I could not really send the story until then in case something out of the ordinary happened – the meeting broke up in disarray, they decided after all to issue a communiqué, or the Israelis bombed the place. Many a foreign correspondent has come to grief by filing his story too early and then seeing in horror the event he has been covering abandon its charted course and go its own way.

But if I waited until the end of the conference before cabling my story, the foreign news desk might not be able to handle it in time to make Sunday's paper. I decided on a compromise. I would send the story in several 'takes', or sections. I would write the first take immediately and deliver it in person to the cable office. Then I would return to the hotel and write the second take, and so on. This would both alert the staff on foreign desk at the *Sunday Times* as to the importance of the story and allow them to begin processing it as it arrived so that when the last take was received the whole thing could go into the paper in a matter of minutes.

I wrote the first take, putting at the end of it the standard phrase 'more to come' so as to warn London that this was only the first part of the story and that, in due course, more would follow. Then I took it to the cable office where an Indian clerk accepted it, counted the words, inspected my cable credit card, stamped everything twice and popped my message into a pigeonhole to await transmission – or so I thought.

I did this five times, delivering the last take announcing the closing of the conference and wrote at the bottom of my last page 'ends' to signal to London that this was the end of the story – just in time for the edition. The Indian clerk read it through. Then he said, 'This word "ends", sir. Does this mean this is the last page?'

'Yes.'

'So now I can transmit the other pages?'

'What other pages?'

'The other ones you have been bringing me earlier today.'

'You haven't sent them?' I shouted.

'No, Sir.'

'Jesus Christ, why not?'

'Because you wrote on them "more to come" so I knew you hadn't finished and so I kept them until you did.'

And he gestured towards the pigeonhole where all my earlier messages were neatly stacked, awaiting my magic word, 'ends', before they could be sent. Shades of Addis Ababa, O. D. Gallagher and *Scoop*.

I changed them all from ordinary cable rate to urgent but it was no use. The edition went without my story and I got a hint of what I had missed when I returned to London the following week. The *Sunday Times* business editor, Peter Wilsher, met me in the corridor. 'That was an alarming picture you sent us from Kuwait,' he said. 'If the Arab world uses its oil as a weapon, it's going to play hell with our economies.'

He was, of course, absolutely right. In the autumn of 1973, the Arabs quadrupled their oil prices provoking an international economic crisis. It had taken longer than expected, but the scenario I had described for the *Sunday Times* seven years earlier had turned out to be correct. But everyone would have forgotten about it by then, and anyway I had only myself to blame because I had forgotten that a foreign correspondent is only as good as his communications – I should have taken the time to explain to the well-meaning cable clerk what I was about. All in all, the Six Day War was a triumph for the *Sunday Times*, but one in which I played no part.

CHAPTER EIGHT

LAWRENCE OF ARABIA

Leonard Russell looked after the section of the *Sunday Times* known as the Review Front. Sometimes this was given over to major news events but usually it was reserved for book serialisations, Russell's speciality. He knew instinctively what the paper's readers liked and he knew how to present it to them. Publishers, however, regarded him with ambivalence. On the one hand, to have a book chosen for serialisation in the *Sunday Times* was a great coup – even though Russell was notorious for paying as little as possible for serial rights. On the other, they knew that Russell would 'gut' the book, ruthlessly extracting the most interesting parts, then stitch them together with invisible seams. At the end of reading a Russell serialisation, the publishers suspected, most readers would say, 'Well, I've read that book. No need to buy it.'

Russell, a neat, sandy-haired man with a quizzical half-smile, seldom appeared in the office before late afternoon and then only stayed an hour or so. Most of his work was done in the study of his fine Georgian house near Hyde Park, in which he lived with his wife, Dilys Powell, the *Sunday Times* film critic, and a tiny dog which disconcerted visitors by frequently attempting sexual congress with Russell's gammy leg. 'Ha, ha,' Russell would chuckle. 'He's feeling his oats again.'

Russell was old-school *Sunday Times*, having joined the paper from the *Daily Telegraph* in 1937, and as associate editor was more concerned with planning the paper's strategy than with week-to-week news. So I was puzzled when his long-suffering secretary, Eileen, rang me one Friday afternoon and said Russell would like to see me. Could I pop in when it was convenient? I took a seat opposite him, he 'borrowed' a cigarette from Eileen (he was trying to give up smoking, so he smoked only hers), then said, 'Tell me, have you read *Seven Pillars of Wisdom*?'

'Years and years ago.'

'Michael Cudlipp tells me you're going on holiday next week. Take it with you and read it again and when you come back we'll talk about it. I might have an interesting assignment for you. Where are you going, by the way?'

'Morocco.'

'Just the place to read Lawrence. Full of Arabs.'

Puzzled but intrigued I added a copy of *Seven Pillars* to my luggage and, with my wife Yvonne and three young children, set off for a quiet holiday in Casablanca. I saw myself sitting outside Rick's Café in the morning, reading *Seven Pillars* over coffee and croissants, joining the family at the beach in the afternoon and returning to Rick's for drinks in the evening. It all turned out to be very different, not the sort of thing that should happen to a journalist but rather to the people he usually wrote about.

At Casablanca airport we were all full of pre-holiday elation until the immigration officer took us out of the queue and into his office. 'Your wife is an Indian citizen,' he said to me, ignoring her but checking her passport. 'Indian citizens now require a visa to enter Morocco. You and your children are free to stay but Madame must leave on the very next plane.' I argued in vain. Neither the travel agent nor the airline, which had inspected our passports in London, had said anything about Indian citizens needing a visa. (We learnt later that Morocco was showing Islamic solidarity with Pakistan which had just lost a border clash with India.) I recruited the aid of our French friends with whom we planned to stay – Baudoin and Yvonne Matignon – who had been waiting in the airport reception hall. They suggested that a handsome contribution to the Moroccan Immigration Officers' Holiday Fund would help but the officer ignored my hints and remained adamant – Madame must leave Casablanca on the very next flight. 'Okay,' I said. 'She'll go back to London on the next flight, get her visa and be back tomorrow or the day after. Will you be happy then?'

'The next flight is not to London,' he said. 'The next flight is to Lagos, Nigeria.'

Now we were really in trouble. My wife could go to Lagos, a place she had never visited and where she knew no one. We could leave the children with the Matignons and go to Lagos together. Or we could all go to Lagos. These were the sort of decisions a special correspondent of the *Sunday Times* was supposed to be able to make in a flash, but no option really appealed. Suddenly I thought of *Seven Pillars* tucked at the bottom of my suitcase. How would Lawrence of Arabia have handled a situation like this? Article Twenty of his famous 'Twenty Seven Articles', a manual telling British political officers how to deal with Arabs, came to mind. 'Keep always on your guard: never say an unconsidered thing . . . watch yourself and your companions all the time.' I had already said several unconsidered things. The question was how to retract them and start again. My two-year-old daughter, Marisa, beat me to it. 'Mummy,' she said. 'I feel hot.' My wife felt her forehead and then inspected her glands. 'Mother of God,' she said. 'She's got mumps.'

Everything now happened very quickly. The immigration officer, obviously a father himself, relented a little. Madame would not have to go to Lagos after all. There was a Moroccan Airlines flight leaving in ten minutes for Madrid. Madame could take that, get a visa from the Moroccan embassy there and return the next day. We handed all three children over to our French friends, promising to be back soon, and were then given an armed escort across the tarmac and put on the Madrid flight. Our last sight of the children was through the window of the airport observation lounge where all three appeared to be crying silently.

In Madrid we quickly discovered that the Moroccan embassy was closed indefinitely because of a dispute between Morocco and Spain over the border in the Sahara. The telephone lines were down between Madrid and Casablanca so we could not even ring our friends to see how Marisa was. The *Sunday Times* correspondent in Madrid, Tim Brown, fixed lunch with a first-secretary at the British embassy. 'Just ask his advice,' Tim said. 'He's been around and he's worth listening to.' The embassy man did not hesitate. 'Abandon your holiday in Morocco. Just forget all about it,' he said. 'You could spend a week running around here or back in London trying to get a visa for your wife. Leave her here in Spain. Go back to Casablanca and pick up your kids. And then have a nice holiday on the Costa del Sol.' In an hour it was all arranged. I put my wife on a plane to Málaga. From there she would take a bus to Algeciras, the Spanish port opposite Tangier, and wait for us. I flew off to Casablanca to pick up the children from the Matignons, take a plane to Tangier and then the ferry to Algeciras. It looked foolproof.

When the holiday was first mooted I had asked Yvonne Matignon whether it was safe in Morocco and she had replied, 'Absolutely.' It was a little puzzling therefore to arrive at her house in the suburbs of Casablanca to discover that it was surrounded by a fifteen-foot-high wall topped with barbed wire and that the gate was guarded by a watchman armed with an automatic shotgun. Neither was it reassuring to retire for the night – after a happy reunion with the children – to be woken several times by the sound of automatic gunfire, apparently at close quarters. I tackled the Matignons about it over breakfast. The armed guard had been hired because theft of French property had become rife since independence. And the shooting?

'The King's birthday is coming up,' Baudouin Matignon said. 'The tribesmen have come in from the countryside to celebrate and they like firing their guns into the air.'

Well, that's all right then, I told the children as, against my instincts – which were to get out of the country as fast as possible – I allowed the Matignons to persuade us to drive to a seaside resort for the day and leave for Spain on Monday morning. The drive was pleasant but the children and I were puzzled by the number of dead dogs we noticed by the roadside, mostly lying flat on their backs with their legs pointing rigidly skywards. Did Moroccan dogs have poor traffic sense or were Moroccan drivers particularly brutal? Eventually I asked Yvonne Matignon. 'No, they haven't been run over,' she said. 'There's been an outbreak of rabies and dogs have been dying like flies. Your children have had their rabies shots, haven't they?' No they hadn't, so I spent the rest of the day on the beach manoeuvring them away from stray dogs, trying to remember how long you had after a rabid dog bit you before you began foaming at the mouth. Even making sandcastles turned out to be perilous. I had just constructed a masterpiece when a muscular Moroccan youth deliberately kicked it to pieces, scattering our group with sand in the process. Baudouin Matignon remonstrated with him. The youth laughed. 'C'est notre pays maintenant,' he said.

Next morning we caught the 9am Moroccan Airlines flight to Tangier. The plane's final destination was Madrid and the stopover at Tangier was only for half an hour. After twenty minutes waiting at the luggage carousel without any sign of our six suitcases, a sudden sense of unease made me approach a member of the airline staff. 'There was no hold baggage from Casablanca,' he said. 'Absolutely nothing.' There was little time to argue with him because out of the corner of my eye I could see a line of Madrid-bound passengers leaving the terminal to board their flight. Back to Lawrence of Arabia's Twenty Seven Articles, this time Number Four – never openly disagree with statements put forward by an Arab but 'after praise modify them insensibly causing the suggestions to come from him until they are in accord with your own opinion'.

'Of course there's no hold baggage from Casablanca,' I said. 'But would it be possible that the baggage of my three children, all travelling without their mother, has been placed in the hold for Madrid?'

'This is possible,' he said.

'Of course you are too occupied with important things to check that this is so. But apart from guarding my children, I have nothing to do.'

'Then why don't you go to the plane and see for yourself?' he said.

'What a good idea,' I said and, mentally thanking T. E. Lawrence, I left nine-year-old Aliya in charge of her brother and sister and joined the line of embarking passengers. Out on the tarmac, past the guard cradling his Kalashnikov, around the plane's steps, and then a quick duck under its belly to the open luggage hold where two men were loading bags for Madrid. Another outing for Article Four ended when one of the Moroccan workers suggested that my suitcases could be at the end of the hold and that if I wanted to crawl inside to check, he did not mind. So I did, and he was so pleased that he had been right, that when I had dragged them through the rope netting to the hold door, he helped me lower them to the tarmac. Then back past the guard with the Kalashnikov, who I was convinced was going to shoot me as a suspected terrorist but who expressed not the slightest interest in a mad foreigner who had suddenly become an airport luggage loader. Sweaty but triumphant, I staggered into the terminal where a Frenchman who had obviously not read *Seven Pillars* was in heated discussion with the airline staff over why his luggage from Casablanca had just taken off for Madrid.

After that it was all easy. Even getting three small children, one with mumps, and six suitcases on the bus to the docks (we would have needed two taxis, and while in Morocco I was not going to be parted from my children or my luggage ever again) did not faze me. Safely on board the 2pm ferry, we waved goodbye to Tangier, admired the view of Gibraltar and were soon approaching Algeciras. I had noticed that a dignified old Moroccan had been staring at us throughout the voyage and now he spoke, 'Pardon me, Monsieur,' he said, 'but is it permitted to ask: where is the mother of these children?' I began to explain, thought better of it, and then was able to point across the narrowing gap of water where the mother of these children was waving wildly from the pier. He nodded in satisfaction while I pondered the lessons. One: never split the family. Two: reporting other people's misfortunes does not necessarily equip you to handle your own. And three: say what you like about Lawrence of Arabia, he certainly knew how to handle Arabs.

Over the next two weeks amid the delights of southern Spain I managed to re-read *Seven Pillars of Wisdom* and on the first day back at the office went to see Russell again. 'What did you think of it?' he said. I told him I had found it heavy going and that I was uncertain how much of it was true and how much invented. 'You wouldn't describe yourself as a fan of T. E. Lawrence, then?' Russell said.

'Not really.'

'Okay,' Russell said. 'Now listen to this.'

Russell said that for some years a Scotsman called John Bruce had been going around Fleet Street trying to sell his life story. He claimed that he had joined the Tank Corps with Lawrence of Arabia, had become close friends with him, and had been engaged by Lawrence to beat him from time to time with a birch. Most newspaper offices had sent Bruce packing without even bothering to hear more or make any checks. Those who had bothered to check began with T. E. Lawrence's sole surviving brother, Professor A. W. Lawrence. Professor Lawrence told them that Bruce was an unstable, deluded nuisance. The few who had continued their enquiries had then received a letter from the solicitors for the Lawrence Trust, a City firm called Kennedy, Ponsonby and Prideaux. The solicitors would point out that they had warned Bruce to desist from his allegations and that Scotland Yard had been informed of his activities. No newspaper had ever persisted beyond this point.

But Bruce had not given up. After a serious illness and the loss of his job with an engineering company had eaten into his savings he had written to the *Sunday Times* with his story. The letter had made its way to Russell who had decided on the spur of the moment to hand over the matter to Insight, then flush with reporters. Colin Simpson got the job. Simpson was a former army officer (hence his nickname, 'the Major') who entered journalism via the antiques trade. He had made his name with a typical Insight story – the antique dealers' 'ring'. This was an arrangement between antique dealers not to bid against each other at auctions – thus keeping prices low – but to leave it to one dealer to secure the item and then to bid among themselves for it later at a private auction. Simpson had brought to Insight many of the skills of a military tactician – intelligence, reconnaissance, deception, and then the swift and decisive blow. I had already worked with him on one story, a reprise of the dealers' ring. Hearing from one of his spies that a ring would be operating at a country house auction in Lincoln, he sent me along posing as an Australian dealer seeking to fill a couple of cargo containers with 'good English brown'. He had already identified the likely site of the private auction – a barn in the grounds of the house. Bruce Page and Simpson were to conceal themselves in an attic over the barn and listen to the proceedings through a hole they had bored with an auger in one of the barn's beams. I was supposed to stumble on the private auction by accident and then in my pose as the Australian dealer persuade the locals to let me join the ring's auction. The moment Page and Simpson heard the dealers begin bidding among themselves they were to burst in, I was to reveal my true identity and the dealers were to raise their hands and plead a fair cop. Unfortunately, if there was a ring operating, the dealers went somewhere else and after a cold couple of hours we went back

123

to the office and wrote that investigation off as one of the many that did not work out.

But Russell's hunch that Simpson was the man for the Lawrence story was absolutely right. Simpson got on the train and went up to Chester to see John Bruce. The meeting was a fascinating one. Bruce was cautious but convincing. He claimed that he could authenticate all his claims about his relationship with Lawrence but he did not want to give away too much until a financial arrangement could be agreed – he said he had a family, his future was uncertain, and he had been disappointed in earlier relationships with other newspapers. Simpson took Bruce through his life: date and place of birth, army service, the times and occasions when he claimed to have met Lawrence. Back in London, Simpson checked the army records. There he discovered that Bruce had indeed been in the Tank Corps during Lawrence's period of service. And although Bruce had joined the Corps in Aberdeen while Lawrence had done so in Bovington, they had arrived at the Corps depot at Bovington together. This lent considerable weight to Bruce's claim that he had joined at Lawrence's instigation and that Lawrence had 'arranged everything'. Simpson then went to see Bruce again and took him through his story a second time, persuading him to expand it, getting him to dredge his memory for incidents that would provide corroborating information. Then, and only then, did he telephone Professor A. W. Lawrence. The professor began what Simpson later described to me as 'a well-rehearsed denial'. Simpson cut him short. 'I think I'd better tell you, Professor Lawrence, that the *Sunday Times* has checked out Bruce's story and we've decided that it is true.' There was a pause. 'Hmmm,' said Professor Lawrence. 'I think we'd better have lunch.'

They met at an Italian restaurant in Soho. Considering the luncheon's purpose – to discuss whether to make public the sexual perversion of a national hero, the brother of one of the men at the table – it was a remarkably pleasant and civilised affair. Simpson told A. W. Lawrence why he believed Bruce. Lawrence said that he had realised that one day Bruce's story would come out. He was concerned now only that it was not presented in a sensational tabloid manner and that his brother's sexual difficulties were treated with understanding and sympathy. If he could be assured of this, then he could offer something in return.

'What would that be?' said Simpson.

Lawrence said that transcripts of letters written to and from T. E. Lawrence had been lodged in the archives of the Bodleian Library at Oxford and embargoed until the year 2000. He would be prepared to open the collection for Simpson to examine.

'Done,' said Simpson. And there and then he got Professor Lawrence to write out on a paper table napkin the crucial part of what must rank as one of the most unusual contracts in literary history. It read:

The Keeper of Western Manuscripts, Bodleian Library.

> Dear Hunt,
> Will you kindly allow Mr Colin Simpson to read anything he may wish in the collection of T. E. Lawrence material you are holding incommunicado till 2000.
> Yours sincerely
> A. W. Lawrence

This was the stage the story had reached when Russell had first spoken to me. He said he was planning three review fronts on Bruce's revelations. 'There's an enduring interest in T. E. Lawrence,' he said. 'People can't get enough. There's too much work for Simpson so I'd like you to help him.' At the moment Simpson was in Oxford, going through the Bodleian material.

'It's a gold mine,' Russell said. 'Simpson rang me today. The papers are in a complete mess but he's found a letter from Lawrence to the Home Secretary asking for the deportation of a fellow called "Bluebeard" who ran some sort of buggers' club in Chelsea. Bluebeard apparently sold his confessions to a German magazine and Lawrence wanted this stopped too. Simpson's going to keep on at the Bodleian and you can start mapping out three parts of about 4,000 words each.'

There was more work than anyone had imagined. For instance, Lawrence's masochism turned out to be very complicated. He had persuaded Bruce to birch him by spinning Bruce a tale of an ogre of an uncle who wanted Lawrence punished for past misdemeanours and physically conditioned to bear pain and suffering that might occur in future wars. The uncle would instruct Bruce when to birch Lawrence. He would then post him the birch and demand, in return for a payment, a detailed written report on how Lawrence had stood up. Bruce was no fool, so Lawrence had taken the trouble to choose a real but distant relative for the role of the uncle and this had to be checked out just in case it were true. It was not, of course, and the written reports went to Lawrence himself who apparently got an additional thrill in reading about his own birching.

The first article appeared in the *Sunday Times* on 9 June 1968 and caused a sensation. Lawrence's supporters all over the world were outraged and hastened to say so. 'It is with shock verging on disbelief that I found that you had opened your pages to tarnish the hero image of Lawrence of Arabia,' wrote Sheldon A. Jacobson from Vancouver, Washington. 'It suggests the hate literature of Hitler and Nasser.' An anonymous writer in *The Times Literary Supplement* said, 'This is instant history and instant history like instant sauce and instant coffee is fit for consumption, but not for connoisseurs.'

Nearly thirty years later neither Simpson nor I have entirely escaped the legacy left by this series of articles on Lawrence of Arabia. Hardly a week passes without a Lawrence fan from somewhere in the world – usually the United States, which seems to crave Imperial heroes – challenging us on some obscure point in the articles, pointing out contradictions, demanding more detailed sources, or offering alternative explanations for Lawrence's behaviour. Television producers write asking for names and addresses of people who knew Lawrence who might still be alive; authors new to the Lawrence scene, and about to recount his story yet again, write to seek permission for quotations; and foreign publishers, particularly Arab ones, seek local language rights.

But as well as the flood of complaints, there also came approaches from publishers making what appeared to us to be enormous bids for the book they thought must already exist. The highest bid was $65,000 from McGraw-Hill of New York, and with offers from Nelson in Britain and eight foreign language publishers, the gross advances for a book as yet unwritten totalled over $100,000 (more than half a million in today's money). Russell was delighted. 'We'll write the book,' he said, 'make a packet, and then serialise it all over again in the paper.' And that is exactly what we did. Russell had no trouble convincing the editor, Harold Evans, and Bruce Page. They quickly realised that this was a way of financing Insight's investigative journalism. You did an investigation using the newspaper's money; when you ran the articles, the book offers rolled in and you used the publisher's advance to repay the paper. Eventually Evans even formalised the idea with a memorandum setting out how the book income would be divided – half to the newspaper, 40 per cent to the authors and 10 per cent to the rest of the editorial staff who had helped in any way at all – so that no one would feel left out. This bewildered the cashiers who found it hard to understand why journalists should be paid again for doing what they were already being paid to do. But Evans was never one to allow accountants to interfere with his editorial imperatives.

We could not devote a 120,000 word book to Lawrence's sexual inclinations so we set out to look with a fresh eye at every aspect of Lawrence's life, arguing that if he had managed to keep his sex life a secret, there could well be other secrets relating to other parts of his life. But wasn't he entitled to keep all aspects of his life secret if he so desired? I had discussed this with Russell. His attitude was that Lawrence had written a semi-autobiographical book which had placed his life in the public eye. The very publication of the book was inviting criticism – of its literary style, its contents, its purpose. We were perfectly entitled, therefore, to say, 'Just a moment. You've concealed from your readers vital information about who you are and what motivated you. You've misled them.' But he admitted that he liked the idea that Lawrence had fooled so many eminent people – Churchill, Trenchard, Curzon, the Bernard Shaws. 'Pity they're all dead,' he said. 'Just imagine their faces if they could have read that their old chum T. E. used to sneak off to a buggers' club in Chelsea and paid rough trade to flog him.'

I was more interested in the repercussions that I felt Lawrence's sexual drive might have had on his actions in the Middle East as a servant of Imperial Britain. But whether one accepted Russell's justification or mine, we both thought that Lawrence's secret sex life was too important to skim over, especially when it became clear – and even clearer in later biographies – that Bruce was not the only man employed to flog Lawrence: there were at least three others.

We ignored all the other biographies and started from scratch, taking nothing for granted, and employing straightforward journalistic practices. Take, for instance, the whole Bey of Deraa story as told in *Seven Pillars* – how Lawrence had been captured at Deraa and then tortured and sexually assaulted, first by the Bey and then by Turkish soldiers. Re-reading this passage for the third time, I was struck by how improbable it all seemed. And the explicit detail of his description of the whip used to beat him – was this not typical of sadomasochistic literature? I began to wonder what the Bey of Deraa himself had to say about this. It seemed surprising that no one had approached him before for his version.

We were three years too late. Hacim Muhittin Bey had died at Izmir in Turkey in 1965 but we located his family in Istanbul without difficulty, spoke with his son, Targan, examined the Bey's diaries and interviewed some of his associates and several of his enemies. Targan remembered his father referring to Lawrence as 'my opponent who wants to capture Deraa' but said that he had never at any time mentioned having met Lawrence and gave no indication he had even so much as known what he looked like. Everyone in Turkey said that Hacim Muhittin Bey was an aggressive heterosexual – even his enemies, who might have supported the *Seven Pillars* account in order to pay off old scores, were adamant that, whatever else he may have been, he was not a homosexual. The result of our research was, admittedly, inconclusive, but it did cast some doubt on Lawrence's version.

Encouraged, we broadened our approach. *Seven Pillars* was Lawrence's personal account of the Arab Revolt. What about the Arab view? The serialisation of the articles in the *Sunday Times* had encouraged Suleiman Mousa, a Jordanian historian, to contact us. He was in London doing research for a book on the Hashemites, the family of the leader of the Arab Revolt, the Sharif of Mecca, and had been working through the Foreign Office archives in the Public Record Office looking at recently released material about Lawrence and his role in the Arab Revolt. We engaged him to extract anything he thought of interest and to provide an Arab interpretation if we asked for it. To cover Lawrence's post-war life, we brought in Arabella Rivington, a middle-aged Englishwoman who had become fascinated by Lawrence and was planning to write a book to be called *T. E. Lawrence, 1918–1935*. In the meantime she was prepared to make her extensive files available and to do further research in the areas in which she had become an expert. She balanced Mousa, in that she considered Lawrence to have been one of the greatest Englishmen who ever lived, and she could be relied on to defend his reputation.

We began looking for anyone who had served with Lawrence, anyone who had known him, any new diaries, papers, correspondence, memoirs, unpublished manuscripts. Simpson, Arabella Rivington and, occasionally, a *Sunday Times* reporter travelled the country interviewing people while the *Sunday Times* network of correspondents tackled inquiries for us around the world. Soon a new picture of Lawrence began to emerge. Far from having an emotional attachment to the Arabs, he did not care for them as a race; far from devoting himself to uniting their divided tribes so that an Arab nation would emerge, he believed that it was in Britain's interests to keep the Middle East divided; far from furthering the cause of Arab freedom and independence, he was intent on making the Arabs part of the British Empire. This double-dealing and the betrayal it involved left Lawrence with a lasting sense of guilt which explained much of his behaviour in later life.

The thrust of our conclusions could not be kept quiet and we began to run into opposition from Professor Lawrence, with whom we had a contract (mainly to do with our use of copyright material); with Kennedy, Ponsonby and Prideaux, who were determined to enforce the contract to the letter; and with an American psychiatrist, Dr John Mack, of Harvard University. One clause of the contract obliged us to help Mack who was also working on a book on Lawrence. He criticised some of our draft chapters, saying that we did not have the psychiatric expertise to understand what had driven Lawrence. In what was, in retrospect, a naive response, we promptly engaged a leading British psychiatrist, Dr Denis

Leigh, of the Maudsley Hospital, to examine Lawrence's medical records; read all our research material; meet John Bruce; and, in effect, do a post-mortem psychological analysis of Lawrence. He concluded that most of Lawrence's problems could be put down to physical causes, of which exhaustion was a principal one.

Kennedy, Ponsonby and Prideaux were the most difficult to deal with. We needed their permission to quote from any of Lawrence's published works and this was extracted with great and painful difficulty. They also insisted that we seek permission from the writers of letters to Lawrence and if the writer was dead – as was often the case – then from the literary executor, and if there was no literary executor, then from the heirs or their lawyers. This proved enormously time-consuming and in one case involved tracking down the widow of an army colleague of Lawrence's to a small pension in Tangier and persuading her to sign a letter authorising our use of a letter her husband had written forty years earlier.

We finished the book in July 1969 and Leonard Russell serialised it again in the *Sunday Times* in August, this time in four parts. The first British print run of 25,000 copies was already sold out when the book was published in September. Once again there was a wave of outrage, backed this time by hostile reviews of the book, one of the most outspoken of which was in the *Sunday Times* itself. Professor Elie Kedourie, an expert on Middle Eastern affairs, said the book 'does not add to knowledge but only promotes and deepens those feelings of guilt in which so many of the intellectual classes in this country like to luxuriate'. We entered into an abortive public correspondence with Professor Kedourie over what our documentation did or did not prove. In retrospect, it would have been better to have remained silent.

Some of the reviews raised questions of literary principle as relevant today as then. Literary editors tend to give biographies to a reviewer who knows about the subject and is competent to spot flaws in the book. But the reviewer has usually gained this competence because he or she has already written a biography on the subject, or – worse still from the author's point of view – is currently working on one. In the first instance the reviewers will naturally tend to feel that the new work does not measure up to their own. In the latter case, they will resent the fact that they have been beaten to publication.

So when Anthony Nutting, former Minister of State for Foreign Affairs under Anthony Eden, reviewed our book, generally unfavourably, he began with these frank and illuminating words: 'It is never an easy task to review a book by another author on a subject about which one has written a definitive work of one's own.' Then the 1970 autumn issue of the *Middle*

East Journal carried a very unfavourable review by Dr John Mack. Yet nowhere in the review did Dr Mack mention that he himself was engaged in writing a biography of Lawrence. This was eventually published in 1976 as *A Prince of Our Disorder* and won a Pulitzer prize. (In 1995 Dr Mack announced that he had discovered that aliens from outer space had regularly been abducting hundreds of thousands – 'if not millions' – of human beings, carrying out research on them, and then returning them to earth. He should have stuck with Lawrence of Arabia.)

Throughout the research and writing of the newspaper articles and then the book I remained puzzled as to the reasons for Lawrence's fame – even today, he and Winston Churchill are probably the best-known Englishmen in the world. The Arab Revolt was a sideshow in the First World War, and Lawrence's role in it a minor one lasting less than three years. When he left Damascus in 1918 his life still had seventeen years to run, all of it an anticlimax to his desert adventures, and a disappointment to his friends and supporters. True, his supporters talk about the intellectual who was also a man of action, the single-minded embodiment of the English Imperial dream, the latterday Crusader, the Prince of Mecca, who, if the war had not ended too soon for him, might well have realised Napoleon's dream and have ridden into Constantinople with most of the tribes of Asia Minor at his side; author, savant, soldier, intimate of poets and kings; a man who could move Churchill to write, 'I fear that whatever our need we shall never see his like again.'

But how did it all begin? How did Lawrence first become famous? If it is all a legend, then how did the legend get started? When I asked Elizabeth Monroe why Lawrence was remembered, she replied, 'Because he could write.' But *Seven Pillars of Wisdom* (subscribers' edition) was not published until 1926 and the abridged version *Revolt in the Desert* not until the following year. Yet Lawrence was already world-famous by 1920. The real answer, of course, was there all the time, although its details have only recently emerged. A journalist made Lawrence famous. A journalist started all the legends. Lawrence of Arabia was the first product of a media/propaganda/public relations/showbusiness partnership – a combination of amoral talents that later developed until it was able 'create' prime ministers and presidents, one of the more dubious phenomena of the twentieth century.

Propaganda began the operation. When the United States entered the war in April 1917, the American people showed a marked reluctance to take up arms, so to inspire the nation to fight President Wilson set up a Committee on Public Information under the chairmanship of a journalist,

George Creel. One of Creel's first acts was to propose sending a correspondent to gather stirring stories in Europe to stimulate enthusiasm for the war. The man chosen was Lowell Thomas, who had cut his newspaper teeth working on the *Chicago Evening Journal* alongside Ben Hecht, author of the classic *The Front Page*.

It did not take Thomas and his cameraman Harry Chase long to realise that there was little propaganda value in the mechanised slaughter on the Western Front, so the author John Buchan, then director of information at the Foreign Office, guided him towards the Middle East where the British army was about to capture Jerusalem. There Thomas found a story with powerful emotional appeal for an American audience. The war in the Middle East could be presented as a modern crusade for the liberation of the Holy Land from the Turks and the emancipation of its Jewish, Arab and Armenian communities. At the centre of the story would be a modern Richard the Lionheart.

Thomas sought out Lawrence and cast him for the role. He arranged to spend a few weeks with him and the Arabs and for Chase to film and take photographs of Lawrence – the ever-popular image of him in flowing Arab costume is largely due to Chase's work during this time. But then – like Hemingway who saved his best Spanish Civil War experiences for his novel *For Whom the Bell Tolls* – Thomas did not waste his Middle East experiences on propaganda stories for the American press, especially as the war was nearly over. Instead, back in America, he wrote a script that he read to audiences as they watched a screening of Harry Chase's film, all to the accompaniment of appropriate music.

He opened this show at New York's Century Theatre in March 1919 where its success inspired a British impresario, Percy Burton, to bring it to London, and put it on at the Royal Opera House in Covent Garden. On the ship to Britain, Thomas had refined his show with the help of Dale Carnegie, who later wrote *How to Win Friends and Influence People*. It was now an extravaganza, an assault on the senses and the imagination which combined all the techniques for doing this in a way that had never before been attempted.

The curtain rose on a theatre-set featuring moonlight on the Nile with the pyramids in the background. After a pop version of the muezzin's call to prayer (adapted and sung by Mrs Thomas), a chorus line did the Dance of the Seven Veils. Then there were slides, film footage and Thomas's commentary, accompanied by music from the band of the Welsh Guards while clouds of eastern incense wafted from glowing braziers. Chase had devised a projection technique for his film that used three arc-light projectors simultaneously, and a fade and dissolve facility that heightened the drama of the presentation.

Thomas began by saying, 'Come with me to the lands of history, mystery and romance,' and referred to Lawrence as 'the uncrowned King of Arabia' who had been welcomed by the Arabs for delivering them from four hundred years of oppression. The show was an enormous success. It later toured the world, was seen by four million people, and is estimated to have made Thomas $1.5 million (more than $20 million in today's money). Lawrence became famous virtually overnight.

But there was more to the whole business than was realised at the time. A hidden political agenda was involved. The impresario Burton was encouraged to produce the Lawrence of Arabia show by the English-Speaking Union, of which Thomas was a member and whose committee included such notables as Churchill and the newspaper proprietor Lord Northcliffe. The Union's aim was to emphasise the common heritage of Britain and the United States, to draw the two countries closer together and forge a common sense of future destiny. If Lawrence could be portrayed as an old-style British hero and, more importantly, a representative of the new, benevolent British imperialism, the American liberal misgivings about Britain as a greedy, oppressive power in the Middle East might be dispelled.

These are the origins of Lawrence's fame, a role he was only too happy to play while all the time professing to hate it. (One of the more perceptive biographies of Lawrence, that by Michael Yardley, is aptly titled *Backing into the Limelight*.) But the truth is that the blame for the continuing tragic history of the Middle East, of which Operation Desert Storm was the most recent example, is largely due to the likes of Lawrence, servants in the Imperial mould, and those like Thomas, who promoted them.

CHAPTER NINE

MUSSOLINI, HITLER AND ME

O. D. Gallagher once told me that part of the thrill of working for the *Express* at its pre-war peak was that you could spend the morning interviewing a talking dog in Balham and that afternoon be on your way to Shanghai. I thought of him one Tuesday in February 1968 when, after I had spent the morning ringing football managers to ask about escalating transfer fees, Bruce Page said he would like me to leave for Milan that evening. It was a delicate assignment, he said, and it was possible that even if I were successful, nothing would appear in the paper. The previous Sunday the Thomson Organisation had announced that it had been the victim of a confidence trick. Two businessmen had offered 'Mussolini's wartime diaries' for sale and Thomson had paid over some money before discovering that the diaries were fakes created by two women from a town outside Milan called Vercelli. But there were still some unanswered questions about the whole deal and Insight had decided to take a further look at it.

I spoke some Italian but not enough to handle an assignment like this, so in Milan I went straight to Eugenio Grignani, an Italian I had met when he was a student in London in the 1950s, and through him hired a bilingual young lawyer still studying for his final exams. Now I had a local lad on my side. Together we went to the Criminal Investigation Department of the Milan police, told the duty officer what we were interested in, and half an hour later were sitting opposite a young inspector who seemed to think we knew a lot more than we did.

'Have you come here with *carta bianca* from your company to see how much of your money you can get back?' he said. 'Is that your mission? If so, I cannot help. Pending any criminal charges, that would be a civil matter and you should engage an Italian lawyer.' I said that no, I was not there to try to get back Thomson's money. I was only interested in what was happening. 'You mean now?' he said. 'Well, we may decide to charge the due donne di Vercelli. The difficulty is that they have a receipt saying that they sold – and I quote – "items written in the *style* of Benito Mussolini". This may absolve them from a charge of attempting to defraud. On the other hand, both have convictions for forgery in an earlier and similar case.'

I was confused by all this, but if I were to fire questions at him, it would expose my ignorance and he could well decide to shut up. The law student caught my eye and then looked pointedly at the door. 'I'd better ask London for instructions,' I said. 'I'll use the public phone in the hall. I'll be back in a couple of minutes.' Instead, I waited in the hall and soon afterwards the door to the inspector's office opened and the law student joined me.

'I told the inspector that you hadn't briefed me properly about the case and because of that I was having trouble interpreting for you,' he said. 'So he filled me in.' From what he repeated to me of the Milan police version and from what I later learnt from the *Sunday Times* editor-in-chief, Denis Hamilton, I was able to piece together what had happened. As far as I know, the whole story has not been told before – the Thomson Organisation was too embarrassed and the confidence tricksters, for obvious reasons, have kept quiet.

It began just before Chritmas, 1966, when Charles Kean, a Polish-born arms dealer, approached a former *Sunday Times* Insight editor, Clive Irving, then no longer with the paper, offering to sell on behalf of an old business acquaintance, one Ettore Fumagalli, some eighteen Mussolini diaries for $12 million. The diaries were in the possession of two women in Vercelli but Kean had some photocopies. Preliminary checks convinced Irving that the offer was worth pursuing, so he went to the only source he knew which would have the capital and prestige to handle the diaries if they proved to be authentic: the Thomson Organisation. After a meeting at Hamilton's London flat on 27 January 1967, Hamilton agreed to put up £5,000 to finance further investigations in return for an option to buy the rights to publish the diaries if they were genuine.

Fumagalli was reluctant to agree to the investigations because, he said, the two women of Vercelli had already been sent to prison once for selling copies of Mussolini's speeches and were terrified that they would be prosecuted again for allowing valuable state papers to leave the country. In the end Fumagalli persuaded Irving to sign a document in the London offices of solicitors Slaughter and May, acting for the Thomson Organisation, stating that he would never reveal the names of the Vercelli women in connection with the diaries.

Thus in one operation Fumagalli had explained the earlier imprisonment of the two women – preventing an examination of the circumstances of their trial which would have exposed the whole operation – and had involved Irving in the conspiracy of silence about the transaction, thus obviating the risk of anyone who knew about the earlier forgeries warning Irving. The next step was to speed everything up to prevent long and detailed checks, consultations and reflection. A contract drawn up by a Bahamas-based corporation called C. B. C., in which a Thomson subsidiary was a major shareholder, required that Fumagalli was to hand over Mussolini's diaries for 1939–42 for 'identification, translation, and evaluation' in return for a deposit of £6,000. At the end of six months, Thomson would have to negotiate a final purchase price for the diaries or return them. But Fumagalli and Kean were having none of this. Kean threatened to catch the next plane to New York 'to see *Life* magazine and *Look*, or better still, to get a Texan millionaire friend to finance the whole deal'. Fumagalli then started negotiations in Milan with the powerful *Corriere della Sera* group to sell the diaries to them and informed Thomson of what he was doing.

As a result, the two men, in a series of demands to the Thomson group (the last at a meeting in the office of Slaughter and May on 22 May), were able to escalate the initial payment from £6,000 to £50,000, with a further £75,000 to be paid out a month later towards a total purchase price of £245,000. As Irving agreed later, 'We had all been expertly conned into worrying more about competitors than in standing up the diaries.'

None of this would have mattered if the diaries had been genuine. The trouble was that no one would say that they were. Irving had three academic experts on modern Italian history look at them. They were excited. 'If these are real,' said one, pausing to wave his hand at a shelf full of works on twentieth-century Italy, 'then all these books will have to be rewritten.' But at the end of their examination, all they could say was that there was nothing in the text – in terms of dates and facts – which exposed the diaries as fakes, nor anything in the handwriting, the feel, the smell or the appearance of the volumes themselves.

Irving had the paper check done by a world expert who expressed reservations about one diary but could not fault the others. The ink and the binding were also tested and appeared authentic. In short, no one was able to say that the diaries were forgeries; no one was able to say that they were genuine. Even Vittorio Mussolini, the dictator's son, flown from Rome at Thomson's expense and presented with a Jaguar car as payment for his opinion, vacillated from belief to disbelief and then back to belief in the space of hours. (He did, however, sign a legal release renouncing his claim to the diaries.) So Thomson went ahead with the deal, paid out the amounts agreed with Fumagalli, and continued with the authentication process.

The dénouement came in Milan. *Corriere della Sera* thought to check its library, discovered references to the previous trial of the two women from Vercelli, and obtained a court transcript. There it all was – evidence of the techniques they had used to 'create' Mussolini documents. The diaries were clearly forgeries. Thomson started legal action against Fumagalli, and rather than wait for another newspaper to run the story, Denis Hamilton decided that the *Sunday Times* itself should break it, disclosing only the essential facts on 18 February 1968.

What was left for me to discover? I decided to start with the two old ladies of Vercelli – the Panvinis. They lived in a modest apartment in a small block of flats. Rosa Panvini, who was eighty-four, received me sitting up in bed, and her daughter Amalia, who was about fifty, bustled around making coffee. They were happy to talk about the diaries, they said, as long as we emphasized that they had never pretended that they were anything other than fakes, curios constructed for the market in Mussolini memorabilia. Whatever Fumagalli said about them was his own business. Rosa even produced a receipt signed by Fumagalli saying he knew he was purchasing 'historical reconstructions'. According to the receipt the amount he had paid was the equivalent of £2,000.

'Fine,' I said. 'I accept your conditions. Let's start with how you do it.'

Rosa launched into a long account, with her mother nodding approval from time to time. 'I do the research and Mama does the writing. I go to the library and I look up the old newspapers. There was something in them about Il Duce nearly every day – Il Duce flies from Rome to Milan; Il Duce opens a new building; Il Duce makes a speech. Then I come home and I imagine what went through Il Duce's mind as he was doing those things and I write it down and put in some flowery bits. Like, "Today I flew from Rome to Milan. As our glorious countryside passed far beneath us, I considered how lucky I was to be leader of this historic country, this ancient bastion of civilisation." It's easy. Then I give it to Mama and she writes it in Il Duce's handwriting.'

'Show me,' I said.

The old lady sat up straighter in bed. Her daughter plumped the pillows behind her, then went to the table and came back with a bound journal, a steel pen and a bottle of ink. She put another pillow in front of her mother who used it like a desk. The old lady took the pen and gripped it between her thumb and second finger, instead of the first. 'I hold the pen like this,' she said. 'It's easier to do his writing this way.' She dipped the pen in the ink and in a cramped and laborious manner began writing in the journal in the hand that was so like Mussolini's that it had fooled the experts.

'But what about the paper?' I said. 'The paper can be analysed and dated. How can the diaries appear to have been written by Mussolini when the paper is of the wrong date?' Rosa smiled. 'But it's not,' she said. 'We bought these journals at a bankrupt sale of stationery things that were all made before the war.' I thought for a moment. 'The ink,' I said. 'The ink may be pre-war ink but it will be fresh on the paper instead of dried and old.' Rosa shook her head. 'We put the journals in the kitchen oven on a low heat for ninety minutes. It ages the ink perfectly.'

I shook my head in admiration. No wonder the experts had been fooled. There was nothing in the content of the diaries that jarred historically because it had all been taken from contemporary reports. The old lady had perfected Mussolini's handwriting. The paper and binding was of the right period, and the two women had stumbled on a simple way of aging the ink good enough to pass scientific tests.

The more I went into the story, the worse it looked for the Thomson Organisation. Vittorio Mussolini, it turned out, would authenticate anything for money – an Italian journalist told me that Vittorio had confirmed for an American collector of Mussolini memorabilia that a pair of outsized woollen underpants had definitely belonged to his father. Irving accepted his share of the blame. As he reported to Denis Hamilton, 'The architects of this swindle were clever and lucky. Lucky, because there was enough legal activity in Italy to have had a reasonable chance of making somebody connect this activity with the earlier notoriety of the Panvini affair. But they didn't. Lucky, because nobody thought to take the elementary step of searching the cuttings for background on the characters involved. No need to comment on that. And clever because they manufactured enough of a climate of obvious intrigue to conceal the real intrigue which lay beneath it.'

Yet with the outlines of the confidence trick clear to me, there were still many unanswered questions. Who was the mastermind? The Panvinis told me that they had started work on the diaries in the early Fifties, long before Fumagalli came on the scene. 'We were commissioned,' Rosa said. 'Who by?' I asked. 'I am not able to tell you that.' And she steadfastly refused to give me a name or even a hint. Who eventually pocketed Thomson's money? The legal action which Thomson started failed to find out. Fumagalli insisted that the diaries were genuine and everything that had occurred was simply an anti-Fascist plot to make certain that nothing favourable to Mussolini was published in the British press. He hinted that the British Secret Intelligence Service had scuppered the deal because the diaries revealed close links between Mussolini and Winston Churchill. Then he disappeared, saying that he was on to an even richer vein of Mussolini papers. The Italian police showed little interest in pursuing him, their attitude being that if a foreign newspaper was foolish enough to buy Mussolini diaries and in doing so risk breaking Italian law, then it had to accept the consequences when the diaries turned out to be fakes. I think that once it had got over the excitement of nearly having a world publishing scoop, this was also the attitude of the Thomson Organisation.

Comparing notes with a reporter from *Corriere della Sera*, I discovered that the approach to his newspaper group had not come from Fumagalli – as we had thought – but from Padre Enrico Zucca, the priest who had been Mussolini's confessor, now head of the Convento Sant' Angelo, the Milan convent where Mussolini's body was hidden after his supporters had snatched it from an unmarked grave. Padre Zucca remained a fervent supporter of Mussolini and Italian neo-Fascism and had somehow made his convent into one of the wealthiest in Italy. Padre Zucca agreed to see me so I did a little research into his background. He was a financial adviser to the Balzan Foundation, set up in Switzerland in 1952 in memory of an executive of *Corriere della Sera*. Under Padre Zucca's guidance the bank account of this foundation grew so rapidly that he felt obliged to deny publicly rumours that its funds had been swollen by the 'treasure of Dongo', the gold which Mussolini is said to have had with him when captured by partisans at Dongo on 27 April 1945.

I wanted to ask Padre Zucca if it was possible that the diaries were part of an operation to rehabilitate Mussolini's reputation and earn some money to support neo-fascism in Italy. But two hours before my appointment with him, his assistant telephoned to say that Padre Zucca had suddenly been taken ill and would be unable to meet me. As I wrote for the *Sunday Times*, 'The story leads off into a murky underworld where forgery, the press, and the secret political manoeuvres of neo-Fascist groups rub shoulders.'

Over the next fifteen years I sometimes thought about the Mussolini diaries because I had a little project I wanted to tackle one day when things in Insight were slack. Mussolini's diaries had last been seen in the possession of a Japanese diplomat who had been serving in Italy towards the end of the war. Japanese records would show who had been stationed in Italy at that time, so it should be possible to track down the diplomat, find out if he were still alive, and ask him what he did with the diaries. Is it just possible that they are in a box under someone's bed in Tokyo or Osaka, grandpa's foreign papers that he brought back from the war and no one can read? I had fantasies of delivering the *real* Mussolini diaries to a beaming Lord Thomson and claiming the glory for Insight. But there never seemed to be the time even to get the project started and by 1981 the Thomson motivation was no longer there because that was the year when Thomson went and Rupert Murdoch took over the *Sunday Times*.

I played a small part in Murdoch's negotiations to buy the paper. He telephoned me at my tennis club one Monday afternoon and asked if I could meet him in his office at the *News of the World* the following morning. What could he want? Just after he had bought the *News of the World* I had telephoned him and told him that a London publisher wanted me to write a biography of Murdoch. 'The time's not ripe yet,' he had said. 'Maybe later.' I told the publisher that it would be a difficult book to write without Murdoch's collaboration. 'It could be done,' I said, 'but he wouldn't like it and I don't want to make him angry – he might own the *Sunday Times* one day.'

In Murdoch's office we chatted for a few minutes about the old days in Melbourne before he came to the point. 'You know I'm after Times Newspapers,' he said. 'I don't think I can pull it off if the journalists oppose my bid. How do they feel about me?' I said, 'Hang on a minute, Rupert. I don't mind answering that, but don't forget I work for Harry Evans. I'll have to tell him about this meeting.' 'Of course,' he said. 'No problem.'

So I told Murdoch that as far as I could judge, the *Sunday Times* journalists – I could not speak for *The Times* – preferred the bid from the consortium Evans was trying to put together. But if that did not happen, then Murdoch was the next choice. He seemed pleased, closed the interview and escorted me to the lift. The reason for his pleasure was revealed only later – he had already planned to offer Harold Evans the job of editor of *The Times* and he was confident that Evans would accept. There was no real threat, therefore, of an opposing consortium. However, for a brief moment, there was trouble from another quarter. I had underestimated the opposition from the *Sunday Times* journalists to the Murdoch takeover and they considered legal action to force the government to refer Murdoch's bid to the Mergers and Monopolies Commission. An Australian barrister, Geoffrey Robertson, QC, advised them that they had a good case and estimated that if each member of the *Sunday Times* chapel (union branch) contributed £400 to a legal fighting fund, that would be enough to mount the action. To Robertson's disappointment, £400 each proved too much for the journalists and they voted not to oppose Murdoch, which was probably just as well because the Trade Secretary, John Biffen, had secretly told one *Sunday Times* journalist that the Commission could only make a recommendation and he did not care what it recommended – he was going to approve Murdoch's takeover anyway.

The transition from Thomson to Murdoch at first made little difference at the *Sunday Times* – apart from a new accounting practice called 'zero budgeting'. Under Thomson each editorial department submitted a figure for what it expected to spend that year. Naturally the figure was inflated to cover emergencies. If there was none, then as the end of the accounting year approached reporters were dispatched all over the world in a rush to spend the budget in case the accountants used any under-spend as an argument to cut the next year's figure. Murdoch ended this overnight. 'If you give journalists a budget,' he said, 'the buggers will spend it all.' Instead each department head would have to seek approval from a financial manager for every project. This did not apply to Murdoch, of course. He was the boss. He could spend what he liked on what stories he liked, which is how we got into the Hitler diaries affair.

In December 1982, the right-wing historian David Irving telephoned me at the *Sunday Times* and said, 'I've got some amazing news for you. Some very important wartime diaries have turned up.'

'Oh, no,' I said. 'Not Mussolini's diaries again.'

'No,' Irving said. 'Hitler's.'

I had known Irving for some time and had been to several of his parties which I had enjoyed because of the eclectic mix of people they attracted. His politics were very different from mine but I found him an interesting and engaging writer, unpredictable, obsessional and given to occasional bursts of eccentricity. (His wife, a Spaniard, told me that she had made the mistake one summer afternoon of telling Irving that an ice-cream van in Oxford Street had charged her £5 for an ice-cream cone. Irving had immediately abandoned his work and spent the rest of the day scouring the streets of London for the van to demand his wife's money back.) I had written about Irving, and now and then he had offered me slivers of information, spin-offs from his research, because he knew of my interest in wartime propaganda. He told me that he preferred to talk to me rather than to my British colleagues because 'you're not encumbered by all the ingrained attitudes that come from an English upbringing, especially a wartime one.' So what was he offering now?

Irving said that a set of Hitler's papers, including some diaries, had turned up in Germany and might be for sale. Would the *Sunday Times* be interested? I said that I was sure it would but I was going to Australia on a long assignment soon and if he wanted a quick, official answer then he should let me have all the details as soon as possible. That night Irving's Rolls-Royce pulled up outside my house and he delivered a letter. It said that on a recent visit to Germany he had met Otto Guensche, the SS major who had burnt Hitler's body. Guensche had told him that he had seen what he called 'the Stuttgart diaries' which showed, among other things, that Hitler had known about Hess's flight to Britain in 1941. Guensche had said that without a doubt the diaries were genuine. Irving concluded by offering to act as a go-between 'to set up or conduct negotiations with traditionally awkward German personalities as might prove necessary in an attempt to secure this material'. In return he wanted a commitment from the *Sunday Times* to pay him 'a finder's fee' equal to 10 per cent of whatever the *Sunday Times* eventually paid for the diaries.

This was an editorial decision that would have to be taken at top level, so the following morning I told my immediate boss, Magnus Linklater, of my conversations with Irving and handed him Irving's letter. Linklater thought it would be unwise for the paper to become too involved with Irving because of his right-wing reputation. I argued that it was only someone like Irving who would have contacts in old Nazi circles and if there were any diaries, that was where they would be. Linklater said he would take it step by step, not committing the *Sunday Times* to anything until Irving had produced more information about the diaries and their authenticity. I left it to him to tell Irving this and went off to Australia.

I arrived back in London on 14 April 1983 and went into the office on the following Tuesday morning. Eric Jacobs, the editor of the Review Front, asked me across the road to the Blue Lion that evening for a welcome home drink and to catch up on office gossip. I had a few ideas for his section but he casually said he did not think he could accommodate them. 'The Front's been booked for a secret project,' he said. I pressed him to reveal what it was. 'Don't tell anyone,' he said, 'but Rupert's bought Hitler's diaries. They're going to be running every weekday in *The Times* and on our Review Front on Sundays.'

'Which Hitler diaries?' I said.

'I dunno,' Jacobs said. 'Is there more than one lot?'

Linklater had gone home so I had to wait until the following morning to learn what had happened. These were not the Irving Hitler diaries, Linklater said. These were the *Stern* Hitler diaries. 'How do we know that they're not the same ones,' I said.

'We don't,' Linklater said. 'But *Stern* has checked them out and it swears that they've passed all the tests.' He added that he had followed up on the Irving Hitler diaries as far as his budget would allow – he had sent Gitta

Sereny, an authority on Nazi Germany and a tireless investigator, to Hamburg to see Gerd Heidemann, the *Stern* reporter who had found the diaries – but in the end had been forced to call a halt when nothing conclusive emerged. Then, out of the blue, *Stern* had approached the *Sunday Times* with an offer, Murdoch had become involved, and the deal was going through at boardroom level. It would be announced on Friday.

I suddenly felt so apprehensive that I needed an urgent pee. In the toilet, staring at the porcelain wall and deep in thought, I became aware that someone had come in and was standing beside me. It was the editor, Frank Giles. With the awkwardness that accompanies all conversations in toilets, I told him that I was worried about the diaries, reminded him of the Mussolini diaries fiasco, and said I felt that the paper was being stampeded into publishing without proper checks.

Giles looked thoughtful. 'You're right to be cautious,' he said. 'But don't worry. It doesn't concern us. Murdoch's going to run them in *The Times*.' I said I would still like to set out my concerns. Could I write him a memorandum to show to Murdoch? 'All right,' Giles said. 'But keep it down to one page.'

I went back to my desk, got out the files, rolled a sheet of paper into my typewriter and began to write. I summarised what had happened with the Mussolini diaries and drew attention to some of the similarities with the deal negotiated with *Stern*. I could not be too specific because I did not know exactly what the *Stern* deal was. But when I had finished this section, I was on confident ground – the lessons I felt that the *Sunday Times* should have learnt from the Mussolini diaries. I set them out point by point:

1 You cannot rely on expert authentication. Thomson engaged five experts. Not one said that the diaries were fake.
2 You cannot rely on people close to the subject. Vittorio Mussolini, Mussolini's son, said that he thought the diaries were definitely his father's.
3 You cannot rely on legal protection. Slaughter and May did the negotiations for Thomson. They did not succeed in recovering a single penny when the diaries turned out to be fakes.
4 Beware of secrecy and being pressed to make a quick decision. The Mussolini con men were able to bring off their sting by pressing Thomson to make a quick deal. Absolute secrecy was essential, they said, to prevent the Italian government from stepping in. Both manoeuvres prevented proper examination of the background of the salesmen and the provenance of the diaries.

I then moved on to what I felt should have been done to check the authenticity of the Hitler diaries. Since I was in the dark about what checks *had* been made, I had to head this section *Questions to Consider*. I wrote:

1 What German academic experts have seen all the diaries? Has, for instance, the Institute of Contemporary History seen them?
2 What non-academic British experts have seen all the diaries? Has David Irving seen them?
3 How thoroughly has the vendor explained where the diaries have been all these years and why they have surfaced *now* – the fiftieth anniversary of Hitler's accession to power?'

Then I tried to sum up all my reservations.

The crux of the matter is that secrecy and speed work for the con man. To mount a proper check would protect us but would not be acceptable to the vendor. *We should insist on doing our own checks* and not accept the checks of any other publishing organisation.

It turned out that I was right on every major point. *Stern*'s authentication procedures had been pathetic. Its fear that it had not secured the copyright of the diaries had fostered a climate of intense secrecy which then infected everyone with whom the Germans had dealings. No German historian had been allowed to see the diaries. There was no explanation as to where the diaries had been kept for more than thirty years. And, most crucial of all, Times Newspapers had not carried out any checks of its own – apart from sending the historian Hugh Trevor-Roper (Lord Dacre), a Times director, for a brief look at the diaries in their Zürich bank vault. Instead we had taken everything another publishing organisation had told us on trust.

I delivered the memorandum to the editor that afternoon, not knowing that it was too late: Rupert Murdoch had already bought the diaries. And yet we might still have escaped unscathed. Giles had told me at our informal meeting in the toilet that I should not worry because the diaries would begin running in *The Times*, not the *Sunday Times*. I learnt now that the plan was for them to start in *The Times* on Monday 25 April. This would have given the *Sunday Times* five days to mount our own concentrated checking operation before we would have published anything the following Sunday and – as later events proved – twenty-four hours would have been sufficient for us to have destroyed the authenticity of the diaries.

But on Friday, I learnt that the plan had changed. I was at a lunch at the

Dorchester for the presentation of the U.K. Press Awards – Gitta Sereny and I had won the award of Colour Magazine Writer of the year – and we found ourselves at the same table as *The Times* editor, Charles Douglas-Home. Douglas-Home stunned us by saying that Murdoch had just altered the schedule. *Stern* had changed its regular publishing day from Thursday to Monday so as to prevent *Newsweek*, which had seen the diaries, from scooping them, so Murdoch had decided that Sunday 24 April would be the perfect day to break the story.

I left the lunch as soon as possible and hurried back to the *Sunday Times* to check that this was true. Linklater confirmed it. Giles had called him to his office that morning and had told him to prepare a story on how the diaries had been discovered and to decide which extracts to use and how best to present them. Linklater had protested. He needed time to allow *Sunday Times* journalists to make their own independent checks. Had Giles not read Knightley's memorandum?

'I know, I know,' Linklater reported Giles as saying. 'But I don't want to hear about all that. The deal's been signed and we're going to have to do it.'

'We've still got today and tomorrow,' I told Linklater. 'Maybe we can do something. Where are the diaries?'

'*Stern* won't give them to us,' Linklater said. 'We'll have a few photostats later today. But they won't hand over the actual diaries until next week, and maybe not all of them even then.' I said it was impossible to do proper checks without at least one of the diaries. The whole thing was beginning to run with a momentum of its own, out of control.

'There's one thing you can do,' Linklater said. '*The Times* is running an article by Trevor-Roper tomorrow saying that the diaries are genuine. Why don't you talk to him?' I rang him immediately. He told me later that he was getting ready for a visit to the opera and that what I had to say spoiled his evening for him. I began by asking him what had convinced him that the diaries were genuine.

'The one thing that impressed me most,' he said, 'was the sheer volume of the material. I asked myself whether it all could have been constructed out of the imagination and incidental sources. I decided that it could not.'

I said, 'But those two old ladies in Milan did eighteen volumes of the Mussolini diaries.'

'The Mussolini diaries? Remind me again what happened with those.'

I gave him a quick summary.

'But I know Hitler's handwriting. I know his signature. I know the changes in it between 1908 and his death. It seemed to me that an operation of forgery on that scale was heroic and unnecessary. And don't forget we're dealing with a very reputable magazine, one of the wealthiest and most widely read in Europe. The directors of *Stem*, one must assume, do not engage in forgery.'

I had recorded the call so that I could better absorb what was said. After hanging up I played it through twice. I had to admit that Trevor-Roper had gone a long way towards convincing me that my worries were groundless. He had examined the diaries; I had not. He had an idea of their content; I did not. He had met and spoken with the *Stem* people; I had not. I decided that it was inconceivable that Trevor-Roper could be so emphatic about the diaries' authenticity without good cause.

At an editorial meeting later that afternoon I got to read translations of some of the diary extracts. I found them interesting but not exactly sensational – Hitler had allowed the British army to escape at Dunkirk; Hitler knew of Hess's flight to Britain. I was wondering whether the rest of the material was going to be any better when my telephone rang. It was Murdoch's secretary: would I come over to his office in *The Times* building to see him? Gitta Sereny was waiting outside Murdoch's office when I arrived and we went in together. Murdoch was in an ebullient mood. He spent a few minutes asking about my Australian trip and chatting about Australian politics. Then he got down to business.

'So which bits of the diaries are you going to run on Sunday?' he said.

Gitta Sereny said we thought we would start with Dunkirk because that would interest British readers. Then we would jump ahead and do the Hess material, then flash back to Hitler's opinion of Chamberlain.

'Hang on a minute,' Murdoch said. 'All this in the first part?'

'Yes,' I said. 'Hit the reader with all of the best bits at once.'

'Jesus,' Murdoch said. 'You're being pretty free with my money, aren't you?'

That would have been the moment for me to have said, 'Rupert, I hope you haven't wasted it. I presume you've read my memo about what happened with the Mussolini diaries.' But I kept quiet. The atmosphere was one of such enthusiasm, and Murdoch exuded an air of such boyish fun at the thought that in thirty-six hours his newspaper would be scooping the world, that it was hard not to get carried along with it all.

So I turned up for work on Saturday and threw myself into my part in preparing the diaries for publication. Even now, with the *Sunday Times* deadline only ten hours away, *Stem* continued to be difficult. They were getting ready for publication the day after us but would not let us talk directly to Gerd Heidemann (possibly because Heidemann might well have blabbed about his next project – an interview with 'my good friend Martin Bormann') and they still would not let us have free access to the diaries themselves. Antony Terry, the *Sunday Times* correspondent in Germany had to winkle extracts out of *Stern* piecemeal, translate them, and then telex them to London. As we read them not only did my unease return but Linklater and Paul Eddy, the Insight editor, actually considered – admittedly not for long – refusing to handle them and then resigning. Would Hitler, a man with a serious, brilliant mind, have sat down after the July 1944 bomb plot on his life and written in his diary: 'Ha, ha, isn't it laughable. This scum, these loafers and good-for-nothings. These people were bunglers'? Linklater tried to put his fears at rest by telephoning Trevor-Roper in Oxford. 'I wanted to hear from the mouth of the expert himself that the diaries were genuine. He said he was 95 per cent certain that they were.'

So Linklater asked me to write an article setting out the reasons for the diaries' authenticity and their importance to history, 'a sort of why you should read them, why you should believe them, and what difference they are going to make to our attitudes to the period'. I agreed to do it as long as my name was not attached to it; it was to appear without a by-line. I wrote it and gave it to Linklater. An hour later he came back to me. 'Frank says this is going to look odd without the name of the writer. The reader is going to say to himself, "This guy's telling me I should believe these diaries but he doesn't believe enough in them himself to put his name to the article." Frank wants to put your by-line to it.'

I stalled. I went off to see John Whale, the *Sunday Times* religious affairs correspondent and a great moral force on the paper and asked him what I should do. John said, 'It seems to me that you've written this in an objective manner and that you've covered yourself if the diaries turn out to be fakes. I think it is okay to put your name to it.' So I did. My mistake was the first sentence which returned to haunt me. I wrote: 'Hitler's diaries have been submitted to the most rigorous tests to establish their authenticity.' I would have liked to have been able to write, 'The *Sunday Times* has submitted the Hitler diaries to the most rigorous tests . . .' Instead I had to take *Stern*'s word and *Stern*'s word turned out to be worthless.

Given that few of us had our hearts entirely in the work, the *Sunday Times* did a professional job in presenting the diaries. The front page had a picture of Gerd Heidemann holding the diaries, superimposed on an enormous close-up of Hitler. The story of the finding of the diaries ran over on to page two, with further articles on pages sixteen, seventeen and eighteen. There were photographs of Hitler, Eva Braun, Goebbels, Himmler and Bormann, and extracts from the diaries themselves. The whole thing was headed with the words 'WORLD EXCLUSIVE'. It was a masterpiece of display. The deputy editor, Brian MacArthur, held up the page proofs and showed them to the newsroom. 'Look at that,' he said. 'You'll never see another front page like that as long as you live.'

A little after 7pm I wandered into the editor's office for the customary glass of wine while we waited for copies of the first edition. The others were already there, discussing with Giles what we should do the following week. The feeling was that part of our coverage should be devoted to rebutting all the attacks on the diaries' authenticity and that the best person to do this would be Hugh Trevor-Roper (Lord Dacre) himself. Giles promptly rang him. We could hear only Giles's side of the conversation and since it was routine none of us was paying much attention. Suddenly a marked change in Giles's tone of voice made the whole office fall silent. 'Well, naturally, Hugh, one has doubts. There are no certainties in this life. But I take it that these doubts aren't strong enough to make you do a complete one hundred and eighty degree turn on that? Oh. Oh. I see. You *are* doing a one hundred and eighty degree turn . . .'

I slid down in my chair until my head rested on the back. Linklater put his head between his knees and kept it there. MacArthur, who had been standing, steadied himself against a door jamb. Giles hung up and stared at the ceiling. Then he recovered. 'Well, Hugh's changed his mind. What are we going to do?' We discussed it for fifteen minutes. We could stop the presses and remake the paper, rewriting everything so as to avoid committing ourselves to the diaries' authenticity. For example, the centre-spread headline 'HITLER'S SECRET DIARIES' could become 'ARE THESE HITLER'S SECRET DIARIES?' Normally, the editor could remake the paper as he pleased. It was unusual to stop the presses, but he could do that, too, if he wanted, without any need to consult the proprietor. But this was Murdoch's own story. He had chased it, fought for it, outmanoeuvred the *Stern* people to get his hands on it and paid a lot of money for it. When Murdoch rang later in the evening, as he usually did, Giles could hardly say, 'Oh, by the way Rupert, we decided not to run your Hitler story.'

So while Giles got Trevor-Roper back on the telephone, just to make certain he had not misunderstood him, and then to insist that he should not yet publicly announce his change of mind but save his reasons for the *Sunday Times*, MacArthur volunteered to ring Murdoch to tell him what had happened. He did it from the office of the editor's secretary and came back looking surprised. 'I told him about Dacre,' he said. 'He's not worried. He doesn't want to remake the paper. He just said, "Fuck Dacre." So there we are.'

Only much later did I learn what had happened with Trevor-Roper between our telephone conversation on Friday, his talk with Linklater on Saturday morning, and his about-turn on Saturday night. He and I had a quiet dinner in Rules to talk about it and he said his mistake had been to sign the document of confidentiality which *Stern* had thrust at him in the bank vault in Zürich. 'It deprived me of that most essential facility every academic cherishes – the freedom to consult his colleagues. I could speak to no one who had not also signed the confidentiality document. I would dearly have loved to have consulted some German colleagues, particularly Eberhard Jaeckel, but I felt that to do so would break the agreement I had signed. I had to make the decision on my own.'

Trevor-Roper said that his conversation with me on the Friday had disconcerted him, particularly my reference to the large number of forged Mussolini diaries. Maybe a forger would not be content with six Hitler diaries and *would* forge nearly sixty. This set him to thinking about points he had previously dismissed, others which were 'just too neat' and his generally poor impression of Heidemann. If *Stern* could employ a man like Heidemann, was it to be trusted? By the end of the opera his confidence in the authenticity of the diaries was beginning to unravel.

Some time on Saturday morning – he could not remember exactly when (but logic would suggest after his conversation with Linklater) Trevor-Roper rang Charles Douglas-Home. 'He was the person who'd employed me,' Trevor-Roper explained. 'Apart from your call, I'd had no dealings with the *Sunday Times*.' He told Douglas-Home that he now had very serious doubts about the diaries and regretted that Times Newspapers had ever done the deal with *Stern*.

In his book *Selling Hitler* the author Robert Harris offers the following explanation as to why Trevor-Roper's change of mind did not reach the *Sunday Times* until Giles telephoned him after the paper had gone to press. 'A fatal breakdown in communication now occurred. Douglas-Home believed that Trevor-Roper's doubts were relatively minor; if they were serious, he assumed the historian would pass them on to the *Sunday Times*. But Trevor-Roper was relying on Douglas-Home to spread the word of his unease around Gray's Inn Road. He did not think of calling them direct . . . He sat at home in Cambridge and waited for Knightley or Giles to ring him.'

But there was more to it than this. Few outsiders appreciated the chasm that existed between *The Times* and the *Sunday Times*. The two newspapers may have been joined by a bridge that crossed Coley Street but as far as the *Sunday Times* was concerned, *The Times* might just as well have been back at Printing House Square, Blackfriars. There was no editorial collaboration, little socialising, no sense of sister papers shoulder-to-shoulder against the rest of Fleet Street. *The Times* regarded *Sunday Times* reporters as vulgar, self-promoting and ostentatious. The *Sunday Times* considered *The Times* journalists as elitist, insular and ineffective. Worse, the *Sunday Times* blamed *The Times* editorial chapel for the departure of Thomson – and thus for the arrival of Murdoch. They argued that *The Times*'s demand for a 22 per cent wage increase when the papers resumed publishing in 1980 after a one-year shutdown – during which all journalists were paid a full salary – broke Kenneth Thomson's will to continue publishing the papers. The respect of both editorial staffs for the editor-in-chief, Denis Hamilton, had maintained an uneasy truce between the two papers but now Hamilton had gone.

This does not mean that Douglas-Home said to himself after receiving Trevor-Roper's sensational telephone call, 'Let's see how the *Sunday Times* copes with this one.' He just would not have considered it his duty to ring Giles and pass on the warning. *The Times* was *The Times* and the *Sunday Times* was another newspaper, and what it was planning to publish on Sunday was none of his business. Linklater, who was at Eton with Douglas-Home, did not blame him for failing to warn us. But I never forgave him.

On the Tuesday after publication, an interval filled with attacks and abuse over the diaries, the *Sunday Times* editorial chapel called a special meeting to consider its attitude. The newsroom, which had had nothing to do with the story, proposed a motion attacking the editor (who had declined to address the meeting) and the management of the paper for publishing the diaries, and dissociating the chapel from the whole affair. There were angry speeches, some reporters arguing that even if the diaries were genuine, the *Sunday Times* should have nothing to do with publishing them; to do so would be an insult to the millions who had died as a result of Hitler's policies.

Linklater spoke against the motion saying that if the diaries were genuine then the *Sunday Times* had a duty to publish them; they would aid our understanding of an important period in history. I suggested that we should not rush to a decision until the authenticity of the diaries was decided. We were pressing *Stern* to allow us to see the diaries. As soon as they agreed we would carry out our own checks and resolve the matter one way or the other. Why not delay passing any motion until then? The chapel narrowly agreed.

Stern was too busy defending itself that week even to consider giving the *Sunday Times* access to the diaries, so we were forced to go to press on Sunday knowing little more than we had the previous week. We switched the emphasis to the controversy over the diaries with a muted front page story:

> Hitler's Diaries – the trail from the hayloft
> *Stern* challenges David Irving
> 'No shred of doubt,' says Heidemann

It was not until the following Friday that *Stern* agreed to lend us two volumes of the diaries. A courier flew in from Hamburg and took them straight to Murdoch's office. Linklater borrowed one and gave it to me. It looked like any book-keeper's journal, about A4 size, with stiff black covers. If Hitler had handled this, then none of his mystique was communicated to me. I shoved it into a large envelope, took a taxi to the City offices of Hehner and Cox and there asked Dr Julius Grant, a forensic scientist, to submit it to whatever tests he felt were necessary to determine when it had been written.

'We'll start with the paper,' he said. 'That's the easiest.'

He took an ordinary sewing needle and gently teased from the bottom of one of the pages a thread of paper so tiny it was impossible to detect any damage to the page. He handed the diary back to me. 'That's all I need for the moment,' he said. 'Come back in a couple of hours and I'll be able to tell you the result.'

When I returned Dr Grant was smiling. 'This diary is definitely a forgery,' he said. He explained that most commercial paper is a mixture of recycled paper and new. New paper is a pristine white but recycled paper tends to be grey. To make the mixed paper as white as possible, manufacturers use a bleaching agent and the presence of this agent can be detected by various scientific tests. Dr Grant said that he had positively identified the presence of the whitening agent.

'How does that prove the diary is a forgery?' I said.

'Because the whitening agent was not invented until 1953 and Hitler, I think we agree, died in 1945. This paper was manufactured at least eight years after his death.'

When I got back to the office I learnt that *Stern* had finally got around to commissioning a similar test and had got the same result. And since we now had two diaries in our possession we had arranged for Professor Norman Stone, one of Hitler's most recent biographers and one of the few German scholars in Britain who could read the Old German script in which the diaries were written, to come into the *Sunday Times* and look at them. He sat in my office the rest of Friday and all day Saturday, reading avidly and chuckling from time to time.

'Listen to this entry,' he said. 'It's for 30th January 1933, the day Hitler came to power. "We must at once proceed to build up as fast as possible the power we have won. I must at once proceed to the dissolution of the Reichstag, and so I can build up my power. We will not give up our power, let there come what may." Does that sound like Hitler to you? It's almost illiterate, like a Charlie Chaplin Hitler.'

So late on Saturday evening – we had put off the moment as long as possible – we gathered in Brian MacArthur's office to work on the paper's apology to its readers for having been fooled. MacArthur was acting editor, Giles having gone on holiday, and he carried responsibility for the statement, but we all worked on it. The first sentence was my suggestion:

> Serious journalism is a high risk enterprise . . . When major but hazardous stories seem to be appearing, a newspaper can either dismiss them without inquiry, or pursue investigations to see if they are true. No one would dispute that the emergence of authentic diaries written by Adolf Hitler would be an event of public interest and historic importance. Our mistake was to rely on other people's evidence.

The statement was widely attacked as 'a remarkable piece of self-justification masquerading as an apology'. Robert Harris wrote, 'The Hitler diaries affair was not an example of "serious journalism", but of cheque-book journalism, pure and simple.' The *New York Times* asked, 'What has happened to the *Sunday Times*? Rupert Murdoch has, for one thing, with his talent for turning what he touches into dross.' The then *Village Voice* columnist, Alex Cockburn, had this to say about me:

> I found it especially delightful that it should have been Phillip Knightley who was detailed to write up the wonders of the Hitler diaries . . . This Knightley wrote *The First Casualty*, a book about war reporting which waxed high and mighty in moral tone about left journalists of the 1930s, including my own dear father [Claud Cockburn]. Knightley let it be known that he had a low view of those who allowed political principle to get in the way of observation of reality and proper deference to the British empirical tradition. It seems that Knightley now has some explaining to do. He was given the assignment of hyping the Hitler diaries at short notice and he performed nobly in the service of Murdoch. Friends now let it be known that he cherished doubts. He has the choice. If he cherished no doubts he was a cretin. If he did cherish doubts, he was a whore –

or so at least it would appear on the basis of the ethical principles outlined in *The First Casualty*.

I replied that I had written the story about the diaries based on information provided by *Stern* magazine which I believed to be true. It had turned out not to be. Cretin? No. Whore? No. Too trusting of colleagues? Yes. My criticism of Alex's journalist father was that he deliberately invented stories (i.e. wrote lies) to further a political aim, a different matter altogether.

It was difficult to respond to all the criticism at the time because everyone at the newspaper was anxious to forget about Hitler and the diaries and move on.

But serious journalism *is* a high-risk enterprise. Harold Evans was worried if a Monday passed without the *Sunday Times* receiving a writ from someone – he felt that the paper could not have been doing its job the previous week. In its day the *Sunday Times* made some powerful enemies, ones with resources at their disposal far greater than those available to the newspaper – Distillers, the Vestey family, McDonnell Douglas. The risk in each case was that we might have made a mistake and would be punished for it.

Next, there is nothing wrong with cheque book journalism – you just have to be discriminating about what you are paying for. The *Sunday Times* could never have revealed the thalidomide scandal had it not written cheques to two sources of information. Information is a valuable commodity, many people who have that information realise its worth and want to be paid for it. If there is no other way of obtaining it, what is wrong with doing so? Other businesses do it all the time, so why should editors be ashamed and defensive when such payments become necessary in the newspaper industry?

But then the Hitler diaries affair was not cheque book journalism, anyway. It was a publishing deal, one publishing house, Gruner and Jahr, *Stern*'s parent company, selling the foreign language rights in a property it owned to another publishing house, News International. It happens all the time. Most of the blame for the Hitler diaries affair was heaped on Murdoch. But as a proprietor of a publishing empire, what did he do that was wrong? He bought the English language rights to what the owners of another publishing empire assured him was a genuine publishing scoop. He cleverly forced the German vendors to lower the price. He wisely included a clause in the contract that obliged the Germans, when the diaries turned out to be false, to refund every dollar he had paid.

True, he rushed to publication before his own journalists had had a proper chance to check the diaries for themselves, but the publication schedule was forced upon him by *Stern* and he had no control over *Stern*'s timetable. True, he did not stop the presses when his one expert revised his position. But he had to weigh the vacillating opinion of Trevor-Roper, for whom he had little time anyway, against the legal assurances and teutonic efficiency of the entire Gruner and Jahr empire.

The failure was journalism's, not Murdoch's. It began with the German journalists. Heidemann had been employed by *Stern* for twenty-eight years. He was a researcher rather than a journalist and was incapable of writing a report himself. He ran in neo-Nazi circles, had had an affair with Goering's daughter, called the war criminal Klaus Barbie his friend, gave parties for leading ex-Nazis, and collected Nazi and other military memorabilia – he boasted of having Idi Amin's underpants. Although he was in debt to *Stern* for a year's salary, he was seldom in the office and no one knew from week to week where he was. He was fond of going on expensive foreign jaunts that produced no editorial copy but no one ever brought him to book for wasting the firm's cash. When he persuaded *Stern*'s management to embark on the Hitler diaries project and lay out nearly a million pounds, no one thought it necessary to tell the editors. Secrecy and deceit seemed to be an integral part of *Stern*. What sort of a magazine was this?

But was Times Newspapers that much better? The lack of co-ordination between *The Times* and the *Sunday Times* allowed each editorial department to offload responsibility for the diaries' authenticity on to the other. Frank Giles knew nothing of his paper's earlier negotiations with David Irving over the diaries or of Gitta Sereny's trip to Hamburg to see Heidemann. 'This may seem to the outside reader, and with good reason, a pretty weird way to run a newspaper or any other sort of office,' Giles wrote later. '[But] one of the more questionable practices to have grown up over the years in the *Sunday Times* was for important departments to have become quasi-autonomous empires of their own. This was especially true of the Features Department with whom Irving made contact.'

So, without Denis Hamilton as editor-in-chief, there was no one who knew the whole picture, no combined editorial control, no one to urge caution on Murdoch, no one who could have ordered a joint *Times/Sunday Times* assault on the diaries' authenticity which, as events proved, would have crumbled within twenty-four hours.

The forger, Konrad Kujau, may have been an uncultured petty criminal – his most successful earlier forgeries had been luncheon vouchers – but, perhaps only unconsciously, he hit upon the nerve end that excites all journalists. Kujau had a whole archive of Hitler material – papers, notes, orders, letters – some of which was genuine. But it was when he spoke of 'diaries' that his newspaper contact, Heidemann, became so excited. This is because the word 'diaries' implies something written regularly, probably daily, and confessional in nature, just the stuff on which journalists thrive.

So Hitler's diaries will not be the last of this sort of journalism. In 1994 we had the diaries of Jack the Ripper – fake, of course. What next? Martin Bormann's? Elvis Presley's? The one certainty is that there will always be a newspaper with no memory of the past ready to buy and serialise them.

CHAPTER TEN

THE THALIDOMIDE SCANDAL: WHERE WE WENT WRONG

In journalism schools and media courses they use the thalidomide scandal as an example of campaigning journalism at its finest – fearless journalists take on a huge corporation which is behaving badly towards child victims of the corporation's horror drug and after a long, bitter battle win for them decent compensation. But, in truth, that is too simple and the reality much more ambivalent. It has taken me twenty years to face up to fact that the *Sunday Times* thalidomide campaign was not the great success it was made out to be and that the full story is as much about the failures of journalism as its triumphs. It is hard for me to write this because the thalidomide campaign was one of the high points of my career and that of many others – there has been nothing to equal it since and it is still with us. We remain involved with the thalidomide victims, their parents and the professionals who were caught up in the tragedy. But when some of us get together and look back at the fight on behalf of the children we end up discussing two crucial questions: Did we do it right? Would it have been better to have kept out of the whole affair?

Thalidomide had been discovered by accident in 1954 by a small German company called Chemie Grunenthal and appeared to be a dream sedative. It had none of the drawbacks of barbiturates, then the fashionable drug, and best of all, it was impossible to take an overdose – an important marketing point in those suicide-by-overdose Fifties. Anxious to capitalise on their discovery, Grunenthal had sold the drug all over the world, aggressively promoting it as an anti-morning sickness pill for pregnant women and emphasising its absolute safety – it would harm neither the mother nor the child in the womb.

The latter guarantee turned out to be wrong. Thalidomide crossed the placental barrier and with devilish precision sabotaged the developing limb buds of the foetus, so that children were born with hands emerging direct from their shoulders, and feet emerging direct from their hips and, in a few horrific cases, with both abnormalities. It was eventually withdrawn in 1961 after an Australian obstetrician, Dr William McBride, made the link. But it was too late to prevent a major disaster and some 8,000 babies around the world were born with thalidomide deformities. No one was prepared and few could cope. In Britain, where the drug was marketed by the giant liquor company Distillers, some hospitals kept the baby from its parents, then sent it home swaddled in baby clothes for the mother to discover there what her child looked like; some fathers took one look at their offspring and walked out of the hospital and out of the marriage. Freddie Astbury's father remembers the doctors telling him – but not his wife – that Freddie had no head and would not live more than a couple of days. Then a little later they gave him the good and the bad news: we've found your son's head, but he has no legs. Then came the final version: Freddie has a head but no arms and no legs.

Even the specialists found this type of deformity hard to handle. Dr Gerard Vaughan, in charge of the Children's Unit at Guy's Hospital, London, remembers, 'I have never seen such a reaction among my staff as when they were faced with the thalidomide children. They were horrified. I had great difficulty in getting them to carry out a psychological test or examination. They were repelled in a way I have only witnessed on the faces of people going into a major burns unit for the first time. And these were doctors and nurses.' But they felt under pressure from some community conscience to put the tragedy right and many of the thalidomide children underwent operation after operation to try to make them look as normal as possible. Vaughan says, 'It was a kind of collusion between doctors and parents to expiate their guilt.' Other children needed surgery just to survive. Patrick Pope, who had major internal abnormalities, was operated on forty-two times. 'My son keeps asking me, "Mummy, please don't let me have any more operations," ' his mother, Julia Pope, wrote in a letter to the *Sunday Times* in 1973.

This was a terrible tragedy, but governments declared that since the testing and marketing of the drug had met all the legal requirements of the time, what had happened was not their responsibility. Road deaths, air crashes, major fires and other disasters are all customarily followed by searching public inquiries, but the biggest drug disaster of its kind was left to the law. Civil legal actions were instituted by the parents of the damaged children and vigorously contested by Chemie Grunenthal and Distillers. But far from opening up the whole matter to public scrutiny, these legal actions – except in the United States – closed everything down. No newspaper felt it could examine the thalidomide tragedy without pre-judging the outcome of any eventual trial and in most countries this was a serious legal offence: contempt of court, punishable by imprisonment. So, in a terrible failure of journalism, newspapers carried stories on the lines of 'Look how well these plucky children are getting on,' while the truth was that the thalidomide children and their desperate parents were suffering agonies in a silence imposed upon them by the system.

The drug's makers felt no such inhibitions. In July 1962 *The Times* and the *Guardian* carried on the same day remarkably similar stories that were basically a comprehensive exoneration of Distillers. *The Times* headline said 'Thalidomide Tests Showed No Sign of Danger'. The *Guardian* story began, 'Neither the British manufacturers of the drug thalidomide nor the doctors who prescribed it for expectant mothers who gave birth to deformed babies were in any way to blame for the present epidemic of congenital abnormalities.' The source for both stories turned out to be Distillers itself. The *Guardian* journalist, Dr Alfred Byrne, was at least frank with his readers and stated openly that he had reached his conclusions 'after inspecting the files of the makers' and interrogating their medical advisers for several hours.

The origins of *The Times*'s article were more difficult to locate but I finally tracked down the journalist who wrote it to his house in Hampstead. He was called Duncan Burn and he was not, as you would suppose, the paper's medical correspondent, but its industrial one. He said that he wrote the article because his speciality was innovation, and innovation was involved in the risk in launching new products. He too said he had had access to the files of Distillers and had spoken 'frankly and openly' with its executives and medical men. Burn left *The Times* the day before his article appeared, took a job as adviser to the Central Electricity Generating Board and then, some years later, went to work for . . . Distillers.

So what was going on behind the scenes? The lawyers acting for the British families who had sued Distillers, believing that they had a weak case, reached a settlement with the company in 1968/69 – the company would pay 40 per cent of what it would have paid if the children had been able to win a negligence action in court. When it came to a test case to decide how much would represent the 100 per cent, the judge rejected evidence from John Prevett, an actuary with the London firm of Bacon and Woodrow, and even refused to allow for inflation . . . because the government had promised to control it! This so outraged Prevett that he wrote two articles in the *Modern Law Review* attacking the court's decision and pointing out that even the full 100 per cent award for the armless and legless boy in the test case would not have been enough because the money would run out when he was twenty-seven – and he was receiving only 40 per cent of that. All this emerged in open court and routine court reporting should have been sufficient to expose the disaster. But Fleet Street treated the awards like a pools win. True, the *Sunday Times* ran a leader page article under the headline 'What Price a Pound of Flesh?' but as the editor, Harry Evans, later admitted, 'It was inadequate in the light of the Prevett memorandum: the thalidomide story concerns some shortcomings in journalism as well as a legal débâcle.'

When the *Sunday Times* campaign on behalf of the thalidomide children eventually got under way in 1972 it had two main themes – that the level of damages settled in 1968/9 was immorally low irrespective of whether Distillers was 100 per cent liable, and since the children would get only 40 per cent then the damages were laughably inadequate. And secondly, that the claim by Distillers that they had followed the best practices of the time because no one then tested drugs on pregnant animals was simply untrue – other drug companies did. But we could have discovered all this four years earlier in 1968. Prevett's articles in the *Modern Law Review* were basically what he had said in the witness box and the reason he had written them was that no journalist would listen to him. All the scientific material to rebut Distillers' defence was available to anyone who had the inclination and time to find it. How could the thalidomide children's case have gone steadily down the drain during those years without our noticing it? When the *Sunday Times* team looked back after the campaign was over, the team leader, Bruce Page, warned that we had no right to feel triumphant. He asked, 'What excuses can we offer for having totally missed the whole bloody thing till it was practically too late? I'm not too happy with my own: they go along the lines of saying that I was in America in 1968, largely concerned with Robert Maxwell in 1969, Bernie Cornfeld and the IOS scandal in 1970, and Ulster in 1971. I hope this will do, but it's nothing to brag about. We were, after all, demanding very high standards for other kinds of human organisations. Why should ours be any lower?' Then, half in jest, he said any book we wrote on the campaign should be called, 'How the *Sunday Times* Gradually Recovered From Its Own Mistakes and Did Something about the Thalidomide Scandal – Just in Time'. It wasn't, of course – it was called *Suffer the Children*. But Page, as always, had a point.

I suppose that at the back of all our minds was the inconvenient fact that we had come to the thalidomide scandal via what critics of the press call 'cheque book journalism', the buying of information. Critics argue that buying stories encourages the informant to say anything in order to get the money. But some information can only be had for cash – you have to approach each case on its merits. Evans rightly considered the thalidomide scandal so important that to get the information we needed he wrote out not just one cheque but two. One was for Henning Sjöström, a leading Stockholm lawyer who had approached the paper in 1967 with an offer we could not refuse. Sjöström was representing the hundred and five Swedish thalidomide children in their case against the drug's distributors in Sweden, Astra. A criminal prosecution had been launched in Germany against executives of Chemie Grunenthal on charges that included the German equivalent of manslaughter, causing grievous bodily harm, and selling drugs by misleading statements. Sjöström had gained access to the documents that the German authorities had seized from the Chemie Grunenthal when mounting this case. No German newspaper could publish what Sjöström had gleaned from these papers because of the contempt of court rule. But a German court's jurisdiction did not extend abroad, so there was nothing to stop a foreign newspaper from doing so. To make any impact, it would need to be a big newspaper and preferably one in a country that had a large number of thalidomide children itself. The answer, Sjöström decided, was the *Sunday Times* of London.

Sjöström's proposition was not as simple as it looked because he wanted to be paid for the documents – his agent proposed £2,500. The *Sunday Times* had to weigh the propriety of paying for information it would use to break the laws of a friendly country against the public interest in knowing the truth about a major medical, commercial and legal scandal. The difficulty of the decision was reflected in the fact that although Harold Evans eventually decided to pay, he was defensive about it. But first he had to have an idea of what he would be getting for his money, so I went off to Stockholm to join up with the *Sunday Times* German correspondent, Antony Terry. We would size up Sjöström, Terry would translate a selection of the German documents, and we would plan an article which Evans would run either on the eve of the German trial, or immediately if the trial were to be abandoned.

Antony Terry was a legend in Fleet Street. He had learnt German in a POW camp and had later been with British military intelligence in Occupied Germany. He had covered hot spots all over the world for two foreign editors and two proprietors: Ian Fleming and Lord Kemsley and then Frank Giles and Lord Thomson. 'The secret of survival in dangerous situations,' he would say on the rare occasions you could persuade him to talk about his past, 'is never to pretend to be anything other than you are.' So Terry had gone off to wars and risky assignments in Africa and South America dressed as what he undoubtedly was – an English gentleman.

Younger correspondents might wear battle fatigues; Terry wore a dark suit, a bowler hat, and an English rose in his lapel.

We learnt enough in Stockholm for Evans to decide to go ahead with the Sjöström deal and Terry brought the Grunenthal documents to London in three suitcases. The next step was daunting – to translate them all. Bruce Page set up a little unit in one of the many spare rooms in the old part of Thomson house, moved the Grunenthal files into it, engaged a German translator, and arranged for a researcher and a floating staff of two or three journalists to process the material. The translator did a literal translation of each Grunenthal document and passed it to a journalist who made a decision on its relevance and then summed it up in a sentence or two. The journalists handed their summaries to the researcher who filed them along with the original document and the translation, and then cross-indexed them with a card system she had started. You could follow the development of thalidomide at Chemie Grunenthal week by week in the chronological index, or, say, through the eyes of the managing director or the chief chemist under their names. It took nearly a year of painstaking, time-consuming work. But that, rather than the dramatic, television-style confrontation, is the real basis of investigative journalism.

The journalists were dragged off for other, more urgent assignments; there were periods when only the translator and the researcher were in the 'thalidomide room'; there were doubts about the value of such expensive, long-term projects. Yet by the end of it everyone working on the story had mastered the history of this dreadful drug and probably knew more about its development than individual Grunenthal executives – Page could more than hold his own with experienced pharmacologists when discussing thalidomide's scientific aspects.

In January 1968 I took the boxes of cards that made up the Grunenthal index out of the thalidomide room and transferred them to my house. There, away from the distractions and gossip of the office, I began to write the narrative. The problem was the plethora of material. Newspaper readers sometimes wonder why some facet of a story has been ignored, why the journalist has not considered all the alternative explanations for what has occurred. The answer is that journalists write to length. A book ends when the author has said all he wants to say. An academic paper ends when the point has been made. Except in rare circumstances, the length of an article written by a journalist is determined by the amount of white space left on a particular page or pages after the advertisements have been allocated. If that space will hold, say, 2,000 words, then that's it, that's what the journalist has to write and this inevitably means leaving things out.

Harold Evans had said that he was prepared to devote four pages to the thalidomide story – an exceptional amount of space. But four pages with display (headlines, photographs, diagrams) is still only about 10,000 words, the equivalent of a long chapter in a book. This is why it took me nearly three months to write a draft of the story, paring down the details without distorting events, discarding sections that, although interesting, drifted away from the mainstream. Then, because Insight was a team operation, its then editor, Godfrey Hodgson, took over and ran the draft through his typewriter adding the drive and drama to the story that, because I had now been so close to the project for so long, I had underplayed.

The *Sunday Times* published it on 19 May 1968, a week before the German trial. 'There has been nothing remotely comparable in Germany, in scale or emotional intensity, since Nuremberg,' the article said. Well, that might have been so in Germany, but in Britain the trial passed almost unnoticed. British newspapers consulted their lawyers and were warned that since the issues being decided in the German court impinged on those concerning the British thalidomide cases, it would be dangerous to publish anything except reports of what went in German courtroom. Even these were brief, and eventually the British press once again lost interest.

But four months earlier the *Sunday Times* had written out another cheque, this time to Dr Montagu Phillips, a consulting pharmacologist and chemical engineer. Phillips had been engaged by solicitors representing the British thalidomide families to act as their professional adviser, to look at the case and if necessary be the expert witness for them. As part of the British legal process called 'discovery', the children's solicitors had been able to obtain from Distillers all their files relating to thalidomide and had passed them to Phillips for evaluation. Outraged by what he read, Phillips had simmered away, waiting for his moment in court. But the years had passed and it began to look as if the case would never be heard and the issues never debated. So Phillips had gone to an acquaintance, John Fielding, a business reporter on the *Sunday Times*. He said he would let the *Sunday Times* see the 10,000 documents Distillers had been obliged to disclose and the newspaper could assess for itself what had caused the disaster. Phillips's genuine anger was one reason he had decided to do this, but money was another. He argued that he was a professional witness, we would need his help to intepret the files, and he wanted to be paid for it.

Harold Evans hesitated, again weighing the inevitable accusations of 'cheque book journalism' against the public interest in the telling of the story. Evans eventually offered Phillips £8,000 (then about $20,000) for sight of the Distillers documents and technical advice, a logical and defensible decision. Phillips accepted and the team that had handled the

German documents now began much the same process with the British ones. Again I took time off from the office and wrote a narrative of how thalidomide came to be marketed in Britain, some hundred and twenty pages that became known in legal circles as 'the draft article'.

It told an even more remarkable story than the German one. Who would have believed, for instance, that one of the reasons Distillers had become involved with thalidomide was the belief that the drug might eventually become an alternative to whisky? A director of Distillers had read in the *Sunday Times* of 10 June 1956 an article by Aldous Huxley in which he predicted the benefits the inhabitants of his Brave New World would enjoy from a new drug which, in his novel of that name in 1932, he had called 'Soma'. 'Will the pharmacologist be able to do better than the brewers and distillers?' Huxley asked, with what has turned out to be remarkable prescience. This question so excited the Distillers director that he dashed off a memorandum suggesting that the company should move quickly to realise Huxley's prediction. 'The ultimate target would be the production of the ideal tranquillising agent to replace alcohol among those people who would prefer to "transform their minds" by this alternative means.'

I worked on the article only intermittently because the continuing legal restraints offered little chance of early publication and it is hard to get excited about a story which might never appear. It was not until April 1971 that I could report to Page and Evans that I had a 12,000-word draft ready and had identified a number of people as candidates for interviews. The article sat in the *Sunday Times* office while the British legal processes ground slowly on. Then a West End art dealer, David Mason, the father of a thalidomide daughter, Louise, angered by the paltry compensation sums Distillers were continuing to offer and by their condition that, if even only one parent objected, then the offer would be withdrawn from all, became the touch-paper that ignited the *Sunday Times* campaign. He decided to go public. At first he did not know how to begin, but a friend of his was an acquaintance of the editor of the *Daily Mail*, David English, so Mason went there with his story.

The *Mail* printed three articles on Mason's theme that he was being legally blackmailed into accepting compensation he thought inadequate: 'My Fight For Justice, by the Father of Hearbreak Girl, Louise', said the headline on the first article. Then, abruptly, the articles stopped. Distillers' lawyers had complained to the Attorney-General that the articles constituted contempt of court. He agreed and warned the *Daily Mail*, and – to English's lasting regret – the paper ceased publication of the story. The rest of the media, which had interviewed Mason and confirmed his account, took fright and carried nothing. Even the BBC backed off. The television programme 'Twenty-Four Hours' thought it could get round the contempt problem by doing just a series of interviews with thalidomide parents. Distillers threatened action and the BBC cancelled the programme. When Mason went to court and won the right to refuse the proposed settlement, there was a brief flurry of headlines about that aspect alone, and then silence once more. I became convinced that my draft article would suffer a similar fate, and, not quite knowing what to do about it, I went to see Mason to lure him away from the *Mail* and get him on our side. In his book *Thalidomide, My Fight for Louise*, Mason tells how he was at first wary of me:

When Knightley sat down in the chair opposite mine, I said, 'Now, Mr Knightley, what can I do for you?' His reply I found disconcerting. He said, 'It's not so much what you can do for me, but what I can do for you. We've been watching your case with a good deal of interest, and I'm here to offer you the resources of the *Sunday Times*.' I said, 'Oh, that's very nice. Will you excuse me one moment.' I shot downstairs, grabbed my secretary's arm and said, 'For God's sake ring up the *Sunday Times* and ask if they've heard of a fellow called Phillip Knightley.' The offer made by the man in my office sounded just too good to be true. I was highly suspicious about my visitor. I went back to the office and humoured him until my secretary phoned and assured me Knightley was one of the *Sunday Times* Insight team, and that his office expected him to be at the gallery. Knightley had really done his homework on me. With other reporters I had had to start right at the beginning and lead them by hand. But this man seemed to have been following the path I had trodden step by step. When he left I felt cautiously elated.

In the background all this time, but about to play a major part, was the *Sunday Times* legal manager, James Evans. Evans was an old Kemsley man who had been persuaded by Denis Hamilton to become a full-time employee of the *Sunday Times* after Hamilton had decided that you could not run an investigative newspaper with part-time legal advice – the traditional 'night lawyer'. Most night lawyers developed a protective mind-set that inhibited good journalism. This was because they quickly discovered that a night lawyer who said, 'I'm afraid we can't publish this . . . too risky,' never got into any trouble, whereas one who said, 'This is risky but I think the chances of being sued are minimal,' and then turned out to be wrong was not going to last long. But a full-time legal manager would have a loyalty to the newspaper and would, hopefully, become involved in the journalistic process from the beginning.

James Evans turned out to be the ideal man and much of the success of the *Sunday Times* during its golden years was in part due to him. A handsome man with high rosy cheeks and a most unlawyer-like friendly manner, he was not only deeply interested in journalism and its problems but was constantly seeking new legal stratagems that would help journalists get their stories into their paper. He was there to be consulted as the story developed, to advise on what extra work might be needed to make it legally watertight and then to work through the writing with the journalist, fine-tuning phrases and sentences to lessen the libel risk, testing the journalist's sources and his proof, until finally he would say, 'We can't get rid of the risk altogether and he may sue but I don't think he'll go into the witness box.' He was right nine times out of ten. We had consulted him all along the way with the thalidomide story and he knew the legal minefield we were trying to cross but he could see no safe way through it.

I brought Mason into the *Sunday Times* and he met Page and Harold Evans. Then, just briefly, the project lost its momentum. We were still going to do the story, but it was not top of the news list. I thought Mason understood this, but as seen through his eyes, the *Sunday Times* was either slipping into the same state of procrastination that had marked the parents' legal case against Distillers or, like the *Daily Mail*, was being frightened off by Distillers and the Attorney-General. Mason is a shrewd man, with an art dealer's skill in reading people. He had learnt enough in his relationships with newspapers to know how to galvanise us back into action. He rang me at the *Sunday Times*. 'I've just heard that the *News of the World* is looking at the story,' he said. 'Apparently Rupert Murdoch is very interested in it.' He let me simmer on that for a few days and then rang me again. 'The *News of the World* is going to run a series,' he said. 'Rupert doesn't give a damn about the Attorney-General. It's due to start the Sunday after next. They want to interview me. What do you think?'

I knew Murdoch well enough to decide that Mason's story was believable. And indeed, later Murdoch was behind the thousands of posters that appeared around the country overnight – including on the doors, windows and railings of Distillers' elegant London headquarters in St James's Square – savagely attacking the company. The national press got copies of these posters with a press release saying that they were a private campaign aimed at hitting Distillers where it hurt – in its pockets. The release was not signed, gave no address or telephone number, and the posters did not give any indication of the printer, who could be prosecuted. Police ripped them down and began a search for the originator. They never found him, because Murdoch had gone to elaborate lengths to keep the operation secret. A senior *News of the World* executive, Graham King, organised it. He first resigned from the *News of the World* so that he would be acting as a private individual, and a few days after the posters appeared, stuck up at night by small groups of volunteers, he left for a convenient appointment in Australia. (He later returned to the *News of the World*.)

I told Mason to stall the *News of the World* and I went to see Harold Evans. I caught him outside his office talking to Denis Hamilton, so I brought them both up to date with what Mason said was happening. Evans was determined not to lose the story. 'I'm tempted to publish anyway,' he said. 'I'll go to jail. That's what I'll do. I'll go to jail. Bloody hell, it'd be worth it.' Hamilton shook his head. 'We can't have the editor of a serious newspaper breaking the law,' he said. 'If the law's bad, campaign to change it. But we can't break it.' He turned to me, 'Are you sure the *News of the World* is going to run the story?' I said I was not. I knew only what Mason had told me and it was possible that he was simply putting pressure on us to act, but if he were to be right, how would we feel after so much effort and money when the *News of the World* scooped us?

Evans decided that he would get James Evans to look again at the legal problems and if necessary take an outside opinion on what could be done. If Mason's information was correct, we had ten days. James Evans needed only three. The law of contempt prevented us from campaigning in the newspaper for a better settlement for the thalidomide children because we would have to discuss the merits of their case and this was the prerogative of the courts. It did not matter that there had been no substantive hearings and that nothing had happened for years. A writ had been issued, the case had not been settled, and as far as the law was concerned, it was an ongoing matter.

But Evans the lawyer had been struck by a remark made by Lady Hoare, who ran a charitable trust for thalidomide children. She said that the parents resented being made to feel that they were going cap in hand for charity 'rather than moral justice from the wealthy Distillers'. The words 'moral justice' gave James Evans an idea. Suppose the *Sunday Times* were to campaign for a better settlement for the children on purely *moral* grounds. We would not discuss the issues in the case, make no attempt to apportion blame, but simply say that these desperately disabled children *deserved* better compensation than Distillers had so far offered. 'Without in any way surrendering on negligence,' James Evans wrote in a draft leader for the editor, 'Distillers could and should think again.' With this as the basis of the campaign, we could go on endlessly about the wretched lives that the children were being forced to lead. True, this might be seen to be putting pressure on one party in a case to settle but it would be moral pressure and nothing to do with the merits of the matter. 'If the Attorney-General moves against us,' James Evans said, 'we'd have an arguable defence.'

James Evans's plan appealed to everyone. To sustain the campaign we would need as many human interest stories about thalidomide children as we could get, so reporters were sent up and down Britain to interview all the most desperate cases that we could find. Most of these reporters were women, the prevailing view in journalism then still being that a tragic human interest story needed a woman's touch. Marjorie Wallace, the leading human interest writer, quartered the United Kingdom, doggedly and courageously working her way through the alphabetical list of victims, staying where possible with the families, learning first-hand about their problems. She had reached the 'Ws' and reported to Bruce Page that she had found a child who could well be the worst afflicted in the country, Terry Wiles. Page asked me to accompany Wallace to write about Wiles. Since she was quite capable of doing it on her own, I suspect that he wanted me to meet a thalidomide child, perhaps to add fire to the draft article, to remind us all that at the end of the formula and the marketing ploys, a human being takes the drug and its consequences.

If so, he could not have chosen a better case. Few human beings could have been given a worse start in life than Terry. His mother had taken Distaval (the name under which thalidomide was marketed in Britain) when she was pregnant. Terry was born without any limbs at all, just a trunk and a head. One eye hung halfway down his cheek and had to be surgically removed. Then as if to torment him, Nature gave him a high IQ and an inquiring mind. Yet – and we came across other examples of this – Terry's tragedy had drawn from others a courage and compassion that make one proud of the human species. Terry's mother, thinking he would not survive, abandoned him at the East Anglian hospital where he had been confined. His father had long since gone, so Terry spent his first five years in an institution for severely handicapped children. There, one day, he was visited by Leonard Wiles, a 60-year-old van driver, who had been asked by one of Terry's aging relatives to be the boy's guardian. He began taking Terry to his home for visits and four years later Wiles and his wife, Hazel, a large, volatile woman eighteen years his junior, the sister of Terry's mother, legally adopted this armless, legless, half-blind little boy whose only obvious attraction was his bubbling good spirits and sense of humour.

Terry's affliction now revived in Leonard a long neglected engineering skill that enabled him not only to devise and build mechanical devices to make life easier for his adopted son, but helped him find a satisfaction in his own life that he had previously missed. 'Just looking at a child like Terry turns you into a kind of visionary,' he said. He designed many gadgets, but the most remarkable was his Supercar – a chair that, working on the principle of a fork-lift truck, could raise Terry from ground level until he stood six feet high and could talk to people face-to-face, transforming him from the fairy-tale frog into the prince.

I have to admit that I had deliberately avoided meeting a thalidomide child as, I suspected, had other reporters and even the editor. I had three young children of my own and I was not anxious to be reminded how lucky my wife and I had been. So my first encounter with the nine-year-old Terry was traumatic. Leonard Wiles drove Marjorie Wallace and me to the local village school where Terry was a pupil. We waited by the car while Leonard went into the classroom to collect him. Wallace and I were chatting when suddenly Leonard appeared carrying Terry in his hands like a damaged doll. He fumbled to open the car door, found he could not manage it, and simply thrust Terry at me saying, 'Hold him a minute.' I did my best. There were no armpits, so was around the chest the best place? But this meant that Terry's face was only inches from mine. Should I look at him? Should we talk? What should I say? I took the coward's way out and passed him to Wallace for whom, by now, thalidomide deformities were no surprise, and the two were quickly immersed in conversation.

By the end of the afternoon, after watching Terry eat his own supper with a mechanical spoon he manipulated to his mouth with his shoulder, and hearing his account of the detective stories he enjoyed writing, I was more at ease. But the idea of signing up for day-to-day life with him for an indeterminate number of years left me with two powerful emotions – admiration for the Wiles, and a conviction that anything the *Sunday Times* needed to do in order to bring the real face of thalidomide before the world and obtain for people like the Wiles the only thing that could ease their burden, money, was absolutely justified – so I bear my share of responsibility for the fact that it was money that later created so many problems for the thalidomide children.

When the paper published the opening shot in its campaign, the skill of the two Evans in their respective fields, Harold in journalism and James in law – was immediately apparent. The headline: 'Our Thalidomide Children: a Cause for National Shame' grew out of James Evans's draft leader, polished by Harold Evans. Harold wrote the 'our' – to try to make readers feel personally responsible for the state and fate of the children; the *national shame* was to make them blame the government. At the end of the article was a tactical smart-bomb aimed and primed by James. It read, 'In a future article the *Sunday Times* will trace how the tragedy occurred.' This put

Distillers on notice that we had learnt enough to reconstruct the history of thalidomide and were going to publish it. If they kept quiet this might go against them if they then moved after the event. If they tried to stop us before publication – prior restraint – the public would wonder what they were trying to suppress. And with these few little words James Evans had lifted any risk of Evans the editor going to jail – the paper had not *published* anything, only announced that at some future date it *intended* to do so – and had shifted the onus for testing the law of contempt on this issue from the *Sunday Times* to Distillers, or as it turned out, the Attorney-General.

At the urging of Distillers, the Attorney-General applied for an injunction to restrain the *Sunday Times* from publishing the draft article. He got it, we appealed, he appealed, we appealed again – and the lawyers loved us. The story of this mammoth legal battle through the British courts all the way to the House of Lords – where we lost – and then on to Europe has been told in detail elsewhere. Suffice to say here that it might have all ended with the House of Lords decision had Marjorie Wallace not gone to Ireland to look for thalidomide children there. Officially there were two victims in Ireland but Wallace suspected that there would be more, probably labelled an Act of God, hidden away and cared for in convents. She found more than ninety. During the search she met the renowned jurist Sean McBride, then a European Commissioner. McBride told Wallace that even if the *Sunday Times* had reached the end of the legal road in Britain, there was still Europe. She told Evans of McBride's view and five years later Evans, Wallace, Elaine Potter and I found ourselves in Strasbourg listening to the European Commission rule that when the British government banned the draft article it had violated our right of free speech protected under the European Convention of Human Rights. We presented this as a triumph, but it was a flawed one. We had fought valiantly for the right to publish an article that we knew all along we could never publish anyway.

During the early stages of our legal struggle with Distillers and the British government, the Attorney-General said he wanted Distillers to see the draft article. The *Sunday Times* sent it to the chairman of Distillers, Sir Alexander McDonald, emphasising that it was only a draft, and asked for his comments. Distillers complained to the Attorney-General that publication would be contempt, and this was the beginning of the legal battle that got all the publicity. But, in a completely separate action, Distillers moved to gag us another way. When the company's lawyers read the draft article they immediately realised that we had seen their internal documents. It did not take them long to work out that the documents had reached us via Dr Phillips and that we had probably paid for them. So they began an action both for their return and for a permanent injunction to prevent us from using any information the documents contained.

They had a winning case. The practice of discovery is an integral part of the British legal system designed to save the court's time: if each side has read the other's documentation before the hearing begins, surprises and delays are less likely in the courtroom. But the system depends on each side knowing that its documentation will remain confidential within the court process and each set of lawyers pledges such confidentiality. Distillers argued that the lawyers for the thalidomide children were bound to respect the confidentiality of their disclosure of the company documents and that when the children's lawyers engaged the services of a professional adviser, Dr Phillips, then the obligation of confidentiality automatically passed to him. He had no right, Distillers argued, to pass copies of the documents to the *Sunday Times* and, since we were planning to publish them, the courts had a duty to restrain us so as to protect the whole discovery process.

We had only one defence. An exception to the confidentiality rule might be made if disclosure documents reveal acts of such iniquity that publication would be justified in the public interest. I prepared for James Evans a paper arguing that a company (Distillers) had marketed a drug (thalidomide) with advertising that stressed that it was safe for pregnant women, and that drug then caused those women to give birth to grossly deformed children; that the company, in its greed for sales, had ignored early warnings that the drug might cause such deformed births. If this was not iniquitous behaviour, what was?

It was no use. In August 1974, Mr Justice Talbot ruled that even if it could be proved that Distillers had been negligent in marketing thalidomide in Britain, such negligence would not constitute an exception to the need to protect confidentiality. 'The protection of discovery documents is paramount to the public interest for the proper administration of justice,' the judge said. The fact that we had paid Dr Phillips for the documents did not help our case. A decision that would have appeared to approve – for whatever reason – a professional witness's decision to sell to a newspaper documents revealed under discovery would have set too dangerous a precedent. We considered an appeal but all advice was that it would be a waste of time and money.

So when we went to Strasbourg it was with the knowledge that no matter what the European Court decided we would still not be able to publish the draft article. Our win therefore appeared a hollow victory – the British Attorney-General had infringed our right to freedom of expression by stopping us from publishing the draft article because it was in contempt of court. We were now free to publish the draft article – except that a permanent injunction for breach of confidentiality prevented us from doing so. In the history of newspaper publishing had a single article ever run into such a wall of complex legal blocks? But the European Commission, perhaps unfamiliar with British court procedure, perhaps accidentally, perhaps out of mischief (I like to think the latter), attached the whole draft article as an appendix to its decision. It thus became a court privileged document – we could publish as long as we did not change it, and on 31 July 1977 we celebrated by printing the Commission's ruling and, along with it, the draft article. It was exactly as I had written it six years earlier even though by now it was outdated and wrong in parts because of further research and new facts that had emerged during our legal battle. Anyway, by then the campaign was long over, and journalism pure and simple had won a proper settlement for Britain's thalidomide children. Or had it?

Well into the *Sunday Times* campaign there was evidence that far from convincing Distillers that they should pay up, we had only made them more determined to stick to their guns. In fact, Sir Alexander McDonald suggested that the *Sunday Times* might make things *worse* for the children. He said that if our campaign caused negotiations with the parents to break down, Distillers might decide to withdraw its compensation offer entirely and instead stand on the legal issues. McDonald was not impressed by our argument that Distillers had a moral obligation to pay more. Writing to an unhappy shareholder, Tony Lynes, then one of the leaders of the Child Poverty Action Group, who had urged Distillers to pay more, McDonald said, 'Even if the directors had agreed with you (which they do not) that there were overwhelming moral reasons for giving away £20 million as you suggest, you must realise that directors of a public company which acted in such a way and on such a scale might at once become subject to legal proceedings at the hands of those shareholders who disagreed.' Sir Alexander said that it was all very well for a shareholder to take a moral stand that involved him in little responsibility towards others – 'and I would observe in passing that it is even easier for a newspaper editor'. There was, however, a great difference between individual shareholders giving away funds to a charity and the directors of a company giving away funds for moral reasons which did not have the unanimous approval of shareholders, and when legal reasons did not justify it – a view which had more support at the time than we realised.

If this attitude was shared by a majority of the shareholders then the campaign would probably collapse, so Lynes began testing it. He was soon joined in this task by Roger and Sarah Broad, neighbours of mine, who had read the first article in the *Sunday Times* and then came to me and asked how they could help. The Rowntree Trust provided them with the

£8,000 they needed to buy a list of shareholders from Distillers (thirty-two volumes) and the cost of postage to circularise them. Among them were big insurance companies and a number of city and town authorities. The Broads gave the names to the *Guardian* which asked these local authorities for their views on the stance adopted by Distillers. Most said that they would support a move for an emergency general meeting to discuss the issue. But it was the stance taken by Legal & General Assurance Society that proved decisive. It had no fewer than 3.5 million shares in Distillers worth £6 million and it told the *Guardian* that it would support a more generous settlement. The *Guardian* led the paper with this scoop, creating a stir in the City – never before had an institutional investor taken a public line on such a controversial matter.

Harsh commercial pressure was also building up. The Wrenson chain of shops and supermarkets announced a total boycott of Distillers products and in Washington, Ralph Nader, the consumers' campaigner, met David Mason and together they laid down an anti-Distillers barrage at a press conference. Nader said he would consult consumer and union organisations and within a month expected to be able to announce a boycott of Distillers products throughout the United States. This made headlines in Britain and in the next nine days nervous dealers in the City knocked £35 million off the value of Distillers' shares. Distillers surrendered. It might well have weathered the *Sunday Times* journalism campaign but the hostility of its own shareholders and the damage that a commercial boycott would have caused were more than it could bear.

They do things differently in America and there the thalidomide story was impressive. There was no need for a newspaper campaign for victims because the drug regulatory system worked and thalidomide never went on sale – although it was used for clinical trials. A McBride-type hero, Dr Frances Kelsey, of the Food and Drug Administration, was not pulled down but was honoured by President Kennedy. None of the comparatively few victims was denied the right to go to law because of the expense, the lawyers were vigorous and resourceful and forced the American manufacturers of thalidomide, Richardson-Merrell, to provide adequate compensation. The American legal system even managed to accommodate twenty-six non-American thalidomide victims who would otherwise have received nothing.

Dr Kelsey stopped thalidomide from being marketed in America because she felt – correctly as it turned out – that Richardson-Merrell had not been wholly frank with her about the drug's side effects. When she read in the *British Medical Journal* that the drug could cause peripheral neuritis she became concerned that it might also cause damage to the foetus. She was still firmly holding out against Richardson-Merrell's attempts to bulldoze her into approving the drug when the first reports of its effects on the unborn child were revealed.

The American contingency fee system – a lawyer can take your case without an initial fee but instead takes a percentage of any damages eventually awarded – encouraged lawyers to fight one case, that of Peggy McCarrick of Los Angeles, right through to a jury trial, a landmark in the thalidomide litigation around the world. On 18 June 1971, by a majority of ten to two, the jury found that Richardson-Merrell had been negligent and awarded Peggy $1.5 million general damages and $1 million punitive damages. (This was reduced on appeal and eventually Richardson-Merrell negotiated a private settlement with Peggy.) Settlements averaging about $500,000 were soon common for most of the American victims.

But Richardson-Merrell had sold thalidomide in Canada and twenty-six Canadian victims who came from the province of Quebec were left out. There the French-derived Civil Code's statute of limitations required that personal injury cases had to be started within a year of the injury. But it took longer than a year for the parents of the victims to realise that thalidomide had been responsible for their deformities. No appeal was possible and the Quebec children had lost hope. I told them that if anyone could help them it would be Arthur Raynes, a Philadelphia attorney who had been involved in the thalidomide actions in the United States from the beginning. Raynes discovered that Richardson-Merrell had a wholly owned subsidiary in New Jersey which had manufactured thalidomide for its parent company. And New Jersey was one of two states (the other is California) that had a doctrine of governmental interest – that is, if Raynes could prove that the Quebec cases concerned the state government of New Jersey, then those cases could be tried there, irrespective of where the injury had actually taken place. So on 25 June 1973, the U.S. District Court, Newark, New Jersey, began hearing the case of Denis Henry, an 11-year-old Quebec boy whose physical damage caused by thalidomide prevented him from ever being able to laugh or cry. Judge James A. Coolahan started proceedings with one of those ringing declarations that occasionally lift American legal proceedings from the mundane to the heroic. 'This court cannot realistically ignore the fact that the defendant's New Jersey activities played at least some part in the general thalidomide tragedy which occurred in Canada . . . The infant plaintiff was only one victim of this tragedy. Thus Denis Henry's cause of action is clearly brought in New Jersey as a test case in the hope that this court will apply the state's favourable statute of limitations law. This court will not shatter that hope.'

There were appeals and out-of-court negotiations but Judge Coolahan had set the tone, and when Raynes video-taped most of the Canadian thalidomide children and ran some of the tapes for Richardson-Merrell's lawyers (one of the lawyers was so upset he had to leave the room), the battle was as good as won. Some of the Canadian children eventually received the highest awards in the world. Raynes got $15 million for the twenty-six Quebec children and the Cleveland law firm of Spangenberg Traci got for a child in British Columbia a record $990,000. (Richardson-Merrell refused to pay $1 million on principle.)

So America handled it better but it still appeared that, one way or another, our newspaper campaign in Britain had achieved all its aims. The children got a decent financial settlement; the process for licensing drugs for sale in Britain was tightened, the law on contempt was reformed and – although we did not boast about it – we had stood up to Distillers' attempt to use the power of its advertising budget. (The *Sunday Times* advertising manager, Donald Barrett, had warned Harold Evans that Distillers was the paper's largest single advertiser, spending £600,000 a year. Then he added, 'I know that won't stop you and it shouldn't.' Immediately the *Sunday Times* began its campaign, Distillers cancelled all its advertising.) But as the years passed some of us became painfully aware that the power of this dreadful drug to blight the lives of all who came in contact with it had not ended with the *Sunday Times*'s campaign.

To start with, some of the parents found the exposure in the press a painful experience. 'We have not sought the publicity which has been thrust upon us, although we are naturally grateful for the support which has followed,' wrote Alec Purkis in a letter to the paper. 'The glaring limelight has undoubtedly caused further distress to the affected parents and the children – most of the latter now read newspapers extensively.'

Next, there was discontent over the way the compensation was paid. Individual payments were made directly to the victims according to the severity of their deformities, but £32 million (£27 million from Distillers and £5 million from the British government) was paid in instalments into the specially created Thalidomide Trust. The trustees decided from the start that most of this money should be allocated to individual accounts, the sum being decided according to the severity of the deformity. But, because of British tax laws relating to charitable trusts, the money could not be paid directly to the victims. They had to apply to the Trust for amounts to cover specific needs. If their account was in credit, then the Trust would buy the item requested. No one was *entitled* to any sum of money – only help for needs *as judged by the trustees*. There were inevitable resentments. Parents who had fought for ten years for the compensation and thought that the

Sunday Times had won it for them were disillusioned to discover that the money did not come directly to the children. They accused the Trust of encouraging a 'begging bowl' regime and of being high-handed and autocratic in dispensing the money. The Trust administrators admitted that there was some truth in this. One, Allan White, said, 'It's an awful business playing God. But, as I tell them, unless they can convince me that what they need is genuine, how can I convince the trustees?'

Then in 1995 it became apparent that the Trust was going to run out of money, probably by 2009. We had been dazzled by the fact that our campaign had played a part in forcing Distillers to increase its original offer from £3.25 million to £32.5 million. It had occurred to no one that many of the victims would understandably be so determined to live as much like normal people as possible – no matter what the cost – that even £32.5 would not be enough. Fortunately, the Guinness group, which had taken over the Distillers company and had inherited the tragedy – but certainly not any legal or financial responsibility – promptly topped up the Trust in 1996 with another £37.5 million and the government added a further £7 million.

But there was already evidence that although the money brought physical comfort to the thalidomide children it did not always bring happiness. One victim, Graham Tindale, complained, 'People look on us as though we're football-pool winners.' Disturbing stories of greed and envy began to emerge. One limbless thalidomide victim was attending a special school along with seven other thalidomide victims who were less severely handicapped. When the seven learnt how much the limbless boy was to receive in compensation from Distillers, they attacked him, kicking him with their artificial legs as he rolled helplessly across the playground.

Allan White told Marjorie Wallace that the compensation money attracted gold diggers. 'The girls in particular are vulnerable. Some collect the most dreadful types and if we know that 90 per cent of what we are giving out is going on these leeches, we have to refuse. We get a lot of stick for doing so, but, in the end, the girls are often grateful. When the money dries up, the chap disappears.'

The most hurtful situations arose when a young thalidomide man or woman wanted to marry or live alone away from his or her parents. If they had put some of their compensation money into a house with their parents and then they wanted to realise the cash, the parents risked becoming homeless. In 1979 Freddie Astbury took his mother to court to remove her as a trustee of his £30,000 private trust and to evict her from the specially adapted house he had bought. He claimed that his mother was drinking heavily, had tried to sabotage his marriage, and had even punished him by removing the batteries from his electrically powered wheelchair. His mother, Ruby, then forty-nine, had to go to a hostel for the homeless. She was very bitter. 'I looked after Freddie for twenty years,' she said at the time. 'But now I am rejected and abandoned.'

Freddie Astbury was not the only one to become estranged from his parents. Terry Wiles met and married a divorcee, renounced Leonard and Hazel Wiles on television, and went to live in New Zealand, cutting off all contact. Leonard Wiles died of diabetes in 1996. Just before his death he learnt that Terry had met his natural mother. According to Hazel, Leonard's last words were, 'How did Terry get on with his Mum?'

As time passed, the curse of thalidomide seemed to home in on all who had had anything to do with it. One of its victims was William McBride, the Australian obstetrician who first alerted the world to the dangers of the drug. McBride became an international hero. He was awarded the Gold Medal of the French Institut de la Vie and used the prize money to set up Foundation 41 (named for the forty weeks of pregnancy and the first week after birth), a private research institute to study the causes of mental and physical handicaps in babies. He was awarded a CBE (1969) and the Order of Australia (1977). He was Australian of the Year (1962), Father of the Year (1972), a member of the Senate of Sydney University, a member of the board of the Women's Hospital, Sydney, and a greatly sought-after speaker in Australia, Europe and the United States. Until 1987, the world was McBride's oyster. Then the curse of thalidomide struck.

After he had accepted the gold medal from the Institut de la Vie, a fellow Australian, Professor Jacques Miller, told him that he had made more enemies on that day than he would in the rest of his life. And Miller put his finger on the canker later to consume McBride: so many scientists spend their lives in laboratories without ever making any notable discovery that they become resentful of those who do succeed, particularly those they regard as non-scientists. They believed that McBride had got lucky with thalidomide, that he did not deserve the accolades that had come his way, and that he should shut up, stick to obstetrics and leave the scientific study of the embryo to scientists. McBride, busy looking at other drugs taken by pregnant women, ignored them.

In March 1980, McBride announced that a morning sickness drug, Debendox, marketed by the American giant Merrell Dow, was 'capable of causing deformities in a small percentage of the embryos of women who took it early in pregnancy'. In June 1982, McBride published a paper on Foundation 41 experiments with a related drug which appeared to support this finding. But one of the research assistants who had worked on the experiment, Phil Vardy, discovered that McBride had changed some of the original figures in the experiment. Vardy said later, 'I concluded that I had proof of scientific forgery.' He consulted his solicitor and then had an 'unsatisfactory' meeting with McBride. Four months later – in October 1982 – Vardy resigned from the Foundation.

And there the matter rested for five years. Then in 1987, Dr Norman Swan, a British-born paediatrician who had ambitions to be a journalist, broadcast a radio report in the ABC Science Show accusing McBride of scientific fraud. In the uproar that followed, Foundation 41 requested a retired Chief Justice of the Supreme Court, Sir Harry Gibbs, to examine this accusation and on 2 November 1988, he concluded, 'McBride did publish statements which he either knew were untrue or which he did not genuinely believe to be true, and in that respect he was guilty of scientific fraud.'

The Complaints Unit of the New South Wales Health Department stepped in to finish McBride off. The unit director, Merrilyn Walton, added to the scientific fraud charges another eight charges relating to McBride's work as an obstetrician. Broadly, she accused him of performing without clinical justification caesarean operations on thirty-eight women between 1976 and 1988. A Medical Tribunal hearing to rule on these charges began on 6 November 1989. Meant to last six weeks, it went on for three and a half years and grew into a monster beyond anybody's worst nightmare. It became the world's longest medical disciplinary proceeding and probably the most expensive (about A$10 million). McBride's forty-six days in the witness box made him a contender for the longest cross-examination in legal history.

Since McBride freely admitted changing the original figures in the experiment because he believed they were wrong and he was correcting them, the fraud charges became instead a long and complex argument about scientific protocol. The medical malpractice part of the hearing swelled into a minute examination of thirty-eight pregnancies, with McBride, medical experts and several mothers undergoing detailed cross-examination on almost every aspect of childbirth. It became clear that this was essentially an argument about the politics of childbirth because none of the patients or the babies had died and not one of the patients involved had made any complaint against McBride.

The thrust of the prosecution case was that McBride, a doctor of the old school, had not recognised the arrival of the non-interventionist theory of obstetrics, which held that there were too many caesarians in Australian hospitals and that thousands of women were being deprived unnecessarily of the experience of natural childbirth. McBride said in his defence that many of his patients opted for caesareans because they were older, first-time mothers, or had histories of infertility and were desperate that nothing should go wrong.

Dr Douglas Keeping, Professor of Obstetrics at Queensland University, who prepared an independent assessment of the thirty-eight McBride caesareans, told the tribunal, 'It is my genuine belief that the clinical case against McBride ... is a vicious persecution, ill-conceived, without substance, and thoroughly reprehensible.' But others thought differently. One doctor, British-born Howard Chilton, told the tribunal that McBride was 'totally evil and without morals' and said he was proud of being a part of 'getting' him.

With appeals, McBride's ordeal went on for six years. At the end of it he was struck off, removed from the register of medical practitioners for 'being of bad character' and labelled a liar and charlatan. All his hospital appointments and his private practice, from which he had delivered nine thousand babies, ended. He had heart by-pass surgery in 1992. His house was daubed with paint and Australian journalists who had once fêted him competed to denigrate him. McBride believes – and he is not alone – that the origin of his troubles is that he became a threat to powerful drug companies: 'They have a vested interest in keeping their drugs on the market. I have a vested interest in protecting unborn babies; it's as simple as that.' After sitting through some of the hearings and watching McBride, with whom I had been at school, steadily dragged down, I prefer Truman Capote's explanation: 'People simply cannot endure success over a long period of time. It has to be destroyed.' But there is a tide in the sea of human frailty and I believe that it will one day turn in McBride's favour. When it does, the names of Norman Swan and Merrilyn Walton and the Medical Tribunal of NSW will fade while the story of Dr William McBride, his triumph with thalidomide and then his Calvary, will be read for many years to come.

Once we knew about the thalidomide scandal, we had to write about it, imperfect though the *Sunday Times* campaign was. But we cannot claim all the credit for the outcome. The truth is that the power of the press is greatly overrated – a proposition we had occasionally discussed in the Blue Lion pub on a Saturday night when the *Sunday Times* had gone to bed. Page's view prevailed – that a newspaper editor could have *some* influence on policy in Ulster, the success of a play, the outcome of an industrial dispute or, for that matter, the behaviour of a big corporation like Distillers. But he could not have *decisive* influence on anything; the power to report or not to report could not be compared with the power of judges, ministers, civil servants, corporate directors or trade union leaders.

The other lesson from the thalidomide campaign is that editors and newspapers move on and the pages that made up their successful campaigns become faded library clippings. But for the reporters in the field, the victims they met and the stories they wrote remain part of their lives, not easily put aside. I continue to fight for Dr William McBride's rehabilitation. Not a week passes for Marjorie Wallace, now director of the mental health charity SANE, without one of the thalidomide victims ringing, writing or calling on her.

The thalidomide children have grown up, some have married, and some have children of their own. Most of these are normal, healthy human beings. But at least twelve have thalidomide-type deformities, raising the spectre that the drug's effects could be passed down the generations – that the thalidomide children could have thalidomide children. McBride, who has always said that the thalidomide tragedy is greater than anyone has realised, believes this to be so and in 1995 offered evidence to the annual conference of the European Teratology Society that thalidomide binds to the DNA in the cells. Other experts reply that some children were accepted as thalidomide-damaged who in fact had alternative explanations for their deformities and some of these may have been genetic. But if McBride turns out to be right, we will have to face the fact that the curse of thalidomide will be with us for ever.

CHAPTER ELEVEN

LIBEL: PAY THE POLICE, COLLECT FROM GOLDSMITH

Australians love literary luncheons and at the peak of the visiting author season there are often two or three a week. About four hundred people pay £20 a head for a light meal and a few glasses of wine and then settle down to hear an author talk about his favourite subjects – himself and his latest book. Afterwards you can buy a copy in the hotel lobby, meet the author and get him or her to sign it for you. I know that there are literary luncheons elsewhere in the world but Australian ones have an intensity that the others lack – these are *important* local events and if the author does not perform as expected, then the audience – since Australians are nothing if not blunt – will let him know. Frank Moorhouse forgot this in 1995 and used his literary lunch to launch an attack on the Australian literary establishment for not giving him a prize. Whereupon a woman in the audience shouted that he was 'a whinger' and walked out. She said later that she had come expecting to hear a couple of jokes and an outline of Moorhouse's book, not a literary political speech.

I had been warned what was expected so when I went back to Australia in 1987 to promote a book about the Profumo affair that I had written with Caroline Kennedy, I arrived at the Holiday Inn-Menzies hotel in Sydney with a speech written, revised and polished. Not that it was difficult to make it interesting. The perennial fascination that the Profumo scandal has in Britain – hardly a year passes without it being rehashed in one form or another – is replicated in Australia. And I had something new to advance: the theory that Stephen Ward, the London society osteopath who introduced Christine Keeler to both John Profumo, the Secretary of State for War in Harold Macmillan's government, and her other lover, the Soviet spy Yevgeny Ivanov, was a victim of the scandal rather than a perpetrator. Ward, who committed suicide while on trial for procuring and living on the earnings of prostitution – charges that I believe were politically motivated, although the investigating officers had no idea of this – was a flawed hero in our book rather than a villain. Little did I know, as I went for a last nervous visit to the lavatory before the speech, I was about to become a victim of the scandal myself.

I emerged from the lavatory and walked towards the podium. As I drew level with one of those large potted palms that hotels scatter about their public areas, a burly, grey-haired man stepped from behind it and blocked my way. 'Phillip Knightley?' he said. I admitted it, and, thinking he was a reader, held out my hand. He pushed a folded piece of paper into it and said, 'This is for you.' It was a writ, returnable in the High Court of NSW, alleging that I had libelled a detective sergeant in the Metropolitan Police, London, and one of the police officers who had investigated the Ward case. I just had time to consult a newspaper solicitor who was at my table. 'For God's sake don't mention the Ward case or the Profumo scandal,' he said. 'It could increase the damages.' Not mention the case? My whole speech was about the case.

I apologised to the audience. I said that I had just that moment received a libel writ, that I had reason to believe that the former Scotland Yard detective who had issued it was in the audience with his solicitor and that therefore I could not talk about my book. Instead I would talk about the British establishment and who was and who was not a member and then we could switch to Australia and discuss who were members of the Australian establishment. The audience's disappointment at the change of subject was lessened by the excitement in the centre of the room where some press photographers had located the former detective sergeant and his solicitor and were busy taking pictures of them, much to the annoyance of the solicitor who was scribbling notes on paper napkins threatening writs if any photographs were published without his client's permission.

This was the beginning of a legal nightmare that occupied a lot of my thinking time for the next three years, that cost hundreds of thousands of dollars, that involved my skulking around the back streets of Notting Hill Gate with brown paper bags stuffed with £5 notes and that, in the end, produced a decision so contrary to logic that when I tell people about it they are reluctant to believe me.

The origins of the case against Stephen Ward remain obscure to this day. The little we know comes from an account – leaked in 1982 by the Security Service, MI5 – of a meeting called in the spring of 1963 by the Home Secretary, Henry Brooke. Others there were the head of MI5, Roger Hollis, the Permanent Under-Secretary at the Home Office, Sir

Charles Cunningham, and the Commissioner of the Metropolitian Police, Sir Joseph Simpson. Brooke asked Hollis if it might be possible to prosecute Ward under the Official Secrets Act over Christene Keeler's allegation that Ward had asked her to find out from Profumo when Germany would receive nuclear warheads. Hollis thought not. Simpson agreed with him but then gratuitously added that it might be possible to get a conviction against Ward on a charge of living off immoral earnings. The two service heads went away reluctantly agreeing to see if they could come up with any charge against Ward that might stick.

My own view about this remarkable meeting is that the government realised that the Profumo scandal was not going to end while Stephen Ward continued to blab about it all over London. If he were given a good fright, this would make him realise that he had been interfering in delicate matters and that his only hope of survival would be to withdraw and shut up. On the other hand if Ward still persisted, there was still nothing to be lost by prosecuting him. Conviction of a criminal offence would largely discredit what he had to say and there would be the added benefit of allaying public disquiet: there had been a scandal, but the government was acting, someone was being prosecuted over it, and it could soon be disposed of and forgotten.

There was certainly top-level interest in the progress of the police investigation. One of the police team, Sergeant Mike Glasse, told us, 'We had to file a progress report each day. At first we had to make only one or two copies, but this soon increased to ten. When I queried the need for so many I was told copies were going to the Prime Minister, the Leader of the Opposition and other prominent people in and out of Parliament. I was told that this was because of the many names which were being mentioned during the investigation, some of whom were MPs, judges and churchmen, and so the Prime Minister had to be kept informed.'

Intrigued by this investigation, Kennedy and I did our best to find and interview all the police officers involved. One had died. We located and spoke with two others. But the fourth eluded us. Scotland Yard told us that he had taken early retirement and, according to the gossip, had gone to live in Australia. What would a former detective in the vice squad in the West End of London, right at the cutting edge of law enforcement, do in Australia? He would, we reasoned, hardly settle for a mundane nine-to-five job. He would most likely stick to his last and join the Australian police. But each state in Australia has its own force, so we had to check all six; no trace of him. The Registrar of Deaths did not prove any more useful.

The one force we did not check was the Commonwealth Police, because my memory of them was of men in brown uniforms who guarded

Commonwealth property such as buildings and airports – more security guards than real policemen. But, it turned out, that was the force our man had joined. Even worse for our case when it eventually came to damages was that he turned out to be a hero – he had helped rescue a girl at Sydney airport when a mentally disturbed man held her hostage with a knife at her throat. We knew none of this when Caroline Kennedy and I sat with the publisher's libel lawyer at the last conference before publication. 'Any further worries?' he said. I thought for a while. 'The fourth detective,' I said. 'We can't find him. Caroline believes that he must be dead. But just suppose, just suppose he turns out to be alive and well and living in Australia, and we haven't interviewed him? Where would we stand?'

We argued about it for a while and then Caroline and I decided that since we had spoken with the other detectives we need not worry.

How wrong we were. We knew nothing about the NSW libel bar, one of the most active and aggressive in the world, so although the writ I received at the literary luncheon surprised me, it was run-of-the-mill stuff for Sydney. Our publishers, Jonathan Cape, carried libel insurance and the insurance company agreed to defend the case jointly with Rupert Murdoch's newspaper, the *Australian*, which had serialised extracts from the book. The *Australian*'s solicitors briefed another top libel barrister who, by a coincidence that seems to happen often in the legal world, was in the same chambers as the detective's barrister. In fact, he had an office just along the corridor. Lawyers think nothing of this but clients wonder why in such cases disputes cannot be settled at a tenth of the cost over a lawyers' long lunch.

Instead all the parties set out to re-investigate the whole Profumo scandal from scratch. Caroline Kennedy and I flew to Australia for conferences. Then our Australian lawyers flew to London for conferences. And while they were there, they asked to meet, and perhaps take statements from, all the people who had given us information about the scandal, sometimes in confidence. This was delicate ground. Take Lucky Gordon, Christine Keeler's one-time West Indian boyfriend, and an important figure in the scandal. Gordon works as a musician/cook at a Notting Hill recording studio and, like the musicians he cooks for, keeps irregular hours. When we were doing the original research for the book, Kennedy and I had many a late-night drink with Lucky in Notting Hill clubs. We had failed to do a deal with him because he would not show us the 'sensational' letters he says he still has until we agreed how much we would pay for them, and we said we could not tell what they were worth until we saw them. But we had parted friends.

I was now expected to go to Gordon and say, 'Look, Lucky, some

Australian lawyers want to talk to you. They may want to take a statement from you. You may be an important witness in a case they are defending. They want you to come into their London office tomorrow morning at nine and you might have to spend all day there, even if it means taking time off from work. Oh yes, and they're not going to give you a penny for this. Not even your fares.'

I thought Lucky would say, 'Man, you've got to be joking.' But when I did approach him, he was more subtle – he brought in an intermediary. I had a telephone call from Frank Critchlow, of the famous Mangrove restaurant in All Saints' Road. 'You've got to see this whole thing from Lucky's point of view,' Frank said. 'Everyone's making money out of this except him. Right? Christine's sold her story ten times over. Your book's done well and your lawyers are all getting fat fees. What's Lucky ever got? Fucking nothing, man. That's what. Now you want him to lose a day's pay to go and talk to some lawyers. Okay, he'll do it for you. But he wants to go to Jamaica for Christmas and he's saving up for the fare, so what about those lawyers giving Lucky an early Christmas present?'

I said I would talk to them. In case they agreed, how big a Christmas present should it be?

'Two hundred,' Frank said. 'Cash. Bring it to me at the restaurant tonight. Have a meal. Bring the lawyers if you like. And I'll get hold of Lucky and tell him to come along. If he can't make it tonight, I guarantee he'll be in the lawyer's office tomorrow morning.'

I went into the solicitors' offices off Gray's Inn where the Australian lawyers had set up their temporary headquarters and I broke the news to them and their colleagues at a conference that afternoon. They were all horrified. 'I'm an officer of the court,' one of the English lawyers said. 'I can't be a party to paying money to a potential witness.'

'Then he's not going to make a statement,' I said. 'Why should he?'

'In the interests of justice.'

I tried not to laugh. 'You've given me a list of people you want statements from. I'm doing my best to get them. You want to talk to Ronna Ricardo. She's a working girl, or she was. She's terrified of policemen, lawyers and journalists – in that order. Have you any idea how hard it was to get her to tell us anything in the first place? Now I come back to her and tell her that some lawyers want to see her in their offices. Why should she do it? What's in it for her? What's in it for Lucky Gordon?'

'Your case will be seriously weakened without a statement from Mr Gordon.'

'Okay,' I thought. '*I'll* pay him the money. I'll pay it out of my own pocket.'

The idea of dinner at the Mangrove appealed to one of the Australian lawyers and he agreed to come with me. I did not pass any money to Frank or Lucky while he was there and made no mention of it in front of him. I drew out £200 in five pound notes from the bank, put them in an old brown paper bag and, with the lawyer and my wife, turned up at the Mangrove at eight o'clock. I tried to park outside the restaurant but the space was blocked by a large enclosed trailer with Italian plates and locked steel doors, the sort of vehicle used to move whole households around Europe. It had been detached from the prime mover and looked abandoned.

I complained about it to Critchlow. 'It's those antique dealers in Portobello Road,' he said. 'They ship English furniture to Italy. The Italian drivers who come to pick it up park their trucks anywhere. It was there this morning when I came to open up. The parking warden said it's too big to tow away, wheels too big to clamp. I rang the police but they've done nothing.'

It was a great evening. The restaurant filled quickly and the atmosphere was suspiciously relaxed. The lawyer asked Critchlow about the heavy fragrance that hung between the low ceilings and the diners. 'Joss sticks,' said Critchlow. 'Neutralises the curry smells from the kitchen.' Lucky arrived and was charming and co-operative with the lawyer, who left early, looking very pleased, pleading jet lag. At midnight I followed Critchlow into the kitchen and handed over the bag full of money with only the chef watching. Then my wife and I shook hands with Critchlow and Lucky and thanked them for an excellent dinner. The fact that it had, in effect, cost me more than £50 a head scarcely seemed to matter. Contentedly full of flying fish, meat patties and West Indian rum, we walked past the abandoned truck trailer, heading for home.

We had just reached the end of the street when there was a shrill whistle and suddenly the whole of All Saints' Road was ablaze with floodlights that appeared to be mounted on rooftops all the way along the street. Seconds later the steel doors of the trailer burst open, a ramp thudded down, and dozens of uniformed policemen, some with dogs, poured out. The lead policemen crashed through the doors of the Mangrove, which erupted with shouts and screams, while the others ran to seal off the street. The light was so bright and the action so choreographed that it was like watching the shooting of a street scene in a film – especially as a police cameraman was busy videoing the whole thing.

'Jesus Christ,' I said. 'It's a drugs raid. Let's get out of here.'

It was not until we reached home that I realised what a narrow escape I had had. What if I had still been in the restaurant when the police arrived. I could imagine the Notting Hill detective giving evidence against me in court: 'And in the kitchen I saw the defendant holding out a brown paper bag towards a man I know to be Frank Critchlow, the owner of the premises. I seized the bag which I immediately saw contained money. This was later counted at the station and was found to amount to £200. I asked the defendant why he was giving this money to Mr Critchlow and he replied – may I consult my notebook, Your Worship? – he replied, "It's a contribution to Lucky Gordon's Christmas trip to Jamaica." I suggested to the defendant that he should not be facetious in his replies to my legitimate enquiries and he said, "No really, officer. You see, Lucky's a possible witness in this libel case in Australia about a retired Scotland Yard vice detective who was involved in the Profumo affair but then joined the Commonwealth Police and we need a statement from Lucky but the lawyers wouldn't give him any money so . . ."'

It all made no difference in the end. Lucky Gordon kept his word and made his statement. In Australia our lawyers started to defend the case. Our main problem was that we had taken a risk over the fourth detective and this had not paid off. The fault was ours and there was a very real prospect we would lose. We had not spoken to him, we had not tried hard enough to find him, and I felt he was right to complain. There was also another problem, a commercial one. If we went to court it would be a virtual re-hearing of the Old-Bailey trial of Stephen Ward. We would have to round up all the usual witnesses and bring them all to Sydney. 'Sydney!' I said when they told me this. 'You saw the trouble we had getting them to Gray's Inn.' The hearing would probably last three weeks to a month. A conservative estimate of the cost would be one to two million dollars. As might be expected, our insurance company was shouting, 'No. Settle, settle.' So our Australian lawyers played legal poker with the other side's lawyers – a game that went on almost to the steps of the High Court – and then our lawyer went along the corridor to the other side's lawyer and made him an offer his client could not refuse. He accepted and it was all over. Or was it?

The London publishers had withdrawn the book the moment they heard I had collected a writ at the Sydney literary luncheon. There were many people who still wanted to read it. I argued that now, three years later, the case had been settled, why not go ahead with the paperback publication? I would go through the book and remove or change every single sentence that the detective had objected to, using his own statement of claim as a guide. 'Great idea,' the publisher said. 'Do it and then we'll show it to the libel lawyers just to make sure you haven't missed anything.'

It took me a week. Then it took two months to hear from the lawyers because they sent the revised manuscript to their Australian colleagues. Finally one of the London lawyers telephoned and said, 'You'd better come in to discuss this. It's much more complicated than we imagined.' First, he said, editing the detective out of the story was no guarantee that he would not sue again. Even if his name did not appear at all he could claim that he was easily identifiable because of the first publication and thus was for ever associated with the case. 'Okay,' I said. 'We sacrifice the Australian market and publish only in Britain.' That would not help, he said. The detective could sue in Britain. 'Sure,' I said. 'But he'd have to come to London to do it. And since he now lives in Australia we could deter him by asking for security for our costs. Would he really go to all the expense of coming to London, engaging a British solicitor, and then hanging around for a possible trial on the remote chance he might get a few quid more?'

The lawyer looked grim. 'Well, this is the bad news,' he said. 'It appears he would not have to come to London to sue. He could sue in Australia.'

'Sue in Australia over a book published in London by a British publisher?' I said. 'Sue in Australia over a book not even sold in Australia?'

Apparently that was so, the lawyer said. His Australian colleagues had gone deeply into the law on the matter. Egalitarian Australia had done its best to make the little man the equal of the big corporation in the eyes of the law. The detective could go to the High Court in Australia and say he wanted to sue a big British company and that big British company was trying to force him to bring the action in London. But London was not a convenient forum for him, so could he please bring the action in Australia, where he lived and where the big British company had a subsidiary? And there would be a good chance that the court would allow him to do so. If he then won damages, these would be assessed on the number of copies that the book had sold elsewhere in the world.

'It's all very interesting,' the lawyer said, 'but it's academic anyway. The libel insurers say they've paid out once on this book so they won't give you cover on the paperback. I don't think the publishers will carry the risk themselves. And if they're not covered, you're not covered. Would you be prepared to risk it?' The answer was no. And that's the inside story of why – to the relief of a lot of people – there has never been a paperback version of *An Affair of State*, the only book to tell the inside story of the Profumo scandal.

I suppose my mistake was not to have Lord Goodman on my side. The previous year I had had a lot of trouble with my book *The Second Oldest Profession: the Spy as Bureaucrat, Patriot, Fantasist and Whore*. It had started in the United States. 'You can't use the word "whore" in the title of a book in America,' the publisher said. 'People are not going to walk out of a store with a book that has a dustjacket with the word "whore" on it. They just won't. "Whore" is a very emotive word here. It has biblical overtones.'

'How about bureaucrat, patriot, fantasist and hooker?' I said. 'Or bureaucrat, patriot, fantasist and lady of the night?'

He was not amused. 'Why don't we just change the entire subtitle,' he said. 'I suggest "Spies and Spying in the Twentieth Century".' I tried to point out that the original subtitle was meant to be pejorative, that it described what the author felt about spies, whereas his subtitle, accurate though it was, sounded like the contents of a catalogue. I lost – a bad omen.

The book had been out a week in Britain when the publishers, André Deutsch, got a writ from Anthony Simkins, a retired officer of Her Majesty's Security Service, MI5. I had written that Mr Simkins had been a great help to Rupert Allason, otherwise known as Nigel West, when he was writing his history of MI5: *A Matter of Trust. MI5 1945–1972*. I had this from a good source close to the service but now both Simkins and Allason said it was wrong, which left me defenceless, and Mr Simkins had engaged the services of the Queen's solicitors, Farrer and Company, so he was serious.

André Deutsch, the founder of the firm, a man not easily intimidated, looked at the writ, saw Farrer and Company, and immediately telephoned Lord Goodman. We were in Goodman's Portland Place flat an hour later, sitting in the lounge in front of a low coffee table, waiting for Goodman to finish dressing. Deutsch reached for his cup of coffee, found that the table was too far away, and so was kneeling on the carpet alongside the table when Lord Goodman swept in. He looked down at Deutsch. 'Get off your knees, André,' he said. 'It can't be that bad.'

'It is, Arnold,' Deutsch said. 'And it's only Wednesday.'

Yet when we left half an hour later the clouds had lifted. Lord Goodman had rapidly grasped the detail, put himself in Simkin's place, and had decided on a strategy. 'Forget about what the writ says. The truth is you've hurt his feelings,' he said. 'He appears by name in a book that says some spies are whores. We've got to let him know that you don't think he's one of them. You think he comes under the patriot label.' He had ushered us out with encouraging phrases – 'meet face-to-face . . . reasonable people . . . clear up a little misunderstanding . . . offer to make a few changes next printing . . . small donation to charity . . . nothing to worry about.' No wonder Harold Wilson thought Lord Goodman could solve the Rhodesia problem.

Two days later we had a meeting with Simkins and two of the Queen's solicitors. Our team was André Deutsch, his then partner Tom Rosenthal, and me – three a side with Lord Goodman as referee. The meeting was in the conference room at Goodman Derrick's offices. The round table was no suprise but a conversation I overheard between Lord Goodman and his assistant was. There was a small annexe outside the conference room with tea-making equipment. As we trooped into the conference room, Lord Goodman turned to his assistant and said, 'Serve tea as soon as you can, then lock the door when you leave.' He must have seen my questioning glance and explained: 'I've found, Mr Knightley, that more compromises are reached by exhaustion than by rational argument.' The sound of the key turning in the lock certainly gave an edge to our discussion.

Lord Goodman turned out to be absolutely right. Early in the conference Simkins said I had called him a whore. 'Not at all,' I said. 'A patriot, Mr Simkins, a patriot.' Goodman was also right about the terms of settlement – a correction in later editions, a modest payment. Unfortunately, Lord Goodman died in 1995 but he remains my model for a good lawyer.

It was a pity that Sir James Goldsmith did not have Lord Goodman's advice in 1976 when – going against my own belief that journalists should not sue for libel – I brought a defamation action against him. Goodman could have saved us both two years' effort and considerable legal costs because the whole business was a mistake, a genuine one on Goldsmith's part but one which he refused to admit.

It happened in the middle of Goldsmith's long-running battle with *Private Eye*. He had initiated sixty-three actions against *Private Eye* – which he said he loathed – including one for criminal libel, the first against a newspaper in this country for nearly a century. The actions split the chattering classes. Those who supported *Private Eye* on freedom of expression grounds contributed to its 'Golden Balls' fund to fight Goldsmith. Others who disliked the public schoolboy anti-Semitism of the magazine, the 'Snipcock and Tweed' jokes, thought it was about time it had its come-uppance. As the crunch hearings got underway there was a lot of side-switching, and during one of the actions in July 1976, two important witnesses changed sides from *Private Eye* to Goldsmith, and then failed to turn up in court for cross-examination by *Private Eye*'s lawyers. One of them, a City public relations executive called John Addey, was rumoured to have left the country rather than appear in the witness box.

What was going on? All the newspapers had teams of reporters trying to find out.

A *Sunday Times* journalist, Anthony Holden, who had been covering the trial, learnt on the Friday afternoon that Addey had returned, so he telephoned him at his City flat and Addey agreed to see him. It was Holden's story but he was concerned that with such a sensitive matter it might be better if he had another journalist with him on the interview to act as a witness in case there should later be any dispute about what was said. I agreed to go with him.

Addey was an interesting man – intelligent, well-connected, and mischievous. He got on well with Holden, known in the *Sunday Times* office as 'Golden Holden' because of his handsome blond looks, his Midas touch with stories, and his luck at the poker table, where he was a player of international standard. Addey told us that on legal advice he could say nothing about the case but he offered us some background information providing it was not attributed to him. Then he and Holden moved on to high-class London gossip and all the people they knew in common. I sat and listened. When it came time to leave, Addey said, 'I'd better get your names straight. Have you got a card?' We gave him one of Holden's cards with my name handwritten on the back of it. As we started down the stairs, Addey leaned over the bannister rail and said to Holden, 'I'm sure we've met before, but I can't think where.' And Holden said, 'It was probably at one of those [Private Eye] luncheons.'

Holden's story, based on the High Court judgment, but also containing a lot of background material provided off-the-record by Addey, duly appeared on Sunday, 18 July, under the heading 'Goldsmith v Private Eye: the curious case of the two missing witnesses'. As was the *Sunday Times* custom, I shared the by-line with Holden, although, apart from suggesting a couple of introductory sentences, I had had little to do with it. The article infuriated Goldsmith and on Monday morning he wrote to Lord Shawcross, the chairman of the Press Council, to complain, saying that it raised an important point of journalistic principle. He said, 'One of the authors of the *Sunday Times* article was Mr Phillip Knightley, who is also an occasional *Private Eye* collaborator. Presumably when newspapers write about a legal action, they normally do so as independent commentators. While the action is in progress before courts, editors do not knowingly open up their columns to one of the litigants so that one side of the case can be publicised. If they were to do so, no doubt they would consider it fair to disclose this fact. Perhaps editors should consider maintaining a register of interests similar to that asked of MPs or of company directors. In this register would be disclosed the other interests of journalists, and in this way editors could avoid the direct conflict of interest that occurs when a commentator, even when wishing to be objective, is also an undisclosed party to the action or linked to such a party.' A public relations company acting for Goldsmith sent copies of the letter to thirty-eight newspapers around the country, to the Associated Press, the Press Association and Reuters and to the main television stations.

The accusation about being a *Private Eye* collaborator was simply not true. I had written nothing for the magazine for eight years and had not even attended a *Private Eye* luncheon in that time. I had even been attacked in the magazine's columns myself as 'that bearded Australian bore'. Therefore I had no relationship with the magazine to disclose and no conflict of interests arose – even if I had written the *Sunday Times* article, which I had not. What's more, three years earlier I had voluntarily done exactly what Goldsmith had suggested in his letter to the Press Council – I had registered all my outside interests with the *Sunday Times* managing editor.

Holden and I discussed Goldsmith's letter and it did not take us long to work out what had happened. Addey must have told Goldsmith about our call on him, including Holden's joking remark about *Private Eye* luncheons. Then, probably upon checking the visiting card, he had inadvertently confused me with Holden. This was an honest mistake and, believing the whole matter could be quickly put right, I wrote to Goldsmith saying that he had got it wrong, would he therefore please write another letter to Lord Shawcross saying so, and would he also release this second letter to all the newspapers who had received copies of the first one. Then we could forget about it. I had not reckoned with Goldsmith's steely determination. He replied, in effect, that he stood by what he had written, that he would say it again, and if I continued to object he would see me in court. So, with the backing of the *Sunday Times*, I issued a writ, but instructed the solicitors to keep pointing out to Goldsmith's lawyers while the process ground towards the courts that I would drop the whole matter if he just wrote to Lord Shawcross admitting he had made a genuine mistake. Instead he began making widespread enquiries among my colleagues, friends and enemies to try to substantiate links between me and *Private Eye*.

There were none, and two years and a lot of money later (John Mathews QC appeared for Goldsmith and John Wilmers QC appeared for me, and neither man came cheaply), Goldsmith admitted his mistake, said he had written the letter in good faith, genuinely believing at the time that I was a co-author of the article in the fullest sense of the word and that I *was* a collaborator of *Private Eye* at the time the article was written. He now accepted my assurance to the contrary and apologised. A week later my post contained a handwritten cheque for £7,500 signed 'James Goldsmith'. I spent a large chunk of it on a dinner party at the Connaught for Holden, the *Sunday Times* legal department, and the outside lawyers. It was nice to have the money and to be able to say that I am the only journalist ever to have bested Goldsmith in a libel action, but looking back on it all now, I am not convinced I made the right decision to sue. I should have let Goldsmith's complaint make its way through the Press Council, which would have cleared me. And Goldsmith should have called in Lord Goodman who would have sorted it all out over a cup of tea.

My experiences with English libel – on both sides of the fence – convince me that it is basically a gambling game invented by lawyers to attract clients. It is a not a game for the less well-off and there is a means test to pass before you can be admitted to the casino – like Lloyds, you have to show that you can afford to lose before being offered a chance to win. I could never have risked the cost of suing a millionaire like Sir James Goldsmith had I not had the backing of the *Sunday Times*. (Ironically, Goldsmith himself recognised this and in 1987 acted to put the little man on even terms with the powerful. He set up a multi-million pound fund to help individuals bring or defend libel actions which they could not otherwise afford. I was happy to read his reasons: 'I completely fail to understand a culture which provides state funding if you lose a finger, but not if you are deprived of your reputation. I profoundly reject the idea that defending your reputation should be the preserve of the rich.' If only the fund had been in existence in 1976 I could have applied for help to sue James Goldsmith.)

In a real casino the odds can be calculated, but in a libel action there are irrational influences at work, especially in jury trials. At about the same time as he defamed me, Goldsmith wrote and published a number of statements to influential people that Michael Gillard, then a reporter for Granada Television, was a blackmailer. Gillard naturally sued. At the trial, Goldsmith produced only one witness – himself. He admitted that he personally had not been blackmailed by Gillard, but said that in 1976 John Addey – the same John Addey from my libel case – had told him that he, Addey, had been blackmailed by Gillard.

There was a problem here. The previous year Addey had retracted this allegation in the High Court, admitted that there was no truth in it, and agreed to pay Gillard £5,000 damages. Goldsmith waved this aside. He said he still believed Addey's original assertion and claimed that Addey had retracted only because he was poor, gutless and a secret homosexual. Goldsmith said he was being victimised and bullied by a coterie of journalists whose 'rotten core' was *Private Eye*. The techniques the magazine employed were 'lies, intimidation and blackmail . . . A group of people have acquired a certain power and they frighten people.' For his part, Gillard called witnesses to show that at the time of the alleged blackmail, he and Addey were good friends and that Addey had been grateful to him for his help. The jury chose to believe Goldsmith and threw out Gillard's action against him.

So the essence of a libel case is not whether the statement is true or false. The point is: who is going to pay? Most publishers insure themselves twice against libel – once by placing the legal onus on the writer to deliver a libel-free manuscript, and then by taking out a policy with an insurance company. Insurance companies being what they are, their reaction to a libel writ is not to say, 'Well, the author tells us that what he has written is true and he can prove it, so let's fight this all the way.' It is to say, 'How quickly can we settle this one before the lawyers' meters start whirring away.' The truth and the merit of the book or article thus take second place to the financial aspects of the case.

Next, in all libel actions there are claims about the terrible damage the plaintiff has suffered because of the defamatory statements made about him or her. These are always exaggerated and no one believes them. They are made because they are usually unprovable. To prove that I had been substantially damaged by Goldsmith's letter to the Press Council, the *Sunday Times* would have had to have sacked me, citing the letter as a reason. Or I would have had to have applied to another newspaper for a job and have been rejected, again its editor citing Goldsmith's letter as the reason.

It is much easier to claim that your feelings have been hurt, and often closer to the truth, as my exchange with Simkins in Lord Goodman's office illustrates. And the former London detective did not say in his action against me that he had lost his job, or found it difficult to get another one, as a result of what I had written about him, only that his reputation had suffered. Are these hurt feelings also exaggerated? My counsel, John Wilmers, said that I had found Sir James's criticisms particularly hurtful because my book *The First Casualty* had criticised journalists who failed to reveal any special interest in matters on which they wrote apparently objective reports. Twenty years on I cannot say I remember any stab of pain on reading Goldsmith's letter. All I remember is surprise that he could have got it so wrong and the conviction that once I pointed out his mistake to him he would recognise it and say so. But that was not his style.

I do not think that Wilmers really believed it, either. Goldsmith and his counsel, John Matthews, certainly did not. They settled because that was the way the game was played. Gillard had a much better case than I did. I won, he lost. He lost partly because of the perverse nature of English libel law and partly because of Goldsmith's performance in the witness box – he convinced the jury that his charges against *Private Eye* – 'lies, intimidation, blackmail, frightening people' – must have some substance. Did they?

The experience in 1993/4 of a friend of mine, then a minor TV star, is illuminating. She was the presenter of a BBC programme about the media. She maintained a friendly relationship with several *Private Eye* journalists, exchanged ideas and stories with them and was invited – but did not attend – various *Private Eye* functions. Then for reasons she still does not understand, *Private Eye* suddenly turned against her and ran an item attacking her. It said, in effect, that she was not liked by her BBC colleagues, was incapable of doing her job properly, and kept it only because she was sleeping with the programme's producer. It was true that she was disliked by some of her colleagues and also that she was having an affair with the producer. But she resented the charge that she was not competent at her job and issued a defamation writ against *Private Eye*.

There then began a sustained campaign to 'persuade' her to withdraw her action. Her friends were telephoned and told to warn her that if she persisted her private life and that of her family would be 'put under the microscope' and further damaging pieces might appear in *Private Eye*. Her producer, who at first said he was willing to appear in court and testify about her competence at her job, began to have doubts after receiving similar telephone calls, did his best to persuade her to drop the action, and finally said he could not after all give evidence on her behalf. She went ahead and won a modest settlement but looking back on the affair she now says that she is sorry she sued because the stress and worry that *Private Eye* caused her was not worth it.

I know that one instance of *Private Eye* applying pressure to someone to make them do something that they would not otherwise do hardly constitutes blackmail. But it does make you wonder if Goldsmith was entirely wrong in his assessment of the magazine.

CHAPTER TWELVE

CHARLES, DI AND BABY BILL

I thought I had covered my last Royal Tour in 1953 but thirty years later the weather decided otherwise. I was in Alice Springs, central Australia, to write about Aborigines for the *Sunday Times* magazine when flash floods wrecked my plans. The telephone lines went out, the roads became impassable, the electricity failed and – an unforgivable disaster in the Australian outback – the pub ran out of beer. My photographer partner, Kenneth Griffiths, flew off to visit relatives in New Zealand and I was just settling down to a book by lamplight when the electricity came back and a delayed cable from London reached me: OFFBREAK MAGAZINE ASSIGNMENT COVER CHARLES DIANA ARRIVAL ALICE-SPRINGS. There was a problem here – Charles and Diana were arriving on the Sunday so whatever I wrote for that week's *Sunday Times* would have to be about what they were *going* to do, rather than what they had done. Never mind; this would be an opportunity to discuss Australian attitudes to this new generation of Royals and the growing republican sentiment I had detected in the country.

Did the Sydney shops selling fake posters of Charles and Diana in the nude represent the real feelings of Australians? Or did the leader writer of the *Adelaide News* have it right? 'The majority of Australians are still royalists at heart and they will be out in their thousands to greet the royal visitors and say "G'day, mate".' Alice Springs seemed a good place to find out. Drinking was the town's main recreation, and drunk or sober its citizens, white and black, had a powerful contempt for pomp, politicians and Poms. The imminent arrival of all three, I decided, had signally failed to excite them. The Chief Minister, Paul Everingham, confirmed that no special arrangements had been made for the royal pair. 'No, mate,' he said. 'We thought about it, but I understand their taste is for simple things. They're steak-and-eggs people.' If so, then Alice Springs was the ideal place for them to meet simple Australian steak-and-eggs people like George Smith, the mayor. As well as being Alice's number one citizen, George was also 'Mister April' in a calendar called 'My Mates', produced by a local photographer, Diana Calder. He had posed for the calendar portrait in the mayoral chambers, before a painting of the Queen, wearing nothing but his lace neck ruff. He gave his vital statistics as 42–34–42 and said his ideal woman was 'a beautiful, blonde, nymphomaniac brewery heiress'. Or the Royal couple could have tea with a steak-and-eggs Aborigine, Nosepig Tjupurrula, of the Pintubi tribe, who was introduced to Prince Charles's mother in Adelaide in 1954. Protocol officers spent many hours teaching him how to bow. When the great moment came, the dignitary doing the presentation began, 'Her Majesty, Queen of England, may I present Nosepig Tjupurrula' – only to hear Nosepig interrupting to add . . . 'King of the Pintubi'.

Out at the airport on Sunday morning the weather had improved and the sun was shining. Charles and Diana landed, met some locals and drove off to the Gap Motor Hotel to get over their jet lag. I sneaked on board the press bus that was to take the Royal Tour correspondents to the press centre to file their copy to London. As the bus moved off, the doyen of the Royal Press Corps, James Whitaker of the *Daily Mirror*, took charge. 'All right then. Can we agree what she was wearing?' (The correspondents referred to notes and handouts and then the women ones fired off some technical stuff about Diana's clothing.) 'Good. Now can we agree what Charles said?' (An agreement of sorts was reached on Charles's quotes.) 'And what did she say to that kid?' Nothing had changed in thirty years. Quickly and efficiently a consensus report was developed. This is why if you were to read every single British newspaper during a Royal Tour – though God knows why anyone would bother – you would discover that all the reports are basically the same. The only rivalry that still exists is between photographers – one of the few worthwhile moments on a Royal Tour is to see them elbowing and kicking each other for an advantageous spot. I felt like suggesting that since the Royals are apparently fair game, why not invade their privacy with a bit more flair? I recall the Australian freelance Maurice Wilmott, who was offered a fortune by some Italian magazine for a photograph of four pregnant Royals – or was it five? – at a family gathering at Balmoral. Wilmott hired a caravan and camped out in Scotland, biding his time. He nearly made it. The Royal detectives spotted him disguised as a fly fisherman, casting his way downstream towards the Royals, rod in hand and a fishing basket full of Nikons and long lenses. As the police moved in to grab him, Charles, who had had a hard time from

Wilmott that summer at Cowes, ran down the bank and shouted in his exquisite Royal accent, 'Fuck off, Wilmott' – the only time he has been known to use a four-letter word.

Pondering on what I could write the second week of the tour that would not be in the Whitaker mould, I thought: why not assess the Royals' performance and the audience reaction as if the whole thing was an entertainment, which it is. I envisaged the headline: ROYAL TOUR FLOP – CHARLES FAILS TO FIND FORM. I tried out the idea on a BBC Royal Tour correspondent. I put it to her that perhaps one of the reasons the Royals were making more frequent tours of Australia was an attempt by Buckingham Palace to stem rising republican sentiment. As far as I could make out, it was not succeeding. In fact, Australians were getting a bit bored of seeing so many Royals so often and were finding it hard to raise the energy to get to the top of the street to see Charles and Di drive past. 'In short,' I said, 'I think this tour's a bit of a washout.' She was horrified. No, she said, Australians loved the Royal pair as much as ever. Well, then, let's report the Royal family for what it really is: a very successful British business, Royals (GB) plc. Even the Queen, I am told by sources in day-to-day contact with Her Majesty, occasionally refers to her family as 'the Firm'. Warming to the idea, I said that this would make the Royal press corps do some real work because it would turn them at a stroke into business news reporters: who is the most efficient executive in Royals (GB)? Is it a good idea for Charles to write his own company speeches? Who was censured at the last board meeting? Who's working on long-term strategy and what is it? How does the chief executive officer see the firm in the year 2000?' The BBC woman looked at me as if I were mad.

Nevertheless I tried it. I put it all together in a story which was at least a bit different from all the other mush we were reading at that time. I had already collected the facts. In Sydney, the official welcome to the Royals at the Opera House was attended by 25,000 people – but this was only half the number who, the previous day, had marched through the city in support of nuclear disarmament. In Newcastle 50,000 packed the town's sports centre to greet the Royal couple but 43,000 of them were schoolchildren, bused in from towns as far as a hundred miles away. At a glittering luncheon at the state parliament house in Sydney, two Labor members of the upper house boycotted the event in protest at the Royal visit. It was no accident, I wrote, that the Australian Prime Minister, Bob Hawke, a declared republican, did not get around to meeting the Royal couple until five days into the tour. Even the Australian press, conservative to a paper, was not 100 per cent behind the visit. I quoted Ian Warden, a columnist on the *Canberra Times* and a self-confessed 'mild monarchist' who had written: 'When I see one human being besotted by another for reasons of rank and station, and the aura that surrounds those ranks and stations, my flesh creeps.' The *Sydney Morning Herald* said that if anything in Australia was going to increase republican sentiment it was not going to be the Royal family but 'the way television brings them to us'. I pointed out that the *National Times* had taken the opportunity to rebut the notion that republicanism was all Australia's fault. 'Australia did not drift away from Britain,' it said. 'Britain cut off contact with us.' The paper went on to cite Britain's entry into the EEC and Australia's inclusion in immigration restrictions aimed at the black Commonwealth in the Sixties and Seventies. I was pleased with the piece. It was factual and restrained – I had resisted the temptation to quote the poster I had seen in Sydney's Oxford Street:

> Take Charles and Di and Baby Bill
> And send the buggers back
> To where it was
> From whence they came
> And fuck the Union Jack

The *Sunday Times* was very unhappy with my article. The very fact that it was different from what other correspondents were writing cast suspicion on it. 'If this is true,' I was told, 'then why hasn't someone else also written it?' This was proof, if I needed it, of the dictum of many editors – news is not news until someone else reports it. I fought my corner and in the end a truncated version appeared, but without the sting. Of course, the Buckingham Palace press corps to a man and woman then denied that the tour was a flop or that republicanism was making the slightest difference to the Royals' popularity.

It was a relief to get back to Aborigines, even though the story was not working out as expected. The *Sunday Times* magazine prided itself on having 'big ideas . . . sweeping concepts . . . a dramatic overview of life'. It did not go in for objective journalism – what one editor called 'all that on-the-one-hand-but-on-the-other-hand crap'. So I was in Alice Springs in quest of what the magazine imagined to be a simple but moving story – 'The Australian Aborigines are a dying race, so find, interview and photograph the last Aborigines living in their unspoilt native state . . . Let's do it now before their traditional way of life disappears for ever.' I began by spending a week in Sydney trying to shed a few prejudices. Like most urban Australians I did not know a single Aborigine. The first one I had ever seen was selling boomerangs at La Perouse, a Sydney suburb, one autumn Sunday just before the war. The second was dead under a bridge outside Lismore in northern New South Wales, his head bashed in by a rock from the dry river bed. The congealed blood in his black hair was the same colour as the cheap port wine he and his murderer had quarrelled over. I wrote about it for my newspaper then, the *Northern Star*, but it did not rate a line. Live Aborigines were a problem; dead ones were an ex-problem, not news.

In the years between the first Aborigine and the second, I had absorbed all the conventional falsehoods and prejudices about them. They had thrown spears at Captain Cook when he was only trying to inform them that he was discovering Australia. They could kill one of their own kind by pointing a bone at him: he would just waste away and die. They could track anything in the desert, especially missing white men. They loved a drink but could not hold it. They made faithful retainers if you could catch them early enough; older ones would go 'walkabout' in the bush just when you needed them most. White Australians had tried to give them the traditional 'fair go' but they hated regular work and and blew every opportunity to make something of themselves.

My generation of Australians cringed in the Fifties when visitors brought up the White Australia policy. We hid our heads when the Immigration Minister, justifying the deportation of a Chinese man called Wong who had hoped to be allowed to stay because he had married an Australian woman, made Parliament rock with laughter when he said, 'Two Wongs don't make a white.' We signed petitions against the evil of Apartheid and marched for civil rights in Alabama. But Aborigines? Some of us knew that they were banned by custom from swimming pools in Australian inland towns – 'who'd want to swim in a pool after an Abo had been in it?' – and were banned by law from pubs. Few knew and cared that officially Aborigines were a non-people – at census time counting was limited to 'the non-Aboriginal population'. They did not have the vote; they were not allowed to own land or property; they needed official permission to take a job and their wages were then paid to the local 'Protector of Aborigines', who was usually the town policeman, and he doled out what he felt the Aborigine needed. They had to live where the authorities told them. If this was on a reserve, they could be required to do thirty-two hours' work a week without pay. Any Aborigine who objected to any of this could be sent to one of the prison islands where he could be detained indefinitely. Shipped there in handcuffs and, occasionally, neck chains, he was sometimes allowed to take his family with him. More frequently he was not, because the unstated policy underlying the official attitude to Aborigines was to destroy their tribal culture so as to hasten their assimilation into white Australian society. It is amazing that today Aborigines, separated in this manner, speak with remarkably little rancour of 'catching up' with their families thirty years later.

They were usually taken out of school at about ten because further education was considered to make them 'cunning and cheeky'. Female Aborigines were sexually exploited by white Australians with impunity; in some areas girls as young as seven were taken into prostitution. The men were victims of violence to an extent only just being realised. A Northern Territory anthropologist told me, 'Every Aborigine in this part of the country can state, quite correctly, that at least one of his relatives has been shot by a white man.' Viewed impartially, it is difficult to see how the plight of the Aborigines in Australia right up until the mid-Sixties differed significantly from that of the slaves in the United States in the last century, and it remains one of the great puzzles of history how Australia got away with it for so long.

Perhaps Australians were able to turn away from the plight of the Aborigines by dismissing it as a transient one, the last brutal but necessary step in the absorption of a Stone Age people into the twentieth century. Otherwise, their very different attitude to life would make their survival impossible. As Captain Cook wrote: 'They seemed to set no value on anything we gave them, nor would they part with anything of their own for any one article we could offer them; this, in my opinion, argues that they think themselves provided with all the necessities of life and they have no superfluities.' The missionaries were equally puzzled by Aboriginal attitudes. In 1840, a Mrs C. G. Tiechelmann complained, 'There are amongst the Adelaide natives several who are able to fence their garden, build a house on it, and cultivate the ground, if they liked to do it; but nobody can give them a taste for that for which they have none.' Disheartened by their failure to convert and civilise the Australian heathens, the missionaries decided that if adult Aborigines were beyond redemption, the answer was to catch the children and remove them from their parents' influence. Given a European education at a mission school, they could then fill a useful role in Australian society. This was done with the best of intentions but it assumed that since Aborigines were different, they therefore had no human feelings. Occasionally a missionary would note that a young child taken away from its family would show 'a tendency to pine'. Others felt that they had achieved something when an Aboriginal child became sufficiently well-educated to be employed as a servant in a white household, an envied position. (A well-known painting of the period shows a small Aboriginal boy in a white sailor's suit with a caption that reads: 'Mrs Blair's aboriginal, Flemington, 1836.') The conclusion was that since the Aborigines were unable to resist the impact of such interventions by the white man, they would soon die out. The figures seemed to support this. By the First World War the estimated 300,000 Aborigines in Australia when the first British settlers arrived had dwindled to a mere 60,000. Soon they too, would be gone, victims of the march of history, and with them would vanish any guilt that the white man felt about their treatment. To act now would be a waste of time.

But in 1966 there was a turning point. In August of that year two hundred Aborigines employed at the Wave Hill cattle station in the Northern Territory, owned by the British meat millionaires, the Vesteys, walked off the job and settled on a nearby reservation, announcing that they would not return until they were paid the same wages as white workers. The strike attracted wide attention and television and newspapers were soon showing urban Australia what life was like on an outback cattle station. 'Aborigines lived in huts like dog kennels that scorched in the summer and froze in the winter. Amenities, even of the crudest kind, were non-existent. Medical care was not for Aborigines, nor were toilets, schooling, decent food, or average wages. Their return for toiling from daylight to dark was cruelty and indignity.' Radical white Australians took up the case for the strikers and under their influence the Aborigines changed direction. They decided that they did not want to go back to work anyway – they wanted to start a co-operative venture at Wattie Creek, tribal land within the Wave Hill boundaries. But under Australian law as it then stood, since the Vesteys held a Crown lease on Wave Hill, the Aborigines would be squatters on their own land, so the whole issue of Aboriginal land rights came to the fore. This coincided with Aboriginal complaints about being treated as second-class citizens in an upcoming census, so the government of the day sought to still criticism by holding a referendum: should we alter the constitution so Aborigines can be counted in the census and should we give the federal government the right to make laws for Aborigines rather than the states, as hitherto? The government was stunned by the result – five million voted yes, only half a million no, the most overwhelming acceptance of a referendum proposal in the country's history. Then everything went wrong. In December 1967, the Prime Minister, Harold Holt, accidentally drowned. His successor, John Gorton, was not interested in reform for Aborigines and the next Prime Minister, William MacMahon, represented farming and cattle interests. The stalemate might have gone on for ever if it had not been for the Sixties' mineral boom.

An Aborigine's relationship with the land is private, complicated, and absolutely essential to his existence. The land is Kunapipi, the earth mother, the beginning and end of life itself. The white man's attitude to land – that it is a commodity to be bought and sold, to be built upon and exploited – is incomprehensible to an Aborigine. Mining, with its symbolic penetration of the earth and the removal of its entrails, is a particularly traumatic image for an Aborigine and many had come to regard mining companies as intrinsically evil. So when Nabalco Pty Ltd acquired a special mineral lease from the Australian government to mine bauxite at Gove Peninsula in Arnhem Land, the Aborigines at a nearby Methodist Mission village decided to fight against it in court. The case, Eastern Arnhem Land Aborigines v. the Commonwealth Government and Nabalco, was a major step in the land rights fight. The government made it clear right from the beginning that the Aborigines were not going to win. If the court ruled in their favour, it said, the government would change the law – 'a handful of people cannot be permitted to obstruct Australia's development'. But the government had not envisaged the Aborigines losing in the manner they did. The chief judge of the Northern Territory, Mr Justice Blackburn, held that the relationship between the Aborigines and the land did not amount to proprietorship as it is understood in English law, that the Aborigines could not prove association with the same land since the arrival of the white man in 1788, and that common law did not recognise that Aborigines had any land rights at all before 1788. Reaction in Australia was one of shocked protest, and the judge's recommendation that the law should be clarified made Aboriginal land rights a major issue in the campaign for the 1972 election. The Labor Party, led by the reforming lawyer Gough Whitlam, swept to power and appointed a leading High Court judge, Mr Justice Woodward, as a Royal Commissioner to advise on how best to establish Aboriginal land rights. Whitlam made it clear that the judge's task was not to advise the government *whether* Aborigines should have the rights, but *how*. Woodward recommended that the Aborigines should be able to acquire land rights in three ways. Those already on government land should be given non-transferable freehold title; others should be able to make claims on the basis of tradition to any unalienated Crown land; and the government should be able to recognise a claim on the basis of need.

But with success in sight, the Aborigines were again thwarted. Legislation to enact these historic recommendations was before Parliament in 1975 when Whitlam's government was sensationally dismissed by the Governor-General, Sir John Kerr, and Whitlam lost the subsequent election. The new government, led by Malcolm Fraser, recognised the strength of feeling on the land rights issue and promised to legislate on substantially the same terms. But when the law was finally passed, the third recommendation – a claim on the basis of need – was left out. Nevertheless, the Woodward report and the ensuing act was a landmark, the most substantial advance in the status of Aborigines in two hundred years.

My homework over, I set off with Griffiths to meet some Aborigines face to face. Our plan was to talk to some urban Aboriginal leaders and then head into the outback to find the last ones living in their natural state. We went first to Queensland, the state with the worst history for the treatment of Aborigines in Australia. In Cairns, a lush Queensland town that grew rich on cattle and sugar and is now an international tourist playground, we found the headquarters of the Northern Queensland Land Council, an Aboriginal grass-roots organisation that is trying to co-ordinate the fight for land rights. Its offices, three rooms over a shop, were plastered with posters: 'Land rights, not mining' . . . 'I don't make the problems; why must I pay'. The head of the council was Mick Miller, an articulate and committed Aborigine, who said he wanted us to get the feeling for life as an Aborigine in Queensland before explaining his work, so he arranged a visit to Yarraba, an Aboriginal reserve about twenty minutes' drive from Cairns. Strictly speaking, to do this we should have had written permission from the Queensland Department of Aboriginal and Islander Advancement, the DAIA, but since we had been invited to enter the reserve by the chairman of the Aboriginal Council there, then it would have been difficult for the white DAIA manager to eject us.

Living conditions on the reserve seemed reasonably comfortable. There were shops, a bakery, post office and sports fields. But the Aborigines we spoke with gave off an air of pessimism and resignation. 'We live on handouts,' said Robert Smallwood. 'We're told to get off our bums and do some work, but when we put suggestions to DAIA about work projects they take no notice. The truth is that they don't want us to get ahead.' There was also an air of subtle intimidation. Alfred Neal, a quiet, dignified man in his early fifties, had lived on the reserve all his life, his parents having been sent there 'in one of the big Aborigine round ups in the Twenties.' We wanted to photograph him with his son but the son said no. Neal explained why: the son had recently been sentenced to three months' jail for spitting at the manager. When his lawyer appealed, the sentence was increased to six months. It took a second appeal to have it reduced to two months. 'If the police see his picture in a newspaper, then they'll mark him down as a trouble-maker,' said Neal. 'Then he runs the risk of being pushed off the reserve. They could just pick him up in the police car one day and take him into Cairns and dump him there with nowhere to go.'

Later I checked this with Miller and he agreed that there was nothing to stop the police from doing this. 'The DAIA director is the trustee of all Aboriginal lands in Queensland and every reserve is administered by his department. You stay there at his tolerance.'

Miller said that the Queensland government, then the most reactionary and racist in Australia, had done its best to sabotage the Federal government's land rights legislation. 'For example, to stop the Federal government from acquiring the reserves in Queensland and then passing them on to the Aborigines, the Queensland government has de-gazetted the reserves and made them into local council areas. If the Federal government tries to compulsorily purchase council land, then it risks raising the emotive issue of states' rights. The way the Queensland government runs Aboriginal affairs gives us no immediate hope of getting land rights. We have to rely on the Federal government and when the Federal government moves, the state government will try to make it a racial issue and stir up race trouble.'

It was time for the outback, time to look for the vanishing tribes. We had been advised that it would be unwise to go wandering around the Northern Territory looking for Aborigines. We could get into trouble with the authorities. Even in Cairns we had been stopped by a police patrol car that had followed us on our way to a reservation, cautioned us about exceeding the speed limit and then questioned us about what we were doing in Cairns in a manner that let us know that the police were well aware of the answer. So we went along to a meeting of the Central Land Council in Alice Springs where some eighty Aboriginal leaders were discussing their affairs. We caught the chairman during the lunch break and told him of our plans: we wanted permission to travel through various tribal areas and photograph Aboriginal life. He was sceptical: Aborigines were a much researched race, with researchers getting rich on their publications and the Aborigines getting nothing. But, he said, this was a democratic gathering and so he would give me five minutes after lunch to address the meeting and convince the tribal elders that they should help us.

What could I say that would be any different from what dozens of other city journalists had told them many times? I made a few notes and came to a decision that went totally against the terms of my assignment. When the chairman introduced me and eighty curious faces fell silent, I said that I wanted to write about Aborigines in a way that I did not think had been done before. Instead of treating them as *victims* of the white man I would like to write about them as passive resisters in the Gandhian tradition who had managed to keep their tribal ways in the face of a lot of opposition. At that stage I had no idea whether this was true or not but it was a theory I could test later if we got the permission we were after. As for Griffiths, I said, he was not your usual 'snatch and run' photographer with a motor-driven 35mm camera. He was an artist. He used a huge wooden wholeplate camera mounted on a heavy tripod and often took hours to get the composition he wanted. At this stage, Griffiths held up his camera for the meeting to inspect and there were murmurs of amazement. To see him at work, I said, the whole Land Council was invited to assemble outside after the meeting and Griffiths would take a formal group portrait. There was a brief debate and then a vote which went our way.

It turned out that Griffiths' offer to take the Land Council's photograph probably swung it for us. He took nearly two hours – not just because he worked slowly but because the Aborigines loved the formality of the occasion and wanted to arrange the pose according to age, precedence and tribal relationships. Griffiths set up his camera, the Aborigines grouped themselves and looked expectant. Griffiths disappeared under the black cloth at the back of the camera and after a minute or so emerged to announce himself nearly satisfied. Just to be certain, he took a Polaroid with another camera, but when it emerged, the Aborigines insisted on seeing it, and then decided to re-arrange themselves. This happened twice and it was only when Griffiths warned that the light was failing that the Aborigines could be persuaded that their third grouping would have to be the last one. The result fascinated me and sixteen years later I still study it from time to time. The background is Billygoat Hill, a tumble of red rocks that cascade down to a level patch of gravel in front of the Land Council offices. Three bearded elderly Aborgines sit, legs crossed, at the front, presumably a position of honour. If so, then the lone figure standing way at the back, dressed like a Hollywood cowboy, with chaps, a bandana, a silver belt and a large steel wrist watch, must have done something terribly wrong. In between there is a hill of brown and black faces, blending by some trick of the light into the rocky background. I can envisage anthropologists studying it two hundred years from now.

Armed with our permissions, we still had to decide where to go and sought the advice of the man in the Northern Territory said to know almost more about Aborigines than they do about themselves, Dick Kimber. 'You're looking for what?' Kimber said laughing. 'An Aborigine in his unspoilt native state! If you mean an Aborigine without trousers, then you're wasting your time. Sure, I know it's still a belief – even in Australia – that somewhere out there is a tribe of naked Aborigines. It's just not so. But on the other hand, the fact that they're wearing clothes and travelling around in four-wheel-drive Toyotas doesn't mean that the Aborigines you see are not traditional Aborigines. It just means that they have adapted the most useful of the white man's tools to their own ways. In fact, tradition is stronger because the Red Ochre men, the guardians of ritual, are able to enforce their authority more widely than before – they get around much faster in their Toyotas than on foot.'

This was interesting stuff and part confirmation of my theory of Aborigines as passive resisters. Griffiths and I held a quick conference and decided to split up. Even if there was not a tribe of trouserless Aborigines out there, Griffiths still wanted to photograph Aborigines living in the desert, so he would go off and do that while I spent more time with Kimber and other experts, trying to sort the myth about Aborigines from the reality.

I put the view that Aboriginal culture, language and traditions are dying out to Kimber. 'Not true,' he said. 'There's been a lot of talk about the revival of Aboriginal culture. There is no revival because it has always been there, hidden from white Australia's eyes. The Aborigines reacted to the dominance of the white man by taking their culture underground. They maintained their traditions, languages, ceremonies and songs. And they kept this all secret until recently when, in the changed atmosphere, they began to take a few white men into their confidence.' (Later, back in Sydney, I mentioned this to an Aboriginal activist and not only did he agree but said there was an ancient Aboriginal language spoken only in the bustling inner Sydney suburb of Redfern and that had been kept secret from the white authorities for decades.)

But how could Aborigines keep up their tribal ways and ceremonies when so many of them seemed to be drunk most of the time? Well, to my surprise I discovered that most Aborigines are teetotal. Those who do drink tend to do so on benders, with long periods of abstinence in between. And when drinking does get out of hand, they are quite capable of solving the problem themselves. In the late Seventies, drink was causing serious trouble at Ayers Rock, the famous tourist site an hour's flight from Alice Springs. Every weekend about two hundred young Aborigines would drive in from miles around to drink and fight. Finally, fed up, the local Aborigines called a meeting of tribal elders. The following Friday night all the young men turned up as usual and were just settling down to some hard drinking when the old men emerged from the darkness and dispersed themselves in the crowd, all the time reciting something. To this day no one knows what they said but the effect was instantaneous. The young men got into their cars, drove away and never came back. A year later the local Aborigines voted to close the pub.

The head ranger at the Rock, an Englishman called Derek Roff, cautioned against writing off even the Aborigines we had seen lying drunk around Alice Springs. 'When the time comes for them to be present at a ritual, they sober up and report to the elders – or else. It's much the same with the young kids. You see them behaving like white kids . . . video games and music . . . until the time comes for traditional discipline and they immediately revert to the tribal ways.'

A futile gesture if they are really a dying race. But even this, it seems, is not true. There are officially 330,000 Aborigines in Australia, more than three times the number in the Twenties when they reached their nadir. But even this figure may be an understatement. The census total for Queensland was 50,000, of which 1,400 were in the Cairns area. Mick Miller and his fellow activists made a check count and got 10,000 for Cairns alone. Miller's estimate of the Aborigine population of Queensland is 120,000. If this is anywhere near correct, then it is possible that the Aborigine population of all Australia is now much higher than it was when the white man first arrived. This is not to underplay the high mortality rate for Aborigines. Their average life expectancy is still twenty years less than that of a white Australian and the infant mortality rate three times higher. Skin and respiratory diseases are common, eye troubles rampant, and even leprosy is not unusual. But these are high-profile health problems, preventable with clean water supplies, proper sewage disposal, decent housing and proper nutrition. Aborigines themselves are already tackling them.

On my last day in Alice Springs I was driving Dick Kimber in my rental car from his house to the centre of town. On the roadside we passed an Aborigine standing motionless staring into the distance, like a portrait from some travel brochure. As we drew near he suddenly waved vigorously at us to hitch a ride. 'For God's sake don't stop,' Kimber said. 'He's a terrible bore.' I thought about this all the way back to Sydney. With the inherited prejudices of my generation of Australians I had regarded Aborigines as being many things – drunkards, street fighters, victims, trackers, stockmen – and had attributed to them many character traits – cheeky, cunning, lazy, mysterious, untrustworthy. But the idea that at least one might have such a mundane attribute as being a bore brought home to me something I had unconsciously denied – Aborigines were people, ordinary human beings . . . with as much right to a decent life in Australia as everyone else.

The Australian author Xavier Herbert had realised this long before me. In 1978 he wrote, 'Until we give back to the black man just a bit of the land that was his, and give it back without provisos, without strings to snatch it back, without anything but complete generosity of spirit in concession for the evil that we have done him – until we do that, we shall remain what we have always been so far: a people without integrity, not a nation, but a community of thieves.' If Herbert had written those lines ten years earlier, white Australians would have laughed him off as a 'ratbag'. They no longer laughed. That was the measure of the change I found and a symbol of hope for all Australians.

CHAPTER THIRTEEN

TRIAL BY TV

Journalism in Australia tends to be parochial, centred on the big metropolitan areas and obsessed with politics. I am not the only one to hold this view. W. F. Deedes, the former editor of the London *Daily Telegraph*, had this advice for anyone from Britain visiting Australia for the first time: 'Try not to read the newspapers during your visit. They are usually full of news about political scandals and will give a totally false impression of this fine country.' Since my own training was on a small country newspaper, I knew that there are dozens of wonderful stories in outback Australia just waiting to be written. I had even worked out how to go about it: I would drive into town, put up at the best hotel, invite the editor of the local paper to a long dinner and at the end of the evening ask him to tell me the biggest local story he felt – for whatever reason – unable to publish. Strangely, I found British editors more receptive to this idea than Australian ones and as a result throughout the Eighties I spent more and more time in Australia writing about the strange and exciting things that happened which never seemed to make the Australian press. This was how I came to be with 'Gunna' Geissmann in an air-conditioned pub in the main street of Yeppoon, a small seaside town slap on the Tropic of Capricorn in central Queensland.

Gunna's real name was Eric but his friends called him Gunna because he was always 'gunna' do something but never quite got around to it. Geissmann loved Yeppoon and considered it to be an Australian paradise. He was probably right. The climate is glorious – day after day of cloudless skies and a cooling breeze in summer. The views are magnificent: miles of white sandy beaches, undulating coves, coral islands and deep blue water. The population is about 7,000 and there are no factories, pollution, petty crime, traffic lights or parking meters. The best cuts of meat are cheap and you can buy giant Pacific prawns right off the fishing boats. According to

Geissmann, his life in Yeppoon had an easy, undemanding rhythm in which one day blurred happily into the next. There was no conscious agreement to keep quiet about the place, but on the other hand no one who lived there went out of their way to broadcast the town's charms. They hoped that it would for ever escape the winds of change.

Well, it didn't, and that was why I was interviewing Geissmann. His story began 1970, when Yohachiro Iwasaki, then aged eighty, came to Yeppoon on a visit for his Japanese chamber of commerce. Just north of the town are some 20,000 acres of beachfront land. The locals thought of this – if they thought of it at all – as scrub, dunes and low-grade pasture. Iwasaki looked at it and saw, he said, the Promised Land. 'The beach is ten times longer and wider than Waikiki, and although Disneyworld is larger, it is artificial. I saw in Yeppoon the best and most beautiful natural resort in the world, a venture that would cement for ever relations between Japan and Australia.'

Iwasaki's plans called for five luxury hotels, ten motels, eighty-five holiday units and 1,250 villas providing, in total, accommodation for 18,000 tourists, mostly Japanese. There would be a marine park, botanical gardens, a wildlife reserve, a forest reserve, a bird sanctuary, a coconut plantation, two eighteen-hole golf courses, a fishing area, a picnic park and tennis and water sports recreation centres. In 1978, the Queensland government under Premier Joh Bjelke-Petersen gave the project the go-ahead. At that early stage, had the government or Iwasaki looked more closely at the file of local objections to the project, they might have saved themselves a lot of trouble because one of them was from Geissmann.

Geissmann, who made a modest living by selling worms as bait for fishermen, thought that the development would pollute the area and ruin the fishing. 'Iwasaki says that there will be only a quarter of the resort people on the beach at any one time,' he said. 'Okay. But that's more than 4,000. Most of the time around here you don't see more than four people on the beach all day. I want to keep it that way.' So on the side of his house, on the road running between the town and the Iwasaki land, he pinned an Australian flag with the Union Jack section replaced by the red sun of Nippon. Underneath was a poster which read: 'Tokyo Joh, Realty Iwasaki: get off our backs. Go home. You can buy politicians, but you cannot buy people.' Bjelke-Petersen ignored the libellous suggestion that he had been bought, but the local police 'recommended' that Geissmann remove the poster. When he did, they took no action but marked him down as the town's leading anti-Iwasaki agitator.

When work started on the project on 20 June 1979, Iwasaki gave the most lavish party ever seen in Queensland. The guests included most members of the local shire council, many members of the state parliament – including Bjelke-Petersen, who was photographed embracing Iwasaki – and two hundred and sixty guests from Japan who emerged from the local airport through a specially erected Shinto shrine gateway. Entertainment was provided by traditional Japanese drummers, dancing girls and fireworks. As was to be expected, the party did not meet with the approval of everyone in Yeppoon. Four days earlier, the local newspaper, the *Rockhampton Morning Bulletin*, carried the following advertisement:

VALE YEPPOON
The Capricorn Coast Protection Council will hold a memorial service for Yeppoon, the town that is being sold, and for a way of life that is passing for ever. The public is invited to the service. No free beer, no free food, no fireworks, no dancing girls.'

This was followed on the eve of the party with another advertisement:

ROLL OF HONOUR
In memory of our fallen comrades who gave their lives in vain. When you go home, tell them of us and say, for your tomorrow, we gave our today. President and members of the Yeppoon sub-branch of the Returned Soldiers' League of Australia.

On the lawn outside the RSL offices, rows of small white crosses appeared overnight, one for each local resident who had died in the war against Japan. The divisions in the town deepened and what happened next was probably inevitable. During the night of Saturday, 29 November 1980, someone put a bomb under the Iwasaki motel, then in the final stages of construction, and blew it up.

Early on the Sunday morning, someone telephoned the offices of the *Morning Bulletin* and said that he was speaking on behalf of the Revolutionary Ring for the Liberation of Queensland. 'We did the bombing,' he said. At about the same time, the president of the Capricorn Coast Protection Council was preparing a press announcement saying that Yeppoon used to be a sleepy hollow and a good place to live. 'Now it's the site of Queensland's first terrorism – thanks to the Iwasaki development.'

The prime suspect was, of course, Gunna Geissmann. The police had questioned him the day after the bombing but it had not been a very successful interview. The police explained: 'Gunna was the worse for wear. He told us that he'd got up at eight that morning and had taken a case of beer to a friend's house to pass the time while they waited for the pubs to open.' After that the police left Geissmann alone until 18 February, about three months after the bombing, when they stopped his car on the highway outside Yeppoon and asked him to accompany them to Rockhampton police station. 'No worries,' Geissmann said. 'I'm pretty free this morning.' Two hours later, the police charged Geissmann and his 23-year-old nephew, Kerry, with the bombing. The trial began before an all-male jury on 23 June 1981 and lasted a month during which sixty-eight witnesses gave evidence. But then, curiously, it took the jury only ninety minutes to find Geissmann and his nephew not guilty.

None of this had made the major Australian papers, much less the international press. I became interested only because I was in Australia at the time for my father's eightieth birthday and a Canadian friend, an academic at the University of Capricorn who had been living in Yeppoon, insisted that I should meet Geissmann and learn the real story of how the case against him had collapsed with repercussions that were still echoing around the town two years later. 'They'll love it in Britain,' my friend said.

Geissmann was only too happy to tell his story. The main witness against Geissmann was one of his best friends, Neville Wust, a former professional fisherman. Wust swore that after hearing Geissmann boast in various pubs that he was the bomber, he had decided to go to the police, 'not for the reward money, but from pure motives and a wish to protect the community'. The judge threatened to clear the court when the public gallery shook with laughter at this point. Geissmann chuckled as he recalled the moment and then explained, 'Everyone knew that the wallopers had been able to lean on Wusty because they'd found some suspicious plants growing at his place.'

Whatever Wust's motives were, the police had decided to use him to trap Geissmann. The plan was for him to invite Geissmann to visit him on board his boat 'for a bit of a party', something they had done before. They would take Wust's boat offshore, drop a few fishing lines, and drink large quantities of cold beer and brown muscat, a sweet but deadly fortified wine. After the two men were well into their drinking bout, Wust would steer the conversation around to the subject of the bombing when, hopefully, Geissmann would repeat the confession that Wust claimed to have heard in Yeppoon pubs. This would be recorded by a small tape recorder concealed on Wust's boat and, in case this malfunctioned, heard by the police hiding on shore via a small radio transmitter also concealed on the boat.

The plan worked perfectly. After drinking large quantities of beer and muscat, Geissmann, with heavy prompting from Wust, began to discuss the bombing and, according to the police, incriminated himself. 'No way,'

Geissmann told me. 'I was on to him from the start and thought I'd have a bit of fun with him. I just repeated everything I'd learnt about the bombing from reading the papers.' The police thought differently but they ran into an unexpected problem. When they came to playing back the incriminating tapes to the prosecution lawyers, the prosecution lawyers shook their heads in horror. For Geissmann and Wust had talked about other things during the five hours they had spent together on the boat and their main topic of conversation had been man's eternal one – women. They had discussed in the most intimate detail the sexual talents – real or imagined – of a large section of the female population of Yeppoon and, in a lapse that many regard as unforgivable, they had named names.

'The lawyers didn't know what to do,' Geissmann said. 'They could've got the police to cut out the sex bits but it would've been obvious that the tapes had been fiddled with. So they had to play the whole lot for the jury and it stuffed their case.' It also packed the courtroom. As word of what the tapes contained spread throughout the district, court officials had to organise a queuing system for admittance to the tiny courtroom. Sensing the mood of the jury, Geissmann's lawyer confined his defence to a simple alibi. On the night of the explosion, Geissmann said, he had a few drinks at various Yeppoon pubs on his way home from a pineapple plantation where he had been helping a relative. He had bought a bottle of brown muscat wine to go with his dinner. After dinner he had drunk a further half bottle of muscat from a bottle he kept tucked behind the couch. Then he had got undressed, put on his track suit, had gone to bed and was asleep when the explosion occurred. Three relatives corroborated his alibi. 'It takes a lotta drink to knock Gunna out,' said one, 'but when he crashes he crashes.'

I tried to find out how the jury had reached its verdict. It is against the law in Australia to interview jurors about cases, but the general feeling in Yeppoon was that the jury had little choice but to find Geissmann innocent. 'If they'd brought in a guilty verdict,' my Canadian friend told me, 'then they'd have been accusing Geissmann and three of his relatives of being liars. You can't do that in a small town. Anyway, the feeling was that the police had not played fair, first by getting Geissmann's mate to set him up, then by making the recording and then, above all, by playing it in court. They reckoned that Geissmann was probably guilty, but they let him off anyway.'

The trial did not end the story. There was a series of transfers from Yeppoon police station as a number of officers were packed off to even smaller places. Neville Wust decided to leave town. Geissmann arranged to pay off his A\$38,000 (£19,000) legal bill at A\$694 (£347) a month and then went on a fifty-day hunger strike to try to persuade the Queensland government to take into Crown ownership the Iwasaki resort beach for 150 metres inland from the high-water mark so as to ensure public access.

As we sipped beer so cold it made your lips numb, I found it difficult to decide who was the real Geissmann. Was he the calm, reasonable man, responsible father of eight children he projected in our interview? Or was he the Geissmann of Australian legend – the hard-drinking Aussie, the battling bomber standing up for the little man against the forces of authority, no matter what it took. 'Look, I'm not a racist,' he said, as the rest of the bar pushed closer to hear the Hero of Yeppoon speak. 'But you can't forget the war that quickly. A lot of blokes died to stop the Japs from getting here. Now the Queensland government lets them come and take what they like. I know there's no hope of stopping the resort now, so I'm concentrating on making sure that we still keep the beach. The beach oughta belong to everyone.'*

I filed the Geissmann story and headed back to Sydney for my father's eightieth birthday, travelling by train, my favourite form of transport. Australian relatives painted a gloomy picture of soot-laden compartments, surly attendants and poor food. Instead the compartment had crisp linen, hot showers and a private toilet. The restaurant was adequate, the wine plentiful and I was able to awaken the children in the misty dawn to see kangaroos hopping away from the line. I got into conversation with some Queenslanders who still showed that friendly curiosity about strangers that the more sophisticated southern states have lost. In five minutes they winkled out of me all my vital details and volunteered many of their own in return. A silver-haired old man told me that he too had once lived in London. 'When was that?' I asked him. 'Back in 1899,' he said, 'But the wife went back recently.' How recently? 'Aw, I reckon 1936.' I decided that time does slip by in Queensland without anyone noticing.

At the birthday party, my father made a speech in which he claimed that he had been alive during the most exciting years in history – two world wars, the Russian Revolution, the arrival of the atomic age, man in space, television and the explosive growth of that most desirable of twentieth-century objects, the motor car. To make his point he recalled going to Moore Park to watch a Sydney dentist, and amateur aviator, make a five-minute flight in a primitive aircraft. 'And then I lived long enough to watch on television an American landing on the moon. All in one lifetime.' But the anecdote that most impressed the young car-driving guests, at constant war with Sydney traffic wardens, was how he used to drive his 1928

---

* Geissmann won his battle to keep access free for everyone. He died of a heart attack on his beloved beach in 1991.

Chevrolet Straight Six the fifteen miles from Sans Souci to the centre of Sydney without seeing a traffic light and then park all day in the middle of the city. Now, he said, he was so worried about traffic congestion that he was thinking about buying a motor-bike, although he doubted whether his son and daughter would let him.

When I compared notes with my sister later, she told me that the motor-bike affair was only one example of the role reversal that seems to take place when one's parents enter the autumn of their lives. My father had come to live with her after my mother died. Awakened one night at 3am by a scuffling noise in her kitchen, she investigated and found my father, then only seventy-nine, his shoes hung around his neck by their laces, crawling through the back window. She was in the middle of ticking him off for staying out so late and forgetting his key when her tirade began to sound familiar – my father had said much the same thing to her thirty years earlier when he caught her in similar circumstances. I thought I had better have a word with him. Now that he was eighty, didn't he think he should be slowing down a bit? Not so many late nights, for example. A little less boisterous behaviour in public? (The organiser of a wine-tasting tour had complained that my father had led some of the group in dancing on the cellar tables.) 'Why?' he said. Well, didn't he feel any sense of mortality? 'None at all,' he said. 'I feel the same age I've always felt.' I gave up. A year later my sister had to ban him from giving parties in her house when she was away – she had returned unexpectedly in the middle of one to find that a 65-year-old grandmother had fallen into the swimming pool, two 75-year-old men had had a fight over a woman, the barbecue had exploded, someone had raided my brother-in-law's vintage wine collection and an 80-year-old man had driven his son's car into the hedge.

Fortunately my father had already taken the decision to give up driving. Coming home from visiting a girlfriend late one night he had slowed down as he approached a car slewed across the road, then attempted to drive around it. As he did so he felt a slight bump. He got out to find to his horror that he had run over the hand of a man lying unconscious on the roadway. My father was still standing there in shock when another driver came from the kerb. 'He's okay, mate,' he said. 'And the ambulance is on the way. Look, I hit him first so there's no sense in you hanging around and getting involved. Why don't you bugger off and forget about it.' My father did, but he couldn't forget about it and a week later, after a lot of thought – he knew he would be lost without his car – he posted his driving licence back to the NSW Road Transport Authority with a letter saying he felt he was too old to drive safely any more. Some sensitive civil servant – they do exist – replied the following week. 'Dear Mr Knightley: This is to acknowledge the receipt of your driving licence which has been duly cancelled. May we congratulate you on two counts? First that you have realised that you are now too old to drive safely. Would that others were like you. And secondly, having examined your file, we note that you have driven in the state of New South Wales for sixty years without a recorded accident. The Minister asks me to pass to you his personal congratulations and best wishes.'

Among the guests at my father's birthday party were a lot of relatives and friends I had not seen since I left Sydney for London. I was amazed to learn that some of them had never bothered to take a trip outside Australia, even for a holiday. Were they any the worse for this? Thirty years earlier I would have been certain of the answer but listening to them chatting happily about their suburban lives, full of the optimism that marks Australians as distinctly as their accent, I had my doubts. I had left because I found Australian society stultifying, but as one of my friends warned at the time, 'You can't change your environment by withdrawing from it.' Now those who stayed had the satisfaction of having taken part in the change while we who left changed nothing and were for ever doomed to be labelled, at best, as 'who live in London', and, at worst, as 'the expatriate Australians'.

An enormous amount of beer was drunk at my father's party – a lot of it by him – and looking for heavy drinker stories to repeat at London dinner tables, I persuaded a group at the barbecue to tell me some. 'There's a story about this bloke in today's paper,' my brother-in-law said. 'A truck driver who had been banned three times for being over the limit. The wallopers picked him up asleep over the wheel and his blood test showed an alcohol level four times the limit. He was still in the police cells when there was a bit in the paper about his incredibly high test. Over the next couple of days the cop station got three hundred and forty-five letters and telegrams for him – all congratulating him for breaking the state record.'

I got to wondering why Australians drink so much and a series of advertisements with stylized paintings of rugged, very masculine men swam out of my memory. The slogans on the advertisements went something like 'Reschs, a man's drink' . . . 'Tooths, the fisherman's friend'. There were also a batsman, a Rugby footballer, a golfer. Perhaps some bright advertising executive back in the Twenties had the brilliant idea of associating beer drinking with manliness and male bonding. Or had he merely been reflecting an already established link, something from early Australian history? I had recently been reading about alcohol's role in American history and the theory that settlers in the United States drank a lot because their food was so terrible they needed a strong drink to wash the taste away. Was it the same in early Australia? Certainly not after the first Chinese settlers had arrived. One of my schoolfriends at the party told me about his first Chinese meal. His father was in the Masonic Lodge, a past Master and Grand District Inspector of Workings. Since he was out on lodge business five nights a week, his wife did not consider it worth cooking a proper family dinner so my friend was brought up on Vegemite and tomato sandwiches. Then, when he was eighteen, someone took him to a Chinese restaurant where he ate his first prawn fu yong and realised that there was a whole new world out there.

My father had done much the same for me, so as part of his birthday celebrations we went to Chinatown and ordered a banquet. One of the guests, a Chinese who was born in China but brought up in Australia, was a doctor so I asked him why it is that Chinese seemed to be able to eat so much but never put on weight: 'When did you last see a really gross Chinese?' He admitted that he did not know but said he had noticed that second-generation Chinese in Australia were heavier than the first generation. I asked if it was a change in diet. 'No,' he said. 'More likely the beer.' So I mentioned something that Germaine Greer had once told me, based, she insisted, not on personal research but on what Australian women had confided to her – a lot of Australian men, middle-aged with beer bellies, are impotent.

As it neared time to return to London I was alarmed to find that whereas I had arrived in Australia with the blood pressure of a boy of ten, I was about to leave with that of a man of eighty. What was it about the country that had made me so excited? There was the constant talk of money – an impolite topic of conversation in Britain. No matter how well one had suppressed the sin of greed, it was hard to hear someone in Australia say, 'So I agreed we'd go ahead at a million and a quarter. That leaves me with about two hundred thou for myself,' without wanting to get one's hands on all those dollars that seemed to be floating around waiting to be picked up. Then there was the difficulty of encompassing Australia in six weeks. I wanted to reach out and grab it all at once. I had not been to Melbourne on this trip. Had I missed something? I had not been to Perth for fifteen years. How could I soak up Australia without going to Perth? This frustration raised the blood pressure ten points alone. And then, inevitably, there was the drink. When you are a visitor, your friends work on you in shifts.

Back in London I had a letter from a film producer called Lloyd Phillips. He wrote from Pinewood Studios saying that he would like to make a feature film based loosely on my story of Gunna Geissmann. We reached an agreement and he asked me to call on the scriptwriter next time I was in

Australia to share ideas for the film which already had a title: *The Last Resort*. The scriptwriter was Miranda Downes, a beautiful and talented woman, and during a series of meetings I came to like and admire her.

She told me that she had had a tough life – a failed marriage, bouts of bulimia, lack of confidence, and a series of boring jobs. Then, almost overnight, all had changed. She got a post as production secretary to David Elfick of *Newsfront* fame, one of Australia's most successful feature films. Unimpressed with some of the film scripts she had to type, she mentioned to Elfick one day an idea she had for a film about Fred Burley, an Australian entrepreneur who in the 1920s founded Berlei, the international underwear empire. Elfick badgered her to put down an outline. She did and, to her amazement, got Australian Film Commission funding to write the script. As the words spun out across the page, Miranda Downes finally knew what she wanted to do with her life – she would be a writer.

Talking to her about *The Last Resort* in Sydney in mid-1985, it was hard to imagine that she had ever considered herself a lost soul. In two years she had turned herself into a highly successful scriptwriter. She was working on three scripts and bubbled with ideas for projects that were going to take her at least the next ten years to tackle. She was in love with her work, in love with Sydney, and in love with Jim Gerrand, a documentary film-maker. As she saw me to my taxi, we arranged to meet again in Britain. The next I heard about her, some three months later, was from the producer Lloyd Phillips who rang me at home one morning. 'Mandy's been murdered,' he said. 'Up in Cairns. They found her body on the beach.' Obviously distressed, he kept repeating, 'Who'd do such a thing? Who'd want to kill Mandy?' I remember thinking that this was the first friend of mine who had been murdered.

The details emerged slowly over the next few days. Miranda had taken a break from working on the Geissmann script to spend a few weeks with two British friends, Roger and Elizabeth Lewis, in a house belonging to Elizabeth Lewis's sister at Buchans Beach, a breathtakingly beautiful spot about fifteen miles north of Cairns. Stiff after her plane trip, Miranda decided she would go for a jog on the beach and told her friends she would be back soon. When she had not returned by 11pm her friends called the police. They found her body at 2am, clad only in her T-shirt, face down in shallow water. Later, police dogs located her underwear in the car park next to the beach and her track-suit trousers in a culvert about one hundred metres from the car park entrance. Roger Lewis identified the body at Cairns morgue at 4am.

The cause of Miranda's death was quickly established. She had been rendered unconscious by heavy blows and had then been placed in the sea where she had drowned. But the Cairns murder squad, in this case Detective Inspector Ken Ryan and Detective Sergeants Bruce Gray and Terry Brooks, soon ran into problems. Most murderers are known to their victims; murder, in fact, is largely a family affair. But this was an arbitrary killing, one of opportunity – the murderer had seen Miranda on the beach and had killed her. Why? The removal of her clothes suggested rape but the body had been immersed in sea water long enough to make it impossible for forensic scientists to establish rape as a certainty and to make any attempt at genetic fingerprinting a waste of time. But in the absence of any other motive, the police decided that they were looking for a man whose first sight of Miranda on Buchans Beach that evening – when it was still light and when other people were around – had aroused in him such uncontrollable passions that he had raped and killed her.

Hearing all this second-hand in London I was pessimistic about the police finding, much less convicting, such a man. Surely he would have left Cairns immediately after the murder? But luck plays a part in murder investigations and the Cairns police got a break. The police forensic scientist had described Miranda's injuries as 'heavy blows'. Inspector Ryan, looking at Miranda's body again, hoping for inspiration, suddenly remembered all the car accident victims he had seen. 'Good God,' he said. 'She looks like she's been run over by a car.' The forensic scientist was asked to have another look at the body. This time he reported 'injuries consistent with having been struck from behind by a vehicle'. In fact, one bruise on Miranda's left shoulder looked like the imprint of a car's side mirror. Now the police had a better idea of their quarry – a man in a vehicle on Buchans Beach in the last hours of daylight on 3 August.

To their surprise, someone fitting this description called voluntarily at the police station that same day and introduced himself. He was a stocky, truculent 46-year-old invalid pensioner from Sydney. His name, he said, was Ernie Knibb. He told the police that he had been on the beach the evening of Miranda's death trying out his new Ford Bronco, a large yellow and white, four-wheel-drive vehicle similar to a Land-Rover. He said he had been there 'only a couple of minutes' and he had not seen Miranda.

The police were not happy with Knibb's story but he parried their questions with ease and when he asked if he was free to leave Cairns they had to say that he was. But barely had Knibb left the police station when another girl jogger came forward. Janice Cunningham said that she, too, had been on the beach about the same time as Miranda. As she ran, a man in a four-wheel-drive vehicle passed her going the other way. He had swung the vehicle around and come back alongside her, calling out as he drove past, 'Don't worry. I'm not going to run you down.' So the murder squad had another look at Ernie Knibb and quickly found out that he was not all he seemed.

To begin with, he was only an invalid pensioner in the technical sense. He had injured his leg in a motorcycle accident in Sydney eighteen months earlier and had received A$80,000 in compensation, some of which he had used to buy the Ford Bronco. He had been in and out of institutions and prisons for much of his life and had a string of convictions for minor offences such as stealing and breaking and entering. This was interesting but not evidence, so the Cairns police decided that they would bring in an undercover team, and that this team would follow Knibb wherever he went in Queensland.

Pretending to be 'bikies', the undercover officers went on several drinking sprees with Knibb, trying to draw him by boasting that on their holiday they had raped girls and got away with it. When Knibb ignored them, one of the officers said in desperation, 'Hey, aren't you the bloke they're after for that Miranda Downes murder?' Again Knibb ignored them. They had not reckoned on Knibb's cunning. A man of well above average IQ, he was not about to be trapped into any ill-considered remark.

Detective Inspector Ryan's next move was to try to pressure Knibb openly. He impounded Knibb's Bronco and subjected it to extensive scientific tests which revealed nothing. But he also leaked the story to newspapers, saying that the Bronco belonged to Knibb and that 'our inquiries with this man are continuing'. One newspaper, under the headline, 'We know Mandy's Killer, Say The Police', reported that a Sydney man believed to be the sex killer of Miranda Downes was living in Queensland 'with the knowledge that one false step will put him behind bars'. The story described the man as a 41-year-old invalid pensioner and quoted the Cairns police as saying that, because of lack of evidence, they were 'playing a waiting game'.

Knibb noted the way the police had used the media and struck back by doing the same thing himself. He walked into the offices of the local newspaper, the *Maryborough-Hervey Bay Chronicle*, asked to see a reporter and accused the police of persecuting him. 'I've committed no crime,' he said. 'I'm alone in the world with no one to defend me. I haven't even got a girlfriend. With my crippled leg I can't chase them.' And he even volunteered to remain in Queensland until the Miranda Downes murder was solved. Knibb's initiative scuppered the police plan to keep pressure on him. Worried that they could be accused of trying to solve the case by harassing an invalid, they backed off. The investigation stalled. Time slipped by – nearly a year after Miranda's death it looked as if whoever murdered her was going to get away with it.

Then in January 1986 Lloyd Phillips sent me an article from the Brisbane *Courier Mail* written by a talented journalist, Adrian McGregor. In it he captured the essence of a killing that so many Australians found so disturbing. 'I have approached this beach, this spot, with a sense of portent. It is the same time of day. I am the professional chronicler of Mandy's last days, but as I stand in the sand, my eyes, too, are filled with tears at the sense of loss, at the senselessness of her death. It was so fearfully random. Death just brushed her aside.' McGregor's story aroused nationwide indignation and the Cairns police returned to the case with new vigour. But they got no further. Knibb remained in Maryborough, living in a caravan park for the next three months. He was at Yuraka in Central Queensland in December 1986, some fifteen months after Miranda's death, when Jim Gerrand, Miranda's boyfriend, decided to try more publicity. He gave an interview to my old newspaper, the *Sydney Daily Mirror*, in which he begged the Queensland police to offer a reward in one last, desperate bid to catch the killer. The police refused, but the *Mirror* story was read by Gerald Stone, the executive producer of one of Australia's top current affairs programmes, '60 Minutes', and after discussing it with his staff, he decided to take over from where the police had left off.

On my next trip to Australia, I went to see Stone and he showed me the film that Ian Leslie, a '60 Minutes' reporter, had made on the case and explained how they had tackled it. Leslie flew up to Cairns, talked with the murder squad and came away with an idea for a controversial approach. Knibb's cunning, his ego, his cool assumption that he was clever enough to be able to handle any questioning about Miranda's death – could all this be turned against him? Leslie decided to offer Knibb a nationwide television audience on '60 Minutes' to put to rest once and for all the accusation that he was the murderer. This was, of course, just a TV version of the old *People* approach in Britain: 'You know what they're saying about you in the village, Mr Jones. They're saying you killed your wife. Make a statement denying this foul lie and my paper will print it next Sunday.' But it worked. Knibb could not resist the lure of TV fame and on a boiling hot day in January 1987, under a canvas canopy outside his caravan, he made his first big mistake – he talked to television. Leslie's last question trapped him: would he agree to return to Cairns to re-enact everything he had done on the evening that Miranda had been murdered? Of course, Knibb said. The resulting programme makes fascinating if disturbing television. Knibb begins with a vehement declaration of his innocence. But then Leslie skilfully leads him into describing how, *if* he had been the killer, he would have gone about things so as to get away with it. 'This may sound cold blooded,' Knibb says, 'but I've been involved in crime for twenty-five years. I've learnt a lot more than the police and the psychologists. If I'd done it I would've covered it up.' Knibb says the man might not have intended to kill Miranda; he might not have done anything more than 'several rapes' before, but then got carried away and 'hit her for some reason'. He might not have intended to kill her. 'He might have said, "Oh shit" and thrown her into the water to make it look like an accident.'

On screen Knibb drives along Buchans Beach in his Ford Bronco with Leslie and the cameraman alongside him. Knibb begins to describe the scene that night but now Leslie is interrupting him with telling questions that have been fed to him by the Cairns murder squad. Knibb grows aggressive as a crucial point is reached. Knibb says that he was on the beach for a matter of minutes, obviously not long enough for him to have murdered Miranda and stripped her of her clothing. Leslie interrupts to say that in the earlier TV interview, Knibb had said that he had been on the beach for at least half an hour. Which was it? The camera catches Knibb's fury. He looks straight at it and says, 'Anyone who says I killed Miranda will get a smack in the mouth.'

The reconstructed drive along the beach proved nothing, but Knibb felt that he had been outsmarted and to regain the initiative he volunteered to take a lie detector test and allow the team from '60 Minutes' to film it. The result is like a scene from an old Hollywood gangster story. After a series of innocuous questions, the operator of the polygraph machine moves to highly relevant ones, climaxing with the direct 'Did you kill Miranda Downes?' Knibb replies with an indignant 'No.' The camera then switches to the lie detector operator interpreting the results for Leslie. He says that for all the main indicators – heartbeat, blood pressure and sweat levels – Knibb recorded a significant change when he was asked the relevant questions. His conclusion: in his professional opinion, Knibb had failed the test; he had been lying. The camera immediately swings to Knibb and Leslie asks his reaction to this verdict. Knibb calmly says, 'I was upset when the murder was mentioned. The test picked up my emotional reactions.'

But by now Knibb is in too far to stop himself. He demands that he should be questioned under hypnosis and that this too, should be filmed. The '60 Minutes' team is only too happy to oblige. Apparently in a trance, Knibb introduces a new twist to his story. As he relives that night he says he sees a strange, shadowy figure lurking in the trees. He is immediately afraid; his instinct tells him that the man is dangerous, he is a killer, so Knibb leaves the beach as quickly as possible. This must have been the man who murdered Miranda. It is a persuasive performance, but when the camera turns to the hypnotist, he says that, in his opinion, Knibb had *not* been under hypnosis – he had been faking.

Leslie had passed on to the Cairns detectives all Knibb's answers and they now reviewed the case. They decided that there were important discrepancies between what Knibb had originally told them and what he had said during his TV interviews. Moreover, one of the points Knibb had originally made to them had collapsed. Knibb had asked: 'How could I have subdued a remarkably fit woman like Miranda when I limp so badly that I need a stick to walk?' But now Sergeant John Field of the Blackall police told his Cairns colleagues that he had seen Knibb walking without a stick and without a limp. What happened next is caught for ever on the '60 Minutes' film.

It is 5 February 1987, eighteen months after Miranda's murder. The camera picks up Knibb walking towards the reception desk in a Cairns hotel. It then goes wide-angle to show two burly men come through the hotel door. They are dressed, like many policemen in the Australian tropics, in shorts. They intercept Knibb. One places his hand on Knibb's shoulder and says, 'I am arresting you for the murder of Miranda Downes at Buchans Beach on 3rd August 1985.' He then begins to caution Knibb. All this is taking place on camera and we can hear Leslie's voice-over saying, 'What's happening, Ernie?' and Knibb replying, 'They're saying I killed Mandy. I tell you now they've got the wrong man.' And then Knibb, as if playing the lead in that old Hollywood film, looks right into the camera lens and says in his best James Cagney voice, 'Get my lawyer for me, will you?'

Knibb's trial took place the following September in the Cairns Circuit Court. The Crown case was that Knibb, driving on the beach, saw Miranda out jogging, ran her down with his Ford Bronco, stripped her, probably raped her, and then left her to drown when the tide came in. The television interviews provided the principal evidence against Knibb and the principal prosecution witness was the '60 Minutes' reporter Ian Leslie. The Crown admitted that there was no direct evidence to associate Knibb with the murder but invited the jury to draw an inference of his guilt. It did, and the judge sentenced him to life imprisonment. His appeals on the grounds that the television film should not have been admitted as evidence against him were turned down.

But the case left many uneasy over television's role. Although Knibb gave his TV interviews willingly, and voluntarily went back to Cairns to re-enact that evening on the beach, he did not know that the questions that Leslie was firing at him had been supplied by the police. He was therefore undergoing what was, in effect, a police interrogation without being formally cautioned. Next, although statements made by an accused person under hypnosis would not be admissible in an Australian court, in Knibb's case the Crown was allowed to present them as evidence because it argued successfully that Knibb was only *pretending* to be under hypnosis, a conclusion supported only by the hypnotist's opinion.

The outcome left me with mixed emotions. I had been as anxious as all Miranda's other friends that whoever was responsible for her death should be brought to justice and punished for the crime. But the role that newspapers and television played left me deeply uneasy. Is this what journalists are supposed to do? I know it is only a remote possibility, but what if Ernie Knibb is innocent? Isn't it a dangerous precedent for journalists – and in particular, television – to take over the role of the police when all else has failed? I have no easy answers.

CHAPTER FOURTEEN

THE GREATEST CON TRICK
OF THE CENTURY

In the summer of 1975 I was invited by a man I knew had contacts in the British Security Service, MI5, to have lunch with him at the Special Forces Club in Knightsbridge. He wanted me to meet 'someone from the office' who had a story which might interest me. There was another guest, an aristocratic young man from the City whose role appeared to be that of prompting the MI5 officer – for that is what I took the man from 'the office' to be – when he hesitated over a real or pretended indiscretion. The conversation was all to do with the extent to which the KGB, or the 'Russian Intelligence Service' as they preferred to call it, had penetrated British society. The MI5 officer quickly dispensed with the Wilson government (its penetration was taken as read), slandered Wilson's own loyalties and those of several members of his Cabinet, and then moved on to the Royal family. The thrust of his allegations was that Lord Mountbatten, 'a dodgy character', had managed to slip on the staff at Buckingham Palace a secretary who was either still a member of the Communist Party or had once been, and who was also eminently blackmailable because of his sexual preferences. Further, MI5's efforts to have this person dismissed as a security risk had got nowhere with the Queen – 'but this is understandable given the political views of the Royal Family'. This last statement appeared to be too much even for the young man from the City. 'I say,' he said. 'You're not trying to tell us that the Royals are' – lowering his voice – 'a bit left-wing.' The MI5 officer was triumphant. 'Always have been, old boy,' he said. 'Always have been.'

This was the extent of the revelations, so needless to say I wrote nothing. But when Anthony Blunt, Keeper of the Queen's Pictures and her third cousin once removed, was finally exposed three years later as a one-time Soviet spy, I wondered if the luncheon had not been some convoluted MI5 way of getting me interested in a mole hunt at Buckingham Palace that would 'out' the hapless Blunt. That's the problem with writing about spy matters – you never know at the time who is trying to use you and why. I spent twenty years writing about Kim Philby and his fellow Soviet agents in the Cambridge spy ring – Guy Burgess and Donald Maclean – and in the end only a combination of circumstances that no one could have foretold, the collapse of the Soviet Union, enabled me to answer the questions: what was it all about and did it make any difference?

I got involved with the Philby story in 1967/8 as a member of the *Sunday Times* Insight team. We wrote a series of articles about Philby, a former *Times* war correspondent who was recruited by the Secret Intelligence Service during the war, rose to be SIS liaison officer in Washington with the CIA and the FBI, and was tipped as a possible future head of SIS – before being unmasked as a long-serving agent of the KGB. When Insight began its investigations into Philby, our overriding impression was that SIS had got what it deserved, that a decadent, incestuous organisation, convinced of its superiority, had fallen for the treacherous charm of one of its own. Or, as John le Carré later put it: 'The avenger stole upon the citadel and destroyed it from within.' We had also formed the opinion that the concern of the government and its civil servants was to keep the details of the Philby affair from the British public. So each week when we published our latest revelations in the *Sunday Times* we felt we were striking a blow for freedom of information, the right of the people to know what those who governed them had been up to. We cherished fantasies of 'C', the chief of SIS, tearing open his copy of the newspaper over a Sunday breakfast in one of the better Home Counties, turning quickly to Insight, and then shaking his head at the iniquities of journalists and journalism.

Years later I learnt how different the truth was – SIS knew beforehand what we were about to publish each week. The editor-in-chief of the *Sunday Times*, Denis Hamilton, had come to an agreement with the service. His need to do so was understandable. I met him in the corridor one day after a colleague, David Leitch, and I had used some FBI documents obtained under the American Freedom of Information Act to write about the relationship between Philby and J. Edgar Hoover, the notorious boss of the FBI. 'Ah,' said Hamilton as we approached each other, 'here comes Philby's public relations officer.' He said it in a jocular manner but, sensing his unease, I explained how we had got the story and its importance. He was not impressed. 'I saw too many good men killed during the war,' he said. 'I'd hate it if we put anyone in danger. You see, you can't always tell. You really ought to take advice on stories like that.'

It turned out that this was what the *Sunday Times* had done with the original Philby stories. When Harold Evans had told Hamilton about the Insight investigation, Hamilton had expressed his concern: would publication help the Russians, would it put SIS officers at risk? Evans told him that Moscow already knew the Philby story; it was the British public that had been kept in ignorance. As for the risk, why not assess that after the investigation was complete? Hamilton said he would think about it.

Instead he went to see the Prime Minister, Harold Wilson, who arranged a meeting with the chief of SIS, Sir Dick White. There Hamilton agreed that the *Sunday Times* would show SIS each Insight article before it was published so as to make sure no one was endangered. Sir Denis Greenhill, a deputy under-secretary at the Foreign Office who acted as liaison officer between the FO and SIS, would also act as liaison between the *Sunday Times* and SIS. At Hamilton's urging, Evans met Greenhill secretly to discuss the Philby project. Greenhill said immediately that he was against the investigation: the *Sunday Times* would make a hero out of Philby, Britain's relations with the Americans would be damaged, nothing would be achieved by publication. He wanted to know what was *really* behind the project. Was Evans certain that some members of the Insight team were not pushing a hidden political agenda? Could the team leader, Bruce Page, be a Communist? Evans said that if he was, then he was safely locked up in the *Sunday Times* slave labour camp on the Gray's Inn Road. Of course, by this time the security service had already run checks on the background of all the Insight team members and was tapping our telephones.

Evans met Greenhill several more times. Greenhill never withdrew his objections to the project but as I hacked my way around the retired spy circuit I began to suspect that some sort of accommodation had been reached between the paper and SIS. For instance, Sir Robert McKenzie, a retired SIS officer, had agreed to see me at his London flat and for a while answered my questions frankly. Then I must have touched on a sensitive matter. 'Hmm,' he said, 'I'd better check that one with the office. Give me a ring tomorrow.' All the old spies had been cleared to speak to us, and were reporting back to SIS on the progress of our investigations and the state of our knowledge. It was not, as the CIA London man Bronson Tweedy was to tell me later, 'a controlled operation'; it was simply that SIS was doing its best to turn our investigation to its advantage.

The articles brought an immediate book offer from the publisher André Deutsch who then sold the rights around the world and the Insight team began writing what became *Philby, the Spy Who Betrayed a Generation*. (Someone at the print works left us in no doubt about his political affiliation by sending back a proof of the dust jacket with the title amended to: 'the Spy Who Saved a Generation'.)

We had just about exhausted the supply of old spies in Britain so I went to the United States to look at Philby's time there. After the secrecy of British society, especially in intelligence matters, working as a journalist in America was a joy. I found the CIA in the telephone book, arranged an appointment with one of its public affairs representatives, and was given the names of several retired CIA officers who had known Philby and who might be prepared to talk about him – the decision would be theirs. I went to the FBI and had a long interview with a senior agent – interrupted when the tape recorder in his desk drawer broke down and we had to change offices. I telephoned Admiral Lewis Strauss, who had been chairman of the Atomic Energy Commission, and General Leslie Groves, who had been in charge of the American atomic bomb programme. Both invited me to call on them and spoke freely and at length. I decided that journalists in the United States occupied a privileged position, that public figures felt under an obligation to help them, and that it was a pity that it could not be the same in Britain.

But I also realised that there was an agenda, an anti-British one. The CIA felt that the British intelligence establishment's custom of recruiting officers on the basis of family connections and recommendation by friends – as Philby had been – was hopelessly out-of-date in a world divided by such intense ideological differences and bound to lead to betrayal. The CIA preferred deep investigation of an applicant's past and then annual lie detector tests – as one CIA officer said, 'You've got to flutter them.'*

The FBI believed that the British were incredibly decadent and that the Old Boy network had protected traitors. The agent I interviewed said that Hoover had sanctioned our meeting because the *Sunday Times* had at last exposed the KGB's Cambridge spy ring, but had expressed doubt that any reform would come from it.

Strauss and Groves were bitter that insufficient notice had been taken of them when they complained that the British were lax about atomic security. Strauss told me that he was stunned when he heard that Donald Maclean had a pass that enabled him to wander around the AEC building in Washington at any time without an escort. 'Even General Groves, for heaven's sake, didn't have such a pass at that time,' Strauss said. 'I revoked Maclean's pass immediately and ran into a barrage of protests from the British. In view of the flak I had to absorb, it was no little satisfaction for

---

* At that time the CIA had had no Philby-type scandals. Subsequent cases suggest that the American system for ensuring its intelligence officers' loyalty is no better than the British.

me to find out later how right I had been.' General Groves was caustic about the case of Klaus Fuchs, the British scientist working at Los Alamos who had passed atomic secrets to the Soviets. Fuchs was unmasked as a Soviet spy in 1950 and sentenced by a British court to fifteen years' imprisonment. But Groves could not understand how the British authorities had ever given Fuchs, known to MI5 to have been a Communist, a security clearance in the first place and claimed that Britain had deliberately misled him about the thoroughness of the investigation into Fuchs's background. 'I have to say that the British were sloppy about security in general,' he said.

I duly noted all this down and some of it was published but I confess that I missed a marvellous opportunity when interviewing Groves. If only I had known more about the development of the atomic bomb I might have been able to persuade him to answer some questions that went right to the heart of the American decision to drop it on Japan. These have come up from time to time since 1945 but are best posed in an article by Murray Sayle in the *New Yorker* in July 1995 – the eve of the fiftieth anniversary of the bombing of Hiroshima. Sayle says that Truman wrote in his diary on 24 July after signing an order drafted by Groves: 'This weapon is to be used against Japan between now and August 10. I have told the Sec of War, Mr Stimson, to use it so that military objectives and soldiers and sailors are to be the target and not women and children . . . The target will be purely a military one and we will issue a warning statement asking the Japs to surrender and save lives.' Is this what Groves told the President? If so, as events soon proved, he was not telling the truth.

Sayle said that Groves's motivation can now be easily perceived. 'By the summer of 1945, he headed what was in effect a new branch of the American armed services – a nuclear strike command, with fifteen aircraft and, after 24 July, two atomic bombs. Having made the bombs, Groves saw it as his duty to have them used, so that, among other things, their future effectiveness as weapons could be judged.' The idea of *not* using the bomb as soon as it was ready was never considered. 'Some scholars – especially those not of the wartime generation – have found it hard to believe that the act that launched the world into nuclear war could have come about so thoughtlessly, by default.' What a fascinating interview I could have had with Groves if only I had known something about this at the time. But I did not and I was too wrapped up in the Philby story to be bothered to talk to Groves about anything else.

When the Insight book on Philby was published I wrote to Philby at his Moscow postbox address and sent him an inscribed copy. He replied thanking me. I wrote back, and this was the beginning of a correspondence that lasted the next twenty years. Philby's letters were chatty, informed, and often amusing. When *The Times* and the *Sunday Times* shut down for a year (over an industrial dispute) he confessed to missing the *Times* obituaries and the crossword: '15–20 minutes with my morning tea to crank up cerebration'. He seemed hungry for political gossip from Britain and keen to get news of Mrs Thatcher. '*Pace* the BBC and other media, the Russians do not call her the "Iron Lady". As the Russians have difficulty with English vowels and the "th", she usually comes out as something like "Meesees Tetchy". Perhaps the bonnet fits.' Occasionally he would make tantalising references to 'trips abroad', to 'my weeks in the sun' and to 'sipping stengahs'.

By coincidence, soon after receiving one of these letters, I dined with the former head of SIS, the late Sir Maurice Oldfield, and told him about Philby's remarks and the questions they raised. 'He hasn't been anywhere,' Oldfield said. 'He knows we will be reading his letters to you. [Early in our correspondence Philby had indeed warned me that our letters would be opened 'at each end'.] So he just wants to make mischief, to have us rushing around wasting our resources trying to find out what he had been up to. Kim was always very good at making mischief.' (Oldfield was wrong. I learnt later that Philby had been on a holiday in Cuba.)

In our letters, Philby and I discussed the latest books and television drama. 'I heard about the Granada production ['Philby, Burgess and Maclean'] from several sources, including my eldest daughter who thought well of it "except that the women were too bitchy". We [the KGB] took a video of it, so I shall probably see it soon.' He seemed to prefer factual spy books to spy fiction but read the latest in each genre. 'I have ordered *The Honourable Schoolboy*. From le Carré's introduction to your book, I get the vague impression, perhaps wrongly, that he didn't like me. But we are generous, and have no objection to contributing to his vast affluence.' Then I made a faux pas and our correspondence ceased. The author and broadcaster Andrew Boyle had published *The Climate of Treason*, the book which exposed Sir Anthony Blunt as a former Soviet agent. In an article I wrote for the *Sunday Times* I quoted a line or two of Philby's opinion of the book which he had expressed in an earlier letter to me. Now my letters to him went unanswered for over a year because Philby's KGB superiors objected to my use of a personal letter in a newspaper.

From time to time I had raised the idea with Philby that I might visit Moscow and interview him. He had always said no. His failure to reply to my recent letters suggested that I had been wasting my time. But then I remembered Nicholas Tomalin's advice when I had just started at the

Sunday Times – 'No no is ever final' – and in 1987 I wrote again. I said I had heard that he had been ill (to remind him that he was mortal), that he had been around long enough for a new wave of interest in his life, career and beliefs (a little flattery is never wasted), and that there had been an improvement in the international political climate and he could contribute to this change (an appeal to the KGB). I suggested an early meeting and an interview which would be recorded for BBC television.

Philby did not reply directly but in a letter to one of his children in London he said he had received my proposal but had to say no. 'I have a snobbish block about visual journalism, TV and stills. The clicks and the trip wires, with little men bent double and running backwards, seem to ruin all solemn and moving occasions.' But then, to my delight he added, 'Just Knightley and a notebook might be a different matter.' So I booked a tour to Moscow for the seventieth anniversary of the Revolution and wrote to Philby from India, where I was on a visit, enclosing my Moscow itinerary, and suggesting a drink. I spent the ten days in Moscow waiting for a call in the middle of the night, or the smiling face of Philby at the hotel reception desk. But I had been thwarted by the unbeatable combination of the Indian and Soviet postal systems, as Philby's letter from Moscow dated 13 November 1987, made clear.

Dear Knightley,

Your letter from India took six weeks to reach me, so the chance of a casual drink presented itself too late. However, if you are still interested, I think there is a fair possibility of us getting together for a real talk in the not too distant future.

This would take the form of a telegram from us to you and your wife inviting you to come to Moscow for a few days. I note that you have agreed to come without TV paraphernalia or tape-recorders. Just your wife, yourself and your notebook – in that order.

There are still a few details to be worked out. I put a high value on my privacy, and do not want you to ring my doorbell trailing the whole Moscow press corps behind you. Furthermore, a leakage at your end of the real purpose of your Moscow trip would put the whole enterprise in question.

What did this mean? Was Philby warning me not to tell the British security authorities that I was going to Moscow to see him? But he realised that they would know anyway, because they would have opened his letter and they would be reading any telegrams he sent me. For my part, I felt no obligation to inform them about my trip or its purpose, but I did decide to do everything in as open a manner as possible. When I received a telegram from Philby on 2 December asking if a visit in the second half of January would be suitable I replied by telegram that it would. Likewise, when on 8 January I got another telegram: LOOKING FORWARD ARRIVAL YOURSELF AND WIFE PLEASE TELEGRAPH DATE AND FLIGHT NUMBER REGARDS – PHILBY, I replied by telegram giving these details. I decided that if the British security authorities were not aware by now what was going on then they were not doing their job.

We arrived in Moscow on the evening of Monday 18 January. Temperatures had hovered around zero centigrade for several weeks so instead of the city being covered in snow and ice, it was covered in mud and slush. As we waited for our luggage I had half an eye open for Philby so nearly missed a tall blonde woman in black fur, who appeared at my side, leaned alarmingly close and whispered, 'Mr Knightley?' When I said yes, she did not introduce herself but said simply, 'Come with me.' She was not KGB, as I had hoped, but an Intourist official who put us into an ordinary Moscow taxi which took us to the Belgrade, a modest hotel favoured by Yugoslav businessmen. There was some problem with our reservation and we were put into one room, only to be moved twenty minutes later. ('The microphones in the first room were out of order,' Philby joked later.)

Philby rang as we were unpacking. He suggested dinner that night and said that 'a neighbour' of his would pick us up in the hotel lobby in twenty minutes. The neighbour turned out to be Vladimir, a large, cheerful young man in a black leather coat, an administrative officer in the KGB. He took us to a small black sedan driven by another KGB officer, Boris, who was to take us to all our meetings with Philby. We appeared to take a very complicated route and when I learnt later that Philby had chosen the Belgrade hotel because it was close to his flat, I assumed that Boris, the well-trained spy, was trying to conceal exactly where his boss lived. Several trips to Moscow later, I realised there was a simpler, less romantic explanation – left-hand turns are banned on most major streets in Moscow and it was this that caused us to take so many detours on that first visit.

Over our first whisky I told Philby how well I thought he looked. 'I am well,' he said, 'and that's one of the reasons you're here, one of the reasons I agreed to see you. There has been a rumour which apparently started in Canada of all places that I was on my uppers, ill, abandoned by the KGB and anxious to return to Britain. I wanted you to see for yourself that none of this was true.' That was one of the reasons he had agreed to see me, but what were the others? Over the next six days of interviews and dinners – both at his comfortable apartment and in a private room in his favourite

Georgian restaurant – I tried but failed to find out. When I left Moscow I had three notebooks, some of Philby's own writings, and three rolls of film. (There should have been four but all the photographs I took of our evening in the Georgian restaurant, including a marvellous one of Philby in his red English trouser braces, were missing. Perhaps because of an early start on the 600 grammes of vodka that Philby had ordered, I had forgotten to put film in the camera.) When I went through it all in London I kept looking for a clue to explain Philby's motives. I could not find one. Never mind, I thought. We had arranged to meet again and I will find out next time. ('Come back in the summer,' Philby had said. 'And we can go down to the dacha.') But there was to be no next time. Philby died on 11 May 1988, so I can only speculate why, after twenty-five years of silence, he decided to speak out, and why he chose me.

The truth is that the Canadian rumour that so upset Philby was not entirely wrong, only out-of-date. Philby *had* been ill and *had* been virtually abandoned by the KGB. Since the collapse of the Soviet Union several former KGB officers who knew Philby have written their memoirs and the one point on which they all agree is that for many years the KGB treated Philby abominably. One, Oleg Kalugin, former chief of counter-intelligence, says he was given the job of rehabilitating Philby because the then chairman of the KGB, Yuri Andropov, wanted to attract Western defectors and realised it was important to show that they had a good life in the USSR. I met Kalugin in Amsterdam in 1990 and he told me that Philby had been a pathetic character – drunk, despondent and disillusioned. Kalugin said he had arranged for Philby's flat to be refurbished, found real work for him at the KGB, brought young officers to meet him, sent him on tours of other Communist countries, and, in general, provided a much-needed boost to his ego.

Kalugin only hinted at why the KGB had treated Philby so badly and I had to wait to meet Genrikh Borovik, a Moscow journalist and broadcaster, to find out the details. In the mid-1960s Borovik had written a spy novel but the KGB had killed it without explanation. He was justifiably bitter about this and when Gorbachev ushered in a new era of glasnost, Borovik did not hesitate to remind the KGB that it owed him a favour. He said he wanted to meet a real Soviet spy and write about him. The KGB introduced him to Philby and over the next three years Borovik recorded many hours of interviews with him. After Philby's death, at Graham Greene's suggestion, he asked the KGB for access to Philby's personal file and, to his surprise, this was approved. Borovik was now able to compare Philby's own version of his life as a spy with the KGB version.

The result was stunning. 'Prepare to have your views about Philby and the KGB shattered,' Borovik told me. 'Thank God Philby himself never saw his KGB file. If he hadn't died of illness, it would have killed him.' For instance, it turned out that the KGB did not have a brilliant long-term plan in the 1930s to recruit British university students who would one day hold positions of power, as I for one believed had happened with Philby. It took on Philby simply because it was convinced – mistakenly – that his father, the Arabist St John Philby, was in British intelligence.

And how did the KGB treat this tender ideological recruit? It lied to him about whom he was actually working for and it threw him into the deep end of the dirty espionage pool by giving him as his first assignment the task of spying on his own father. And Philby did it. He gave his KGB bosses unquestioning loyalty, forming close personal relationships with them. In turn, they nurtured and supported him. Then, all of a sudden, they vanished, victims of Stalin's belief that they were traitors. They were replaced by a new wave of intelligence officers all determined not to make the same mistakes as their unfortunate predecessors. They read the files, they came across Philby's name and they went to their bosses to ask about him. And the new KGB, to which Philby had agreed to devote his life, did not even know who he was. Who is he? Where is he? Who recruited him? Mar! But Mar has been executed as a traitor. Who's been running him? Orlov! But Orlov has defected to the West. It is all very suspicious – Philby could well be a plant from British intelligence and will have to be watched all the time. And so entered the splinter of suspicion that remained for the rest of Philby's active life with Moscow.

In his own book and in his conversation with me, Philby presented his career with the KGB as one unbroken line of dedicated service. But Borovik showed me that the Nazi-Soviet Pact of August 1939 had been such a blow to Philby that he had stopped working for the KGB for a year and that, in turn, the KGB wanted nothing to do with him. It only changed its mind when it learnt that without its help, suddenly and unexpectedly and all on his own, Philby had got into the British Secret Intelligence Service. It hastened to get in touch with him again. But, Borovik said, the KGB's initial elation soon turned sour. From the Lubyanka, Philby's entry into SIS looked too easy, suspiciously easy. All right, said his KGB bosses, if you really are in British intelligence, then give us a list of the names of British agents who are going to be sent to work against us in the Soviet Union. When Philby replied, 'There aren't any,' Moscow underlined this sentence twice in red ink and put two large question marks against it. The KGB simply did not believe him.

Philby's loyalty was now tested to the limit. The German invasion of the Soviet Union in June 1941 meant that he could resume the anti-Fascist fight with a clear conscience. But, to his dismay, Moscow seemed uninterested in his material. They kept him busy – writing reports about himself, his father, his wife, his friends, his colleagues. Please write your autobiography again. Who are your closest friends? Tell us again how you managed to join SIS. With the Germans at the gates of Moscow, the KGB was more intent on trying to trip up its best British agent, to get proof that he was an SIS plant, than in exploiting his privileged access to British secrets – further evidence of my belief that intelligence agencies are more interested in the game than in real information.

The KGB even handed his entire file to a trusted desk officer for an evaluation: was he a genuine recruit to the Soviet cause, or was he a British penetration agent, cleverly planted on the KGB? The officer, a woman called Elena Modrzhinskaya, read Philby's files and those of the other members of the Cambridge ring. The first point she raised was the volume and value of the material the ring had been sending to Moscow. Could the British intelligence service really be run by such fools that no one had noticed that such precious material was leaking to Moscow? Was it really possible that Kim Philby with his Communist views, his work for the Communists in Vienna and his Austrian Communist wife, had been recruited for SIS and had sailed through its vetting procedures.

She decided that Philby was a plant. And if he was, all the others probably were too. So the London KGB station was told that Philby, Guy Burgess, Anthony Blunt and John Cairncross were really British intelligence officers who had been inserted into the KGB network. Only Donald Maclean escaped. It was possible he was a genuine recruit but he was being secretly manipulated by the others. This was an astounding conclusion and, of course, totally wrong. But having reached it, the KGB bosses proceeded to cover their backs by continuing to use the Cambridge spies. You can see the twisted logic at work. Elena Modrzhinskaya has made out such a powerful case against Philby and his colleagues that we will have to act on it. But what if, in the end, she turns out to be wrong. We might be blamed. We might be shot. So we will pretend that nothing has changed, let the British spies think that we trust them, and wait to see what happens.

And so the game of deceit and double-dealing continued. The Cambridge spies were deceiving their colleagues, their service, their families and their country in the sincere belief that they were serving a greater cause through an elite intelligence service, the KGB, which fathered them, mothered them, and appeared to trust them totally. But, in turn, they were being deceived by the KGB because it really believed that they were playing a treble game and were all traitors to the Communist cause. This leads me to conclude that the main threat to an intelligence agent comes not from the security services in the country against which he is operating, but from his *own* centre, his *own* people. This certainly applied to Philby because it was the KGB that brought him down.

Readers of previous books on this topic will remember that the big unanswered question in the whole Philby, Burgess and Maclean affair was: why did Burgess go? The FBI and MI5 had been closing in on Maclean and he was due to be interrogated by MI5 on Monday 28 May 1951. Tipped off by Philby that he was in danger, Maclean fled on the Friday, accompanied by Burgess who had arranged the gateway. Other accounts have suggested that Burgess's role was simply to get Maclean out of Britain on the cross-Channel steamer, and then be back before Maclean was missed. But Burgess went all the way to Moscow, never to return. His disappearance immediately threw suspicion on Philby, because they were friends and had shared a house in Washington. SIS recalled Philby to London and, while agreeing that there was no real evidence against him, forced him to retire. Thus his career as a KGB penetration agent was over.

In my talks in Moscow with Philby about this he placed all the blame on Burgess. 'The unplanned part was that Burgess went too. The whole thing was a mess, an intelligence nightmare, and it was all due to that bloody man Burgess. The KGB never forgave him.' The KGB files revealed a very different story. The KGB had ordered Burgess to accompany Maclean to Moscow because Maclean was in such a state that he might not make it alone. But Burgess was assured that the moment he delivered Maclean to Moscow he could head back to London. Instead the KGB kept him there and subjected him to hostile interrogation, determined to discover once and for all whether the Cambridge ring was genuine or not. But by holding Burgess it ruined the career of its best agent, Philby, the man who could have become head of British intelligence. Borovik told me that in his many conversations with Philby about this, Philby could not bring himself to blame the KGB for his downfall. Donald Maclean had no such inhibitions. When he realised what Moscow had done he wrote a furious letter to the KGB accusing it of betraying Philby, of throwing him to the lions. As far as Borovik could discover, the KGB did not deign to reply.

So Philby's interviews with me were a KGB public relations exercise designed to show the world that the KGB treated its Western agents well, that Philby was still as dedicated to the Communist cause as he had ever been, and that the KGB had got the better of Western intelligence agencies in a number of Cold War encounters. A secondary reason was part of the KGB's programme to rehabilitate Philby – to show him that the service appreciated him, and to allow him, in the late autumn of his life, to relive the most exciting moments of his intelligence career. I did not know this at the time, although I suspected some of it, but I would have gone to Moscow anyway. What journalist would have refused a chance to talk to a man whose life exercised such a hold on our imagination, to probe the motives of someone who always put politics above human relations and freely admitted that he admired people who could shed blood for a political ideal?

But why me? It turned out that I was not the first choice. Philby had liked my argument that there was a new generation in Britain which did not know his story, and he used this to convince his KGB colleagues that it would be in the service's interests to allow him to tell it again. But they preferred that he talked to Graham Greene – they knew him better and they felt he would be more sympathetic. (They apparently did not know that Greene was still reporting to SIS.) Philby argued that I would be perceived as being more objective. But in assessing one other factor, the KGB and Philby made a mistake: they both thought I still worked for the *Sunday Times*, whereas I had left three years earlier and had been a freelance in the intervening period. I know now that when the KGB decides to release information to the press, it does not give a damn about the political leanings of a newspaper – all that matters is its circulation. So if Moscow Centre had known that the Philby interviews were being conducted by a freelance with no publication of his own, rather than a staff reporter from a leading British newspaper with four million readers, I think they would have called off the whole operation.

When I later met Rupert Murdoch at a memorial service for Sir Denis Hamilton and in the course of a discussion about Philby made the error of mentioning that the KGB thought I was a staff reporter from the *Sunday Times*, I saw Murdoch's eyes cloud over as he rapidly calculated the discrepancy between the large amount he had paid me for the articles and the modest salary of a staff reporter the *Sunday Times* could have assigned to the story.

Money comes into the story in another way. I did not have to explain to Philby that there was no way I could pay him for the interviews. He understood that the *Sunday Times* had to be able to assure its readers that it had not bought a traitor's story. But I doubt that the KGB did. They saw an opportunity for Philby to earn some hard currency, were puzzled when this did not happen, and when, after the collapse of the Soviet Union, they began making some of their files available to Western authors, the choicest went to the highest bidders, irrespective of their political views.

There was a hidden, twisted thread in the Philby story which I have only now unravelled. It led to the Krogers, an American husband and wife Soviet spy team, to an as yet unidentified KGB agent – an American atomic scientist – and finally to the centre of an event which became a Cold War icon for the Left: the execution of Julius and Ethel Rosenberg. For reasons we did not understand at the time, when the original *Sunday Times* articles on Philby appeared, the KGB responded with an operation to secure the release of Helen and Peter Kroger, who were serving twenty years in a British jail for their role in the late 1950s as communications officers in the spy ring run by the KGB colonel Conon Molody ('Gordon Lonsdale') at the Portland naval base.

The first hint of this operation – the existence of which has been confirmed to me by several former KGB officers involved in it – came from Philby himself in conversation with Murray Sayle, who had been sent by Evans to Moscow when the paper was still considering whether to publish Philby's own book. 'That was an interesting suggestion in *The Economist*,' Philby said to Sayle, 'the idea that I would be prepared to withdraw my manuscript if the Krogers were exchanged for Brooke [an Englishman in jail in the Soviet Union for distributing anti-Soviet pamphlets]. If that were in fact a condition of the Krogers being released, of course I would withdraw my book.'

Sayle said, 'Is that a message for someone? Do you want that passed on?' Philby replied, 'No, it was just an idea I had.' He then went on to try to convince Sayle that the Krogers were innocent. 'We don't dispute that people like Gordon and Colonel Abel [a KGB officer caught in the United States] were our agents, highly skilled professionals, but we cannot agree that the Krogers were the top-level agents that they are being represented as, or indeed our agents at all except in the sense of being friends of Lonsdale's.'

Again, we did not know it at the time, but this was nonsense – the Krogers were two of the KGB's most respected and highly valued agents who had been key players in Moscow's atomic spy ring in the United States and had worked with Abel. Our ignorance can be forgiven because SIS and the CIA, too, did not know then how important the Krogers were, otherwise they might not have gone ahead only nineteen months later with the exchange of the Krogers for Gerald Brooke, a very minor figure in the intelligence war. And yet . . . did it not occur to the Western services to wonder why the KGB was negotiating for the release of the Krogers, two *non-Soviet citizens* – something it had never done before?

I became interested in this husband and wife spy team when, while visiting Moscow in 1990, I learnt from Igor Prelin, a former KGB colonel, that they were living in a state retirement home in Moscow, and that a

KGB film unit had been recording their life stories. I asked if I could see them but instead I was invited to help adapt the Kroger interviews for a Russian-British TV documentary eventually shown in the West under the title 'Strange Neighbours'. It concentrated on the Krogers' life in London, and told how they pretended to be New Zealand antiquarian book dealers, whereas in reality they were busy transmitting Gordon Lonsdale's spy reports to Moscow either on their concealed radio transmitter or with a micro-dot system. But there was another story the documentary did not touch. I had seen the uncut film of the Krogers talking to the KGB and had finally realised why Moscow had gone to such lengths to get them released from their British prison, and why Kim Philby was so eager to play a role in this release.

The Krogers were really Morris and Lona Cohen, two New Yorkers who had joined the American Communist Party in 1935 and, full of idealism almost to the last, served the party cause for more than fifty years. In the KGB film, faces alight with memories – 'We were going to help build a better world for the masses' – they gave the impression of being locked away in a Communist time warp. Morris, the son of a New York peddler, joined the Mackenzie-Papineau battalion of the International Brigades under the name of Israel Pickett Altman and went off to the Spanish Civil war to fight for the Republicans. Recovering in hospital after being wounded by machine gun bullets in both legs, he was recruited by Soviet intelligence officers and sent to a spy school in Barcelona. Back in the United States he married Lona, a high school sweetheart, in 1941. They were such good Communists that Lona checked with the party first to see if it would prefer her to marry Morris or a rich lawyer who had been courting her. 'I told the CP official, "The party always needs money and I can get a lot of it for you without him knowing about it. I know how to do things like that." And he said, "If you marry a rich man you'll have servants, you'll have everything you want, and you'll forget about Communism." And I replied, "Never." And he said, "No, marry the poor man and you can work together." '

The following year Morris joined the American army. But the couple had both been working for Soviet intelligence since 1938, running a seven-man spy ring. Lona recalls on the uncut film how this ring indentified secret Nazi supporters in the United States, stole weapon parts from American arms factories, succeeded in recruiting an agent in the Office of Strategic Services (OSS) and worked with Abel for ten months in 1948. But their most valuable service for Moscow was to do with the Soviet atomic spy ring that had penetrated Los Alamos to steal American nuclear secrets. Lona Cohen, then only twenty-seven, made several trips to New Mexico to collect material from someone working at Los Alamos and then brought the material to her KGB controller, Anatoly Yatskov, in New York. Yatskov said in 1991 that the material was a detailed description and drawing of the world's first atomic bomb which had just been dropped on Hiroshima. In the film interview Lona does not identify the spy at Los Alamos who gave her this priceless information. But in the uncut KGB film, Morris Cohen talks about him at length. However in 'Strange Neighbours', all these references were edited out by the Soviet co-producers. Fortunately, I could remember most of them.

Morris said that he had met a young American in his battalion in the International Brigades in Spain, and that after the Spanish Civil War this young American had become a nuclear scientist and had eventually gone to work at Los Alamos. Morris said that Moscow had given him the job of approaching this old comrade-in-arms to see if he were willing to spy for the Soviet Union. Morris said he had met his friend at Alexander's restaurant in Manhattan and the recruitment had been successful. This was the source in Los Alamos who had provided the material that Lona had couriered to the KGB in New York. Furthermore, Morris said that this scientist had never been suspected and that he was still alive, although not now living in the United States. Morris gave me the impression that the scientist was either not American-born or, if he was, came from a European immigrant family. Yatskov gave other clues. In an interview on the same film as the Krogers he said that his atomic spy ring at Los Alamos was ten strong – five agents he described as 'sources of information', three who collected the material from them, and two senior KGB officers in overall charge. The FBI had caught only seven of them. Did they include the scientist who provided Lona Cohen with the material she couriered to New York? 'The people she had contact with were never exposed,' said Yatskov in 1991, 'and they are living peacefully in their own country now.'

The fact that the KGB had decided to cut this material from the interview with the Cohens/Krogers suggested to me that there were sufficient clues in it to indentify at least the scientist recruited by Morris Cohen. It would be a great story and a boost to any journalist's career to be responsible for identifying the last major atomic spy, an American traitor. But, I calculated, he would be at least seventy-six, his spying career long over, and in the final analysis his information had not changed the course of history – the Soviet Union would have developed an atomic bomb anyway, if not quite as quickly as it had done. Did I really want to set in motion events that could end with this elderly scientist opening his door one morning to a team of agents from the FBI? Anyway, how could I be certain that Morris Cohen had been telling the truth? I sat on my knowledge and did nothing.

Then with the collapse of the Soviet Union and the KGB under threat, there was a concerted effort by the service to boost its image to help its chances of survival. Articles about the service's successes began to appear in Russian publications. One, in *Novoe vremia* (23 April and 30 April 1991), by Vladimir Chikov, a KGB colonel, was headed 'How the Soviet Secret Service Split the American Atom'. Chikov's article quoted a message from a Soviet intelligence officer in the United States sent to Moscow in 1942 or 1943 about Morris Cohen's recruitment of his Spanish Civil War colleague. 'The physicist . . . contacted our source "Louis", an acquaintance from the Spanish Civil War . . . We propose to recruit him through "Louis". "Louis" has already carried out a similar task and very successfully.' Chikov went on to say that the recruitment went ahead and that the physicist became the chief Soviet source within Los Alamos. Since Morris Cohen was in Moscow and safe from the FBI, Chikov had no hesitation in identifying him as the agent 'Louis'. But, significantly, he did not name the American physicist, codenamed 'Percy'.

Although in Chikov's version it is the physicist who first approaches Morris Cohen, the rest of his account served to confirm what Morris Cohen had said in those parts of his uncut film interview. It seemed now only a matter of time before the physicist was identified. Michael Dobbs of the *Washington Post* led the hunt but it was not until 25 February 1996 that he announced that the Soviet agent was Theodore Alvin Hall, a Harvard-educated physicist, now aged seventy, who had worked at Los Alamos in 1944–5. He had been investigated for espionage by the FBI in 1950–2 but was not prosecuted. He left the United States in 1962 for Britain and at the time of writing lives in Cambridge. He has an inoperable cancer and refuses to confirm or deny any involvement in espionage activities.

But is Hall the right man? He is a physicist, which fits Chikov's description of his profession. But that is all. He was born in 1926 which means that he would have been only ten years old at the outbreak of the Spanish Civil War and thirteen when it finished, so he was certainly not in the International Brigades. Yet both Morris Cohen in his KGB film and Chikov in his article are positive that the physicist did serve in Spain. Morris Cohen died in Moscow in 1993, a year after his wife. Anatoly Yatskov, the Soviet intelligence officer who ran them, also died in 1993. While Percy, the physicist, is alive, the KGB will not release anything further about him, especially after their error over the film interview for 'Strange Neighbours'. It is likely therefore, that the identity of this major American spy will remain secret for some years to come. Does this matter?

After talking about it with some American colleagues, I had second thoughts about the importance of the KGB's atomic spy ring in the United States. My colleagues argued that even though the Soviet Union would have developed the atomic bomb anyway, the fact that its spies had stolen America's atomic secrets caused a major shift in American attitudes. The revelation that native-born Americans could be ideological traitors ended an age of innocence, ushered in the McCarthy period, and shattered hopes that science could be international and advances in the field of atomic energy freely shared. It was important, therefore, that Percy be identified before he died in the hope that he would explain his motives to history.

The Krogers had taken Percy's identity with them to their graves, but I went over and over their filmed debriefing looking for clues. They told how they had left the United States for Germany in 1950 after the FBI had started to uncover some of the Soviet espionage ring.

Then, posing as American steel salesmen, they crossed into Czechoslovakia and from there went to Moscow where they trained for a new assignment. 'At first we were told that we would be going to South Africa,' Lona Cohen said in her television interview. 'And the head of government there was Kruger. So we put an "o" instead of a "u" – Helen Joyce Kroger and Peter John Kroger. We studied everything about South Africa. But then they came to us and said, "You won't go to South Africa. You'll go to England." So I said, "Why did we have to study everything about South Africa? Why didn't you tell us earlier?" And they said, "That's orders." So we went to England.' And there they were caught and sent to jail for twenty years. This was largely the result of sloppy tradecraft by Conon Molody (Lonsdale), the KGB colonel they were servicing – he failed to shake off his MI5 followers and led them straight to the Krogers' house which was stuffed with espionage equipment. We can now see why the KGB was so anxious to get the Cohens out of a British jail – they were long-serving agents, arguably the most successful husband and wife spy team in the history of espionage, who had played a vital part in helping the Soviets steal the secrets of the American atomic bomb. But there was more to the story than professional loyalty. There was also guilt, both on the part of the KGB and on the part of Philby.

In 1950, when Philby was British intelligence's liaison officer with the CIA and the FBI, his Washington office was in an annexe of the British embassy. But he also had a small office in the FBI where he would go to read FBI material too sensitive to be allowed out of the building. A lot of this related to the Venona decrypts, the radio traffic from the Soviet Consulate in New York in 1944–5, which American code-breakers had been working on since the end of the war. The Venona material offered a window into the running of the Soviet espionage apparatus in the United States. Of course, it did not reveal names. But it did offer clues to the identity of Western agents recruited by the KGB and by painstakingly putting these clues together the FBI could narrow down a list of suspects and, hopefully, finally pinpoint the agent. American experts who have studied the Venona story say that this one code-breaking success was responsible for nearly all the major spy cases of the postwar period.

Being party to the Venona material put Philby in a difficult and dangerous position – what should he do as he followed the FBI homing in on his Soviet intelligence service comrades? He discussed this with his Soviet control and they made some brutal decisions. If Philby were to use what he had learnt from Venona to tip off those Soviet agents under suspicion so as to allow them to flee, then the FBI would suspect a leak. It would ask: who has had access to Venona? Philby would be included in any list and he would be investigated. There would be no proof against him but he would be compromised, and J. Edgar Hoover, who did not trust the British anyway, would make certain that Philby would never again enjoy the same degree of confidence in Washington. This could imperil Philby's lifelong plan – that he should become the chief of the British Secret Intelligence Service, a coup without precedent in the history of espionage and one which would allow the KGB virtually to control the espionage Cold War. So Philby's knowledge of Venona would have to be used sparingly and this meant helping those agents who were of most importance to Moscow and sacrificing the others. Donald Maclean would be helped because he had provided excellent intelligence from Washington and the KGB hoped he would continue to rise in the British Foreign Office. (He did. In November 1950 he became head of the American Department in London and passed to Moscow, among other things, the assurance obtained from President Truman by Prime Minister Attlee that the United States would not use the atom bomb in the Korean war.)

So Philby kept his Soviet control appraised of the progress the FBI was making towards identifying Maclean and tipped off Maclean in time for him to flee to Moscow in May 1951. He also told his Soviet control that the FBI was getting close to identifying the Cohens. 'In the summer of 1950 we had information from a comrade that the best thing would be for us to leave,' Morris Cohen recalled in his Moscow interview. That comrade was Yuri Sokolov. 'I had orders from Moscow to tell them to get out immediately,' he remembered in Moscow in 1991. 'I went to their flat and in case it was bugged I wrote out the order on a piece of paper. They were gone within the hour.'

But no one tipped off Julius and Ethel Rosenberg until it was too late.

Why? Simply because the Soviets did not consider them to be important. The KGB's assessment of the Rosenbergs was that they were 'minor couriers, not significant sources, who provided no valuable secrets and who were absolutely separate from major networks gathering atomic secrets'. They were not part of Yatskov's ten-strong team. The fact is that in the spy Cold War the Rosenbergs were considered expendable, especially as neither Philby nor his bosses in Soviet intelligence ever expected that even if the Rosenbergs were caught and convicted, the Americans would execute them. But there were counter-espionage pressures influencing the Rosenbergs' fate that Moscow did not know about.

The FBI wanted to smash the entire Soviet espionage apparatus in the United States without revealing Venona – the fact that it had been breaking the Soviet code. So if Julius Rosenberg could be persuaded to make a general confession, the FBI could then arrest all the other agents they knew about only through Venona, but claim publicly that it had been Rosenberg's confession that had led them to these people – *even though it had not*. Julius Rosenberg knew nothing about Venona or the FBI's aims but he resolutely refused to confess so the Justice Department decided to increase the pressure on him. Assistant US Attorney Myles Lane told the Joint Congressional Committee on Atomic Energy, 'The only thing that will break this man Rosenberg is the prospect of a death penalty or getting the chair, plus that if we can convict his wife too, and give her a sentence of twenty-five or thirty years, that may serve to make this fellow disgorge and give us the information on these other individuals.' The judge at the Rosenbergs' trial went further. After consulting the Justice Department he sentenced not only Julius Rosenberg to death in the electric chair but Ethel Rosenberg as well, thus offering Rosenberg the chance of saving his wife's life with his confession. But both refused to budge and were executed on 19 June 1953 after a worldwide campaign failed to convince President Eisenhower to grant them clemency.

So no wonder that when Murray Sayle saw Philby in Moscow in 1967 he formed the impression that Philby 'seemed to feel a personal responsibility to the Krogers to get them out of jail'. It was too late to help the Rosenbergs but perhaps Philby felt he could somehow redeem himself by sacrificing his book – which meant a lot to him – on behalf of another husband and wife spy team. On the last night of our talks in Moscow I said to Philby, 'Looking back on your life, do you have any regrets?' He gave general answers and then suddenly said, 'Professionally I could have done better. I made mistakes and I paid for them.' At the time I thought he was talking about his friendship with Guy Burgess. I now think he was talking about the Rosenbergs.

What did all those articles and books I had written about espionage add up to, what influence had they had, what did it all mean? The conclusions were not comforting. I decided that, like all journalists who write about the world of espionage, most of the time I had been just a pawn in the game, that the billions of dollars spent on intelligence agencies during the Cold War had been largely wasted, that the necessity and value of spies had been a sham, and that history will decide that the spy war between East and West was one of the greatest confidence tricks of the century.

The cases of two American traitors started me on the path to this conclusion – Aldrich H. Ames and Edward Lee Howard, both CIA officers. Ames is currently serving a life sentence in the United States for passing CIA secrets to Moscow. At the time of his arrest in 1994, the CIA called him the worst traitor ever. In return for $3.5 million he handed over huge bundles of CIA documents to the KGB. According to the prosecution at his trial, 'This led to the loss of virtually all the CIA's intelligence assets targeted at the Soviet Union and cost many agents their lives.' Edward Lee Howard slipped out of the United States a jump ahead of the FBI and turned up in Moscow in 1985. Before Ames, Howard was 'the most harmful Soviet agent uncovered with the CIA . . . he largely destroyed the CIA's operations in Moscow'.

Add to these two traitors the case of John Walker, the US navy officer jailed for life for working for the KGB, 'one of the most daring and damaging spies in the history of the Cold War'. The amount of information Moscow obtained from him was 'staggering', and included the activities of the Atlantic Fleet, US codes, and documents from the CIA and the State Department. Not to mention the German Rainer Rupp, codenamed 'Topaz', jailed in 1994 for twelve years after he admitted having passed NATO's most sensitive military secrets to the Communist bloc for more than a decade, including NATO's plans for defending Europe in the event of a war with the Soviet Union. Let us be clear about this. These traitors were not the Cambridge idealists of the Thirties. They were not the atom spies of the Forties. These were spies operating – mostly for money – during the past fifteen years, and according to the CIA, they so thoroughly damaged the West's operations that by 1987 the CIA did not have a single source in the Soviet Union that was producing any worthwhile intelligence.

Yet the West won the Cold War. The conclusion is obvious: intelligence can have played little or no role in this outcome. Economic strength, technological ability, political institutions, geography and population were far more important factors. The simple fact is that the Soviet Union was unable to prevent its citizens from learning about the West and it was obvious from the way the young of Moscow dressed, and from the music they played, that they considered life abroad better than what they had at home. The media, not the spies, won the Cold War.

If you accept this, then you have to accept that the billions of dollars spent on spying have been largely wasted. Ames himself admits that it was all a sideshow, 'a self-serving sham carried out by careerist bureaucrats who managed to deceive policy-makers and the public about the necessity and value of their work'. This was possible because an intelligence agency is a bureaucrat's dream – its secrecy makes it difficult to call it to account and to measure its performance, and it has an ability to expand beyond its wildest dreams. SIS started with one room and four officers. Today it occupies a whole Babylonian palace on London's South Bank and has a staff of 2,000. When the CIA was being set up in 1947, Allen Dulles, a future director of the agency, told Congress he envisaged a staff of about twenty. By the end of the Cold War it had 19,000 employees and a budget of $3 billion.

You might argue that this was well worthwhile, but according to a study by the Royal Institute of International Affairs, the CIA's success rate in predicting Soviet moves was no better than that of America's many think-tanks. The late William Colby, a former CIA director, conceded that the agency never succeeded in its main objective of penetrating the Kremlin. No wonder the CIA's list of failures is so long. It failed to predict the first Soviet atom bomb. It failed to predict the North Korean and Chinese invasions of Korea. It failed to predict the Hungarian revolt, Fidel Castro's victory and the subsequent siting of Soviet missiles in Cuba. It failed to predict the invasion of Czechoslovakia and the invasion of Afghanistan. Above all, the CIA failed even to imagine the collapse of Soviet Communism and the end of the Cold War. Its judgment was equally flawed. It helped to restore the Shah of Iran to power in 1953 but then underestimated support for the Ayatollah Khomeini and was caught by surprise when the Shah was overthrown. In 1961 it sponsored the disastrous invasion of Cuba at the Bay of Pigs (President Kennedy came close to winding up the agency on the spot); it got mixed up in Iran-Contra with its secret support for the Nicaraguan rebels, spied illegally on thousands of Americans opposed to the Vietnam war, never imagined that Saddam Hussein would invade Kuwait, and as recently as 1994 worked secretly to subvert its own government's plans to restore Jean-Bertrand Aristide, Haiti's exiled President, to power.

Overall the KGB's performance was about the same. The respected Russian historian Vladislav M. Zubok published in 1994 the results of his research in the Soviet side of the espionage war and accused the KGB of having had delusions of grandeur. There is evidence that this was true. The

KGB defector Oleg Gordievsky, who at the time of writing is a consultant to Britain's SIS and works for a TV spy game, in reviewing the memoirs of his boss, General Oleg Kalugin, wrote of how the years Kalugin spent as head of the KGB's foreign counter-intelligence became the most important in Kalugin's life as he 'turned his talent and energy towards the destruction of the fabric of American society'. The idea that any KGB general, no matter how brilliant, could sit at his desk in the Lubyanka and mount intelligence operations which would destroy the fabric of American society is clearly ludicrous. Kalugin himself admits as much. 'When people in the West say that Soviet intelligence penetrated the higher echelons of Western government, I know that this is not true.'

Other KGB officers have been frank about the shortcomings of their service. Yuri Modin, the officer who controlled the notorious Cambridge ring in Britain, told me that when he was working as a desk officer in the KGB during the Second World War, he seldom had time to read all the reports that KGB agents abroad sent him. When he consulted his senior officer about his problem, he was told to plunge his hand into the pile of reports on his desk, hope that he hit gold, and file the rest marked 'doubtful' or 'provocation'. After the war some senior KGB officers realised that if Stalin ever found out about this, they might well be shot, so they destroyed much of the evidence. (This explains why the KGB archives have not turned out to be the treasure chest many Western historians hoped for.)

Gems of intelligence that survived the first contact with the KGB bureaucracy then faced Stalin's paranoia. Richard Sorge, a German national but an agent of Soviet military intelligence (GRU) and arguably the greatest wartime spy of all time, kept Moscow informed of Japan's intentions from his base in Tokyo. His information in October 1941 that Japan would strike south to attack the United States rather than westwards against the Soviet Union enabled the Red Army to bring troops from the Far Eastern frontiers of the Soviet Union to defend Moscow against the Germans. Yet Sergei Kondrashov, retired chief of KGB counter-intelligence, told me that he had himself seen in the Moscow archives a message from Sorge on which was scrawled in Stalin's hand, 'Send me no more of this German provocation.' And he said that Sorge had been recalled to Moscow in 1942 but had refused to come. 'If he had, he would have been shot.'

The CIA, FBI, DIA, NSA, KGB, SIS, GCHQ, ASIS, ASIO, MI5, STASI, DGSE – the whole bunch of acronyms and numbers – were all equally ineffective, spy-catchers as well as spies. MI5, Britain's so-called crack counter-espionage service never caught a single spy on its own during the whole fifty years of the Cold War. But wait a minute. What about the 'terrible damage' caused by all those spies listed earlier? Surely this is evidence of a genuine, ongoing intelligence war? Or was it all shadow-boxing, a game between the intelligence agencies themselves, with little or no relevance to government policies and no real influence on events? I tested this at an historical conference on intelligence held outside Frankfurt, Germany, in November 1994. I challenged a panel that included Sergei Kondrashov; his colleague the former head of the KGB, Leonid Shebarschin; former head of East German intelligence, Markus Wolff; and former head of West German intelligence, Heribert Hellenbroich, to name a single important historical event in peacetime in which intelligence had played a decisive role. No one could do so.

Writing about spies and intelligence agencies occupied a large part of my career. I do not regret it. It gave me a chance to meet and talk with – among others – the following spies and spy masters: Sir Dick White, Sir Maurice Oldfield, Stephen de Mowbray, William Skardon and Arthur Martin (SIS and MI5); Harry Rositzke, Lyman Kirkpatrick, Frank Snepp and Miles Copeland (the CIA); Kim Philby, George Blake, Yuri Modin, Anthony Blunt, Oleg Kalugin, Leonid Shebarschin and Sergei Kondrashov (the KGB); Marcus Wolff (the Stasi). They were all charming, pleasant people to be with, but espionage itself is a dirty business riddled with deceit, manipulation and betrayal. True, those involved in it as officers of one service or another – not agents, who risked their lives – found it enormous fun, with opportunities for adventure, travel, good expenses and authorised sex. Few were motivated by ideological considerations, but those who were stand out.

Philby made his lifelong allegiance because he was shocked by the apparent inability of any political system except Communism to make a stand against the rise of Fascism, and the craven policies of appeasement – 'more than the politics of folly, the politics of evil'. Donald Maclean told everyone at Cambridge that as soon as he came down in 1934 he would be off to Russia to help the revolution, probably as a teacher. When he was forced to flee to the Soviet Union in 1951 he made a deliberate effort to integrate into Soviet society and to help build Communism. He learnt Russian, and established himself as one of the leading experts on British foreign affairs. He not only retained his early idealism but lived a life fully in accord with his Communist principles, eschewing all privileges, dressing and eating simply. And although he did not hesitate to speak out against Soviet leaders, interceding personally on behalf of dissidents and giving part of his income to a fund for families of those who had been imprisoned, he did not lose his idealism. When he died in 1983 he was still firmly committed to the idea of each for all and all for each which, he wrote, 'gives socialism its moral leverage'.

Luckily for me, I never had to make the choice. I admired those first fellow-travellers, mostly journalists, who were swept away by the earth-shaking events of the Russian Revolution – John Reed who wrote *Ten Days that Shook the World*, buried in a Hero's Grave in Red Square; Morgan Philips Price, the *Manchester Guardian* correspondent in Moscow, later a Labour MP; Arthur Ransome, of the London *Daily News*, who married Trotsky's secretary. And, I admit, I admired Philby, a man capable of making a political decision and sticking to it above all else – family, friends, colleagues, country. They were all wrong, and today it is easy to scoff at their naivety, deride their choice, and gloat at their downfall. But they made a principled commitment in the climate of the time. I suppose the crunch question is, knowing all you do now, would you have stood with Philby against the Fascists in Vienna in 1934? And for me, the answer has to be yes.

CHAPTER FIFTEEN

A HACK'S PROGRESS?

For two years after Rupert Murdoch took over the *Sunday Times* in 1981 most of the changes were at managerial level. Harold Evans went off to edit *The Times*, as agreed with Murdoch, and the former deputy editor and foreign editor, Frank Giles, took his place. Giles was close to retirement and tended to leave his executives to get on with the job. But how long would it be, we all wondered, before Murdoch moved his own man into the editor's chair – and who would he be? Any idea that Murdoch would recruit him from within the paper vanished when he announced that Andrew Neil, formerly of *The Economist*, would get the job. Neil, a tough, uncompromising Scotsman who worked in shirtsleeves and red trouser braces, shared most of Murdoch's views, and was determined to mould the paper into the image he wanted – as was his right. But I began to worry about whether I would have the same freedom I had previously enjoyed.

The way the *Sunday Times* ran under Evans meant that you could usually pursue each week whatever subject appealed to you. In my twenty years there I can honestly say that I never wrote a story that I was not interested in or did not believe in. This freedom extended to editorial policy. On one occasion in 1969, Kenneth Thomson, son of Lord Thomson, decided that he would like to attend the weekly leader conference where the paper's editorial policy on various issues was decided. Harry Evans and his senior executives and leader writers awaited his arrival with some trepidation – would this be the moment when the proprietor imposed his views on the paper? Thomson sat silently throughout a half-hour discussion on what the paper's attitude should be to the Biafra war. Then he got up to leave but stopped at the door as if with an afterthought. Heads turned apprehensively. 'Say Harry,' said Thomson. 'Where exactly in the paper do these leaders go?'

I had worked for Australian newspaper proprietors and knew better than my colleagues how they behaved. Murdoch, for instance, simply could not understand why journalists should have any say in the running of a paper at all. If he owned it, he could decide policy, appoint the editor, and even write headlines if he wanted to. And if he owned television stations as well, then why shouldn't he promote those stations in the columns of his newspapers? It was the obvious thing to do – use one part of his empire to boost another. His experiences in Britain and the United States made him more subtle in the way he exercised control so when critics accuse Murdoch of dictating policy to his editors they are wrong. It does not work like that. First, Murdoch chooses editors who basically agree with his outlook on life, who think like he does. Next, to keep them up to date on his views, he holds an annual conference for senior editorial staff. In some opulent resort hotel, they all sit around a table for several days and talk. At the end of the conference every editor knows exactly what Murdoch's opinions are on almost everything.

An executive who attended one in Aspen, Colorado, in the late Eighties, described it for me. 'Rupert said, "Well, what do you reckon is the biggest story in the world today?" One by one the editors offered a view. "The success of the Tiger economies," said one "Wrong," said Rupert. "Racial unrest in America," said another. "No," said Rupert. "The international drugs business," said a third. "No," said Rupert. There were another two or three further suggestions followed by silence. Then Rupert said, "The biggest story in the world today is the coming collapse of Communism." And he proceeded to justify his statement. We adjourned soon afterwards for lunch and I nearly got knocked down in the rush for the telephones as all the editors called their offices to order stories about the coming collapse of Communism. That's how it works. Rupert doesn't interfere. He doesn't have to.'

Soon after he arrived, Neil began to prune the editorial staff, and efficiency became much more important. I remember Neil asking me about a highly-talented colleague in my department, 'What has he done this week to justify his salary? What's he had in the paper recently?' Under Evans, reporters sometimes went *months* without getting anything into the paper. This was because Evans was a compulsive recruiter of talent and was always hiring people at parties, in lifts, in pubs, at his club and on the squash court until the *Sunday Times* probably had three times the number of journalists needed to produce it.

But this was one of its strengths. Fierce competition for space in each week's issue meant that section editors had a vast pool of stories to choose from. The ones that made it were always the best, the freshest, the most unusual. And when journalists grew restless at not seeing their names in print, Evans would form them into some special team and send them off to find a long-term project and produce something. Often they did not, but when they did it was a winner, the sort of story that made the *Sunday Times* in the Sixties and Seventies the most interesting newspaper in Britain, a surprise every week. 'I hate the *Sunday Times*,' a left-wing friend once told me. 'By the time I've finished reading it I'm trembling with anger at the corruption and injustices it has revealed, with envy of the glamorous people it writes about, and with excitement at the picture it paints of the world. It completely ruins my Sundays.'

Yet the real savings were not to be made on the editorial side of the paper – under Thomson it accounted for only 11 per cent of the total cost of production. I sensed a hidden agenda, that Neil was getting the editorial department down to a core of loyal journalists ready for Murdoch to confront the print unions and that this battle would be a very nasty affair. Anyway, it was obvious from all this that what I saw as the golden days of the *Sunday Times* were coming to an end – newspapers have their ups and downs like football teams – and journalism for me would never be quite the same again. A minor story crystallised my feelings. I discovered that the millionaire meat family, the Vesteys, had used a loophole left in British import regulations after the ending of Commonwealth preference to divert meat shipments from Australia and New Zealand to Germany. They did this because they got a much higher price in Germany than in Britain, where regulations specified that Commonwealth meat had to be sold to schools, the Ministry of Defence and old people's homes. This seemed to me to be a good story – meat millionaires depriving pensioners, kids and soldiers of cheap meat. The response of my departmental head was, 'But are they doing anything illegal?' And when I said no, but illegality was not the point, the story was buried on an inside page with a tiny headline and no display.

So after a lot of thought I decided it was time to move on. The managing editor, Peter Roberts, tried to persuade me to stay, but as I wrote to him at the time, 'The point is that once you have jumped the river in your mind there is just no going back. It is hard to explain, but emotionally I have already left.' When Murdoch's plans to break the print unions were ready and he announced the move to Wapping with its new print technology, I knew I had made the right decision. I could not have crossed the union picket line, not just because of the cultural baggage I had carried all the way from my copy-boy days in Sydney, but because – and I have not seen this explained before – the print unions had members who were secretaries, telephonists, librarians and messengers, all friends and close colleagues of mine for twenty years, suddenly all sacked. They were on the picket line, too. Yes, the bulk of the picket were men from the machine room, the ones who had so often held the *Sunday Times* to ransom. But how could I have looked Fred the librarian or Sue the secretary in the eye and walked past them into Wapping?

I went to Wapping on the night of Saturday, 25 January 1986 to see the first issue of the *Sunday Times* come off the presses, produced not by printers but by newly recruited members of the Electricians' Union trained secretly in the latest technology by Times Newspapers. There were no pickets yet because the printers had – like many others – underestimated Murdoch. Right on press time, the big TNT trucks rolled down the slipway, past the razor-wire barricades out through the guarded gates and off into the night. I knew then that the printers had lost, victims of their brother trade-unionists and the march of time. The propaganda painted them all as ignorant, venal men. That is not the way I remember them.

One week in 1972 I wrote a story about Judith Todd, daughter of Garfield Todd, former Prime Minister of Rhodesia. Judy had been protesting against the rebel regime of Ian Smith. The authorities tried to silence her by imprisoning her and when in protest she went on a hunger strike, they force-fed her, a messy and degrading experience. In the end she became such a nuisance to the Smith regime that they let her go and she immediately came to London. I had known Judy for years and persuaded her to tell her story to the *Sunday Times*. It was the main feature that week with good photographs and – if I do say so myself – some stirring prose about a young woman who had fought at some cost to herself for the right to express her views on the political situation in her country.

On the Saturday night, at Harold Evans's suggestion, I invited Judy to come to the paper, read a page proof of the story about her, and then see the page sent off for printing. An outsider, particularly a woman, on the composing room floor with its highly organised chaos, was unusual, so I asked George Darker, the head printer, if Judy would be welcome. 'Of course,' he said. We went down to the composing room together, Judy read the page, made a few corrections, saw a Linotype operator set them and then watched the stone hand slip the lead slugs into place, lock up the page, then bang the metal with his wooden hammer to ensure that everything was level and secure. Judy thanked him and we began to walk towards the stairs leading to the editorial department. As we passed George Darker's office at the top of the steps, Darker stopped Judy, took her arm and turned her to look back out over the composing room. Every stone hand stopped whatever he had been doing, took up his wooden hammer and began to bang loudly and rhythmically on his metal form. The noise was ear-splitting. 'What on earth's happening,' Judy shouted. 'They're banging you out,' I said, and explained that it was an old printing tradition, a salute, a tribute, an honour, and that it was accorded only rarely and usually only for other printers, like when a head printer retired. In forty years I had seen it only one other time, on Harry Evans's last day. Judy left, weeping, and I reflected on the fact that these supposedly self-centred Luddites not only knew who she was and what she had done but wanted to express their approval. I miss them.

Deprived of the womb-like comfort of an office, colleagues and a regular salary, I would go often to the empty *Sunday Times* building in Gray's Inn Road to move out twenty years of files from my morgue-like, paper-strewn office. I spent weeks going through them, hoping to find a story I had missed that I could now sell to someone as a freelance. One file contained nothing but hundreds of letters from a Mrs Elizabeth Stroud, a widow who lived in Somerset. She had started writing to me after she had read one of my first articles on espionage. She was convinced that MI5 had her under observation and had tapped her telephone and 'bugged' her house. After making some enquiries I wrote assuring her that this was not so but she was not convinced and continued to send me two or three times a week by registered, heavily sealed post a 'Diary of Suspicious Events' in which she listed everything that happened in her street which she considered unusual. She would then telephone me to make certain that the letters had not been intercepted or opened and for reassurance that none of the events she had described had any sinister significance. I managed not to lose patience with her, reluctantly accepting that this was one of the drawbacks of being a journalist. Our patron saint rewarded me – when Mrs Stroud died in 1996 she left me £2,500 in her modest will.

On one of these visits to Gray's Inn Road, I went down to the composing room where rows and rows of Linotype machines stood cold and silent like tombstones in a war cemetery. There in the middle of the floor was a hill of typewriters, two to three hundred of them, including one I identified as mine. In the old days the paper had a staff mechanic who worked full-time to maintain all the typewriters in the building. Now they were just junk, so much scrap metal, a symbol – if I needed one – that a new age of journalism was upon us.

Thinking about my finances made me panic and I began taking any freelance work offered me. No fee was too small. I did a book review for eight pounds and accepted an annual subscription to a magazine whose editor said he could not afford to pay me in money. Then one day I looked at the contract for a long-overdue book about intelligence services (*The*

Second Oldest Profession) and saw that if I could only finish it, then the delivery payment was double what I had earned in six months as a freelance journalist. I did, and got a further contract for a book about the Profumo scandal (*An Affair of State*). Then my interviews in Moscow with the British traitor Kim Philby came up and resulted in another book (*Philby, KGB Masterspy*). A film producer became interested in making a documentary series from my book about war correspondents, *The First Casualty*, and although he never raised the finance he was very generous with his advance payments. I realised that I was over the *Sunday Times*. I was making a living as an author and a self-employed journalist. I had fulfilled my ambition to crack Fleet Street and a salaried job no longer held any attractions. I was free.

Now, since one of the advantages of freelance writing is that you can do it anywhere, and since cheap air travel had overcome the tyranny of distance that had exiled me from Australia, there was nothing to stop me going off to Sydney for a while. I could try the local scene, take a few trips down memory lanes, show my own children what my childhood had been like, even see some of Australia that I had not had time to see before. I would not be a visitor, I would be a resident.

One of the things that had tempted me back was that other expatriates had told me that there was now a real hunger in Australia for ideas and that it no longer mattered how provocative you were. The *Spectator* had even written, 'Australia loves nothing better than a good row: Sydney makes London seem intellectually obese.' That was not how I found it. In April 1990, on the 75th anniversary of the landing at Gallipoli in the First World War, the *Sydney Morning Herald* asked me to write about it, anything I liked. It seemed to me that the legend of Gallipoli – brave Australian cannon-fodder led to bloody disaster by uncaring English officers – encapsulated the essence of the British-Australian relationship and that thinking about it might help me sort out some of my own problem of deciding what I was and where I belonged – now that I had the choice. It was also an interesting topic because it was Murdoch territory and I had long held the theory that Rupert's contempt for the English establishment came not so much from his Scottish ancestry but from the role of his father, Keith Murdoch, in creating the Gallipoli legend.

This role began in September 1915 when after a brief visit to Gallipoli Murdoch wrote a letter to the Australian Prime Minister, Andrew Fisher, praising the Australian troops and criticising the British – not just the officers, as is generally believed, but the ordinary British soldiers as well. The British troops, Murdoch said, were suffering from 'an atrophy of mind that is appalling . . . The physique of those at Suvla is not to be compared with that of the Australians. Nor, indeed, is their intelligence . . . They are merely a lot of child-like youths without strength to endure or brains to improve their condition . . . After the first day at Suvla, an order had to be issued to officers to shoot without mercy any soldiers who lagged behind or loitered in an advance.' As far as British officers were concerned, Murdoch said, 'the conceit and complacency of the red feather men are equalled only by their incapacity. Along the lines of communications are countless high officers and conceited young cubs who are plainly only playing at war.' Other epithets Murdoch used to describe the British General Staff included 'rude', 'disgusting' and 'chocolate soldiers'. The Australians, on the other hand, were wonderful. 'It is stirring to see them, magnificent manhood, swinging their fine limbs as they walk about Anzac. They have the noble faces of men who have endured,' Murdoch wrote. 'Oh, if you could picture Anzac as I have seen it, you would find that to be an Australian is the greatest privilege the world has to offer.'

This depiction of Australians as outstanding troops commanded by British idiots was picked up by Ellis Ashmead-Bartlett, of the London *Daily Telegraph*, first in his journalism and later in his books. Alan Moorehead continued it in *Gallipoli* (1956) and it was brought to its refined best in Peter Weir's film of the same name, a film which Rupert Murdoch had helped finance. In fact Weir's sentiments about Gallipoli echo Keith Murdoch's and Weir talks about his first visit there in cathartic terms. But – as I wrote in the *Sydney Morning Herald* – there is little truth in the legend. Australian troops were no better and no worse than the many others taking part in the campaign: British, New Zealand, French, Senegalese, Gurkha and Indian. There were acts of heroism and cowardice among them all. In his criticism of British officers, Murdoch did not mention, for instance, that at the landings on 25 April, some Australians were led ashore by teenage British midshipmen, at least two of whom were cadets in their first term at Dartmouth. Nor did he mention that the official Australian war correspondent, Charles Bean, wrote in his diary for 26 September 1915 that some Australian troops had to be driven ahead by the threat of being shot from behind by their officers.

The general opinion at Gallipoli was that the best troops of all were the New Zealanders. As one historian said, 'They combined the élan and dash of the Australians with the meticulous professionalism of the British.' Even the Australian casualty figures, compared with the war on the Western front, were not horrendous. A total of 7,818 Australians were killed during the Gallipoli campaign. This pales when compared with the 45,033 Australians killed on the Western front, the 40,000 British killed at

Gallipoli, the 500,000 Frenchmen lost in the first four months of the war, and the million by the end of 1915.

I wrote that none of this was meant to demean the Australian soldier, but to emphasise that the Anzac legend was not created as a celebration of his fighting qualities, or of Gallipoli as a great victory, which it clearly was not. If this had been the intention, then the taking of Damascus by the Australian Light Horse ahead of both Allenby's British troops and T. E. Lawrence's Arabs – a triumph that made Lawrence hate Australians for the rest of his troubled life – would have been much better material with which to create a legend. Or how about General Sir John Monash's triumphs on the Western front with his hardened Anzac troops in the critical last months of the war? His breakthrough tactics were a powerful factor in the German decision to ask for an armistice and thus a real turning point in history. Yet the Australians who fought on the Western front appear doomed to live for ever in the shadow of Gallipoli. No, the reasons for the legend of Gallipoli have to lie elsewhere.

I wrote that nothing stimulates nationalism like a blood icon and that is what Gallipoli became. The fact that it was a bungled defeat and a tragic waste of life and someone else's fault did not matter; it made the icon even stronger. The important point was that it had happened in the service of Great Britain and this became a focus for a growing sense of detachment from the Mother Country. By 1916 Australians, particularly those of Irish origin, were already showing reluctance to meet British demands for more and more Australian troops. These demands could be met only by conscription and although all but one of the country's political leaders urged a 'yes' vote in a national referendum on this issue, Australians replied with a resounding 'no'. If a man wanted to volunteer to fight for the British Empire, it was his right to do so, but no one was going to force him to go. So over the years the commemoration of Gallipoli on Anzac Day became not only a moment to remember the tragic sacrifice of the country's youth, but to reinforce Australia's growing sense of a national identity independent of the British superstate.

I concluded by saying that now Australia was a nation in its own right, it no longer needed such an icon. It had served its purpose brilliantly but it meant little to a new generation of Australians and nothing to the large non-Anglo-Celtic community. The historic truth would always be there, one to be proud of, but it no longer needed the halo and falsification of myth. 'This should be the last official pilgrimage to Gallipoli and the last Anzac Day; the time has come to let them really rest in peace.'

The article met a wall of hostility. Most of those who objected to it simply repeated all the old arguments I thought I had demolished – the

British generals were incompetent and they sacrificed the Australian troops who were the best fighters ever born. There was one unusual response. Columnist Richard Glover said that celebrating a defeat was in keeping with one of the most consistent themes in the Australian legend – the lauding of failure. 'Any country can make a hoopla about its victories. What makes Australia unique is the way it has always preferred to remember the brave-but-defeated, the underdog and the loser.'

Many of the letters I got were abusive but one from Britain redressed the balance. Mrs Mollie Bush of Tunbridge Wells wrote, 'You mention the Australians being bravely led ashore by two teenage English midshipmen. One was my late husband, Eric. He was just fifteen and was awarded the DSC, the youngest ever to receive it. He also landed the Lancashire Fusiliers and every Anzac Day the regiment still sends me the most lovely bunch of flowers, after all these years.'

Journalism gives its practitioners a chance to educate themselves at someone else's expense so I was constantly on the lookout for someone to pay for my re-education about Australia. The chance came from Rex Lopez, my friend from those days back in the old *Sydney Daily Mirror* office in London. He was now features editor of a new Sunday paper in Melbourne, the *Herald-Sun*, and he offered me a freelance job as a columnist. There I was, back working for . . . Rupert Murdoch, who, of course, owned the new paper. As one of his former editors put it, 'You can run from Rupert but you can't hide.' My briefing was to find interesting people from any walk of life and interview them in depth for each Sunday's paper. Some of them Lopez found for me, but, worried that I would run out of interviews, I read all the newspapers and magazines seeking slices of Australian life and the people who inhabited them. Looking at these clippings again and at the stories that I wrote, I discover that most of the clichés about Australians are true. They are friendly, generous, outspoken, bawdy, irreverent, aggressive and anti-authoritarian. I delighted in watching my fellow-countrymen fulfil all the stereotypes that *Private Eye*, Bazza Mackenzie and Barry Humphries had cast for them. A woman wrote to a Sydney restaurant to complain that although the site, ambience, service and food were fine, the portions were too small and she had left the restaurant still hungry. In Britain such a letter would probably have brought an apologetic, even grovelling reply. The Sydney restaurant owner replied, 'I found your letter to be insulting, offensive, cheap and slanderous and don't give a flying fuck what you think. I can see clearly by your letter that your arsehole must be so tight that you have to shit from your mouth. That's the only excuse I can see for putting such crap on paper. Hopefully my restaurant will remain free of cheap, negative, unappreciative morons like yourself.'

An old friend, the eccentric but much-loved Australian author Hugh Atkinson, died, and his wife arranged a cremation service in the local Anglican church at Cobbitty, a small, historic settlement outside Sydney. This is very English territory – Captain John Macarthur, founder of the Australian sheep industry, once farmed nearby – so everyone expected a dignified but dull service which would have paid proper tribute to Atkinson but which would hardly have captured his non-conformist spirit. The eulogy was given by a long-time friend, Dibbs Mather, who had a different agenda. 'What can we say when we consider the loss of a friend, a colleague, a mentor?' Mather said. 'How do we express the sense of loss, the grief, the awful longing for what might have been? There is a way. We do it with a word, a simple word, a word we all recognise. It is a word that enters the lives of us all. It is a word that expresses emotions across the whole enormous gamut of human feelings, a word that touches all of our loves as well as all of our griefs. What shall we say when we consider that Hugh has gone? We shall say the word, and the word is ... FUCK!!' Atkinson's friends said later that the parson flushed and there was some consternation in the congregation, but at the wake afterwards there was a long, serious discussion over why it had taken so long to bring the magic word into a religious ceremony.

I put in a request to interview the Paul Keating, then the Treasurer and soon to be Prime Minister. His press secretary gave me a day and a time but met me at Keating's office to say, 'Paul's got a bit of a cold' – making me think that the interview was off – only to add, 'so he says do you mind coming out to his house?' When I got there, Keating opened the door in slacks and an old cardigan, took me into the kitchen while he made us both a cup of tea, and then chatted for the rest of the afternoon about everything from music to house prices in London.

I remembered the republican debate as reported in London as centring on whether it would be desirable to replace the Queen as head of state and if so with whom? On the ground, I was pleased to see it was a much more passionate affair. On the 'Midday Show', a high-rating television chat programme, Normie Rowe, a pop singer, Vietnam veteran and loyalist, faced sports commentator Ron Casey, a republican. In no time Casey was baiting Rowe, demanding to know how much blood one had to shed to show one's loyalty to the Crown. Rowe responded by calling Casey 'a really low republican rat'. Both men stood up and Casey landed a hefty right cross to Rowe's chin before security men stepped in and the station had a quick, unscheduled commercial break. Casey said later, 'It was a good punch and I'm proud of it.' Rowe said that when he next had a chance, 'I'm going to thump him harder than he did me.' And 35,000 Australians telephoned the station to discuss the fight . . . and the republican issues.

This Australian willingness to offer physical violence has a ritual-like quality to it – the offer is made so often and is so seldom accepted that it can almost be interpreted as a gesture of friendship. When Kerry Packer, Australia's richest man, bought one of the world's smallest pubs – in Noccundra, an isolated town in south-western Queensland – a news team was sent there to write about this latest acquisition. As the reporter and photographer were getting out of their truck after a long and tiring drive, a helicopter used for mustering sheep landed alongside them and a battered-looking farmer got out. His opening line was, 'Do youse blokes want a fight?' When they assured him that they would prefer a drink he took them into the pub where, in the course of the next seven hours they watched him and his four friends drink eight dozen cans of beer and a litre of rum. The reporter asked for ice in his rum and Coke, so one of the pub regulars called him 'a poofter' and invited him outside for a fight. Later in the day three strangers arrived, and another regular immediately offered to fight them one at a time or all at once.

God knows what the newly liberated, self-confident, ambitious and powerful Australian woman thinks of all this. I went to dinner with a fellow expatriate, his sister and three of her girlfriends. They all had interesting and rewarding careers and they discussed their lives with a frankness that would have been impossible in my youth. One of them had spent a holiday on a cruise to the Pacific islands. On the outward voyage she had been picked up at the bar by one of the ship's entertainers, a ventriloquist. 'Actually,' she said, 'it was his dummy who picked me up. The guy was sitting beside me at the bar with this bloody dummy on his lap and the dummy started talking to me.' The night before the liner docked in Sydney the ventriloquist and his dummy were at the bar again and this time, the girl said, she went with him to his cabin. Then she said, 'But you know I had to stop him half-way through because he'd just flung the dummy in the corner and I had this funny feeling it was watching us.' While we were all laughing about this, another girl said, 'What I want to know is . . . did the dummy come too?'

The rise of the Australian woman has been paralleled by the emergence of so many gays that Sydney has now taken over as the gay capital of the world. I went to a lawyer's wedding reception in the Sydney barracks, a remnant of colonial New South Wales, on the night of the gay mardi gras. A sudden downpour drenched the floats as they made their way along Macquarie Street. In the middle of the best man's speech the reception was

A HACK'S PROGRESS

suddenly invaded by twenty ballet dancers, dressed all in white with feather tutus, beautifully made up, lipstick glistening in the light. But there was not one under six feet and they all had hairy arms, axeman's shoulders and baritone voices. What a story I could have written for Ezra Norton and the old Sydney *Truth*.

I found lots of proof that Sydney still had a large heart. A Russian scientist, Professor Nikolie Vtyurin, was invited to a conference in Melbourne, all expenses paid. On the plane to Australia he met a friend of mine who asked him how long he planned to stay in Sydney. Vtyurin said only an hour while he changed planes for Melbourne. 'You can't come all the way to Australia and not see Sydney,' my friend said. 'Change your ticket and I'll find you cheap hotel room, only about twenty dollars a night.' Vtyurin looked wistful: 'Twenty dollars is what I earn in a month.' My friend and I got to work. One of Sydney's leading hotels gave Vtyurin a free suite overlooking the city. A restaurant specialising in Australian bush food invited him to have all his meals there, no charge. A ferry company gave him a free tour of Sydney Harbour and a Sydney scientist volunteered to drive him around and take him swimming at all the best beaches. I went with them on Vtyurin's last day. He plunged into the surf at Manly and it was difficult to get him out again. 'I have never had a swim in sea water,' he said in explanation. 'And I don't know if I ever will again.'

Talking to other returned expatriates, I discovered that new laws enabled me to apply to have my Australian citizenship re-instated. I had lost it in the Fifties when, fed up with all the visas needed for an Australian passport in Europe I had opted for British citizenship. I went for my interview at the Immigration Department in Sydney. The officer attending me was what Sydneysiders call an 'ABC' – an Australian-born Chinese. 'Now it's important that when you opted for British citizenship you did not realise at that time that this would mean that you lost your Australian citizenship.' I began to explain that I did indeed know this but it would have been difficult to continue to work as a journalist who needed to travel often to Europe and still keep an Australian passport. She cut me off. 'You didn't realise that this would mean you'd lose your Australian citizenship, did you? . . . Did you?' I got the message. 'No, I didn't,' I said. 'No worries.' she said, smiling. 'Your citizenship will be through in a couple of weeks. Welcome back.'

An Australian again, I revisited my schooldays. Sans Souci baths were still there but the water was not as clear and had a thin slick of engine oil from all the million-dollar motor cruisers moored around the corner in Kogarah Bay. You could still order a double chocolate malted milkshake at the milk bar but the malt was not as tasty and the owner was a Vietnamese instead of a Greek. Canterbury Boys' High School had not moved but it now accepted girls. The *Daily Telegraph* and the *Daily Mirror* were still there but they had become one newspaper, a morning and afternoon one. There were no longer any copy boys because what the journalists wrote was moved around the office and to the printers electronically. No one had much time for drinking or any ambition to go overseas so there were no boozy discussions about the best way to get a job on Fleet Street. No newspaper reported the lottery winners any more because the first prize of $100,000 did not seem like a lot of money. The *Sunday Telegraph* beach girl competition had died with Dave Barnes and what photographer would want to persuade a beach girl to drop her bikini top when so many girls no longer wore them anyway. Ezra Norton had long since died and so had Frank Packer and with them the days of the last wild men of Sydney. The eminently respectable Canadian Conrad Black owned The *Sydney Morning Herald* publications and Rupert Murdoch all the others. Two men more unlikely to try to choke and punch each other in the members' bar at Randwick racecourse would be hard to imagine. In short, as I should have known, the Sydney of the Forties and Fifties had moved on.

After a year I began to miss London – as friends had warned me I would. One, a Russian woman with an impeccable Bolshevik background – she is descended from one of the 1917 revolutionaries – had married an English milord and had reminded me that she loves London so much that she refuses to leave Knightsbridge except to ride to the hounds. Then there is the New Zealand editor who says he spent the best years of his life in Fleet Street and now, back in Auckland, weeps every time he sees a No. 13 bus on television. Clive James ended his *Unreliable Memoirs* with a lyrical passage about the attractions of Australia, yet he still lives in Britain. I kept asking myself why Australians as diverse as academic Germaine Greer, publisher Carmen Callil, singer Shirley Abicair, composer Malcolm Williamson, TV producer Nelson Mews, film-maker Di Holmes, psychologist Estelle Bowman, journalist John Pilger, writer Jill Neville and dentist Bill Howell, who have all made their names and could return in triumph, still live in London?

I decided that one of the great things about London is that it has seen it all, and although it will raise a glass of champagne to success, it will look with a kind eye on failure, especially if it is failure with style. I recalled a scientist who lived around the corner from me, a brilliant pioneer in his field with an international reputation. He rode a battered old bicycle around town, dressed like an upmarket tramp, got his newspapers from rubbish bins, and ate in appalling cafés. He did not want a highly paid job in California or Canberra; he did not want to write a bestseller, own a luxury flat, or drive a BMW. He just wanted to live in London in penury.

So back I went to Britain for the fourth time with an assignment from the *Australian* newspaper to travel around the country and then write a long article tentatively entitled 'The End of Great Britain'. The idea was to look at the ways in which Britain had declined since the Fifties and say that this was one of those points in history at which it was possible to say that, whatever else it might be, Britain could no longer be described as 'great'. I thought I would start by contrasting the thriving newspaper industry that I had found in 1954 with what remained today. So as soon as I had settled back into London life, I took a No. 13 bus to the Law Courts, got off and walked down Fleet Street just to recall the old thrill of the unexpected that only an industry as instant and as ephemeral as newspapers could produce. I remembered how you could sniff the printer's ink almost as far as St Paul's, and how, when the presses rolled in unison, the pavement trembled gently under your feet. In the Fifties, Fleet Street reflected life in Britain, the Commonwealth and the great world outside – a daily dose of hope and confidence. Forty years later I saw a tacky, dirty little street lined with expensive wine bars and cut-price electronics shops, great newspaper buildings like the *Daily Express* boarded up like a derelict old factory, and not a journalist in sight. What had happened? One by one all the newspapers had closed their doors and left because there was no reason to be there any more. The old printing system – hot metal and slow presses – meant that newspapers had to be strategically placed: close to a railway terminal for country-wide distribution, and close to the city centre so that vans could get the papers around the capital's breakfast tables. And where the printers had to be, the journalists had to follow, for in the old days the copy went from the journalist to the composing room by hand. But the new technology broke the link between the printing process and the journalist. Today an editorial staff can create a newspaper and feed it to presses anywhere in the country down a telephone line. With no longer any need for newspapers to be centrally located, the new-wave proprietors could not wait to sell their expensive real estate and go elsewhere.

So the news is gathered on the telephone and from the television screen, the background filled in from a databank, and a new generation of journalists interview and write about people they never meet. And since the scattering of their papers, they never even meet each other any more. The gossip, the discussion, the argument, the exchange of information that is such an important part in helping a writer form a view that will add dimension to his reporting is gone. The old Fleet Street hacks were sociable characters. They entertained their contacts and their subjects in the pubs around the Street; they took them to lunch; they invited them to the newspaper office. In those days Fleet Street was full of the hubbub of tomorrow's news in the making. But now who wants to travel to Wapping to meet a reporter? What journalist wants to commute from Canary Wharf for a quick drink in Soho? The journalists' pubs of Fleet Street have been taken over by lawyers and currency dealers. And with the demise of Fleet Street went the sense of adventure that was a vital part of it and the nation's spirit. As today's young reporters plough through Docklands traffic to their aseptic open-plan offices they do not dream that they might soon be on their way to join an expedition to the heartland of New Guinea. They know exactly where they will spend the rest of their day – in front of their computer screens.

Looking at Britain with eyes fresh from the Australian scene, I noticed a harsher national mood, a tougher attitude to outsiders, non-conformists and those less well-off. I did not remember ever being approached by a beggar in the Fifties and if there were homeless then they did not live in doorways. Now I suddenly noticed people eating out of rubbish bins and sleeping in the West End in cardboard boxes – 'the sort of people you step over when you come out of the opera,' said Housing Minister Sir George Young. It had become acceptable to be rich and uncaring. 'The rentier's return is a cruel insult to the working people of Britain,' said the *Spectator*, 'but for the fortunate bourgeois, it heralds an era of indolence and cultivation.' What had happened to those cruelly insulted working people? I took a little tour of the country's industrial heartland to find out.

The Don Valley runs between Sheffield – which once had the heaviest concentration of heavy industry in Europe – and Rotherham, all steel country. On a summer's day, cars passing the smelting works used to wind up their windows as a shield from the heat of cooling ingots. When I drove down the same road I passed mile after mile of black rubble-strewn fields. Only an occasional sign on a derelict building yet to be bulldozed recalled a glorious past – Albion Iron Works, Forgemasters, Bright and Black Bars, Precision and Repetitive Engineers. The area lost 60,000 jobs in three years.

From Sheffield I went to Coventry to visit the Wood End estate. A vast sprawling suburb of concrete and pebble-dash bungalows and terraces, with lots of green open parkland, it has 3,000 households and a population of about 8,000, of whom immigrants number less than 300. This was a white, British-to-the-core housing estate. It was originally built in the early 1950s for the people who had been bombed out of the centre of Coventry, and then for manual workers who came flocking to the area as the car industry boomed. When these jobs vanished, the estate became a monument to much that I now found wrong with Britain.

Eight out of ten of Wood End's residents were 'economically inactive'. The unemployment rate among those of working age was 50 per cent. Nearly half the children on the estate lived in one-parent households. The largest single age group comprised those fifteen years old or younger. The estate lived largely off social security benefits and had detached itself from mainstream life in the rest of the country.

Most of the support services got out at sundown. Among the few exceptions were the vicar of the local Church of England, the Rev. Nerissa Jones, and her husband, Lieutenant-Colonel David Jones. Not that the locals had that much respect for the church. The last vicar had a nervous breakdown after his TV and video were stolen for the sixth time. The church had been badly vandalised, and the glass walls smashed. These had now been replaced with bullet-proof glass.

In the Fifties Great Britain was described as an island made of coal, covered in steel mills, spinning mills and factories, and surrounded by its merchant fleet. There were nearly 700,000 working miners. Bradford clothed the world. There were car plants in forty cities, from Glasgow in the north to Dagenham in the south. The British flag flew on 5,600 freighters. A slogan at the time was, 'Britain delivers the goods', and it was true.

Forty years later there were only 14,000 coal miners and fewer than twenty mines; most of the steel mills had gone; Bradford's spinning mills had been closed or sold to India; the last big British car plant, Rover, had been bought by the Germans, and only 248 merchant ships flew the flag. I don't know how I feel about this. Perhaps it is a good thing that coal mining is virtually finished. It was a dirty, dangerous job and if we can buy coal cheaper elsewhere, then why not? But when you see former miners who once had a purpose in life and enjoyed the comradeship of the work force hanging around pubs in towns without a heart, knowing that they have no future except next week's do-it-yourself project, you have to conclude that there should be more to running a country than economic rationalism. But what about the idea that manufacturing no longer mattered anyway, that Britain's future lay in an expanding services industry, especially financial services? I know an American industrialist and he laughs at this – 'It's a pipe dream. You can't all make a living opening doors for each other.'

I found that Britain's politics had grown nastier and more insular. The blame was always someone else's and no one had the honour to resign any more. Say what you like about the Macmillan government but when poor old Profumo got caught lying to the House of Commons he fell on his political sword without hesitation. The decline in political probity seemed to have spread into the Civil Service, the one sector of British life that in the Fifties held everyone's faith, its honour unquestioned. The pick of the nation's brains took one of the toughest examinations in the world in the hope of entering this elite branch of public life. When I arrived back the newspapers were full of the case of Gordon Foxley, a senior official in the Ministry of Defence who had been convicted of having received £1.5 million ($3 million) in kickbacks from German and Italian defence contractors. During his trial there had been allegations that the Ministry was reckoned to be 'among the most corrupt in Europe'. The Public Accounts Committee, a non-partisan parliamentary body with members from all parties and a Conservative majority, warned that scandals and waste of public money were threatening to destroy traditions of honesty in the nation's public service. The committee gave examples of 'fraud, waste, unjustified golden handshakes, recruiting irregularities, impropriety, mis-management, improper use of funds, and dubious conduct'.

I wrote that Britain might have to resign herself to a steady decline until it reached a natural plateau which, according to a Treasury document, would, by 2015, be somewhere ahead of Portugal but behind Italy, India, Brazil, Indonesia and even Thailand, and then wait, perhaps a century or two, for the turn of history's wheel. Is it the unconscious recognition of this that accounted for another side to the British mood I noticed on my return – a haunting melancholia, a nostalgia for what once was, a fear of the future and an expectation of things always getting worse? All this was brought home to me when a friend sent me a card marking the fortieth anniversary of my arrival in London. It was one of those very English cards with bunches of flowers, a sentimental poem and a list of events that had occurred in Britain in 1929, the year of my birth. The only thing wrong with it was that it was made in Sweden.

When the article appeared in April 1994 it brought bags of complaining letters from all over Australia. Intriguingly, most were from British migrants, some of whom had lived in Australia for twenty years and more. Presumably they had left Britain because they had found something wrong with it, but now in their new country they were angry that someone had criticised the old. Their loyalties were torn and I sympathised with them because so were mine. When they wrote, 'If you hate Britain so much, why do you continue to live there?' I had no answer. All I could do was to refer them to *Alienation*, a wonderful book published in 1960 by MacGibbon and Kee. One of its editors, Timothy O'Keefe, had brought together ten gifted exiles* and asked them why they had become alienated from the land of their birth and why they had then chosen to live in England.

All of them said that living in Britain had enabled them to have a deeper understanding of their own country while at the same time the fact that they had not been born in Britain helped them view it with a fresh and sometimes disturbing eye. Consider J. P. Donleavy's description of escaping from New York after a particularly gruelling visit during which a fellow American had shouted at him: 'If you are as good a writer as you probably are, you have no right to leave America.' Donleavy manages to hold on to his sanity until he is on board the *Franconia*. On the stern of the ship he stands watching Manhattan disappearing into the mist, wondering if he has done the right thing. A steward arrives with beef tea and biscuits. Then Donleavy writes: 'There were tears in my eyes. I said silently, "I'm in England".' I know how he felt. Despite all the harsh things I wrote about Britain in the article, I love the beauty of London, the drive alongside Buckingham Palace up to Hyde Park corner on a crisp December day, the leafless trees stark against the setting sun. Or the sweep of the Nash terraces in Regent's Park, the iron bridges over the Thames, the round pond in Kensington Gardens on a rare bright afternoon, and tea on the lawn at Hurlingham in mid-summer with a string quartet playing selections from musical comedies – 'We'll gather lilacs in the spring again/And walk together down an English lane.' When I leave El Vino at Blackfriars on a late August evening after conversation as stimulating as you would find anywhere in the world, there is a view across the Thames that is magical. In the foreground is the solid presence of the Unilever building where generations of young men had their yellow fever shots before going off to far outposts of Empire. In the middle distance is Sea Containers and further up the river the Oxo tower. Softened by the English twilight the scene is an oil painting, timeless and reassuring. When I look at it I know I am a Londoner. And yet . . . As the plane comes in over the Blue Mountains after that interminable flight from London, and there is Sydney Harbour sparkling in the early morning sun, and I realise in a few hours I'll be caught up in the bubbling, enthusiastic hedonism of a country that feels it is going somewhere, my heart lifts and I know, deep down, I am for ever an Australian.

In truth I am both. One lesson I have learnt in this forty-year-long

* The Indian Victor Anant, the Irishman Brian Behan, the American J. P. Donleavy, the West Indian Merrill Ferguson, the South African Dan Jacobson, the Southern Rhodesian Doris Lessing, Abioseh Nicol from Sierra Leone, the Canadian Mordecai Richler, the Australian Murray Sayle, the New Zealander Patrick Wilson.

journey is that I do not have to decide. I am an Australian who lives some of the time in London; I am a Londoner who lives some of the time in Australia. The narrow nationalism that once seemed to force a choice is over. The other lesson is about journalism and my working life. I know now that the influence journalists can exercise is limited and that what we achieve is not always what we intended. It is the fight that counts. I attended a newspaper conference in Stockholm where everyone was bemoaning the death of journalism, killed by accountants and their demands for cost-effective reporting. We were shamed into silence by a young woman from a small town paper in America's mid-west. The town's citizens had failed for years to persuade the railroad company to install gates at a level crossing. One day the train hit a truck. No one was injured but the reporter said she decided to investigate what other heavy vehicles used that crossing. The answer was three school buses. So she wrote a story saying over a hundred local kids were in danger of death each day. Within twenty-four hours of her paper hitting the streets, the railroad company had agreed to install the gates. 'You don't need money for good journalism,' she said. 'You just need the will.'

She is right, of course. So my advice for the new generation of journalists is to ignore the accountants, the proprietors and the conventional editors and get on with it. And your assignment is the same as mine has been – the world and the millions of fascinating people who inhabit it.

Also available in Vintage

Geoff Mulgan

CONNEXITY

SUCCEEDING THROUGH CONNECTIONS: FREEDOM, BUSINESS AND POWER IN THE NEXT CENTURY

'Energetic and impressive'
Guardian

The world has never been more closely and intricately connected. Our behaviour influences the environment we all share, and we are tied into a global economy and global communication system. This interdependency, or 'connexity', is the defining characteristic of the world today. But despite connexity, human beings have never been more separate. Belief in individual rights is at the heart of the West's world view. We insist on our freedom to choose how to live, who to love, what to consume and what to believe.

In this inspiring and important book, Geoff Mulgan argues that our freedom and connectedness are set on a collision course. This tension has led to crisis: institutions, including governments, sense themselves to be inadequate; individuals are faced with a mass of conflicting information and values. Geoff Mulgan argues clearly and passionately that the only way out of our current impasse is to go beyond our sense of ourselves as isolated units, and recognise the webs of mutual responsibility in which we live.

VINTAGE

Also available in Vintage

Tom Athanasiou

SLOW RECKONING

'Everyone who really cares should read *Slow Reckoning*'
The Times

Most people today try to be environmentalists. They recycle
rubbish, drive a bit less, and shop for energy-efficient products. They think they are making a difference – but they're
wrong. Athanasiou locates the roots of the crisis in the
planetary divide between rich and poor, between developed
and developing nations, and warns of the apocalyptic consequences if we don't undertake radical social and economic
changes to forestall disaster.

'One of the most important books of this decade'
Mike Roselle, co-founder, *Earth First!*

'A well-researched, radical critique...Tom Athanasiou has
written an important and poignant book, addressing the
most urgent political issues of our age. We treat him as a
Cassandra at our peril'
Literary Review

'Lays bare the fallacies of feel-good environmentalism and
roots the environmental crisis in the rich/poor nation divide'
Financial Times

VINTAGE

Also available in Vintage

Graham Harvey

THE KILLING OF
THE COUNTRYSIDE

Winner of the
1997 BP Natural World Book Award

'A scathing attack...he explodes the myth of cheap food with a few simple statistics that even the dimmest politician should be able to grasp, and shows rural Britain devastated by the politics of unthinking subsidy'
John Humphreys, *New Statesman*

'*The Killing of the Countryside* is absolute dynamite...It's so invigorating to hear the case for a truly sustainable, country-side-friendly agriculture mapped out so passionately'
Jonathon Porritt, *BBC Wildlife*

'A forceful, informed and authoritative account of the state of farming and the countryside which could not be more timely with a new government in office'
Bryn Green, *Spectator*

'I fully support this book's profound and Blake-like charge, which is laid not just against the mere farmers and the agricultural community, but against our whole society'
John Fowles, *Sunday Times*

VINTAGE

Also available in Vintage

Naomi Wolf

PROMISCUITIES
A Secret History of Female Desire

BY THE AUTHOR OF THE
INTERNATIONAL BESTSELLER
THE BEAUTY MYTH

'A daring, startlingly brilliant book'
Carol Gilligan

In this provocative and highly personal new book, Naomi Wolf – probably the most outspoken feminist of her generation – takes an uncompromising look at female sexuality and what it means to come of age as a woman.

'The prevailing fantasy is that, while men have a sexual "past", women have none...Wolf, in *Promiscuities*, smashes that taboo, both directly by talking about herself, and indirectly by relaying the confidences of her pseudonymous friends. The result makes fascinating reading'
Mary Ann Sieghart, *The Times*

'At last, a new generation of women writers is addressing the powerful issue of female sexuality. I gulped this wonderful book down in one sitting, like a novel. Brava Naomi Wolf for your courage, your intelligence, your lucid prose'
Erica Jong

VINTAGE

Also available in Vintage

John Pilger

HIDDEN AGENDAS

'A moral interpretation of world affairs in a cynical age'
Independent

In his powerful new book, journalist and film maker John Pilger strips away the layers of deception, dissembling language and omission that prevent us from understanding how the world really works. From the invisible corners of Tony Blair's New Britain to Burma, Vietnam, Australia, South Africa and the illusions of the "media age", power, he argues, has its own agenda. Unchallenged, it operates to protect its interests with a cynical disregard for people – shaping, and often devastating, millions of lives.

By unravelling the hidden histories of contemporary events, Pilger allows us to read between the lines. He also celebrates the eloquent defiance and courage of those who resist oppression and give us hope for the future. Tenaciously researched and written with passion and wit, *Hidden Agendas* will change the way you see the world.

'Pilger is the closest we have to the great correspondents of the 1930s. The truth in his hands is a weapon, to be picked up and used in the struggle against injustice'
Guardian

VINTAGE

Also available in Vintage

Anthony Barnett

THIS TIME

Our Constitutional Revolution

1997 was a turning point in history...

- The May election shattered the Tories
- Scotland voted for a new parliament
- London will have a mayor
- People are turning against old-fashioned monarchy
- A European Bill of Rights is on the way

BRITAIN IS BECOMING A NEW COUNTRY.
WHAT DOES THIS MEAN?
In a groundbreaking look at the experience of 1997,
This Time:

- Asks what the general election really tells us
- Explores the significance of the response to Diana's death
- Shows that the old British system is broke
- Explains what a constitution is
- Advocates a written constitution
- Suggests a strategy for change
- Probes the meaning of English and British identity
- Looks at the choices facing Tony Blair

VINTAGE

Also available in Vintage

Isabel Fonseca

BURY ME STANDING
The Gypsies and their Journey

'A remarkable achievement. A gripping, original work'
Edward W. Said

'Compassionate, amusing, sardonic and highly intelligent'
Michael Ignatieff, *Independent on Sunday*

'Isabel Fonseca's book is literally a revelation: a hidden
world – at once ignored and secretive, persecuted and
unknown – is uncovered in these absorbing pages. She
writes with grace, insight and passion, and peoples her text
with vibrant characters brought vividly to life. It is a
magnificent achievement'
Salman Rushdie

'A passionate and dramatic defence of the defenceless...This
beautifully written story speaks in a way of all who do not
want to submit to the reverses of fortune, who seek their
own place on earth'
Ryszard Kapuscinski

'An utterly fascinating, and even inspiring book'
Edward Mortimer, *Financial Times*

VINTAGE

Also available in Vintage

Damian Thompson

THE END OF TIME

'Damian Thompson's extraordinary book is literally a revelation, a detailed map of the battle-plan of Armageddon...it is superb and often breathtaking'
J.G. Ballard, *Daily Telegraph*

'It is forty years since historical research began to reveal what an important part millenarian and apocalyptic expectations have played in the course of Western Civilisation, but until now nobody has produced a global survey. Damian Thompson has set out to do that, and he has carried it off triumphantly. *The End of Time* is a splendid book'
Norman Cohn,
author of *The Pursuit of the Millennium*

'Delightfully spooky, engagingly quirky, compellingly presented...a book to read with pleasure and contemplate with dread'
Independent

'It covers this vast and fascinating subject without neglecting significant detail, and the lightness of Thompson's touch makes it an engrossing read'
Joan Bakewell, *Sunday Times*

VINTAGE

A SELECTED LIST OF NON-FICTION
AVAILABLE IN VINTAGE

☐	THIS TIME	Anthony Barnett	£6.99
☐	BURY ME STANDING	Isabel Fonseca	£7.99
☐	THE KILLING OF THE COUNTRYSIDE	Graham Harvey	£7.99
☐	WESTMINSTER WOMEN	Linda McDougall	£8.99
☐	HOW WE LIVE	Sherwin Nuland	£7.99
☐	HIDDEN AGENDAS	John Pilger	£8.99
☐	COVERING ISLAM	Edward W. Said	£7.99
☐	THE END OF TIME	Damian Thompson	£6.99
☐	PROMISCUITIES	Naomi Wolf	£7.99
☐	GUNS, GERMS AND STEEL	Jared Diamond	£8.99
☐	SLOW RECKONING	Tom Athanasiou	£7.99

- All Vintage books are available through mail order or from your local bookshop.
- Please send cheque/eurocheque/postal order (sterling only), Access, Visa, Mastercard, Diners Card, Switch or Amex:

☐☐☐☐☐☐☐☐☐☐☐☐☐☐☐☐

Expiry Date:_____Signature:_____

Please allow 75 pence per book for post and packing U.K.
Overseas customers please allow £1.00 per copy for post and packing.

ALL ORDERS TO:

Vintage Books, Books by Post, TBS Limited, The Book Service,
Colchester Road, Frating Green, Colchester, Essex CO7 7DW

NAME:_____

ADDRESS:_____

_____

_____

Please allow 28 days for delivery. Please tick box if you do not
wish to receive any additional information ☐

Prices and availability subject to change without notice.